Lash-Up

Forge Books by Larry Bond

Dangerous Ground

Cold Choices

Exit Plan

Shattered Trident

Lash-Up

Forge Books by Larry Bond and Jim DeFelice

Larry Bond's First Team

Larry Bond's First Team: Angels of Wrath

Larry Bond's First Team: Fires of War

Larry Bond's First Team: Soul of the Assassin

Larry Bond's Red Dragon Rising: Shadows of War

Larry Bond's Red Dragon Rising: Edge of War

Larry Bond's Red Dragon Rising: Shock of War

Lash-Up

Larry Bond

A Tom Doherty Associates Book • New York

LASH-UP

A Forge Book
Published by Tom Doherty Associates, LLC
175 Fifth Avenue
New York, NY 10010

www.tor-forge.com

Forge® is a registered trademark of Tom Doherty Associates, LLC.

The Library of Congress Cataloging-in-Publication Data is available upon request.

ISBN 978-0-7653-3491-6 (hardcover)
ISBN 978-1-4668-1894-1 (e-book)

Forge books may be purchased for educational, business, or promotional use. For information on bulk purchases, please contact the Macmillan Corporate and Premium Sales Department at 1-800-221-7945, extension 5442, or write to specialmarkets@macmillan.com.

First Edition: May 2015

Printed in the United States of America

0 9 8 7 6 5 4 3 2 1

Author's Note

I've lost track of the number of projects I've done with Chris Carlson: novels, games, articles, presentations, and other products that are lost in the fog of memory.

But there's always something new. This is the first time we have "explored the frontiers of technology," in other words, written about something that really hasn't been done yet.

Writing *Lash-Up* was also a new (notice I didn't say "novel") process, because we were expanding a novella that I had written and was first published in 2001, as part of Steve Coonts's anthology *Combat* (see the afterword). I was never happy with having to ignore so many plotlines, and Chris readily accepted the challenge of updating a ten-year-old story by someone else and adding material that would make it complete.

It was fun, although prying Chris's fingers off the *Engineer's Handbook* took a little time. My personal growth came in letting go of something I had created and trusting that Chris would improve it.

Chris did more than simply improve the story, and if you enjoy it, he should get at least half the credit. I could not have done this alone, and even if I could have, it would not have been as good, or as enjoyable to write.

Dramatis Personae

Matheson, Dr. Harold: National Aeronautics and Space
    Administration director
McConnell, Ray: brilliant yet humble engineer at SPAWAR,
    Defender project technical director and flight engineer
Naguchi, Jim: Ray McConnell's coworker and friend
Norman, Carl; General, USMC: Camp Pendleton base commander
Overton, Frank; Rear Admiral, USN: J-2 (Intelligence), Joint Chiefs
    of Staff
Oh, Jennifer; Lt. Commander, USN: communications specialist at
    Navy Information Operations Command
Peck, Everett: Secretary of Defense
Rutledge, Thomas K.: representative from Nebraska's 3rd
    Congressional District
Scarelli, Jim: Lockheed Martin test pilot, *Defender* pilot
Schultz, William; Vice Admiral (later Admiral), USN: Commander,
    Naval Air Systems Command, then Space Force Chief of Staff
Skeldon, Steve; Captain, USMC: *Defender* navigator/co-pilot
Takir, Avrim: Ray McConnell's coworker at SPAWAR
Tillman, Sue; Lieutenant, USN: *Defender* sensor officer
Warner, Michael; General, USAF: Air Force Chief of Staff
White, Rudy: Ray McConnell's boss and a division head at
    SPAWAR

CHINESE
Dong Zhi, Dr.: chief scientist of *Tien Lung* project
Li Zhang; General, People's Liberation Army (PLA): Chief of the
    General Staff and PLA Commander
Pan Yunfeng: President of the People's Republic of China and
    First Party Secretary
Shen Xuesen; General, PLA: commanding general of the *Tien
    Lung* launcher, engineer.
Wen Jin: Senior Agent, Ministry for State Security

Lash-Up

Prologue

The sleek, streamlined object arced gracefully upward, its presence revealed only by the light reflecting off its hull as the sun emerged from behind Earth. Below, a new day was dawning in the Pacific basin, but the vehicle's electronic brain ignored the aesthetic beauty of a perfect sunrise. Its attention was focused solely on its intended target.

Hurled into space at tremendous velocity, the dartlike vehicle was coasting now, its solid rocket motor expended. Only its attitude control thrusters still worked. Settled into its orbit, the vehicle's sensors scanned the space ahead of it, diligently searching for the satellite that the projectile's masters wanted eliminated. Its flight path had been carefully planned, with an interception distance on the order of a few hundred meters. In theory, it would be virtually impossible for the projectile's sensors not to see the target. With cold, calculated precision, the vehicle gazed at the heavens. It didn't have long to wait.

The vehicle's radar picked up the satellite at five hundred miles, and an imaging infrared sensor immediately confirmed the target's identity. The projectile's flight computer calculated a small course correction to ensure optimal warhead performance. Puffs of steam and nitrogen gas from the attitude control thrusters quickly altered the vehicle's course ever so slightly, but it was enough to ensure that it would pass just in front of the oncoming satellite. An arming signal was sent to both warheads.

At a combined speed of nearly nine thousand miles per hour, the two spacecraft devoured the distance between them in just over three seconds. The projectile's radar kept a sharp electronic eye on the target's range, and at two hundred meters, the flight computer sent the firing signal.

The explosively pumped microwave generator detonated first, sending a focused multigigawatt electromagnetic shock wave toward the satellite. It was similar to the electromagnetic pulse, or EMP, created by a nuclear explosion, but a high-powered microwave warhead creates its intense burst of energy at a much higher frequency, making it far more difficult to defend against. Even though the satellite's precious electronics were radiation-hardened, they weren't designed to stop such a massive blast of microwave energy delivered from such a close distance.

Infiltrating through the numerous communication antennas, the intense electromagnetic energy created localized power surges that fried the microprocessor chips and other semiconductor devices on the satellite's sensitive circuit boards. With one short burst, the spacecraft was completely disabled—it could no longer receive, process, or send any data.

Not content with merely lobotomizing its target, the projectile's second warhead detonated, propelling a focused stream of hundreds of tungsten pellets toward the hapless satellite. Striking at a speed of nearly eighteen thousand miles per hour, the tiny BB-sized fragments, along with some copper shrapnel from the first warhead, tore huge holes in the satellite's body, ripped off antennas, and shredded solar panels.

Mangled beyond recognition, the satellite careened past the interception point, a trail of debris following in close formation. With its orbit altered and slowly tumbling from the high-speed impacts, the satellite, nothing more than space junk, continued its flight around Earth.

Unexpected Losses

San Diego, CA
September 16, 2017

Ray McConnell was watching the front door for more arrivals, but he would have noticed her anyway. Long, straight black hair, in her early thirties, casually dressed, but making jeans and a knit top look very good. He didn't know her, and was putting a question together when he saw Jim Naguchi follow her in. Oh, that's how she knew.

Ray stood up, still keeping one eye on the screens, and greeted the couple. The woman was staring at the wall behind Ray, and he caught the tail end of her comment. ". . . why you're never at home when I call."

Jim Naguchi answered her, "Third time this week," then took Ray's offered hand. "Hi, Ray, this is Jennifer Oh. We met at that communications conference two weeks ago—the one in San Francisco."

As Ray took Jennifer's hand, she said, "Just Jenny, please," smiling warmly.

"Jenny's in the navy, Ray. She's a computer specialist . . ."

"Which means almost anything these days," Ray completed. "Later we'll try to trick you into telling us what you really do."

Jenny looked a little uncomfortable, even as she continued to stare. Changing his tone a little, Ray announced, "Welcome to the

McConnell Media Center, the largest concentration of guy stuff in captivity."

"I believe it," she answered. "Those are Sony LED flat-screen TVs, aren't they? I've got a fifty-incher at home."

Ray half-turned to face "The Wall." "These are similar, still just three and a half inches thick. But larger," he said modestly.

"And four of them?" she said with awe. "Impressive, and expensive."

Ray shrugged sheepishly. "Some guys have sports cars; I have my Wall."

Every new guest had to stop and stare. The living room of Ray's ranch house was filled with electronic equipment, but the focus of the room was the quad four-by-eight flat-screen video panel. He'd removed the frames and placed them edge to edge, covering one entire wall of his living room with an eight-by-sixteen-foot video display—The Wall.

Right now it was alive with flickering color images. Ray pointed to different areas on the huge surface. "We've set up the center with a map of the China-Vietnam border. We've got subwindows," Ray said, pointing them out, "for five of the major TV networks. That larger text subwindow has the orders of battle for the Vietnamese and Chinese and U.S. forces in the region."

He pointed to a horseshoe-shaped couch in the center of the room, which was filled with people. "The controls are at that end of the couch, and I've got two dedicated NEC quad-core computers controlling the displays."

"So is this how the big kids keep track of an international crisis?" Jennifer asked.

"Maybe." Ray shrugged again and looked at Jim Naguchi, who also shrugged. "I dunno. We never met any. We're just engineers."

"With a strong interest in foreign affairs," she observed.

"True," Ray admitted, "just like everyone else here." He swept his arm wide to include the other guests. Half a dozen people were sitting around the living room, watching the screens, talking, or arguing.

"There are folks here from the military, like you, and professionals from a lot of fields. We get together at times like this to share information and viewpoints."

"And watch the game," she noted coolly. Her tone was friendly, but a little critical as well.

"That window's got the pool on the kickoff times," Ray answered, smiling and indicating another area filled with text and numbers. "Most of the money on when the Chinese will move is at local sunset, in"—he glanced at his watch—"eight hours or so."

"And I brought munchies," Naguchi added, holding up a grocery bag.

"On the counter, Jim, like always," Ray responded. On one side of the living room was a waist-high counter covered with a litter of drinks and snacks.

Ray explained. "It's my way of feeling like I have some control over my life, Jenny. If we know what's going on, we don't feel so helpless." He shrugged at his inadequate explanation. "Knowledge is power. Come on, I'll introduce you around. This is a great place to network."

Raising his voice just a little, he announced, "People, this is Jenny Oh. Navy. She's here with Jim." Everyone waved or nodded to her, but most kept their attention on the Wall.

Ray pointed to a fortyish man in a suit. "That's Jack Garber. He's with Northrop-Grumman. The guy next to him is Don Engen, a C++ coder at a local software company. Bob Reeves is a Marine." Ray smiled. "He's also the founding member of the 'Why isn't it Taiwan?' Foundation."

"I'm still looking for new members," the Marine announced. Lean, tall, even sitting down, and with close-cropped black hair, he explained. "I keep thinking this is some sort of elaborate deception, and while we're looking at China's southern border, she's going to suddenly zig east, leap across the straits, and grab Taiwan."

"But there's no sign of any naval activity west of Hong Kong," Jenny countered, pointing to the map. "The action's all been inland, close to the border. I'm not in intelligence," she warned, "but everything I've heard says it's all pointed at Vietnam . . ."

"Over ten divisions and a hundred aircraft," Garber added. "That's CNN's count this morning, using commercial imaging satellites."

"But why Vietnam at all?" countered Reeves. "They're certainly not a military threat."

"But they are an economic one," replied Jenny. "They're another country that's trading communism for capitalism, and succeeding. The increased U.S. financial investment makes China even more nervous."

"Out of the blue like this?" Reeves was ardent. "Without any warning, two weeks ago, the Chinese started massing troops on the Vietnamese border, and at the same time issued an ultimatum that effectively turns Vietnam into a Chinese colony. It's clear it took everyone by surprise. Look at the way the U.S. military's scrambling to move ships and planes into the theater. But what's behind it? No incident, no provocation, just 'meet these demands or we invade'?"

"No provocation that we know about," Jenny responded coolly.

Ray McConnell smiled, pleased as any host would be. The new arrival was fitting in nicely, and she certainly improved the scenery. He walked behind the counter into the kitchen and started neatening up, trashing empty bags of chips and recycling empty soda bottles. Naguchi was still laying out his snacks on the counter.

"She's a real find, Jim," Ray offered. "Not the same one as last week, though?"

"Well, things didn't work out." Naguchi admitted. "Laura said she needed more space. She suggested I go to Mars." He grinned.

Ray nodded toward the new arrival. "Where's she stationed?"

"All Jenny will tell me is NIOC, San Diego, the Navy Information Operations Command," Naguchi replied. "She knows the technology, and she's interested in defense and the military."

"Well, of course. She's in the business," Ray replied. "She's certainly involved in the discussion." He pointed to Jenny, now using the controls to expand part of the map.

"That's how we met," Naguchi explained. "The Vietnam crisis had just broken, and everyone at the conference was talking about it between seminars, of course. She was always in the thick of it, and somewhere in there I mentioned your sessions here."

"So *this* is your first date?" Ray grinned.

"I hope so," Naguchi answered. "I'm trying to use color and motion to attract the female . . ."

"Ray! You've got a call." A tall black man was waving to him. Ray hurried into the living room, picked up the handset from its cradle, and hit the VIEW button. Part of the Wall suddenly became an image of an older man, overweight and balding, sitting in front of a mass of books. Glasses were perched on his nose, seemingly defying gravity. "Good . . . evening, Raymond."

"Dave Douglas. Good to see you, sir. You're up early in the morning." The United Kingdom was eight hours ahead of California. It was four in the morning in Portsmouth.

"Up very late, you mean. I see you've convened one of your gatherings. I thought you'd like to know we've lost the signals for two of your GPS satellites."

Naguchi, who'd moved next to Jennifer, explained. "Mr. Douglas is the lead administrator for the SeeSat-L website, a satellite observation group. They're hobbyists, located all over the world, who track satellites visually and electronically. Think high-tech birdwatchers."

"I've heard of them," she answered, nodding, "and of Douglas. Your friend knows *him*?" She sounded impressed.

Naguchi replied, "Uh-huh. Ray's got contacts all over."

Jennifer nodded again, trying to pick up the conversation at the same time.

". . . verified Horace's report about an hour ago. It was space vehicle number sixty-three, a relatively new bird, but anything mechanical can fail, I suppose. I normally wouldn't think it worth more than a note, but he and I were already discussing another GPS satellite that went down earlier. We lost its signal about a week ago."

"Why is Horace looking at the GPS satellite signals?" Ray asked.

"Horace collects electronic signals. He's writing a piece on the GPS signal structure for the next issue of our online magazine."

Ray looked uncertain, even a little worried. "Two failures so close to each other is a little unusual, isn't it?" It was a rhetorical question.

Douglas sniffed. "GPS satellites don't fail as a matter of routine, Raymond. You've only had five go down since the first operational satellites were put online some twenty-eight years ago. That's just over a nine-percent failure rate overall, and with the newer-generation satellites, the failure rate is half that. No, Raymond, this is most atypical. By the way, both satellites were passing over the Pacific basin when the signals were lost."

Ray could only manage a "What?" but Douglas seemed to understand his query. "I'm sending you a file with the orbital data for the constellation in it. I've marked SVN forty-five and sixty-three. They're the ones that have failed." He paused for a moment, typing. "There . . . you have it now."

"Thank you, Dave. I'll get back to you if we can add anything to what you've found." Ray broke the connection and grabbed his data tablet.

While he worked with the system, speculation filled the conversation. "So we turned off two of the birds ourselves?" someone asked. "That doesn't make any sense. What could we hope to accomplish by doing that?"

"Denying their signal to the Chinese," Reeves suggested.

"If so, why only two?" countered Jenny.

"And the most accurate signal's encrypted anyway," added Garber. "The Chinese can only use civilian GPS."

"They've got their own Beidou system," reminded Reeves. "With it's own encrypted signal. They're using it in their equipment. And if they have the gear, they can use the European Galileo, which is even more accurate."

"We need GPS a lot more than the Chinese," said Garber.

Jennifer nodded. "All of our strike planning depends on GPS. Not to mention most of our precision-guided weapons. If we had to go back to the pre-GPS days, it would be a lot harder to run a coordinated attack. We could never get the split-second timing or accuracy we have now, and we'd have to get closer to the targets. That means higher losses from air defenses."

"Here's the orbital data," Ray announced.

The smaller windows on the Wall all vanished, leaving the map showing southern China and Vietnam. A small bundle of curved lines appeared in the center, then expanded out to fill the map, covering the area with orbital tracks. As Ray moved the cursor on his data pad, the cursor moved on the map. When it rested on a track, a tag appeared, naming the satellite and providing orbital and other data. Two of the tracks were red, not white, and were marked with small boxes with a time in them.

"Where are the satellites right now?" someone asked.

Ray tapped the tablet, and small diamonds appeared on all the tracks, showing their current positions.

"Can you move them to where they'd be at local sunset for Hanoi?" suggested Garber.

"And what's the horizon for those satellites at Mengzi?" Jenny prompted, pointing to a town just north of the Chinese-Vietnamese border. "That's one of the places the Chinese are supposed to be massing."

"Stand by," answered Ray. "That's not built in. I'll have to do the math and draw it." He worked quickly, and in absolute silence. After about two minutes, an oval drawn in red appeared on the map, centered on the location. Everyone counted, but Ray spoke first. "I count three."

"And you need four for a good 3D fix," finished Naguchi.

National Military Command Center
The Pentagon
September 18, 2017

". . . and since we no longer have complete twenty-four/seven 3D GPS coverage, the staff is working a new air plan." The assistant J-3 looked uncomfortable, as only a colonel can look when giving bad news to a roomful of four-star generals. "Aircraft navigation errors interfere with our tactics, and weapon-miss distances more than double."

General Warner was the Air Force Chief of Staff. He cut into the conversation, reporting, "The first wave has eighty-three targets, and we've allocated a hundred and fifty combat aircraft and almost two hundred cruise missiles. That part of the air plan has been redone, except for a final check. The follow-up and secondary strikes are next. They'll be harder, since it's a larger set and involves potentially mobile targets."

General Sam Kastner, U.S. Army, Chairman of the Joint Chiefs, was in charge of the meeting. "I just came from the Oval Office, and the president is convinced that Operation CERTAIN FORCE will only work as a deterrent if the Chinese believe we really can stop their invasion."

This meeting of the Joint Chiefs of Staff had originally been scheduled to review the ongoing preparations for Operation CERTAIN FORCE. The buildup had been ordered as soon as the United States and her Asian allies had become convinced that the Chinese troop movements were more than just an exercise. Instead, they were working to understand the effects of the GPS satellite loss on what had been an almost overwhelming advantage.

"It will work," Warner affirmed, standing. He was built like a fighter pilot, short and almost stocky. The air force was the lead service for the operation, since their aircraft would carry out most of the manned strikes.

"Right now, for at least ten percent of the prime night-strike time, we'd be operating without adequate GPS coverage. If we use the remaining time with full coverage, to maximize our strikes, that makes us a little more predicable. If we accept the reduced coverage and fly then, we'll pay for it with proportionately reduced effectiveness. We can still do it, but the price may be a little higher."

Kastner nodded an acknowledgment, scowling, but as Warner sat, the air force general asked, "Did the president mention anything about the negotiations? Do we have a timeline?" In other words, how much time did they have before the Chinese moved?

"No." Kastner answered so sharply it surprised the others. "The Chinese aren't negotiating, so there's been no progress. Just an impossible list of demands, out of the blue, citing territorial claims hundreds of years old, persecution of the Hoa minority in Vietnam, and of course the South China Sea with the Spratly Islands."

"And all the Vietnamese have to do is allow themselves to become a Chinese colony," Admiral Glover finished.

Kastner shrugged. "They're not talking to the Vietnamese—they're not talking to anyone. But it's not an ultimatum, technically. There's no deadline—which, in a way is smart, because nobody knows exactly when the time's up. Most of Asia's in an uproar over this, and the lack of a timeline just adds to the uncertainty."

"We'll get it done, sir." Warner looked over to Glover, who nodded confidently.

Kastner turned to a boyish-looking rear admiral. "Mike, have your people found out anything else since this morning?"

The J-2, or the director, joint staff intelligence, usually had two or three assistants on his briefing staff, but this time he had a small mob of officers and civilians behind him. The admiral moved to the podium.

"Only that both birds were functioning within norms just before they went off-line. Number forty-five was much older, well beyond her design service life. She was the first to go, and, because of her age, no one thought anything of it. Hell, we were surprised she kept on plugging along after last year's solar flare took out three of her siblings. Number sixty-three is a whole other ball game. It was one of the updated Block IIF birds with the longer service life, not quite brand-new, but not over the hill, either. All attempts to restart them, or even communicate with them, have failed. Imaging from telescopes shows that they're still there, but they're in a slow tumble, which they shouldn't be doing . . ."

"And the chance of both of them suffering a catastrophic failure is nil," concluded the chairman.

"Yes, sir. The final straw is that we started warm-up procedures on the two reserve birds, sixty-six and sixty-seven. Or rather, we tried to warm them up. They didn't respond, either. And they're tumbling, too. Both were younger Block IIF satellites, with only three years in orbit."

General Warner asked, "Is there anything that links this to the Chinese?" He sounded frustrated, and surprised that the perpetrator should be so hard to identify. The air force, through the Fiftieth Space Operations Wing, operated the GPS satellites.

"Aside from the timing, and the fact that the active GPS satellites stopped transmitting while over the Pacific, no, sir. We don't know how they did this, either. If we knew how, that would immediately narrow the list of suspects, as well as ways of gathering evidence.

"We know that the DSP infrared satellites detected no launches, and we believe that they also would have detected a laser powerful enough to knock out a GPS bird—although that's not a certainty," he added quickly, nodding to an army officer with a stern expression on his face.

"The Chinese are the most likely actors, of course, but others can't be ruled out. CIA believes the attack was made by agents on the ground or in cyberspace, but we've detected no signs of this at any of the monitoring stations. The navy believes the Chinese have adapted their space launch vehicles for the purpose. Although it's a logical proposition, we've seen no sign of a launch or the considerable effort it would require. And we track the Chinese space program quite closely."

The frustration in his voice underlined every word. "It's possible that the Russians or someone else is doing it to assist the Chinese, but there's no particular reason for them to help China. There aren't that many candidates, and we've simply seen no sign of activity by any nation, friendly or hostile." He almost threw up his hands.

"Thank you, Admiral," replied Kastner. "Set up a Joint Intelligence Task Force immediately. Spread your net wide."

He didn't have to say that the media was also spreading their net. Television and the Internet were already full of rumors—that an attack had been scheduled but called off, that the Chinese buildup was just a bluff, that the United States had already backed down because of the risk of excessive casualties, and others more fanciful. U.S. "resolve" was now an open question.

Gongga Shan Launch Complex
Sichuan Province, China
September 22, 2017

General Shen Xuesen stood quietly, calmly, watching the bank of monitors but wishing he could be on the surface. He had a better view of the operation from here, but it did not seem as real.

It was their fifth time, and he could see the staff settling down, nowhere as nervous as the first launch, but China was committed now, and her future hung on their success.

Everyone saw the short, solidly built general standing quietly in the gallery. It was a commander's role to appear calm, even when he knew exactly how many things could go wrong, and how much was at stake, both for him and for China.

In his early fifties, he'd spent a lot of time in the weather, and it showed. An engineer, he looked capable of reshaping a mountain, and he had Gongga Shan as proof.

Shen had already given his permission to fire. The staff was counting down, waiting until they were in the exact center of the intercept window. The "Dragon's Egg" sat in the breech, inert but vital, waiting for just a few more seconds.

The moment came as the master clock stepped down to zero. The launch controller turned a key, and for a moment the only sign of activity was on the computer displays. Shen's eyes glanced to the breech seals, but the indicators all showed green. He watched the video screen that showed the muzzle, a black oval three meters across.

Even with a muzzle velocity of nearly five thousand meters per second, it took time for the egg to build up to full speed. Almost a full second elapsed between ignition and . . .

A puff of smoke and flame appeared on the display, followed by a black streak, briefly visible. Only its size, almost three meters in diameter, allowed it to be seen by the human eye. High-speed cameras caught the egg as it left the bore and displayed an image on a central screen. Everything appeared nominal.

Shen relaxed, his inward calm now matching his outward demeanor. His gun had worked again.

"Hatching," reported the launch controller. Everyone had so loved the egg metaphor that they used the term to report when the sabots separated from the meter-sized projectile. Designed to hold the small vehicle inside the larger bore, they split and fell away almost instantly. Effectively, the projectile got the boost of a three-meter barrel but the drag of a one-meter body.

Speed, always more speed, mused Shen as he watched the monitors. The crews were already boarding buses for their ride up the mountain to inspect the gun. Other screens showed helicopters lifting off to search for the sabots. Although they could not be used again, they were marvels of engineering in their own right and could reveal much about the gun's design.

The goal was ten kilometers a second, orbital velocity. First, take a barrel a kilometer long and three meters across. To make it laser-straight, gouge out the slope of a mountain and anchor it on the bedrock. Cover it up, armor and camouflage it, too. Put the muzzle near the top, 7,900 meters above sea level. That reduces air resistance and buys you some speed. Then use sabots to get even more speed. You're halfway there. Then . . .

"Ignition," announced one of the controllers. Put a solid rocket booster on the projectile to give it the final push it needed. "She's flying! Guidance is online, sir. It's in the center of the basket. Intercept in twenty minutes."

General Shen had seen the concept described in a summary the Iraqis had provided of supergun technology after the first Persian Gulf war. American technological superiority had been more than a shock to the People's Liberation Army. It had triggered an upheaval.

The Chinese military had always chosen numbers over quality, because numbers were cheap, and the politburo was trying to feed one and a half billion people. They'd always believed that numbers could overwhelm a smaller high-tech force, making them reluctant to even try. Everyone knew how sensitive the Americans were to casualties and to risk.

But if the difference in quality is big enough, numbers don't matter anymore. Imagine using machine guns during the Crusades or a nuclear sub in World War II. Shen and his colleagues had watched American troops run rings around the Iraqis, suffering few casualties while they devastated the opposition.

So the Chinese army had started the long, expensive process of becoming a modern military. They'd bought high-tech weapons from the Russians. They'd stolen and copied what they couldn't buy. They'd gotten all kinds of advanced technologies: supersonic cruise missiles for their navy, advanced radars, exotic aircraft designs.

It wasn't enough. Running and working as hard as they could, they'd cut the technology lag from twenty to ten years. They were following the same path as the West, and it would just take time to catch up.

General Shen had seen the answer. He'd found a vulnerability, then planned, convinced, plotted, and argued until the politburo had listened and backed his idea. If your opponent strikes at you from above, take away his perch. Take away that advantage.

Build a prison camp deep in the mountains, in a remote spot in southern China. Send the hard cases and malcontents there. The state has useful work for them. Watch the prisoners dig away the side of a mountain. You need a rail line to the nearest city, Kangding, two hundred and fifty kilometers southwest. That had been a job in itself. Then add army barracks, the launch control center, and extensive air defenses. It had taken years before it looked like anything more than a terrible mistake.

Meanwhile, design the *Tien Lung*, or Celestial Dragon, to fly in space. And design a gun, the biggest gun in the history of the world, *Lung Mu*, "the Dragon's Mother," to fire it. China's civilian space program had been expanded, and provided a lot of the talent, as well as a convenient excuse for foreign study and purchases.

"Control has been passed to Xichang," the senior controller announced. "Intercept in ten minutes." A look of relief passed over his face. If a screw-up occurred after this, it was their fault, not his. Of course, it was still a week's effort wasted.

Shen longed to be in two places at once, but the gun was his, and Dong Zhi, the scientist who had actually designed the Dragon's Egg, was at the space complex. Xichang was one of four launch complexes associated with China's space program, and they were in the right location and had the antennas to watch the intercepts.

Everyone in the room watched the central display, even though it was only a computer representation. Two small dots sat on curved lines, slowly moving to an intersection point. Then the screen changed, becoming completely black, with the characters for "Terminal Phase" displayed in one corner.

General Shen Xuesen smiled. He had insisted on an imaging infrared seeker for terminal-phase guidance. Not only was it hard to jam, it made the result understandable. Seeing the target grow from a speck to a blob to a recognizable satellite had made it real, both for the leadership who had watched the tests and for the people who had to do the work, who fought the war from Earth's surface.

The image was a little grainy, because of the lens size, but it also had the clarity of space. He could see the boxy, cluttered body of the American GPS satellite and the outspread solar panels, each divided into four sections.

The controller started counting down as the image slowly expanded. "Five seconds, four, three, two, one, now." He uttered the last word softly, but triumphantly, as the image suddenly vanished. A few people clapped, but they'd all seen this before, and most didn't feel the need now.

All that work, all that money, to put two small warheads in orbit. An explosive charge created an electronic pulse that fried the target satellite's electronics. A second warhead hurled a wall of fragments at the unarmored victim. Filled with atomic clocks and delicate electronics, a GPS satellite didn't have a hope of surviving either attack. The carcass would remain in its orbit, intact, but pocked with dozens of small holes, its microprocessors shorted out and smashed.

In fact, the kill was almost an anticlimax. After all the work of getting the vehicle up there, it was over far too quickly.

Skyhook One Seven
Over the South China Sea
September 22, 2017

"We just lost one of the GPS signals," reported the navigator. "Switching to the inertial navigation system." The navigator, an air force major, sounded concerned but not alarmed.

"Is it the receiver?" asked the mission commander. A full colonel, it was his job to manage the information gathered by the electronic intelligence aircraft. Running racetracks off the China coast, it listened for radar and radio signals, analyzing their contents and fixing their location. The digested information was data linked directly back to the joint task force headquarters.

"Self-test is good, sir, and the receiver is still picking up the other satellites, but we just lost one of the signals, and now we're outside our error budget." Each satellite over the minimum required narrowed the area of uncertainty around a transmitter's location. GPS was accurate enough to target some missiles directly or give pilots a good idea of where to search for their objective.

"So we've lost another one," muttered the colonel.

2

Inspiration

CNN News
September 24, 2017

"With the loss of another GPS satellite, emotions at the Fiftieth Space Operations Wing have changed from grim, or angry, to fatalistic." Mark Markin, CNN's defense correspondent, stood in front of the gate to the NORAD complex at Cheyenne Mountain. The Fiftieth's operations center was actually located nearby at Schriever Air Force Base, but the drama of the mountain's tunnel entrance was preferable to Schriever's nondescript government buildings.

Markin wore a weather-beaten parka, zipped up against the chill of the Colorado wind. His carefully shaped hair was beginning to show the effects of the wind as well, and he seemed to rush through his report in an effort to get out of the weather.

"Although it is widely acknowledged that the loss of the GPS satellites is not attributed to any fault of the people here at the Fiftieth, they are still suffering a deep sense of helplessness.

"Since the GPS network became active in 1989, it has become almost a public utility. The men and women here take pride in providing a service that not only gives the U.S. Armed Forces a tremendous military advantage, but benefits the civilian community in countless ways. Even with the fielding of the Chinese and European

satellite navigation systems, GPS remains a critical aspect supporting everyday life, as well as international travel and commerce.

"Now, someone, possibly the Chinese, but certainly an enemy of
the United States, has destroyed at least three satellites. Yesterday's
loss shows that last week's attack was not an isolated incident.

"And the United States seems unable to do anything to stop it."

SPAWAR Systems Center Pacific
San Diego, CA
September 25, 2017

Leaning back in his chair, arms crossed over his chest, Ray sat silently, staring at the GPS Block III satellite model on his desk. His
morning coffee sat untouched, the contents of the mug having long
since cooled. The computer screen was empty, the machine still dark.
Ray McConnell was elsewhere, his gaze focused intensely on the
model satellite, like a monk before the cross. So entranced, he failed
to recognize Jim Naguchi's spoken greeting. It wasn't until Naguchi
knocked hard on Ray's door that he was yanked back to the here and
now.

"Earth to Ray, come in, please," teased his friend as he entered.

"Huh? Oh, sorry, Jim. I didn't hear you," replied Ray with a sheepish grin.

"Obviously. Please tell me you were daydreaming about a scant-
ily clad blonde on some remote beach."

Ray chuckled halfheartedly at Naguchi's off-the-wall remark.
"Hardly, Jim, hardly. My mind has been out there," replied Ray
grimly as he tilted his head toward the satellite model.

"In medium Earth orbit? Well, that explains everything now,
doesn't it?" The sterner tone told Ray his friend wasn't joking anymore.

"What do mean by that?" Ray shot back defensively.

"For the last week you've been shuffling about, depressed and gloomy. 'Morose' would be an apt description. Then I hear from a couple of the guys that you canceled your regular Saturday BOG-SAT at the very last moment, no explanation given. And this morning, you came into the office, said not a word to anyone, and parked your ass in that chair. Both your computer and coffee are stone-cold, meaning you haven't done any work and you blew off the division heads' meeting."

"I sent Jake in my place," Ray interrupted.

"Yes, you did, and Mr. Olsen did a fine job, too. Your job," argued Naguchi. "And Rudy was none too happy about it, by the way. But I digress; my point is that your behavior as of late isn't even remotely normal for one Ray McConnell. Everyone is upset about the GPS satellite loses, but you seem to be taking it personally. Would you mind telling me why you're ripping your stomach lining apart?"

Ray ran his fingers through his hair and let out a low sigh. Naguchi's summary was spot on; Ray had been brooding since he first learned of the two satellites failing. One was an old Block IIR satellite well beyond its service life and was expected to die at any moment. But the other bird was relatively young, with more than half of its life left. Then there were the rumors that the two reserve satellites had mysteriously failed as well. Both of them were just barely three years old.

But it was the most recent failure of a brand-new Block III satellite that really got to Ray. It hadn't been in space three months. Five satellites, of three different types, had suddenly stopped functioning within a matter of a month. This was no systematic engineering fault; someone was intentionally attacking the GPS constellation. There was no other plausible explanation.

The simmering frustration had grown to a full boil when Ray's inquiries to Naval Intelligence were quietly rebuffed. He didn't have "a need to know," he was told. If the U.S. Navy's lead engineer on GPS didn't have sufficient justification for access to the information, then who the hell did? It then dawned on him that maybe the intel types were just trying to hide the fact that they didn't know who was making the attacks. That thought only made him more depressed. Most people within the navigation-satellite community suspected China, but there wasn't a shred of evidence to link them to any of the losses.

After a short silence, Ray threw his hands in the air. "You're right, Jim. This whole thing has been driving me crazy! Nobody seems to know what is going on, and nobody seems to be doing anything about it!"

"And how would you know that, Ray?" Naguchi countered. "We aren't in the operational chain of command, we aren't war fighters, and, the last I checked, the folks in STRATCOM aren't required to tell us R&D wonks a damn thing."

"C'mon, Jim. You, of all people, should know that I have contacts throughout the GPS community, including NNSOC and the Fifticth Space Wing. Everyone is scratching their heads on this one; the satellites were functioning within specs and then suddenly just dropped off-line. The fact that they're all tumbling points to a physical impact of some sort. But there is no evidence of a launch, from anywhere in the world that coincides with any of the events. The 'operators' don't have a clue how the satellites are being attacked, or by whom!"

Ray was the ultimate social networker whose methods went far beyond just the trendy electronic means. He regularly met and talked with people both in and out of his specific technical area. He'd attended professional conventions and other official functions just to meet new people, to exchange new ideas and bounce them around over a beer.

And then there were his BOGSAT sessions, which functioned like a powerful magnet, pulling even more people into Ray's ever-expanding sphere of professional contacts. His Rolodex was rumored to be a proverbial Who's Who of top marine and aeronautical engineers, as well as doctorate-level experts within the IT, communications, and spacecraft-design disciplines—a list that had paid handsome information dividends in the past.

"All right," exclaimed a frustrated Naguchi, "so you have a valid basis for your concern. But that doesn't change the fact that it's not our problem to fix. We don't build the satellites, we don't launch them, we don't operate them, and we sure as hell don't defend them. Those functions are just not in our job description, and you aren't doing anyone any favors, particularly yourself, by moping about and agonizing over things we have no power to deal with."

"I couldn't have said it any better, Jim," came a new voice from behind him.

Naguchi winced, instantly regretting not closing the door before talking to Ray. Turning, he saw their division chief, Rudy White, walk into the office.

"Would you please excuse us, Jim? I need to speak to Mr. McConnell alone."

"Certainly, Rudy," replied Naguchi. Facing Ray, he said, "I'll catch you later, Ray." His expression added an unspoken "Sorry."

Ray nodded his understanding. He knew his friend wouldn't intentionally sandbag him in front of their boss. As Naguchi turned to leave, White added sternly, "Please close the door on your way out, Jim."

Once the latch clicked in the strike plate, White wasted no time and demanded bluntly, "Why weren't you at the division meeting this morning?"

Ray could see his boss was angry, not that that was anything new. Rudy White always seemed to be angry with someone or something. "I was trying to figure out what's going on with our satellites, Rudy. I asked Jake Olsen to attend in my place because he can give the routine project update just as well as I can."

"While that may be true, Mr. McConnell, the government isn't paying him to be the navy's GPS team lead; they're paying you. And as we are getting very close to the delivery date for a major research project, I expect to see more of you, not less."

"The quantum-logic-clock integration study is nearly finished. I just need to wrap up the last editorial corrections to the final report. You'll have it by Thursday, which is the due date, as I recall."

"Was, Mr. McConnell, was. Thursday *was* the due date to get the report to me. But since our commanding officer has had his trip to Washington moved up, the report is now due by close of business tomorrow. A schedule change that you would have been alerted to if you had bothered to read your e-mail or attend the regular division meeting." A sarcastic smirk momentarily replaced White's usual frown.

Ray bit his tongue; nothing good would come from one of his witty barbs. Normally he wouldn't shy away from sparring with White over such a minor schedule change, but not when Ray was clearly in the wrong. "No problem, Rudy. You'll have the final report by early to-morrow afternoon."

The surprised expression on White's face told Ray that his reply was not what his boss had expected. Frowning harder, White said, "Good. I want Rear Admiral Griffith to be well prepared when he attends the navy R&D budget meeting next month. The quantum-logic-clock project has the potential to be the biggest advance in sat-ellite navigation since the introduction of GPS itself. I don't want us blowing it with a substandard report."

Ray ignored White's insult; the man could be quite petty at times. All he was concerned about was his projects' cost, schedule, and de-liverables. As long as everything was on the proper glide path, and his bosses were happy, nothing else mattered. His bureaucratically narrow focus often grated on Ray.

"It won't matter that we can nail position accuracy to within a few millimeters if we can't keep our satellites safe from harm," he said firmly.

"The issue of the GPS satellite failures is being . . ."

"They're not *just* failing, Rudy!" Ray exclaimed. "They're being attacked and neutralized!"

"The jury is still out on that, Mr. McConnell. However, I'll grant that you are probably correct. But even if our satellites are being attacked, it's a matter for the warfighters to handle, not us. We have neither the talent nor resources to address this problem. Even in times of war, there are chains of command and areas of responsibility, Ray."

"But, Rudy, that's my point! No one has a handle on this. It makes far more sense for all the commands to pool their resources and try to solve . . ."

"Ray, I appreciate your concern, truly," interrupted White. "But we're a research and development command, and while we support the warfighters, we're not an operational command. Which means we don't jump into the warfighters' knickers and tell them how to do their job. If they want our help, they'll ask. Until then, SPAWAR Systems Center Pacific is not officially involved. Is that understood?"

"Perfectly," Ray replied firmly. There was no point in continuing the discussion. White simply couldn't conceive that it might be necessary to stray from their well-established lane in the road to solve a national-level problem. One didn't just leap across command boundaries without permission; it wasn't how good organizations behaved. To even suggest such a thing was undisciplined foolishness.

"Good. I look forward to seeing your team's report tomorrow afternoon."

Ray nodded his understanding and watched as White departed. Reaching down, Ray turned on his computer and then grabbed his favorite DO NOT DISTURB sign and hung it on his door. He had a lot of work to do, and he was determined to finish it by the end of the day.

Ray smiled smugly as he e-mailed to White not only the completed final report but also the edited PowerPoint presentation for Admiral Griffith as well. *This should keep Rudy busy for a while,* thought Ray. He then forwarded everything to Jake Olsen, along with a note that he'd be out of the office for a few days. He had a lot of "use or lose" leave on the books, and he wanted to get started on a new personal project. As soon as Ray sent the electronic leave request to White, he bolted for the door.

National Military Command Center
The Pentagon
September 26, 2017

The Joint Chiefs of Staff didn't normally meet at two in the morning, but Rear Admiral Overton's call was worth getting out of bed for.

Most of the service chiefs had been in the Pentagon anyway, trying to manage the crisis, the troops, and the media. Although only five GPS satellites had been lost out of a constellation of twenty-six, it had created periods when there were gaps in 3D coverage over the South Pacific during the night hours, and there was no indication that they'd be able to put a stop to the mysterious losses anytime soon. On the contrary, everyone assumed it would get a lot worse before it got better.

Then there was the continuing problem in Vietnam. The crisis had been rapidly building, and even though the shooting hadn't started yet, indications strongly argued that it was only a matter of time. Unfortunately, U.S. forces could not completely execute their preferred way of war, precision night attacks, without full GPS coverage. The longer the Chinese waited, and with further degradation to the GPS constellation, the window suitable for U.S. strikes would continue to shrink. No one believed this was a coincidence. Had China initiated hostilities by attacking American GPS satellites? Had a war already started out in space?

As they hurried into the command center, the J-2, Rear Admiral Frank Overton, compared the generals' normal polished appearance with the tired, frustrated men in front of him. He was glad he had some good news—sort of.

The chief of staff of the air force and the chief of naval operations were both last, coming in together, breaking off some sort of disagreement as they walked through the door. Overton didn't even wait for them to sit down.

"We finally have proof. It's the Chinese. We figured out how and that led to where," he announced.

Overton's tablet and the large screen at the head of the table showed a black-and-white satellite photo. A date in the corner read "June 2012."

"This is the Gongga Shan prison camp in Sichuan Province, southern China—at least, we had identified it as a prison camp. We named it after the mountain. Gongga Shan is the tallest mountain in Sichuan Province and is part of the Daxue mountain range. The peak rises to a height just shy of twenty-five thousand feet." Using his laser pointer, he showed areas marked PRISONERS' BARRACKS, GUARD BARRACKS, INFIRMARY and so on. "As far as we know, it was built about five years ago and can accommodate several thousand prisoners."

He pressed the remote again, and the first image slid to one side, and a second, of the same area, appeared alongside it. "This was taken about six hours ago. This construction work"—he indicated a long scar on the side of the mountain in the first photo—"has been finished or just stopped. The imagery analysts believe it was finished, because if the Chinese had just abandoned it, the excavation scar would still be there. In fact, if you look in the second photo, the mountain's surface has been restored to its natural state. The original analysis four years ago speculated that the prisoners might be mining, or building an observatory, or putting up a major communications antenna hub. The excavation went across the southern side of the mountain in a west-to-east direction, more than halfway up to the peak."

Admiral Overton paused, looking at the group. A hint of embarrassment appeared on his face. "That initial analysis was never followed up." He shrugged apologetically.

General Kastner spoke for the group. "And the real answer is?"

Overton pressed the remote again. A gray-green infrared image appeared, superimposed over the second photo. "We drilled down a bit to see what they'd been working on. This is a satellite infrared picture taken about an hour ago. We were lucky," he explained. "We had perfectly clear weather and the wind wasn't too high."

Most of the shapes in the image duplicated the buildings and other structures, but one shape was unique: a long, thick, straight line, laid west-to-east along the southern face of the mountain.

"It's 3,280 feet long—a full kilometer—and based on careful measurements, we know it's angled along the mountain face at about eighty-five degrees. At the base you'll see a series of buried structures, including what we think are several bunkers for the launch crew. The buildings at the base are hot, and the entire structure is slightly warmer than the surrounding rock. We think it's made of high-strength reinforced concrete."

"A buried rocket launcher?" wondered the army chief of staff.

"Close, but no, sir. It's a buried gun barrel, a very large gun barrel. There's no discernable large entrance to bring in a missile, nor is there a road or railhead leading up to the launcher. Also, the imagery guys haven't found any evidence of exhaust vents. You'd need those to prevent the rocket exhaust from pressurizing the launcher. But with a gun, that is exactly what you want to do. See these shapes?" He used the pointer to indicate several rounded structures. "We believe these are tanks for the liquid propellant fuel, probably liquid hydrogen. The bore looks to be about nine or ten feet in diameter. It's at the corner of this ridgeline, here. It's been well camouflaged, but it's still a little warmer than the rest of the rock. We haven't finished working out the numbers, but the initial estimate is that it's capable of launching a small rocket-boosted projectile into medium Earth orbit."

Even while the flag officers and their staffs took in the spectacular news, Kastner jumped on it immediately. "Great job, Frank. We're pressed for time, but I've got to know how you found this."

"We're putting together a complete report right now, sir. You'll all have it in a few hours." He paused for a moment, and then added, "To answer your question: elimination and luck. The three active satellites were killed in the same area, just east of Okinawa. We assumed an easterly trajectory, as that requires the least amount of energy to get something into orbit. We then focused our radars on the

GPS birds as they passed by that area during the night. We caught a glimpse of a projectile during the last attack, back-calculated its trajectory to its origin, and tried to find a launching site in the region. We got lucky because we figured they'd start with an established installation, and the Gongga Shan prison camp was on a rather short list. In hindsight, it probably never was anything but a construction site for the gun. We've been looking in all the wrong places for the last three weeks." He didn't sound proud.

Kastner was complimentary but grim. "Well, Frank, I'm glad the intel community nailed it down. As they say, better late than never. But your work has just begun. We need to know a lot more about this weapon. First, is this the only one? It probably is, but I've got to know absolutely. Second, how many more satellites can they kill with it? And third, what would it take to stop it?"

Overton nodded silently, his expression as grim as the chairman's. Nodding respectfully to his boss and the other joint chiefs, he and his staff left. They had a lot of questions on their plate and not much time to get the answers.

Kastner turned to the others. "Immediate impressions, gentlemen? After we finish here, I'll wake the SECDEF. He'll have to give the bad news to the president."

Casa McConnell
San Diego, CA
September 26, 2017

The chime from his computer jolted Ray back to consciousness. Yawning, he looked at the clock on his desktop—two o'clock in the afternoon! He must have fallen asleep soon after he had sent out the "call to arms" by e-mail. Without thinking, Ray reached for the mug by his machine and took a big gulp. "Ugh!" he gasped, almost spitting the liquid out onto his laptop.

"Cold coffee, bad choice," choked Ray. Stumbling over to the kitchen, he put the mug in the microwave and nuked its contents on high. While the coffee returned to a drinkable temperature, Ray leaned over the kitchen sink and threw some cold water on his face. By the time he'd dried his hands and face, the sharp "ding" of the microwave signaled the completion of its assigned mission. Snatching the mug from the microwave, Ray headed back to his computer, sipping the old but now hot coffee. He grunted his approval as he sat down and pulled up his e-mail in-box. He liked what he saw on the screen.

Twelve people had already sent a positive response to his "emergency" summons; they'd be at his house by 7:00 P.M. Several more expressed their disappointment that they were out of town and would miss the kickoff meeting, but each one reassured Ray they'd join the design team as soon as they got back to San Diego. Within seven hours of his e-mail going out, Ray had sixteen top-notch experts committed to helping him with Project *Defender*. The name he'd chosen was, admittedly, a bit cutesy, but it would help keep them focused on their goal—defending U.S. space-borne assets. It certainly wasn't any worse than some of the corny names the Pentagon came up with.

A quick review of the growing roster showed Ray he had a solid team in the spacecraft design, propulsion, communications, and mission-planning cells. But they were weak on command and control and payload (i.e., sensors and weapons). He'd suspected these areas would be harder to fill, as many of the best people wore uniforms, and he'd intentionally not sent the e-mail to anyone currently on active duty in the military. They could get into serious trouble if their chain of command found out what Ray was working on and that they were helping him.

That decision had been particularly agonizing for Ray. He had many close friends in the armed services, particularly the air force and navy, who weren't going to be happy with him for leaving them out of the loop, but he couldn't risk jeopardizing their careers by sending them a direct e-mail that could be traced back to him. If they heard about this project through the grapevine, he'd deal with each individual at his front door.

Ray shook his head as he looked at the command and control group; it was the weakest of the lot by far. He immediately thought of Jenny Oh. She was smart, motivated, and had the very expertise that Ray knew he desperately needed. But she was a naval officer, and that put her out of bounds. Taking Jenny off the Project *Defender* design-team list seemed to bother Ray more than it should have, and he was at a loss to explain why.

Sure, she was as attractive as she was intelligent, but she was a relative newcomer to Ray's circle of influence. She'd only been to two of his weekend BOGSATs, and both times she came with Jim Naguchi. In the grand scheme of things, she was little more than an acquaintance.

The chime from his laptop forced Ray to focus his attention on a new e-mail. Another engineer had pledged his efforts to the cause. *Excellent,* he thought. "Maybe SPAWAR doesn't have the talent, Rudy," muttered Ray to himself, "but I know where to find it."

3

Networking

Casa McConnell
San Diego, CA
September 28, 2017

Chris Champagne had gone to only a few of Ray's BOGSATs. His "discussion groups," famous throughout SPAWAR, were always worthwhile. Although Champagne would have liked to go more often, two preschoolers and another on the way severely limited his free time.

Tonight, though, he'd made the time. In fact, his wife, Sandy, had almost ordered him to. After he'd described Ray's sudden leave of absence and the rumors from the other coworkers, she'd urged him to go and get the straight story.

Champagne was an antenna design specialist on Ray's GPS team. He liked his very outgoing boss and had no trouble working for the man, even though McConnell could be a little fierce in technical "discussions." Champagne was worried about their project, which was suffering in Ray's absence, and about Ray. With the brass so upset about the GPS losses, and Rudy White foaming at the mouth over the final project report, it was no time for Ray to play "missing person."

The map on the car's navigation console showed he was getting close. Ray's street was just around the sharp bend ahead. Champagne signaled and started turning onto Panorama Drive. The last time he had visited Ray's place was over a year ago, when he and Sandy had attended a reception for a visiting astronaut. That had been quite the occasion.

But nothing like this. As he made the turn, Champagne saw the street almost completely lined with cars. This was definitely not typical for the quiet residential community. Champagne ended up parking a block away.

As he hurried up the path, he heard the expected hubbub flowing out the open windows, but it didn't seem as loud as usual. Stranger still, Ray didn't answer the door, and everyone wasn't reclining before the Wall. People seemed to be spread out all over the house. A group of four men huddled around a coffee table in the living room, and he could see another clustered in the kitchen. Ray appeared suddenly from one of the bedrooms, hurrying. He looked tired. As soon as Ray saw the stocky engineer in the doorway, he made a beeline over to him.

"Chris Champagne! It's great to see you." Genuine pleasure lit up Ray's face as he shook Champagne's hand in greeting, but there was a distracted air to it. And surprise.

Champagne saw no point in dissembling. "Ray, what's going on over here? You haven't been at work . . . ."

"I've got bigger fish to fry, Chris. Promise you won't tell anyone what's going on here? Unless I okay it?"

"Well, of course." Champagne wondered what he'd just agreed to. It couldn't be anything illegal . . .

Ray looked at him intently. "No, Chris, I mean it. You can't tell anyone. Treat this as if it were classified."

The word "classified" triggered reflexes. It made Champagne both cautious and curious. He studied McConnell for a moment, then carefully said, "I promise not to tell anyone what I see here." He fought the urge to raise his right hand.

Ray seemed to relax a little and smiled again. "You'll understand

in a minute, Chris." Turning, he called over to the group at the coffee table. "I'll be right there."

One of the men, whom Champagne recognized as Avrim Takir,
a mathematician from the GPS group, popped his head up and answered, "Fine, Ray. We need another ten minutes, anyway." Takir
spotted Champagne and waved but quickly returned his attention
to the laptop in front of him.

Ray led his teammate down the hall into his home office. The desk
was piled high with books, disk cases, and printouts. The center display, a big flat-screen monitor mounted above the desk, showed an
isometric design for an aircraft—no, a spacecraft, Champagne realized.

Used to polished CAD graphics where they worked, he was surprised. This one was crude. Some of it was fully rendered in 3D
space, but parts of it were just wire frames. At least one section was
a two-dimensional image altered to appear three-dimensional.

"*Defender* isn't pretty, but we're a little pressed for time," Ray
declared. He had the air of a proud parent.

Champagne, surprised and puzzled, studied the diagram, which
filled the four-by-eight display. Data tables hovered in parts of the
screen not covered by the vehicle. He started tracing out systems:
Propulsion. Communications. Weapons? He shot a questioning look
at McConnell.

Ray met his look with one of his own. "Here's a question for you,
Chris. What's the best way to protect a satellite? If someone's shooting them down, how can you stop them?"

"They haven't confirmed it's the Chinese . . ."

"It doesn't matter who's doing it!" Ray countered fiercely. "Someone is." He paused and rephrased the question. "Can you effectively
protect a satellite from the ground?"

Champagne answered quickly. "Of course not. You're on the
wrong end of the gravity well, even if you're near the launch site, and
you could be on the other side of the planet."

"Which we probably are," Ray agreed. "Here on the surface, even with perfect information, we can't defend a satellite until something is launched to attack it, so we're always in a tail chase. If we're above the launch site, with the satellite we're trying to defend, Isaac Newton joins our team."

"And this is going to do the job?" Champagne asked, motioning toward the diagram. He tried to sound objective, but skepticism crept into his voice despite his efforts.

Ray didn't bat an eyelash; he seemed used to the disbelief. "It can, Chris. There's nothing startling in here. The technology is all there: an orbital vehicle, sensors, and weapons."

"And you've been tasked by . . ."

"It's on my own hook, Chris. This is on my own initiative," Ray admitted. Then he saw his friend's question and answered it without waiting.

"Because I can't wait for the government to think of it, that's why. The answer is obvious, but by the time they hold all the meetings, write the requirement, and submit a budget proposal, we won't have any satellites left!"

Ray sat down heavily, fatigue and strain showing on his face. "This isn't about just the GPS constellation or the Chinese, Chris. Someone's developed the capability to attack satellites in space. That means they could attack manned spacecraft as well. They can hurt us, or anyone else they don't like. And we know they sure as hell don't like us."

Champagne leaned back against the edge of a table and looked carefully at Ray. "So you're going to design the answer to our problems." He phrased it as a statement, but it was still a question.

"Me and all the other people here," Ray corrected. "Why not, Chris? I've got a good idea and I'm running with it. I might not be in the right bureau, or in the right branch, but I believe in this. Ideas are too precious to waste."

Inside, Champagne agreed with his friend, but practicality pushed that aside. "But you can't build it," he stated quietly.

"Well, that's the rub," Ray said, actually rubbing the back of his neck in emphasis. "I've made a lot of friends over the years. I'm going to shotgun it out over SIPRNET—only within the system," he hurriedly added, referring to the secret-level Internet system capable of handling classified material. "I won't go public with this. It's a serious design proposal."

"Which needs a formal requirement, funding, and research and development . . ."

"And congressional hearings and hundreds of man hours arguing what color to paint it," continued Ray sarcastically. "Look, a small group can always move faster and think faster than a large one. I want to present the defense community with a finished initial design, something so complete they'll be able to leapfrog the first dozen steps of the acquisition process." He grinned. "We can skip one step already. The bad guys are writing the requirement for us."

Ray stood and turned to face Champagne directly. "I know I'm bending rules, but they're not rules of physics, just the way DoD does business. I'm willing to push this because it needs to be done, and nobody else is doing it."

Champagne sighed. "Ray, I gotta tell you: Rudy is breathing fire and brimstone. Jake is handling it okay, for now, but he's not as adept at dealing with our div chief as you are."

"What does Rudy want now? I gave him everything he asked for, and more, and ahead of his revised due date." Ray's voice was strained with impatience.

"He blew up when you didn't come in today, claimed you were AWOL, and ranted about the corrections he needed you to make to the final report. Rudy said he sent you e-mails and tried to call your cell phone."

"I ignored them. I don't have time to argue with him. But I did send the answers to the questions directly to Jake and asked him to put them in the report for me. And none of them were even remotely critical—just more of Rudy's typical bureaucratic editing bullshit! Besides, I'm not AWOL! I filled out a leave slip before I left."

"But didn't bother to wait and see if your request was approved," challenged Champagne.

"I assumed it would be a formality," Ray replied with a sheepish look. "I've got more 'use or lose' leave time than I can shake a stick at, and the fiscal year ends in two days. I'm entitled to a few days off."

"Still, technically you're on unauthorized leave," Champagne concluded.

Ray scowled, sighing heavily. "Technically, yes."

Champagne looked down and shook his head. His boss could be just as pigheaded as White, but the similarities ended there. He also knew that Ray McConnell had a knack for getting things done, even if it looked nigh on impossible on paper. Chuckling, he looked back at Ray and made a wide sweep with his hand. "So who's working on your comm system?"

Ray grinned. "They're in the second bedroom. They've got almost all the electronics nailed down, but there's still lots to do." Ray led him down the hall. "Come on, I'll introduce you." Chris recognized one coworker from a different division in SPAWAR, another was introduced as an engineer from Northrup-Grumman, and the team leader was . . .

"It's good to see you again, Chris," called out a woman's voice. Champagne would need to be blind not to remember Jennifer Oh. She looked over at Ray, and he explained, "Chris is a comms specialist in my division, and SPAWAR is not using all his talents to the fullest."

Jennifer Oh beamed. "That's great! With one more person, we can have two teams and assign each one . . ."

"Wait a minute, please." Champagne held up his hand. "Let me make a call first." He stepped out of the room, looking unsuccessfully for a quiet spot to call from. McConnell saw his problem and motioned for them go outside. With Champagne ready to make his call, Ray started to step back inside, but Champagne stopped him and asked, "Where's Jim Naguchi? If Jennifer Oh is here . . ."

McConnell shook his head. "It's just Jenny. She's shown up every night, and she even brings food. I tried to warn her off, because I don't want to get any active service members in trouble. She didn't take that very well. She insisted on helping and handed me my 'chivalric ass' on a platter. The woman is nothing if not determined, and I'm glad she is. Jenny's a great engineer."

Champagne stopped dialing and closed his cell phone. "Wait a minute. She's been here all the time, without Jim, and she even brings you food?"

"Yeah, you saw. She's leading the command and control group, and . . ."

"Ray, did it occur to you that there might be another reason for her being here?"

"Like what?" Ray asked, genuinely confused. He then saw Champagne's incredulous expression and said, "No, Chris. Not possible."

Champagne ignored his protests and nodded approvingly. "She's a real find, Ray. Brains and looks. Thinks for herself. Of course, we'll have to overlook her poor taste in men." Champagne's brown eyes were twinkling with amusement; a grin ran from one ear to the other.

"I don't have time for that!" protested Ray.

Champagne's grin disappeared, and his expression became deadly serious. "She's making time. Now it's your turn, and if you blow this chance, you'll never find another one like her. Now, beat it. I still have to make that phone call."

Ray said, "Tell Sandy thank you."

"It's not Sandy. I'm calling Sue Langston in the graphics shop. Your illustrations suck!"

Rayburn House Office Building
Washington, D.C.
September 28, 2017

Congressman Tom Rutledge watched images slide across the flat screen as his aide briefed him. "There are—or were—twenty-six satellites, with twenty-four active and two in reserve. The new Block III birds cost 543 million dollars each. The older ones in orbit were less capable and less expensive, but to replace the ones that have been lost, that's the price tag. Lockheed Martin is the prime contractor for the satellites. The air force runs the GPS system out of Schriever Air Force Base in Colorado."

Anticipating the congressman's question, the aide added, "Lock Mart has an office in Papillon with about eleven thousand jobs. It's not involved in the GPS program. Offutt Air Force Base is not involved in the program."

"And neither of those are even in my district," Rutledge remarked, half-complaining.

"Space-related industry in Nebraska accounts for less than two percent of the state's economy, sir."

"Which is why I spend so much time looking at hogs and harvesters," Rutledge groused. "Put the brief on my tablet, Tim. I'll go over it later."

"I'll give it to everybody," Tim Stevens replied, broadly hinting.

Heads nodded around the room. All Rutledge's senior staff had assembled in his congressional office "to sound out this GPS business."

"Doesn't sound like we should be all that concerned," Ben Davis observed. Davis was Rutledge's chief of staff and had been with the congressman since his days in Kearney. Stevens, the senior legislative assistant, had joined the congressman's staff when Rutledge was first elected to the 3rd district seat, six years ago, and the two didn't always get along.

"Tim, what's going to be the effect on the streets of Kearney?" That was Rutledge's favorite phrase, and everyone had learned to be ready for it, as well as not to wince.

"Economically, very little. Civilian GPS won't be affected that much because they don't need the same precision as the military does. Planes need a fix in three dimensions, but plain folks usually only care about two, and they aren't using smart bombs that have to hit within a meter of the aim point. And a lot of civilian GPS sets can now use the Galileo system as well, the constellation the Europeans put up. It's more accurate than ours, actually."

"There's a European GPS?" Rutledge was surprised. "Well, can't the military just switch to the Galileo satellites?"

Stevens shook his head. "They'd need to modify the receivers in each weapon, and it uses a different antenna."

"Can we buy some smart bombs from the Europeans, then?"

"Sorry, Congressman, you have to modify the aircraft's GPS receiver as well. It's not a quick fix, and it wouldn't be cheap.

"Besides the U.S. system, which is actually called NAVSTAR, and Galileo in Europe, there's the Russian GLONASS and Chinese Beidou constellations"—

Davis cut in. "Tom, the biggest effect will be perception. The folks back home won't like China shooting down U.S. satellites, but they already have China pegged as a bad actor. They'll throw it in the same hopper as the hacking attacks and currency manipulation. With no bodies, and no personal impact, Joe Citizen will expect the government to do something, but he doesn't want to go to war over it."

"The last polls in your district showed that public support for the U.S. defending Vietnam was lukewarm, no more than forty-eight percent. In some spots it was as low as thirty-seven percent. If China invades Vietnam, that man on the street in Kearney is going to say, 'That's too bad,' and then see if his latest *Idol* contestant was voted off the show."

Rutledge said, "This all makes sense, but set up a new poll on attitudes about space and China. Make it statewide."

While Davis took notes, Stevens, twenty years Davis's junior, pressed his point. "Congressman, if GPS goes away, the U.S. military becomes less powerful, maybe a lot less. A lot of our influence overseas is based on that power. We could find ourselves dealing with crises around the world."

Rutledge straightened up in his chair and said, "You're absolutely right, Tim, which is why I want Bill to write a series of speeches condemning administration inaction on this latest Chinese outrage." Bill Hamilton, Rutledge's "communications director," nodded and made his own notes.

"Hit on the administration's lack of foresight," Rutledge directed. "And also how they're soft on China. Rather have China's trade dollars than stand firm against their human rights abuses, that type of thing. Be sure to get some solid numbers in there."

Rutledge had a reputation for lacing his speeches with figures, and he'd rarely been challenged. If you picked the right topic, you could find the numbers that made you sound like an authority. You didn't have to stretch the truth.

"There's no sense wasting a perfectly good crisis," Rutledge continued. "This is a national issue, which is just what I want to be dealing with, and since it doesn't affect Nebraska, I've got some flexibility in my message." He smiled in anticipation.

Davis matched his smile. Rutledge had been aiming for a VP seat, or at least a cabinet post, after the 2016 elections, but he didn't have the name recognition. The congressman had dedicated himself to making sure that would not be a problem in three years.

Naval Air Weapons Station China Lake
China Lake, CA
September 29, 2017

Tom Wilcox worked in the test and evaluation shop at China Lake. The entire base's mission was to evaluate new weapons systems for the navy, but his shop was the one that did the dirty work. He spent a lot of time in the desert and would be out there at dawn, half an hour from now.

Wilcox looked like someone who'd spent a lot of time in the desert. Lean, tanned, his face showed a lot of wear, although he joked that was just from dealing with the paperwork. He'd been in his current job for twenty-five years and insisted he was good for that many more.

This morning, he had to inspect the foundations for a new test stand. Before too long, they'd be mounting rocket motors on it, and he didn't want a motor with the stand still attached careening across the landscape.

First, though, he always checked his e-mail. Working on his danish and placing his coffee carefully out of the way, he said, "New messages."

The computer displayed them on his wall screen, a mix of personal and professional subjects listed according to his personal priority system. The higher the rank of the sender, the less urgent the message had to be. Anything from an admiral went straight to the bottom of the pile.

He noted one unusual item. Ray McConnell had sent a message with a medium-sized attachment. He'd known Ray for quite a while as a colleague, but he hadn't seen him since Wilcox had been to SPAWAR for a conference last spring, about six months ago. They'd exchanged some notes since then.

Wilcox noted that it had a long list of other addressees, and it had been sent out at four this morning. He recognized a few of the addressees. They were all at official DoD installations.

The cover letter was brief: "I think you'll know what to do with this. It's completely unclassified, but please only show it to people inside the security system. Thanks."

Well, that was mysterious enough to be worth a few minutes. He downloaded the attached file, waited for the virus and security checks to finish, then had a look.

It was a hundred-page document. The cover page had a gorgeous image of a wedge-shaped airfoil rendered in 3D. It had to be a spacecraft, and the title above it read, *"Defender."*

Wilcox's first reaction was one of surprise and disappointment. He almost groaned. Engineers in the defense community receive a constant stream of crackpot designs from wannabe inventors. The unofficial ones were ignored or returned with a polite letter. The official ones that came though a congressman or some other patron could be a real pain in the ass. Why was Ray passing this on to him?

Then he saw the name on the front. Ray was listed as the lead designer! *What is this? It's not an official navy project. McConnell must have put some real time into this, and he's no flake,* thought Wilcox. Or at least, not until now.

He opened the cover and glanced at the introduction. "We are completely unprepared for the Chinese attack on our satellites. Even if the source of the attacks is found and destroyed, the technology now has been demonstrated. Others, hostile to U.S. interests, will follow the Chinese example.

"*Defender* is a vehicle designed to protect spacecraft in orbit from attack. It uses proven technology. Please consider this concept as an option to protect our vital space assets."

Below that was a long list of names, presumably people who either endorsed the idea or who had helped him with the design, probably the latter. Wilcox scanned the list. He didn't recognize any of the names, and there were none with a rank attached.

He skimmed the document, watching the clock but increasingly absorbed in the design. Ray had done his homework, although his haste was obvious. At least the art was good. Diagrams were important for the higher-ups. They had problems with numbers and large words.

The phone rang, and Wilcox picked it up. "We need you in five," his assistant reminded him.

"I'll be there," Wilcox replied, and hung up.

He sat for another ten seconds, thinking and staring at the screen. All right, Ray's got a hot idea and he wants to share it. In fact, Wilcox realized, he wants me to share it, to send it up the line. He's trying to jumpstart the design process.

Wilcox knew, as did anyone else who worked for the DoD, that it took years of effort just to produce an approved requirement for such a design, and only then did the acquisition process get started. It was supposed to be a carefully crafted document that took into account the needs of the military services as described by law, future enemy capabilities, U.S. manufacturing capabilities (current and future), etc., etc. But sometimes the U.S. didn't have time for such a deliberate and agonizingly slow process.

Wilcox quickly skimmed the file. It was all there. Wilcox saw several pages he'd want to study later in depth, but it looked reasonable. The United States had no way of protecting its satellites. This could do the job.

Taking the few minutes needed, he found ten names in his address book. Most were senior engineers, like him, but a few were military officers of senior rank. *Let's see if they're still capable of recognizing an original idea when they see it*, thought Wilcox.

That morning, Ray had sent his document out to thirty friends and colleagues. All had clearances, and all worked in some area of defense. By lunchtime, eight hours after its transmission, over a hundred and fifty copies existed. By the close of business, it was over five hundred and growing.

Air Force Rapid Capabilities Office
The Pentagon
Arlington, VA
September 29, 2017

Captain "Biff" Barnes was more than ready to leave for the day. His skills as a pilot were supposed to be essential for this project, but he spent most of each day wrestling with the Pentagon bureaucracy.

Biff's given name was Clarence, after his grandfather, but he'd acquired the nickname, any nickname, as quickly as he could. He hated Clarence. Barnes was only five foot eight, but average for a pilot. He kept in very good shape, counting the months and weeks until his desk tour was finished. His thin, almost angular face showed how little fat he carried. His hair was cut as short as regulations would allow. The air force didn't like bald pilots, but he'd have shaved his head if he could.

He understood the work he'd been assigned to do was important but, for him, doing anything other than flying was a comedown. Biff loved being active, always moving, but nothing provided a more satisfying rush than fighting, or at least matching his skills against an opponent in the air. Sports had been an outlet when he was younger, soccer and karate when he was small, then baseball and football in high school. He'd never been a star, but he'd lived to get out on the field, whatever the game was. A wise uncle had taught him chess, another type of conflict, but it lacked the kinetic element Biff needed.

And if you wanted to move, nothing beat a jet aircraft on afterburner. Biff had worked like a madman at the academy, and he'd made the cut. He'd flown F-22s before being assigned to the Pentagon, and he'd been promised an ops-officer billet in an F-22 squadron once this tour was complete.

His Pentagon job was interesting, when he got to actually do it. Assigned to the Air Force Rapid Capabilities Office, he helped design the payloads that were carried into space by the X-37B space plane. The "X" was supposed to mean it was an experimental vehicle, designed to test new aviation or space technology. And the X-37 had started out that way, with NASA, back in 1999, as a reusable unmanned spacecraft. Two would fit in the payload bay of the space shuttle. After riding the shuttle into orbit, the X-37s would be deployed and would maneuver with their own engines, deploy or recover cargo with their own robotic arm, and return to earth, landing automatically.

With the shuttle program gone, the X-37 had been adapted to ride a Delta booster into orbit, which worked well, as did the entire concept. After several successful test flights in the early 2000s, the air force had ordered an improved X-37B from Boeing. The air force hadn't bothered to give it a new designation, like Secret Spaceplane One, or anything. They just called it the "orbital test vehicle." Right.

The air force had needed its own vehicle, since they couldn't use the shuttle anymore, and the X-37B was it. And it was all in-house, which simplified everything.

Only one problem: If the shuttle had been called a "space truck," the X-37B could be described as an "orbital duffle bag." The shuttle could carry a payload of twenty-eight tons and was big enough to hold two X-37s in its bay. The X-37's payload had to fit in the same space as the bed of a pickup truck—a long bed, maybe, but it was a small fraction of the size and weight.

Biff's degree in aeronautical engineering had been helpful, but he'd spent most of his tour learning new ways to make things smaller and lighter. He also spent a lot of time searching for new materials and technologies that could help the air force do that. He'd gotten to look at a lot of exotic hardware up close and visited more labs than he cared to count. It was important stuff. It was the future. But it still wasn't flying.

And he spent way too much time futzing with paperwork, especially now, when anything connected to space was under a microscope. More than one congressman wanted to be briefed on the project. Could it be used to protect the GPS satellites? Why not? Could it be used to launch more satellites? As a substitute for one? What are we spending all our hard-earned tax money on, then? And then it turned out the congressman was angling for contracts in his district.

And that was just the beginning. Some other agency didn't want to provide information he needed. That took some doing to finally pry it loose. The Government Accountability Office wanted to review their phone records. Or some reporter on a fishing expedition filed a Freedom of Information Act request. That had to be dealt with immediately.

Because the project was classified and only a limited number of people could be cleared into the program, everyone involved had to do double or even triple duty. The junior troops, like Barnes, drew most of the nasty jobs.

He couldn't have dodged the latest flap, anyway. A government office concerned with equal opportunity needed to know if Barnes, who was African American, felt his "capabilities were being fully utilized," and it had given him a five-page form to fill out. He'd put it off because of the congressional GPS flap and then spent too much of the afternoon finally filling it out. Biff had used the comments section to share his feelings about his "utilization."

Barnes sat at his desk, closing up files and locking his safe, but still reluctant to go after an unproductive day. He checked his e-mail, at this point even willing to read Internet humor.

The page opened, and the first things he noticed were another two copies of the *Defender* document, from separate friends at Maxwell and Wright-Pat. He'd also gotten one that morning from a pilot buddy at March Air Reserve Base in California—three altogether. He'd ignored it then, far too busy, but his mind was ready for a distraction now.

He opened the file and almost laughed when he saw the cover. Someone had taken the old *VentureStar,* a prototype single-stage-to-orbit space vehicle, and tried to arm it. It was obvious why his friends had sent him so many copies. The introduction touted it as a way of defending the GPS satellites.

A worthy goal, although Barnes had no expectation that this lash-up was anything more than a time-wasting fantasy. Still, he was motivated by curiosity to see what this McConnell guy had done.

Barnes flipped to the section labeled "Payload" and started to read. Whoever this McConnell was, thought Barnes, he didn't write science fiction. He hadn't made any obvious mistakes.

But what about weapons and sensor integration? What about power? Or just flight controls? He started working through the document, answering questions and becoming increasingly impressed with McConnell's idea.

He knew about spacecraft, not only because of his degree, but because he'd actually been selected for the Astronaut Corps after his first squadron tour. He'd flown one mission but then left the program. He hated the constant training, the public relations. And what he really hated was the lack of flight time.

Barnes's stomach growled, and he looked up from the screen to see it was 7:45. He'd missed the rush hour, anyway. Biff said, "Print file," and pages started to fill the hopper. He wanted to show this to his buddies.

Then Barnes pulled himself up short. His friends would be interested, but they didn't all have security clearances, and the cover message had explicitly asked that it not be shown to anyone who wasn't cleared. Respect for the design made him want to respect the author's wishes.

The Vietnam crisis, another exercise in U.S. diplomacy and deterrence, had suddenly transformed itself into a much wider challenge. McConnell proposed this *Defender* as an answer—maybe the only answer, since Barnes hadn't heard of any others.

He looked at the proposal. Did he really buy into it? He did, Biff realized. McConnell and his team knew what they were doing.

Biff sat back down at the keyboard. He had some friends in high places.

Pentagon Briefing Room
Arlington, VA
September 29, 2017

Secretary of Defense Everett Peck approached the podium; a sea of anxious reporters milled about, eagerly awaiting what he had to say. He was not a happy man. Earlier that day, another GPS satellite had fallen silent, and the tracking data confirmed the projectile that destroyed it had come from the Gongga Shan complex. Immediately after the JCS briefing, the president had ordered Peck to call the Chinese out publicly. The secretary was convinced the press conference wouldn't do any good, but at least the cards would be back on the table. Striding up to the microphone, with camera flashes going off all around the room, Peck wasted no time getting started.

"Ladies and gentlemen. I apologize for the lateness of this press conference, but it was imperative that I had my facts straight, and that takes a little time. This morning at eleven seventeen Eastern Daylight Time, another Global Positioning System satellite went off-line. Like the others, it ceased functioning while over the eastern Pacific. But unlike many of the other GPS satellites, we at least now know why. Based on the two most recent events, the Intelligence Community and STRATCOM have conclusive proof that the satellites were intentionally attacked by a new Chinese weapon system."

A low murmur broke out as the reporters whispered to each other. It was expected that China would be identified as the culprit, but the words "conclusive proof" weren't. Peck raised his right hand to silence the mumblings.

"China has installed a very large cannon into the side of the tallest mountain in Sichuan Province in southern China. This mountain, called Gongga Shan by the Chinese, is well situated to launch attacks on any satellite in low-to-medium Earth orbits. The cannon is a kilometer long and has a bore of approximately three meters in diameter, just over ten feet. The intercept projectile is launched from the gun but is also rocket-powered, enabling it to reach our GPS satellites in orbit 12,550 miles above the earth.

"This act of aggression by the Peoples' Republic of China was unprovoked and is in keeping with their overall campaign to conquer Vietnam. We see these attacks as an attempt to limit our ability to respond to their military buildup along the Vietnam-China border.

"Make no mistake: This is a hostile act perpetrated by the Chinese government against the United States. The president prefers to resolve this escalating crisis diplomatically, and has already delivered a strong letter of protest to the Chinese ambassador. However, the United States retains the right to protect its territory and interests, by military force if necessary, and that right extends to the heavens."

4

Suggestion

CNN News
October 1, 2017

Mark Markin stood in front of a map of China and Vietnam, a familiar image after weeks of confrontation. He read carefully from a data pad.

"Xinhua, the official Chinese news service, today released a statement claiming a victory over 'an American plan to seize control of Southeast Asia.'"

Markin's image was replaced by the Chinese Premier, Hua Peng, speaking to a crowd of cheering citizens. Thin, almost scrawny, the elderly leader spoke with energy in Chinese. English subtitles appeared at the bottom of the image as he spoke: "In response to preparations for a massive attack on Chinese territory, the forces of the People's Liberation Army have hamstrung the imperialist aggressor by destroying his military satellites. Deprived of their advantage and given pause by our new technological superiority, the Americans can no longer freely play the role of bully in Asia. The territorial disagreements between the People's Republic of China and the Socialist Republic of Vietnam has waxed and waned over the last fifty years, and America did not see fit to become involved. But now, after Vietnam's blatant escalation, the United States has shown nothing but unbridled aggression against the Chinese people. We could not allow this to continue and took measures to safeguard our people without causing harm to American citizens."

Markin reappeared, looking concerned, and said, "U.S. defense officials have refused to comment officially, but it has been the working assumption that the Chinese were responsible for the disabled spacecraft. The officials also were unable to say how or when U.S. military forces would react to this news.

"Sources at the State Department were slightly more forthcoming, but only about the reasons for the Chinese announcement. They believe that the Chinese are openly challenging the U.S. in a field that has long been considered exclusively American: their military-technological edge. By denying the United States the ability to wage its preferred way of war, China has, without bloodshed, wrestled the advantage away from Vietnam in the ongoing South China Sea crisis.

"There was no comment from the White House, except that the president and his advisors are considering all options to protect American interests."

SPAWAR Systems Center Pacific
San Diego, CA
October 3, 2017

Ray McConnell came back to his office and shut the door quickly. He was shaken, almost physically trembling, after his meeting with Admiral Carson.

Rear Admiral Eugene Carson was not just the head of Engineering and Integration, which was Ray's group, or even of Systems Center Pacific, but of the entire Space and Naval Warfare Systems Command. It had taken Ray two days to work his way up the chain, first with Rudy White, his own division head, then Dr. Kozak, the chief engineer for Ray's center, and so on. With increasing force, he'd made his case for *Defender*.

Rudy White, his first stop, was more than displeased. "I've already discussed this *Defender* business with you, Ray. Why haven't you put some of that creative energy into your work here?"

"Because China's shooting down GPS satellites," Ray had responded. He'd worked with White for years, and in spite of Rudy's concerns, Ray knew he could press his point. "*Defender* can stop that. We've got the basic design finished, and I need to show it to the navy officially."

White laughed cynically and shook his head. "So it's ready to be built, then?"

"Rudy, please. I'm not that big a fool. I can't build this, but we—the government, I mean—should be building it now. I want to brief this to Admiral Carson, and higher if he'll let me. I have to convince them that this is how we can protect our GPS constellation."

"This has no chance of getting picked up by the navy or anyone else. You know that, don't you?"

"*Virtually* no chance," Ray corrected him. "So, there's no harm in trying."

"Hmmm. You've neglected your team's duties, in fact disrupted my entire division, and now you want my permission to take this up the chain."

Ray responded flatly. "Yes. We need *Defender*."

"I'm not convinced," White answered, "and I'm a lot easier than Admiral Carson will be." Ray's division chief paused, then announced, "All right. You're a good engineer, Ray, and you've done good work here. I'm hoping *Defender* is only a passing madness. Your proposal is clearly outside my ability to judge its merits," he concluded, "at least that's what I'll put down as my reason for letting you see Dr. Kozak. What she does with this is up to her."

"Thanks," Ray responded gratefully.

"Maybe this will get it out of your system," White answered. "It better," he warned. "I need you here, Ray. Jake's stepped up in your absence, and done a great job. Don't give me a reason to replace you."

Dr. Rebecca Kozak had been even less helpful, wondering aloud if *Defender* was SPAWAR property, since several SPAWAR employees had participated in its design. Ray had been nonplussed, hoping to appeal to her engineering sensibility. Instead, she stopped his presentation on the second slide and began asking questions about *Defender* as intellectual property. How many people from SPAWAR had been working at his house? How many from other government agencies? Could he guarantee that no work had been done on government time by anyone involved? Ray was unsure whether Kozak was greedy or simply trying to cover her bureaucratic behind.

Seeing she was circling the wagons, Ray decided to play the doctor's game. Kozak had been shocked when she heard about the several hundred copies of the design now circulating through the defense community, including the Pentagon.

"I'd be delighted to have SPAWAR officially take ownership of *Defender*." Ray fought hard to keep a straight face when he saw the look of horror. Kozak hadn't been able to get him out of her office quickly enough.

Word of Ray's ascent up SPAWAR's chain of command became news in its own right, independent of *Defender*. Some of his coworkers actually came by his office to see "if the stories were true."

By the end of the first day, he'd managed to get as far as Admiral Griffith, in charge of space systems. The admiral, a submariner, was fascinated by the idea, and was more than willing to approve a meeting with the SPAWAR vice commander, Rear Admiral Gaston, for the next morning.

The vice commander had been the final hurdle. He'd been more than aware of *Defender*'s popularity. "You realize that you have no credibility as a manned-spacecraft design engineer," Gaston explained coolly. He'd been polite, but a little condescending.

"I didn't think I had to be qualified to have a good idea, sir."

Gaston shook his head. "I disagree. Without the proper credentials, why should anyone waste their time looking at this design of yours? People have 'ideas' all the time. There was an article on carbon nanotubes in the last issue of *Popular Science* magazine, so we've been getting suggestions from interested citizens to use nanotubes in our structures, 'because they're so light and strong.'" He sounded amused, but irritated at the same time. "As if that was all it took, or we didn't understand the potential of what may be the greatest engineering revolution of the new century."

Gaston smiled. "Some of them even want to be paid. And I would happily pay them, if they could solve the manufacturing and design issues required to actually use carbon nanotubes. The genius that can do that will be well paid."

He gave Ray a hard look. "Are you a genius, Mr. McConnell? You don't seem to be. The difficulty is always in making an idea a reality, and you just don't have a clue what that requires. As far as the navy is concerned, you're no different than anyone off the street. And you've submitted it to the wrong agency," he added.

"I know that this isn't SPAWAR's area, sir, but I'm a SPAWAR employee. I didn't want to go outside my own chain of command."

Gaston nodded, smiling approvingly. "Quite right. Your actions have been correct, although"—he glanced at his tablet—"your supervisor's concerned with the timing of your leave during a crucial phase of a key research project. That can't be simply ignored. Your official work has suffered."

"This entire effort has been on my own time, sir. I didn't want to do it on navy time. And anything purchased to support the design process was paid for out of my pocket; not a single penny came from the Treasury."

Gaston scowled. "We're on navy time now." He sat silently for a moment, pretending to consider the issue, while Ray fretted.

To be truthful, Gaston had made up his mind before McConnell ever walked in the room. He'd just wanted to interview the engineer himself before letting him go on to Carson.

Defender was too widely known, at least at the lower levels. It was a miracle the media hadn't picked it up already. It was the kind of grassroots concept reporters loved. No matter that it was impossible—a ridiculous idea that could never be built. If he said no, then he'd be blamed as one of the people who prevented it from happening. Better to let McConnell hang himself. Gaston didn't have to support it, just pass it on.

"All right, I'll forward it. But 'without endorsement.'"

Ray had begun to hope.

The meeting with Rear Admiral Carson had begun poorly. The admiral had granted him fifteen minutes between other appointments and appeared distracted. Ray had started his pitch, but Carson had cut him off after only a few words, chopping with one hand as if to cut off the stream.

"I'm familiar with the design, Mr. McConnell," Carson had said with irritation. "I've received three copies in the past two days, besides this one. I'm also familiar with the problem. I've spent most of the last week in Washington answering questions about our own vulnerability and what SPAWAR could do to counter it.

"I've also been fully briefed about the Chinese antisatellite threat," he said finally. "The current estimate is that the Chinese can't possibly have many more of the kill vehicles."

He walked over to where Ray sat, almost leaning over him. "I've also looked over your personnel file. I was looking for your academic credentials. They're bad enough: no doctorate, a master's in electrical engineering, and an undergraduate degree in physics. What made you think we'd take a manned spacecraft designed by you seriously?"

"I'm not the only designer, sir. This was a collaborative effort, and some of the people on the design team have doctorate degrees in aerospace engineering and experience in the field."

"However true that may be, Mr. McConnell, you're the one vouching for the viability of this design. Correct?"

Ray nodded silently.

Carson picked up his data tablet and checked something on the screen. "And then I found this: After your master's degree, you applied for the astronaut program. Correct?"

Ray nodded again. "Yes, sir."

"And you were turned down. Then you joined the air force. You served six years as a junior officer and, during that time, applied three more times to become an astronaut. Also correct?" His tone was more than hostile.

"Yes, sir. Each time I missed by just a few percentage points. I hoped . . ."

"You hoped to get into space with this half-baked fantasy!" shouted Carson, pointing to *Defender*. "Did you plan on scoring the theme music for your little adventure, too?"

"Admiral, I've always been interested in the space program, but that doesn't have anything to do with this. I just want to get this idea to where it will do the most good."

Carson had sat, glowering, listening while Ray protested.

"Your idea is worthless, Mr. McConnell." He tapped the tablet again. "Instead of helping SPAWAR deal with a real crisis, you've created this fantasy. At best, it's a distraction at a very difficult time. At worst, it's a personal attempt at empire building, and a very crude one at that. What's worse is that you've managed to involve others in your scheme, magnifying the disruption.

"Although you've broken no rules that I'm aware of, I am directing the inspector general's office to review your activities and your work logs to see if any of your fantasizing has been done on government time. If that is the case, docking your pay will be the weakest punishment you will suffer. Now get back to work and hope I never hear about *Defender* again!"

Sitting in his office that afternoon, Ray struggled with his feelings. He'd created *Defender* because he'd seen the need for it. Why didn't the chain of command see that need as well? Was he wrong? Maybe he really didn't know enough to do it by himself. But he'd had lots of help in designing *Defender*. And he'd gotten lots of mail back, some critical, but more supportive, much of it even offering to help.

Was it time to sit down and shut up? He liked his job and the people he worked with. Did he really want to lose everything over *Defender*?

With his morale bordering on despair, Ray looked at his overflowing in-box. Mechanically, he reached for the first large folder at the top of the pile, but before he could grab it, his phone rang. Ray didn't recognize the number on the display, not that it mattered. This was his work number.

"GPS Team, McConnell speaking," he answered.

"Ray, it's Jenny. How did your meeting with SPAWAR go?"

Ray quickly pulled the handset away and looked at it with utter amazement. How the hell did she know he'd just finished his meeting with Carson? He'd only learned the time of his appointment after getting into work that morning.

"Ray, are you there?" squeaked a tiny voice.

"Yeah, I'm here," he replied suspiciously. "And would you mind telling me how you knew my meeting ended just a few minutes ago?"

"I have my sources, Mr. McConnell," teased Jenny.

"Uh-huh, anyone I know?"

"I'm not at liberty to discuss it. Besides, why should I give away a perfectly good advantage in our relationship? So, how did the meeting with Admiral Carson go?"

"In a word, terrible."

"Oh, that bad?" Jenny's tone had changed to concern.

"Let's just say that Custer had more success than I did."

"Ouch! What did he say?"

Ray had a strong urge to vent his frustration, but then recalled

Admiral Carson's threat about working on anything *Defender*-related during working hours. "Ah . . . Jenny, look, this really isn't a good time to talk right now."

"Understood. When and where?"

"Tonight, eighteen hundred. The Blue Cantina."

"I'll be there."

The Blue Cantina
San Diego, CA
October 3, 2017

Ray had eaten here before and thought the restaurant was one of the better ones in town, even if the management went way overboard with the "blue" theme. The dark blue plates set off the colorful entrées well, but the blue walls, floor, and even furniture were a little overpowering.

The food was excellent, and they'd spent most of the first hour on small talk and joking about what else the management could paint or dye blue. Officially, this was their third date, but the first two were over pizza or Chinese carryout at Ray's house working on *Defender*'s design. Ray still smiled thinking about it.

"I'm so sorry, Ray." Jenny sounded as disappointed as Ray felt. "But to be honest, it's a typical bureaucratic response from a risk-averse flag officer." It was supposed to be a "night off" for the *Defender* design group, but she'd changed her plans so she could meet him for dinner. Her mere presence made him feel better.

"You're right," he admitted. "A purely bureaucratic reaction. He shredded it, put a match to it, and stomped on the ashes." Ray tried to smile, but it wasn't in him. His attempt at humor was too close to the truth. "I knew it was a long shot, but I didn't expect the command to be hostile. Indifferent, yes, or even negative, but I'd hoped for some understanding. Admiral Carson would have thrown me in the brig if he could justify it."

She laughed, in spite of his grim expression. "You're joking." He liked her laugh.

Ray shook his head. "That's no joke, unfortunately. He's siccing the IG on me, to see if I've wasted any navy time on this quote 'half-baked fantasy' unquote."

"That's not good." She paused, then asked, "So, you've gone all the way up your chain of command with no success?"

"I'd call that an understatement," he replied.

"Well, then it's time to try another chain," she said forcefully. "Let me make some calls."

"What?" Ray was horrified. "Jenny! I'm poison now. If the IG finds out you're actively helping me, they'll want to talk to you. Please, just ditch anything you have with my name on it."

Ray saw the surprised expression on her face and quickly corrected himself. "No! I don't mean like that." He took her hand. "Finding you may be the only good thing to come out of this mess, but I don't want you to get in trouble because of my foolishness."

"It's my choice, Ray. I believe in you and *Defender*."

"But if you get in trouble, I'll feel terrible . . ."

"Since when are you responsible for me?" she asked sharply. There was an indignant undertone in her voice that he hadn't heard before. "If I help, it's because I think *Defender* is worthwhile, not because I'm some love-struck female."

Ray grinned. "Darn. I was hoping for 'love-struck.' "

"Don't change the subject," she snapped angrily. "You're not responsible for my actions," she repeated.

"It's just that it was my idea, so of course if you get involved . . ."

"*If* I get involved? Who's been over at your house five out of the last six nights? Who helped design the command and control suite?" The undertone was growing in strength.

Ray tried a different approach. "Jenny, right now your name is one of many on a list on page two. Making phone calls will show up on the IG's radar . . ."

"Are you so afraid the IG will find something? Is there anything for him to find?"

"No, not a thing!" he protested.

"Then maybe you don't think *Defender* is worth a few risks?" The infuriated undertone was now her only tone.

In spite of it, Ray pressed on. "By me, not by anyone else, and especially not by you!"

"I don't need your protection," she responded sharply. "So *Defender* is your personal property, then. You want all the credit."

"I don't want any of the credit. I just want it to be built!"

"None of the credit, but all of the risk? Then you're a martyr."

"No, wait . . ."

She held up a hand, stopping his protest. "Doing anything important means taking risks, and in the case of *Defender,* more than most." She sharpened her tone, aiming the words straight at Ray. "Are you really committed to making it happen? You'll do whatever it takes?"

"Yes, of course," he answered immediately.

"Then accept the risk and move forward. You know, I'm going to make those calls whether you want me to or not. You don't own *Defender* anymore, and I don't need your permission."

"Yes, Jenny. You're right. I'm sorry."

Her tone softened. "I know some people on the NAVAIR staff. Admiral Schultz is a pilot and an 'operator,' not some bureaucrat. I've worked for him in the past, and I think he'll give you a chance."

Ray didn't know what to say except, "Thanks, Jenny. I just hope this doesn't backfire."

Office of the Chief of Staff of the Air Force
The Pentagon
October 4, 2017

General Michael Warner was an unusual chief of staff. He flew bombers, not fighters. In an air force that gave fighter pilots most of the

stars, it was a sign of his ability not only as an officer but as a politician. Looking more like a banker than a bomber pilot, he had an almost legendary memory, which he used for details: of budgets, people,
and events.

Pilots lived and died because of details. They won and lost battles
because of them. And the general kept looking for some small detail
that his deputy, General Clifton Ames, had missed. The three-star
general had put the target analysis together personally.

Ames had nothing but bad news. An overhead image of the Gongga
Shan launch site filled the wall screen. "I've confirmed there's no way
the navy can stretch the range of their Tomahawk missiles. But even
if they could, there's no way a Tomahawk warhead can penetrate that
much rock. Not to mention, the warhead is pretty small and will have
a limited damage potential. Of course, our conventional air-launched
cruise missiles aren't any better. And even if we could adapt a ballistic missile with a conventional warhead, they aren't accurate enough
for this type of target."

His tablet PC linked to the screen, Ames indicated various features of the site as he talked. "The Chinese built this installation expecting it to be attacked by cruise missiles. There are two air bases
with multiple J-15 fighter squadrons within two hundred miles, supporting multiple combat-air-patrol stations, and the Chinese have
recently started orbiting airborne early-warning aircraft. The facility
is also heavily defended by long- and short-range SAMs and triple-A.
They've mounted modern air-search radars on elevated towers to give
them additional warning time of an attack. They've even constructed
tall open-framework barriers across the approach routes a cruise
missile might use." He pointed to the large girder structures, easily
visible in the photograph.

"The gun and all vital facilities are hardened, and then there's the
matter of the barrel itself. Given its three-meter bore, intelligence says
the barrel thickness is at least a foot. Damaging that will require a
very precise strike—the very capability we're now losing.

"To get an eighty-percent chance of success would take twelve

B-2s, each carrying two GBU-57 Massive Ordnance Penetrators." Ames knew he was talking to a bomber pilot and watched for Warner's reaction. The chief just nodded glumly, and Ames continued.

"And the worst part is that unless we damage major portions of the gun, the Chinese could have it back in operation again within a few months, possibly a few weeks. We're certain the barrel is constructed in sections, like the Iraqi gun design. If a section is damaged, you remove it and replace it with a spare section. We've even identified in the imagery where they probably keep the spares."

Even as he said it, Ames knew that a bomber strike wasn't a viable option. Stealth bombers aren't invisible to radar, but the detection range is reduced to the point where the aircraft can easily avoid them, flying through the gaps in the coverage. But in this situation, there was no way for a stealth bomber to fly around all the defenses. The radars, fighters, SAMs, and guns were all huddled too damn close to each other.

"What about losses?" Warner asked.

"Using the standard engagement models for this kind of dense, overlapping defense," Ames replied, "there's a good chance we'll lose forty to fifty percent of the bombers. And part of the flight path is over very unfriendly Chinese territory." The implications for search and rescue were not good.

"All right, Cliff. Send this on to the chairman's office with my respects. And my apologies," Warner muttered.

"Sir, I've been looking at the *Defender* concept," Ames offered. "One of my friends in STRATCOM passed it to me with an analysis by a former colleague of his in the Rapid Capabilities Office. I think we should consider it."

Warner had heard about *Defender*, of course, but hadn't had time to do more than dismiss it as a distraction. "Are we really that desperate?" the chief asked.

Office of the Chief of Naval Operations
The Pentagon
October 4, 2017

"I am not going to go into the Joint Chiefs of Staff and propose that we adopt some crackpot design that came off SIPRNET!" Admiral John Kramer was so agitated that he was pacing, quickly marching back and forth as he protested.

Admiral William Schultz, Commander, Naval Air Systems Command, sat quietly in his chair. He'd expected this reaction and waited for Kramer to settle down. Schultz was calm, sure of himself and his mission.

"I've spent some time checking out this design, John, and the lead engineer. Both are okay. There are some technical questions that need to be addressed, but nothing McConnell's team has proposed is science fiction. The man certainly isn't a 'crackpot.' Sure, he had a lot of help. And it is most assuredly an unofficial submission"—Schultz leaned forward for emphasis—"but it's a reasonable first shot."

He sat back, straightening his spine. "It's also the only decent idea I've heard in almost two weeks."

Kramer and Schultz were both pilots and had served together several times in their navy careers, but where Kramer was tall, and almost recruiting-poster handsome, Schultz was only of middle height, and stockier. And his looks would never get him any movie deals. His thinning sandy hair was mussed whenever he put his navy cover on, while he was sure Kramer kept his hair in place with mousse. Kramer was a good pilot, but he'd also done well in staff jobs, a "people person." Or so he thought.

Used to the convoluted, time-consuming system-acquisition methods of the Pentagon, the CNO continued to object. "Even if we did propose it, and even if it were accepted, where would we get the funding?"

"Somewhere, John, just like we've always done before. The

money's out there; we just have to decide what's the most important thing to spend it on."

Schultz continued, mentally assigning himself three Our Fathers and three Hail Marys. "Look, I've heard the air force is buying into *Defender* in a big way. They think it can work, and as far as they're concerned, if it's got wings, it belongs to them."

Kramer looked grim. The air force was shameless when they talked about "aerospace power." He nodded agreement.

"Let them get their hands on any armed spacecraft, and the next thing you know, we'll lose SPAWAR. Remember the time they tried to convince Congress that we should scrap our carriers and buy bombers with our money?" Kramer frowned, listening carefully.

Schultz pressed his point. "Do we have any viable alternative for stopping the Chinese, sir?"

Kramer shook his head. "The launch site is out of Tomahawk range, and they wouldn't do any good even if they could get there. The president has already said that he won't authorize the use of a ballistic missile, even with a conventional warhead—too much ambiguity. And even if we could use them, you'd need lots of missiles. The way that site is hardened, I'm not certain a nuke would do it."

"Air Force B-2s could reach it," Schultz said quietly. "But they can't be sure they'd get any out alive. The defenses are incredibly thick, and the Chinese are expecting us to use cruise missiles or bombers. This is a better option, John, even though it looks a little crazy."

"Then that's what we'll try to sell," Kramer decided reluctantly.

5

Summons

CNN News
October 5, 2017

Jane Suzuki was CNN's lead correspondent in the western Pacific. She was already a household name in the broadcasting field when her coverage of the 2011 Great East Japan Earthquake and Tsunami not only earned her several prestigious journalism awards but also cemented her place in the public consciousness. For many Americans, she was their window into Asia.

For this report on the China-Vietnam crisis, she'd chosen a spot on the plaza in front of the National Diet Building. Most Americans wouldn't recognize the structure, so she started her broadcast by letting the camera pan over the building and describing it as the Japanese equivalent of the U.S. Capitol.

"And the Japanese government is only one of several Asian powers watching China with growing concern. I've spoken not only with the Vietnamese ambassador, who is 'alarmed,' in his words, but also the South Korean and Taiwanese representatives here. They all used different words to express their greatest fear: Is this the end of the U.S. security umbrella?

"In the last decade, China's economy and armed forces have undergone spectacular growth, and her foreign policy has become expansionist, aggressive, almost belligerent. Nobody here in Asia believes that the GPS attacks are an isolated or impulsive action. Earlier I spoke with Professor Eji Watanabe, of the China Study Group, here in Tokyo."

Watanabe was seated behind his desk, a cluttered bookshelf in the background. His English was heavily accented, and the network had added subtitles. "American military power has dominated East Asia since the end of the Great Pacific War. China wishes to end that, so they create a crisis. First, they concentrate troops to threaten Vietnam. As expected, the U.S. responds by marshaling its own forces in the region as a deterrent. Next, the Chinese reduce U.S. military effectiveness by making bloodless attacks on their GPS satellites. Now, China waits for America to react again."

The camera panned to include Suzuki in the view. She asked, "But why is China doing this? Why Vietnam?"

Watanabe answered instantly. "Because Vietnam is vulnerable. Her small military is no match for China's in either size or quality. There's a history of conflict between the two countries, with invasions during both centuries in the past and as recently as 1979. And that doesn't include the Chinese seizures of Vietnamese island territories in the South China Sea in 1974 and 1988. But most importantly, Vietnam is not a U.S. ally, so the American commitment to protecting Vietnamese security is nowhere near as strong as if it was, say, Japan or the Philippines.

"The Americans reacted predictably to the Chinese troop concentration by massing their own forces as a counterbalance. But now, because of the loss of their GPS satellites, the American military is weaker and risks greater losses if the U.S and China actually fight."

The reporter asked, "Is that the Chinese goal, to conquer Vietnam?"

The expert shook his head. "No. The Chinese did not do this to gain territory, although if this dispute goes as they have planned, they will gain Vietnam and much more. By increasing the potential cost in blood for something of marginal interest, China is betting America will turn away and lose face."

Watanabe continued. "The Chinese wish to replace American military dominance in the region with their own. Economic influence follows from military influence. China doesn't want a war with the United States. That would be costly for China, even if it wins. Instead, they are taking a page from their own master, Sun Tzu: 'Hence to fight and conquer in all your battles is not supreme excellence; supreme excellence consists in breaking the enemy's resistance without fighting.' If they challenge the United States, and she does not or cannot respond effectively, nations in the region will see China as the new leader in the Pacific."

Suzuki asked, "Don't some Asians resent American military dominance anyway?"

Watanabe smiled. "Certainly, but small nations do best when they have powerful friends. America has been an ally and trading partner for over seventy years to Japan, South Korea, Taiwan, and the Philippines. Even nations that are not U.S. allies have benefited from the stable security environment created by America's military might." He sighed. "Nobody expects to flourish under a Chinese hegemony, but if American power fades, we will be forced to accept the new situation and adapt."

He straightened is his chair. "The next move is America's. What will they do? What can they do? Even doing nothing is a response, but we are all hoping that Washington will act, and act wisely."

Casa McConnell
San Diego, CA
October 5, 2017

Ray automatically reached for the controller to turn off the TV, but then stopped himself. It was only noise, but he needed to hear other voices. The house was empty. He'd sent out an e-mail two days ago, telling everyone about Admiral Carson's warning and urging them all to stay away.

Canceling the design sessions went head-on against the urgency he felt, the urgency that had driven him. There was still so much to be done, but continuing to meet would be in open defiance of Carson's order. The admiral was angry enough to cashier not only Ray but anyone associated with him.

The place seemed dark and empty, although he'd turned on lights all over the house. It was just a typical three-bedroom rambler with a red tile roof, like every other home in Southern California. Ray liked having other people around and was happiest when his home was stuffed to capacity—for a party, a football game, a hearty discussion, or sharing his dream to build *Defender*.

Reflexively, he started to pick up the place. As busy as they'd been, packing materials from recently purchased computer equipment had been pushed into corners for later disposal. Paper plates and cups, takeout boxes, and empty bottles covered the tables, along with scribbled notes and printouts. Every horizontal surface was equally covered with litter. Many of his walls were heavily adorned with yellow stickies or early versions of *Defender*'s plans. As crammed and chaotic as his house was during those days and nights when the design team was going full bore, Ray had to admit those were good times. The vacant rooms, with the sound from the TV echoing off the walls, were crushingly depressing.

By rights, he should start breaking down the work-group centers throughout the house. The living room and bedrooms each had chairs clustered around a table with a networked workstation. Even the bedroom he actually used for sleeping had been taken over by the propulsion group, with his bed pushed to one side.

But he couldn't do it. It would mean abandoning *Defender*. Carson was just plain wrong, but the man had the power and authority to block any progress. Instead, Ray had to find a way around Carson's prohibition, somehow change his mind or get him overruled . . .

The phone rang while he was outside, trying to find more room in a grossly overstuffed recycling bin. The sound surprised him, because after his "stay away" e-mail, he wasn't expecting any calls. He caught it on the fourth ring.

"Hello."

"Ray McConnell?" The voice was that of an older man.

"Speaking," Ray replied.

"Mr. McConnell, this is Vice Admiral Bill Schultz. We have a mutual friend, Jennifer Oh."

An admiral? Calling him? Ray rooted through his memory, and when the caller mentioned Jenny's name, made the connection.

"Admiral Schultz? Commander of NAVAIR?" Surprise mixed with curiosity. Schultz was a vice admiral, a three-star flag officer, and outside the SPAWAR chain of command. As one of the navy's materiel commands, Naval Air Systems Command had frequent contact with Ray's organization. Still, by contacting him directly, Schultz was completely bypassing the traditional chain of command.

"Ray, I've taken a good look at the *Defender* proposal you and your friends put together. I want you to come out to Washington so we can talk about it."

Astonished but jubilant, Ray wanted to cheer, then remembered Admiral Carson's direct order. "That's really great, sir, but I'm afraid I can't get any leave . . ."

Schultz cut him off. "Jenny explained everything. You'll travel on official government orders; the CNO's staff has already cut them and made the travel arrangements. The CNO has also spoken with Admiral Carson, so there won't be any issues with your chain of command."

Oh . . . my . . . God! thought Ray. Carson must be apoplectic. After screaming at Ray that he never wanted to hear about *Defender* again, it must have been quite the shock when the CNO told him the navy wanted to have a closer look. Ray tried to imagine the various shades of purple that Carson's face passed through upon hearing the CNO's instructions.

"Effective immediately, you are on temporary rotational orders to

NAVAIR," continued Schultz. "Everything has been e-mailed to both you and your supervisors. You don't go back to work until I'm done with you. You're on a flight out early tomorrow morning, and pack for an extended stay. And of course bring anything you need to make your case for *Defender*."

Schultz hung up, and Ray just stood there, processing the news. Things to do and stray thoughts whirled about in his head, and after turning in place twice, he forced himself to stop and prioritize his list. He had plenty of time to pack. He wouldn't even try to sleep.

But first, he had to call Jenny.

The Pentagon
Arlington, VA
October 5, 2017

Captain Biff Barnes had paused only long enough to make sure his uniform was perfect before hurrying up two floors and into the E ring. He fought the urge to run. A direct summons to report immediately to the chief of staff of the air force filled him with questions, and some trepidation. He couldn't remember making any major screwups, so his conscience was clear. Besides, if he'd committed some transgression, any punishment would have been handled by his chain of command. No, Biff was convinced something else was behind this unexpected call from on high.

The Pentagon has not only five sides but also five floors and five rings. The floors are of course numbered, and the rings have letters, going from the innermost, A, to the outer ring, E. Those two rings are the only ones with windows that have anything worth looking out to. The ones on the inner ring face the concrete-walled, five-sided courtyard, while the outer ones actually face the outside world. The coveted E-ring offices are occupied by the higher entities: the secretary and assistant secretary of defense, the service chiefs, and their associated hangers-on.

Biff had to show his badge just to get into the same corridor as the chief of staff's office, but as the enlisted security guard examined his credentials, a four-star general came down the corridor toward them. The captain braced, and, seeing his reaction, the guard turned and then came to attention as well.

Tall, with salt-and-pepper hair, the general's stern-looking face broke into an unlikely smile as he waved his hand, telling them, "At ease," as he reached out to shake Biff's hand. "Captain Barnes, I'm Clifton Ames."

As in the vice chief of staff of the air force, Biff thought. He fought the urge to remain at attention and ventured, "Then am I reporting to your office, sir?"

"No, Captain," the general replied, shaking his head. "We'll be meeting with General Warner, but not in his office." Ames set off at a brisk pace, and Barnes followed, automatically falling into step. The general didn't speak, and Biff held his questions, for the moment.

Ames stopped in front of an unremarkable-looking door and punched in a key code. As the door opened, the general remarked, "You can reset that to your own code, of course."

What the—

Before Biff could finish that question in his mind, a better one appeared. Why was General Mike "Spike" Warner, Chief of Staff of the Air Force, waiting for him in an empty office? The door closed behind Barnes and Ames, and Biff felt a sense of foreboding, especially when he saw a hard copy of the *Defender* file lying in front of Warner on the desk.

Warner was younger—well, he looked younger than Ames—and tall, especially for a pilot. No wonder he'd picked bombers. His hair was still jet-black, and the word was that he was as good a politician as he was a pilot.

"Captain," Warner asked abruptly without an introduction, "did you send the *Defender* document to General Wissmann at STRAT-COM?

"Ah, yes, sir. I met the general while I was in the astronaut program. He was a colonel then, part of the old Space Command . . ."

"And in your e-mail, you pointed out several issues with the design, but also said they were not insurmountable. You thought"—Warner paused to read from a sheet of paper—" 'It was better than anything else I'd heard of,' and asked the general about the best way to get the air force to consider *Defender*."

Biff could only nod. "Yessir, that's correct."

"Well, your idea worked, because General Wissmann sent it to me and said some nice things about you as well. Do you still think that *Defender* will work?"

"Realistically, it's the only way to go, sir." Then he added, "Unless there's something in the 'black' world I'm not aware of." The armed forces ran a lot of 'black' programs, top-secret projects with advanced technology that were shielded from public scrutiny. The F-117 had been one of the most famous; its debut in Desert Storm was dramatic and devastating. Was there one that could deal with this threat?

"Nothing that will help us, I'm afraid." Warner shook his head, half-musing to himself. "The X-37's operational, but she was never supposed to be more than a first step. She doesn't have the payload, in any case."

Looking at Barnes directly, Warner continued. "Yes, Captain, there is technology in the classified world that would help us—in anywhere from five to twenty years. The Chinese have jumped the gun on us." He sounded angry.

The general complained. "We should own this crisis, and we just don't have the tools to deal with it! And now some SPAWAR employee and his buddies in their free time have come up with this, and we're all taking it seriously?"

Barnes waited for the general to continue. When it appeared he'd run down, the captain offered, "Well, sir, at least he's former air force."

Warner laughed, a little grimly, then glanced at the wall clock. "All right, then, Captain. As of now, you are the U.S. Air Force's point man on the *Defender* program."

Barnes answered, "You want me to develop a plan to actually build *Defender*." He phrased it carefully, as if testing the concept.

Warner replied, "We're going to stop the Chinese and protect U.S. space assets by any means necessary." He gestured to *Defender*. "Including this. The question's changed, Captain. It isn't, 'Will it work?' anymore. I'm asking, 'How do we make it work?' And you're going to answer that."

General Ames added, "I've told your boss, Major Pierce, that we're borrowing you for a few days. You'll work here, alone, for the time being. The three people in this room are the only ones who know the air force is taking a hard look at *Defender*. I don't want to imagine what the media would do if they found out, but it wouldn't be good. And for heaven's sake, we can't let the navy hear about this. If they think we're treating *Defender* seriously, they'll try to stick their oar in the water." Ames smiled at the metaphor.

Warner said, "There's a National Security Council meeting in two days. I need a to-do list by then. What are the real problems? You don't have to solve them all, but we must know if there are any showstoppers before we present this. If we can show them a coherent plan for actually building *Defender*, and the NSC approves it, I'll put every resource the air force has behind it."

He stood, offering the desk to Barnes. As the two generals turned to leave, Warner said, "The face of warfare is changing, and I want the air force to lead the way."

Gongga Shan
Sichuan Province, China
October 6, 2017

General Shen Xuesen stood nervously in the launch center. It was hard to maintain the unruffled demeanor his troops needed to see. He needed all of his willpower to look calm and relaxed.

High-level visitors at such a time would make anyone nervous, and they risked being a significant distraction for the launch team. A television crew was unthinkable, and yet there they were. It was a state-run crew, of course, and they were being carefully supervised, but they brought lights and confusion and, worst of all, exposure.

Now they were filming an actual launch. Beijing had even asked if they could film the intercept, but Shen had refused absolutely, on security grounds. He understood the propaganda value of a *Tien Lung* vehicle smashing a satellite and offered to supply tapes of previous shots. They all looked alike. Who would know?

But the producer wanted shots of activity in the launch center, and the reporter would add his narration. At least the general had been able to avoid an interview, again citing security reasons.

CNN News
October 6, 2017

The oval opening erupted in flame, and a dark blur shot upward. Mark Markin's voice accompanied the video. "Released less than two hours ago, this dramatic footage from Gongga Shan Mountain in China shows the launch of a *Tien Lung,* or Celestial Dragon." Markin's voice continued as the scene shifted to a more distant shot. The mountaintop, a rugged texture of browns, was capped by a small white cloud of smoke that lingered in the still morning air.

"That is their name for the spacecraft, or 'ASAT vehicle,' as U.S. officials describe the weapon. They also confirmed the destruction of another GPS satellite just a short time ago, the time of loss consistent with the launch shown here.

"This footage was released through Xinhua, China's official news agency. The narrator claimed that China had now demonstrated military superiority over the United States and that their superiority had halted American aggression in the region."

The mountaintop and its fading smoke were replaced by a

computer-drawn representation of the gun, angled upward inside a transparent mountain.

"Intelligence officials here believe that the gun is based on the work of Dr. Gerald Bull, a Canadian engineer who fiercely advocated using large guns to launch spacecraft into orbit. To further his goal, he developed large artillery pieces, at first for scientific purposes with the U.S. and Canadian governments. When funding for those programs ended, he worked for the South Africans developing advanced long-range artillery, then for communist China, and finally the Iraqis under Saddam Hussein.

"In return for improving the ballistics of Iraq's Scud missiles, Hussein financed Bull's idea for Project Babylon, a gun that would launch satellites into space. The full-sized design was to be one hundred fifty meters long and had a one-meter bore. That program ended with Bull's assassination in 1990, likely by the Israelis.

"The Chinese experimented in January 1995 with their own supergun near the Taiwan Strait. Experts have already pointed out many similarities between Bull's Babylon guns, the first Chinese weapon, and the current Dragon Gun."

Computer animation showed the process of loading the projectile, the launch, and sabots falling away from the projectile before a rocket booster fired.

The animation disappeared, replaced with Markin, an image of a GPS satellite behind him. "This brings the number of GPS satellites known to have been destroyed by China to a minimum of five. Unsubstantiated rumors suggest the total is more likely seven satellites destroyed. While American officials have wondered publicly about how many *Tien Lung* vehicles the Chinese can build, China threatened during the broadcast to destroy the entire GPS constellation unless 'America abandoned its plans for Pacific hegemony.'"

The Pentagon
Arlington, VA
October 6, 2017

General Warner had made sure the office was fully supplied, and Barnes had started work immediately. To avoid questions, he hadn't even returned to his own desk. There were a few personal items he'd retrieve later, after everyone had gone home, but he didn't need them to work on *Defender*.

He was already familiar with the design, and even remembered a few rough spots that were going to require some research, but while his mind leapt ahead, spurred by urgency, he forced himself to organize a proper study of each subsystems group: space frame, propulsion, life support, and of course weapons. He really wanted to start there, but when he thought about it dispassionately, weapons were just cargo. First things first: the thing had to fly.

Luckily, Lockheed Martin had done most of the heavy lifting when they designed *VentureStar*. It had been designed as a reusable single-stage-to-orbit vehicle. No expendable boosters, and, like the shuttle, it was good for more than one flight—potentially hundreds. It was what most people imagined when they heard the word "spaceship," but it was still at the ragged leading edge of human technology.

Like the shuttle, *VentureStar* was intended to be a "space truck," hauling heavy cargoes to orbit and landing like an aircraft. Her revolutionary Aerospike engines were powerful enough to lift her into orbit without boosters, and she was a lighter, more efficient design. The shuttle had been built in the sixties and seventies. *VentureStar* was at least twenty years newer.

Barnes's study quickly led him to what had caused the *Venture-Star*'s cancellation. The biggest problem had been the composite cryogenic fuel tanks, new technology that made NASA decide it was too expensive to continue the program. But Lock Mart had continued to develop the fuel-tank technology on its own dime and appeared to have found a solution.

Of course they hadn't applied the fix to the *VentureStar* prototype, which was mothballed at a storage facility at Edwards Air Force Base. It was ninety-five percent complete, according to what he could find out, although it was only "eighty-five percent assembled." Biff lost a little time finding out that while some parts had been fabricated, they hadn't been integrated with the space frame yet.

That was fine. He'd built kits as a kid. This was just bigger and a whole lot more complicated. With really expensive glue.

At least there weren't any hydraulics. Everything was done with electric motors—the landing gear, control surfaces, everything. Eliminating an entire system like that simplified the design and saved a lot of weight. It was just a good idea when they designed *VentureStar*, but it was vital now.

While he studied the individual systems and made notes, a question kept pushing into his mind from the side. It wasn't his first priority, but if he did come up with a plan, the next question would be, How soon? General Warner would expect at least a rough timeline.

Barnes added "power" to the list of systems. *VentureStar* burned liquid hydrogen and oxygen, which was nice because it could then use fuel cells to generate electricity, since the cells also used hydrogen and oxygen. And their output was water, which could be used by the life-support system.

But while McConnell's fuel cells were state-of-the-art, in his work Barnes had seen new fuel-cell technology that increased energy efficiency from sixty percent to over eighty percent. They were new, and expensive, so they hadn't been adopted commercially, but for this application they were worth it. Fewer cells meant saving critical weight, but he hadn't looked at the power requirements yet . . .

By one in the morning, he knew enough about *Defender* to go home and sleep, after stopping off at his old office. He ignored a note on his desk from Major Pierce telling Biff to call him ASAP. It would be better if explanations came from someone with stars on their shoulders. He didn't even consider pulling an all-nighter. He had all day tomorrow to work on the plan.

Unmarried, Biff lived in a two-bedroom apartment in Crystal City, right off the Metro. He didn't have to risk his beloved Porsche in Pentagon traffic or fight for a parking spot. Two levels belowground, covered snugly, it waited patiently for the next weekend drive to Ohio or North Carolina or Connecticut. The challenge was finding two different routes, there and back, and of course doing it in as little time as possible.

On the way back to his apartment, Biff thought about *Defender* and Ray McConnell. Normally, one of his first phone calls would have been to the guy who created *Defender*, but that was out of the question—he worked for the navy, and Barnes had been specifically ordered to keep their sister service in the dark. For the same reason, he hadn't called Lockheed Martin, although there were many questions he'd like to ask them. Biff had started a list, for those two and others.

McConnell was evidently a great organizer, and he wasn't afraid to push a good idea. Putting it on SIPRNET had taken some courage. He had to be an aerospace engineer of some sort, and probably at a senior level. Biff hoped he'd be able to meet McConnell some day, possibly soon. It would be interesting.

6

In Decision

United Flight 1191, en route to Washington, D.C.
October 6, 2017

Ray McConnell closed the window with the news feed on his tablet and put his head back against the seat, shaking it in frustration. Usually, he liked winning a good debate, but he wasn't reveling in the prospect that he was right this time. Ray knew that those "American officials," the talking heads spewing their nonsense on the cable news programs, were indulging in wishful thinking. China's space program had a good base of design and operational experience. The kill vehicle, the *Tien Lung*, was not trivial, but it was well within their capabilities. The GPS satellites were completely unprotected and had only the most limited ability to maneuver. From a technical viewpoint, it wasn't a problem.

And logically, if the Chinese leadership had committed themselves to this premeditated confrontation, would they only have a handful of bullets for their gun? *I'd have dozens stockpiled, and factories making more,* Ray mused.

It was bad news, although it helped strengthen his case.

He said it again. His case. Schultz had called him from Washington last night, telling him to come out ASAP, on navy orders. Sitting in his house, still depressed about his meeting with Carson,

Schultz's call had struck him like lightning. Ray hadn't known what to think or hope.

He'd then spent most of the night trying to organize the jumble of material that represented the *Defender* design. If Schultz wanted to talk about *Defender*, he'd want to see more than just the document that had been circulated on the net. There was a lot of supporting information behind the team's initial work, but in the rush to get the basic document produced, they'd planned to put together the supporting annexes "later."

And an admiral wanted to see it. Correction, at least two admirals wanted to see it. The CNO was also directly involved. Ray knew he had a lot of work to do. He'd seen enough Pentagon briefings to know what was expected. Ray finally quit at 5:00 A.M. and took a taxi to the airport. He could sleep on the plane.

Waiting at the gate, Ray dashed off an apologetic e-mail to Jake Olsen, explaining what he could and promising to make it up to his deputy somehow. Ray was pretty sure it would take something more than a fruit basket.

Rudy White wouldn't find out about Ray's absence until he came into work at seven thirty. Although Ray had official orders authorizing his travel, Rudy would still not be happy. Fortunately, Ray's flight would be an hour in the air by the time his supervisor read his e-mail.

At the gate, Ray fidgeted, impatient and distracted. He typed, of course, trying to organize the thoughts crowding into his mind, but he kept checking the clock. It moved at an agonizingly slow pace.

Finally, it was time to board and then take off, but he found he still couldn't relax. Ray realized that his stress had nothing to do with the flight, or the design, but with the thought of *Defender* actually becoming real. He'd been so emotionally braced for failure that he hadn't prepared for success. It was time to start looking forward.

Ray paused to think about what it would mean for him personally. If *Defender* flew, it would, of course, mean professional validation. But would the powers that be let him be part of the program in some way? He was pretty sure he'd need a new job. His prospects at SPAWAR were problematic, even if *Defender* succeeded.

Once they were at altitude, Ray opened his tablet and continued to work and, now, plan for the future. Sleep was impossible. Thanks to Schultz's call, the odds of *Defender* being built had improved from "slim" to "small." Ray wanted to make them even better.

Triggered by a keyword search, the news broadcast had popped up, interrupting his work, but he'd welcomed the information. It reminded him what this was all about.

"Ladies and gentlemen, this is the pilot. We've just received word that Air Traffic Control has rescheduled our arrival into Dulles to five forty-five instead of four thirty-eight this afternoon. There's no problem with the weather, but, because of the recent problems with the GPS system, they've just announced they'll be spacing aircraft farther apart near the airports, as a precaution. United apologizes for the delay. Passengers with connecting flights . . ."

Ray smiled. For once, he was glad for the extra time in the air.

Dulles International Airport
Sterling, VA
October 6, 2017

Outside baggage claim, a balding man in his fifties, not particularly tall, was holding a sign that read, "McConnell, R."

"I'm Ray McConnell," he announced, and the other man offered his hand.

"I'm Bill Schultz." He smiled warmly, easing Ray's surprise at being met by the head of Naval Air Systems Command in civilian clothes.

"We're keeping your visit low-profile, for the moment," Schultz explained as they headed for the exit. "There's a JCS brief tomorrow morning, and you're going to pitch *Defender*."

"To the Joint Chiefs of Staff?" Ray asked, shocked. He discovered it was possible to be both pleased and terrified at the same time.

There was a navy car waiting at the curb, and Ray's bags went in the trunk.

Once they were in the car and moving, Schultz explained, "We'll spend tonight and tomorrow morning putting together your presentation. Then you and Admiral Kramer will present *Defender* as a navy program at ten hundred hours."

Concern growing, Ray protested. "You haven't even seen what I brought out."

"Have you discovered any fatal flaws in the concept since we spoke last night?" Schultz was smiling as he asked, and when Ray quickly shook his head, continued. "*Defender* is really all there is. If it doesn't work, the Chinese win, so we are going to make it work."

Relieved, Ray sat back in his seat and asked, "Where are we going?"

"First to get some dinner, then to the Pentagon. I've got a room at the Marriott Courtyard in Crystal City reserved for you. If we get enough done tonight, I might let you sleep a few hours." Schultz was still smiling, and Ray could only hope for the best.

They ate at a sports bar a few blocks south of the Pentagon while the navy driver took Ray's bags and checked him in to his hotel. "There aren't many good and fast restaurants around here," Schultz apologized, "but I found this place a few weeks ago. We've been pulling a lot of late nights recently, and I can't stand delivery pizza."

Schultz asked about how Ray had come up with the idea for *Defender*, how he'd found people to help, and then what the reaction had been within SPAWAR to his proposal. "Jenny passed on what you told her, but now I want all the gory details."

As Ray gave a complete account of his climb and fall on the bureaucratic ladder, Schultz listened carefully, almost to the point of taking notes. Alternately frowning and smiling at his supervisors' different reactions, he remarked, "Pay attention tomorrow. You'll hear the same thing from officers who should know better. I've never met Admiral Carson, but I know the type. Anything that falls outside the wiring diagram is at best a distraction, and possibly a threat. Your idea was so big that it could only be a threat, to him and to SPAWAR.

"But you're here, thanks to Jenny," he continued. "So, how long have you two been going out?"

The sudden change of subject surprised him, and Ray had to pause before responding. "A few weeks. She showed up at the design sessions, and one thing led to another." He shrugged, embarrassed for no good reason.

"Part of the reason—no, a big part of the reason I brought you out here was because of her support. She's sharp, and I valued her judgment when she worked for me as a junior officer. If she thought you were worth something, then that was good enough for me."

"I won't disappoint you, Admiral."

Schultz laughed softly. "I'm not the one you have to worry about disappointing."

Office of the Chief of Staff of the Air Force
The Pentagon
2215 hours
October 6, 2017

Captain "Biff" Barnes tapped his tablet, and the file collapsed down into a small spaceship icon. His presentation had condensed McConnell's hundred-page design document down to fifteen minutes. It had been a long fifteen minutes, with Warner, his deputy, General Ames, and a small gaggle of generals and colonels watching intently.

Warner had called together his "brain trust" to hear about *Defender* and tear it apart, if they could. They hadn't said a word, which Biff took to mean there weren't any showstoppers. That didn't mean there weren't any questions.

"What about her radar signature?" one general asked. "Can you add radar-absorbent material?"

Biff shook his head. "We don't know about its heat resistance. There's been testing of some advanced RAM concepts to about Mach 5, but *Defender*'s going way above that. We can't even put it on the nonaerodynamic surfaces, because the material is so dense. We don't have the weight margin."

A colonel suggested, "How about adding a gun?" Others in the room almost laughed at the suggestion, but he defended the idea. "I'm uncomfortable with the weapons suite. It's all untried technology. We know a gun will work in space."

"We considered it, sir," Barnes answered. "And it sounds like a good idea. Without air friction or ballistic drop, you've got a flat trajectory out to many times its normal range, and it doesn't even have to be an explosive projectile. The *Tien Lung* ASAT vehicle is most likely unarmored. So we looked at a long twenty-millimeter barrel firing shells loaded with something like double-ought pellets.

"The problem is the weight of the installation. You can't mount it in the nose, like a traditional aircraft, because any orifice in the front compromises the heat shield. And rigidly mounting the gun means that the spacecraft has to be precisely aligned with the ballistic path of the projectiles. It's hard enough to get the right angle on a target a mile away. Here, the target will be much farther out." Biff noted all the fighter pilots nodding in agreement. "Aiming would also use up reaction mass as the attitude-control jets fired.

"It would have to be mounted in the bay, on a remote two-axis mount. By the time you're done, the weapon and its mount take up just as much space and weight as a railgun or a laser, and have over twice as many components. Since the flexible mount would be a new design, the biggest chance of failure lies there. Clearing an ammunition jam would mean an EVA."

Lieutenant General Towns was the Vice Chairman for Strategic Plans and Programs, and, like the rest of the officers there, this was his first encounter with *Defender*. He'd been furiously taking notes during the meeting, only half-listening to Barnes's briefing and the discussion. He listened to another question about launch support before speaking up.

"I don't understand how we're going to be able to present this as a complete design. Captain, you've fitted all these components together, but I'm seeing pieces of four different programs at different stages of development. I see two civilian technologies that haven't been certified for military use. And since this will be a major defense acquisition system, we need to go through the Joint Capabilities Integrated Development System and develop a requirement, which we then have to demonstrate can't be met with existing systems or a change in strategy."

Towns gestured toward the screen. "We can only proceed with the design, which Captain Barnes is presenting here, after that is approved. I'm ignoring the fact that several of the programs Captain Barnes talks about are compartmented and will have to be formally approved for fielding, or were you planning on keeping them on the 'black' side, Captain?"

General Warner cut in as Barnes started to answer. "Hank, that's not fair. I directed the captain to use whatever technology he could find to describe a viable weapons system. Which he has done," Warner declared approvingly.

The chief of staff continued, speaking carefully. "Having determined that an armed spacecraft is the only way to defend the GPS constellation, and having identified technology that will allow us to construct said spacecraft, my intention is to present the secretary of defense with an air force program already at the design-readiness-review stage. This will enable us to move on to Milestone C, production and deployment, expeditiously."

Towns scowled. "So we're just going to ignore the first two-thirds of the acquisition process, not to mention most of the DoD regulations? And what about competitive bidding? Using *VentureStar* makes Lock Mart the sole-source prime contractor, and you've also identified specific components for the rest of the design. The entire thing is sole-sourced!" He almost shuddered.

Warner smiled. "Hank, you're in this room because of all the problems you just stated. Take your best people and have them write the world's shortest, simplest requirement. Have another group work on the justification for sole-source contracts, another group . . ."

Lt. General Towns nodded impatiently. "I understand, sir. My staff will get on it immediately. Other programs will probably suffer, of course." That remark forced him to pause for a moment. He then asked, "And where will the money for this wonder program come from?"

"From those other programs, of course," Warner answered quickly. "But as long as the Chinese are shooting down GPS satellites, anything connected with *Defender* is the most important thing in the air force." Biff noted a lot of frowns, but the general ignored them.

"This is a critical moment in military history. The Chinese have opened the door to a whole new type of warfare. We knew it would happen eventually, but we were in no rush to get there, until now. Just as the airplane changed the way ground troops operated, spacecraft will change the air force. Regardless of whether *Defender* is ever built, we must review everything we do—tactics, hardware, and especially future programs. Anyone who doesn't think there will be changes hasn't fully grasped the situation."

Caesar's Diner
Crystal City, VA
0830 hours
October 7, 2017

Ray had wanted to get his breakfast to go, but Schultz insisted on their sitting down and eating in the restaurant. McConnell had protested. "I still haven't solved all the power-management issues, and . . ."

The admiral cut him off. "Pace yourself, Ray. Five hours of sleep is only going to get you so far. And you can't solve every engineering problem before today's briefing. Besides, there are bigger things to think about."

Ray's expression as he worked on a steak omelet managed to ask the obvious question, and Schultz explained. "What part of the navy is going to run the program? I'm head of NAVAIR, and I don't want it. I'd love to see some of the R&D folks at China Lake involved, because they've been very creative in the past. But this is way bigger than they can handle. And what about when it's on the ground? We'll need Marines to guard it, of course. Then there are launch-preparation considerations to be worked out. How long does a complete turnaround take under 'combat conditions'? Can we work to shorten it?"

They took turns taking bites and exchanging ideas and questions. Schultz's questions caught Ray flat-footed. He hadn't given the slightest thought to how *Defender* would fit into the military once it was built.

During the ten-minute drive from the diner to the Pentagon, Schultz told Ray, "My goal is to present the JCS with a complete concept, not just of how this spacecraft will function, but how it will be supported and commanded."

The admiral's statements had surprised Ray, but also excited him. They assumed *Defender* would be built and take its place as a part of America's military.

"For instance, we can't run this kind of mission from Houston, or any of the existing space-command centers. That means we should have a rough idea of what that center should be like. We get enough of those questions answered before they're even asked, and the JCS will let us build your baby."

Answers to the admiral's questions swirled in his mind, competing for attention as they passed through security and headed for Schultz's office. Ray couldn't wait to start.

First Floor, E Ring
The Pentagon
0950 hours
October 7, 2017

"Bringing in a graphic artist was inspired, Captain." General Warner was almost beaming.

"I knew he could get those diagrams done more quickly than I could, and they'd look a lot better."

"What? I've found a pilot who wasn't an art major?" Warner joked. "The important thing is that a dedicated artist let you concentrate on the content, while Sergeant Epperson made it look great."

Warner's aides had gone ahead to load the briefing and prepare the hard copies, and the two officers headed for the elevator down to the National Military Command Center, the "war room."

As they rode down, the general said, "Biff, regardless of whether the JCS buys *Defender* or not, you've done a stellar job, and I'll make sure Major Pierce knows about it. I know you're looking forward to flying again, and I think you're going to make an excellent operations officer. Unless you want to stay with the *Defender* program," Warner added.

And miss a chance at ops officer, third in command of a fighter squadron? Barnes failed to suppress a wide smile. "Thank you, sir. I'll do my best today."

Warner laughed, a little grimly. "I just hope the Joint Chiefs have a sense of humor."

National Military Command Center
The Pentagon
October 7, 2017

Ray looked around the fabled war room. Every available chair was filled, most by someone wearing a uniform with stars on it.

The Joint Chiefs themselves sat on both sides of a long table, with the chairman at the head on the left. A briefer's podium stood empty at the head, and behind the podium, the entire wall was an active video display.

Several rows of chairs to one side of the main table were filled with a gaggle of aides, experts, and assorted hangers-on, including Ray. Nervously, he typed on his tablet PC, working on the design that was never finished.

The vice chairman, a navy admiral, stepped up to the podium, and the buzz in the room quickly died. "Gentlemen, the Chairman."

Everyone rose, and Ray saw General Kastner, the Chairman of the Joint Chiefs of Staff, enter and take his seat. McConnell wasn't normally awed by rank, but he realized that this collection of stars could really make things happen. They literally were responsible for defending the country, and that's what they'd met to do.

The vice chairman, Admiral Blair, clicked a remote. A chart appeared on the screen. It was titled "Protection of Space Assets."

"Gentlemen, our task today is to find a course of action that will protect our satellites from Chinese attack. Any solution we consider"— and he started to tick off items on the list—"must address the cost, the technological risk, the time it would take to implement, and any political repercussions." He glanced over at Kastner, who nodded approvingly.

Blair continued. "Above all," he said, scanning the entire room, "it must work, and work soon. The material costs alone already have been severe, and the potential effects on American security are incalculable.

"For purposes of this discussion, while cost should be considered, it is not a limitation. Also, the president considers these attacks by China an attack on American vital interests, although he has not made that decision public."

Nor will he, Ray thought, *until we can do something about them.* So cost wasn't a problem—just shut down the Chinese, and do it quickly.

Blair put a new slide up on the display, listing some conventional methods of attack. "You've all sent analyses indicating that these are not viable options. Our purpose is to see what other means you've developed since then."

Kastner stood up, taking Blair's place at the podium. Blair sat down at his left. The chairman looked around the room. "To save time, let me ask a few questions."

The chairman looked at the chief of naval operations. "Can we use a missile to shoot down the kill vehicle?"

Admiral Kramer answered quickly. "We'd hoped that would work, sir, but we're sure now that we can't. We had two Aegis ships in a position to track the last ASAT shot seven days ago. We've been analyzing the data since."

"The *Tien Lung*"—Kramer pronounced the Chinese name carefully—"is too fast. Our SM3 missile can shoot down a ballistic missile, but as hard as a missile intercept is, it's easier than this. At least a ballistic missile is a closing target, but the ASAT vehicle is outbound the whole way. It's a tail chase from the start. Even if we launched at the same instant, the intercept basket is nonexistent."

"Does the army concur?" Kastner looked at the army's chief of staff. The army also had an active antiballistic-missile system.

"Yes, sir. It's simply impossible from the surface of the earth." General Forest didn't look pleased.

Ray realized the general had just told the chairman that the army didn't have a role in solving the crisis. Of course, the commandant of the Marine Corps looked even unhappier. This was one beach his men couldn't hope to storm.

General Kastner announced, "I'm also allowed to tell you that there are no special assets that might be able to destroy the launch site using unconventional methods."

In other words, Ray thought, *they can't get an agent into the area.* He didn't even want to think about how he'd destroy the launcher. Talk about *The Guns of Navarone* . . .

Which meant they were getting desperate. Ray saw what Kastner was doing: eliminating options one by one. He knew about *Defender.*

He had to know. Ray didn't know what to feel. Was this actually going to happen? Fear started to replace hope.

General Warner finally broke the silence. "Sir, the air force thinks we can make the *Defender* concept work."

Admiral Kramer shot a surprised look at Schultz, sitting next to Ray. Then both looked at McConnell, who shrugged helplessly. He was equally surprised and confused. Warner's aide began typing commands on the display, and Ray saw *Defender*'s image appear on the wall. This was becoming a little too surreal.

Others in the room thought so as well, although for different reasons. A low murmur rose and quickly fell, and Ray saw many shaking their heads in disbelief. Just because all other options had been eliminated didn't mean they'd automatically accept this one.

"Captain Barnes from our Rapid Capabilities Office has put together a presentation on the design." Ray saw a black air force captain with astronaut's wings step up to the podium. As he started to speak, McConnell suddenly felt irritation, an almost proprietary protectiveness about the ship, especially when he saw that the graphic on the front had been changed to add U.S. insignia and "USAF."

It was *his* idea. Ray wanted to speak up, then silenced his inner voice. This was what he'd wanted, to have his idea accepted and adopted. After all, the goal was to stop the Chinese and protect U.S. satellites. *Remember the big picture*, he thought. But the irritation persisted.

Barnes seemed enthusiastic about the design, and had to be some sort of engineer. He spoke knowledgeably and had resolved some design issues. Ray wasn't familiar with all of the gear Barnes had added, but he understood its function. Some of the changes made sense, but the captain completely missed the boat on others. Ray tried to be fair. Nobody knew *Defender* as well as he did, or, at least, that's what he wanted to believe.

Ray spoke softly to Schultz beside him. "He's made some mistakes. Power management will not work like that." Schultz lifted one eyebrow in response but didn't say anything. The admiral pulled out his tablet and typed quickly. Kramer, watching the presentation from the long table, glanced down at his pad and tapped something, then looked over at Schultz, nodding. They watched the rest of the brief in silence. There was nothing about the larger questions that Vice Admiral Schultz had raised earlier that morning.

The last slide read "Questions?" and General Forest started to ask a question, but Admiral Kramer spoke up. "Excuse me, General, but Mr. McConnell, the engineer who led the *Defender* design team, is here, and can add to what Captain Barnes has presented."

Schultz nudged Ray, and the engineer stood up and moved toward the podium. As he passed Admiral Kramer, the naval officer muttered, "Go get 'em, Ray." The engineer had never felt less like getting anyone in his life.

As he approached the podium, Captain Barnes shot him a hard look, seemingly reluctant to leave. Ray said, "Hello," conscious of the captain's sudden obsolescence, and tried to smile pleasantly. Barnes nodded politely, if silently, picked up his notes, and returned to his chair.

Ray was acutely aware of the many eyes on him. He linked his tablet to the screen and transferred his own presentation to the display. He used the moment's fiddling to gather his wits. He'd given dozens of briefs. This was just a little more impromptu than most. And much more important.

"As Vice Admiral Schultz said, I'm Ray McConnell, and I led the team that produced the *Defender* concept. It uses the Lockheed Martin *VentureStar* prototype with equipment currently available to detect launches, maneuver to an intercept position, and kill the attacking ASAT vehicle. It also has the capability to attack the launch site from medium Earth orbit."

Barnes had said that much, Ray knew, but he'd felt a need to also make that declaration, to say to these men himself what *Defender* was and what it could do.

He opened the file and rapidly flipped through the large document. McConnell realized that the pilot had done a pretty good job of summarizing *Defender*, so he concentrated instead on the work that had gone into selecting and integrating the different systems. That was his specialty, anyway, and it improved the credibility of his high-tech offspring.

A message appeared on his tablet from Admiral Schultz as he talked. "Are there any army or Marine systems in the design?" Ray understood immediately what Schultz was driving at. There wasn't a piece of army or Marine gear anywhere on the ship, and Ray mentally kicked himself for not understanding the importance of Pentagon diplomacy.

Ray spent most of his time explaining the command and control scheme and how the spacecraft would be supported on the ground. By the time he finished, he felt positive as he assured the assembled generals that there were no insurmountable problems in building *Defender*. He glanced at Barnes, but the captain was head down, typing.

"Thank you, Mr. McConnell." Kastner rose again, and Ray quickly returned to his seat, barely remembering to grab his data pad. "I'm much more confident about *Defender*'s ability, and possibility, than I was at the start of this meeting. It is my intention to recommend to the president that *Defender* be built, and soon."

Ray felt a little numb. Schultz gave him a small nudge and smiled.

"We haven't really discussed the political implications of arming spacecraft." General Forest's tone was carefully neutral, but his expression was hard, almost hostile. Would he fight *Defender*?

Kastner was nodding, though. "A good point, Ted, and part of our task." He looked around the table. "Admiral Kramer?"

"I believe the Chinese have solved that issue for us, sir. They've fired the first shot, and said so proudly and publicly." He smiled. "I think *Defender*'s name was well chosen."

General Warner added quickly, "I concur. There's no guarantee that the Chinese will stop with just GPS satellites, and there's every likelihood that their capabilities will expand. More frequent launches, and the ability to destroy satellites in higher orbits. That puts our communications satellites, even our nuclear-warning satellites, at risk. Consider the political implications of *not* acquiring this capability."

"All of our public statements will emphasize that we are taking these steps only as a result of Chinese attacks," Kastner stated.

Admiral Kramer quickly asked, "Should *Defender* even be made public? So far, it's only been circulated on SIPRNET, so we can keep its existence classified. With enough warning, the Chinese might be able to take some sort of countermeasure."

Kastner considered only a moment before answering. "All right. My recommendation will be that *Defender* remain secret until after its first use."

General Warner announced, "I'll have my people look for a suitable development site immediately. With all the air force bases we've closed . . ."

"Your people aren't the only ones with runways, General. This is a navy program. Mr. McConnell is a navy employee," Kramer interrupted.

"And that's why he put his design on SIPRNET, because of the tremendous navy support he was receiving." Warner fixed his gaze on Kramer, almost challenging him to interrupt. "It was my understanding that he offered this design to the DoD as a private citizen. Certainly the air force is the best service to manage an aerospace-warfare design. We'll welcome navy participation, of course."

"The navy has just as much technological expertise as the air force. And more in some of the most critical areas . . ."

Ray understood what was going on even as it horrified him. *Defender* would mean a new mission, and, if it worked, a lot of publicity, and more important, money. That mattered in these lean times, but the implications went beyond just a bigger slice of the pie. A revolutionary capability could have a significant impact on the defense industry, recruiting, and even the manned space program. It could also change the future in ways they couldn't even guess. But now they were arguing over the prize like children.

"The army's experience with ballistic-missile defense means we should be able to contribute as well." General Forest's tone wasn't pleading, but his argument almost did.

Kastner spoke forcefully. "We will meet again at zero eight hundred hours tomorrow morning. Every service will prepare a summary of the assets it can contribute, and any justification it might feel for wanting to manage the project."

Oh, boy, thought Ray. *It's going to be a long night.*

7

Genesis

CNN Early News
London, England
October 8, 2017

Trevor West stood outside Whitehall while morning traffic crept past him. His overcoat and umbrella provided some protection against the typically rainy London weather, but the brisk wind fought his words. He spoke loudly and held the microphone close.

"After an emergency meeting of Parliament this morning, in which the prime minister spoke at length on China's intentional disabling of the American GPS constellation, Her Majesty's government has issued a stern condemnation of the Chinese attacks and has demanded that they cease immediately. The official démarche, presented to the Chinese ambassador approximately half an hour ago, protests not only the attacks themselves but also the militarization of space.

"The Chinese ambassador received the diplomatic note without comment. The American ambassador was provided with a copy of the démarche and welcomed the British support, stating that the United States was doing everything in its power to defend its interests and property.

"Ministry of Defense sources are unsure what the Americans plan to do about the Chinese attacks. MoD officials believe a direct attack on the launcher in southern China would be quite difficult given the Chinese air defenses and how deeply buried the gun is in the mountainside. And, of course, the GPS satellites themselves are entirely defenseless.

"One source speculated that the Americans may try to threaten Chinese interests elsewhere in Asia, pressuring them into stopping their attacks. They say they've even seen some signs that this may already be occurring. Of course, military pressure risks widening the conflict—including open hostilities between the United States and China.

"MoD officials refused to speculate what Her Majesty's government's position would be in such a situation."

Office of the Chief of Staff of the Air Force
The Pentagon
October 8, 2017

Biff Barnes leaned back in the large leather chair and rubbed his eyes. He tried again to focus on the plans for *Defender*'s fly-by-wire system—no luck. All the lines, numbers, and letters had become fuzzy. Standing, he stretched and suppressed a large yawn. It had been a long night. He and a dozen other officers had spent it in the posh executive conference room, laboring nonstop to transform the *Defender* design concept into a proper air force acquisition program. The large flat-screen displays at the end of the conference table showed the overall *Defender* design side by side with the standard DoD chart showing a program's plan of action and milestones. Blueprints, data printouts, and tablet PCs covered the table, mixed with an army's worth of empty Styrofoam coffee cups, Chinese takeout boxes from the night before, and doughnut boxes from that morning.

The past forty-eight hours had compressed into an indistinguishable blur. First, the mad rush to meet with the chief of staff, and then essentially being drafted to be the air force's lead on the

Defender program. The run-up to the JCS meeting that followed was just as fast-paced, with Barnes preparing and then presenting a logical argument for why *Defender* was not only plausible but was their best chance to level the playing field with the Chinese. And, oh, why the air force should own *Defender*. But the navy had effectively upstaged the air force and him with Ray McConnell. Like any fighter pilot, Biff didn't take being outmaneuvered well. It was also his first real run-in with honest-to-God interservice rivalry.

Of course, Biff was well aware of the competition between the various services. No one who served in Washington, D.C., could miss it, but he hadn't been a participant in a bare knuckles fight at the general-officer level before. Barnes considered himself a damn fine pilot, but he had no delusions about his place in the grand scheme of things. He was just another minor cog in a much greater machine.

And yet he suddenly found himself dragged into the "stratosphere," the highest levels of the U.S. Air Force, tasked to do new and challenging things. Things that had never been done before, and those things would change the very nature of the air force. Biff found it all very exciting, and at the same time somewhat unsettling. The risks were considerable, but then so, too, were the potential rewards. The fighter pilot in him eagerly embraced the challenge. But in a dark corner of his mind, a small voice asked if this was going to help or hurt his chances of making major.

When the air force contingent had left the JCS meeting eighteen hours earlier, General Ames had come up to Barnes and said, "You did a good job on your presentation, Clarence."

Barnes, already in a foul mood, interrupted. "Please, sir, just 'Biff.'" Why was the general getting on a first-name basis?

Ames smiled. "Fine then, Biff. Who knew the navy would back *Defender* as well? I certainly didn't expect they'd bring in McConnell himself to argue their case. All things considered, you did very well."

"Thank you, sir." Biff was unsure where this was going, but the hairs on the back of his neck were starting to tingle. His instincts told him to check his six o'clock.

"I need someone to put that presentation together, Biff. I'll give you as many of the staff as you need, and you can set up in my conference room. We've got until zero eight hundred tomorrow to come up with a strong argument that will sell General Kastner on the air force owning *Defender*."

"Maybe you should get a lawyer," Biff suggested. He was half-serious.

"No, I want a pilot, and you're the only one in sight who's also been an astronaut."

"General, with all due respect, sir, I'm just a captain. I'm not even senior enough to make coffee in this building. Won't my lack of seniority be a significant disadvantage?"

Ames chuckled. "Normally, Biff, I'd agree with you. But right now, under these circumstances, the chief of staff is more interested in your expertise than your rank. As far as he's concerned, you're the right man for the job. Everybody else's opinion is irrelevant. And if more 'senior' officers have to work for you to bring this task to a successful conclusion, well, they'll just have to get over it."

By now they'd reached Ames's office, but Biff didn't respond immediately. Finally, the general asked him flatly, "Do you want the job?"

Biff knew he could say no if he wanted to. He believed Ames was a fair enough officer not to hold it against him. But Barnes was still mad at the navy, and McConnell in particular. "Yes, sir. It's in the bag." He grinned, a fighter-pilot grin.

General Warner's guidance to Biff and his team was to pitch *Defender* as an accelerated-acquisition program, which compressed or eliminated many steps of the acquisition process. This strategy would provide the justification to get a high-risk program approved, but would also appeal to the "sense of order" that the SECDEF was comfortable with. Warner was quite certain the CJCS would not make the final decision on *Defender* all by himself; the SECDEF would have his say, and he was a lawyer by trade. Biff wasn't completely convinced that approaching the problem as if it were a trial was the right thing to do, but the chief of staff was a bomber pilot and a savvy Pentagon warrior, more accustomed to a by-the-book, deliberate planning approach.

Barnes walked through the executive-level briefing one last time, correcting minor grammatical mistakes and checking on the animation. Color and motion were useful tools in grabbing, and retaining, a senior officer's attention. The presentation itself was deceptively small when one considered all the effort that had gone into it. The whole thing could be given in less than forty-five minutes—attention span was also an issue—but the supporting documentation would need a wheelbarrow. Biff was staring at the final slide, wondering if he'd missed anything, when General Ames hurried into the room. He'd checked on their progress several times during the night, and Biff started to report when Ames cut him off.

"Turn on the news," Ames ordered a lieutenant at the far end of the room. The junior officer looked for the remote and grabbed it, then fumbled for the power control.

". . . as yet there has been no response to the Chinese demands. The State Department spokesman only repeated earlier demands by the U.S. government that the Chinese stop their attacks."

The CNN defense reporter, Mark Markin, stood in front of a sign that read U.S. DEPARTMENT OF STATE.

"To repeat, the Chinese have now stated their conditions for stopping the attacks on the NAVSTAR GPS satellite constellation. The U.S. must reduce its forces in the region to below precrisis levels, especially in South Korea and Japan. According to their official statement, this is 'to remove the immediate threat of U.S. aggression against the People's Republic of China.' If the U.S. does so, the Chinese will agree to cease their attacks. The Chinese ambassador also hinted that they might also restart the stalled talks on human rights, intellectual property rights, and other long-standing disputes."

Ames said, "That's enough," and the lieutenant turned it off.

The general looked at Barnes. "The answer's 'hell, no,' of course, but you've gotta love the way they're taking it to the media. And some of the reporters aren't helping the situation by making us sound completely powerless to do anything." Ames sounded disgusted.

Biff clicked on the SAVE button, closed the file, and announced, "We're ready, sir. Let's clean up and go get us a program."

Chief of Naval Operations Conference Room
The Pentagon
October 8, 2017

Ray had managed to get about three hours of rest, and that only because his eyes simply couldn't focus on the screen any longer. Suffering badly from jet lag, he fought dozing off with a powerful combination of caffeine, sugar, and adrenaline. The urgent need to whip together their pitch for the chairman kept them all going at a feverish pace. Working like a rented mule, Ray struggled to finish *Defender* in one night, while the CNO and his staff put together the case to keep her a navy project.

Ray smiled at the irony. He had done the nigh impossible; he'd won. He'd made the case for *Defender*. By all rights, he should be on cloud nine right now. Not only was *Defender* going to be built, but the services were fighting over who would run it! Maybe it was fatigue, or the thought that his baby could be taken away from him, but he wasn't feeling optimistic, let alone happy.

Schultz had gotten no sleep whatsoever, and looked it. But they'd all gained a second wind right after the Chinese ultimatum. Dogged determination could substitute for sleep, for a little while anyway.

The admiral took a slug of lukewarm coffee as he reviewed the staff's work, scribbling furiously on paper copies of the slides. Schultz was approaching the impending meeting as if it were an airstrike. Identify the "enemy's" center of gravity and pound the dog poop out of it. In this case, he was targeting the air force's likely approach to the *Defender* ownership issue.

Having served nearly two years in the "Five-Sided Funny Farm," Schultz had a strong hunch that his air force colleagues were going to default to their tried-and-true acquisition practices. And while the NAVAIR commander had great respect for the air force chief of staff, he knew Warner tended to be more bureaucratic than most and would probably follow a more traditional path. They'd go with an accelerated program, to be sure, but it would still look more like a regular acquisition program than Schultz wanted. There were two ways to tackle the air force's pitch: go longer, or shorter. The admiral chose the latter.

"All right, people. The air force will almost certainly put together a dog and pony show that would make Cecil B. DeMille green with envy. It'll be a colorful production of epic proportions, loaded with graphics and animation that will use every second of their one hour. We could match them, but that would leave our audience in a PowerPoint-induced stupor. So we're going with brevity and simplicity." Schultz pulled up his single guidance slide on the large flat-screen display and, pointing toward it, gave the staff their running orders.

"While Mr. McConnell puts the final touches on the *Defender* design, the rest of you will build a rapid-development program based on an urgent operational need. We're going down the UON route because, once approved, it becomes one of DoD's highest priorities. This means we'll get the funding and resources necessary to develop, build, and deploy this new capability in a matter of months, not years.

"Since time *is* our enemy, I want our pitch to be short, clear, and concise. No bells and whistles, just the bare minimum it takes to make our case to the chairman and the SECDEF. Now turn to!"

By 0740, the navy's brief arguments had been assembled into several one-inch binders, one each for the CNO, the chairman, and the vice chairman. Everyone else would get stapled black-and-white copies of the slides. Ray had timed Schultz's last dry run—twenty minutes max. That had to be one of the shortest policy-decision briefs he'd ever seen. As the staff started cleaning up from the marathon planning session, Admiral Kramer and Vice Admiral Schultz, now in a fresh set of pressed khakis, walked into the conference room.

"Ready, Ray?" Schultz asked.

"Ready as I'll ever be, sir."

"Very well. Let's go and clip some air force wings, shall we?"

National Military Command Center
The Pentagon
October 8, 2017

Both groups arrived at the NMCC's briefing room at the same time. Quietly, the air force and navy members shuffled through the door and took their seats. Ray found himself seated directly across from Barnes, and he gave the young air force officer a weak smile as a greeting. Ray couldn't help but notice the bags under Barnes's eyes, a testimony that he'd been up all night as well. *He looks like hell,* Ray thought. He then self-consciously rubbed his hand on his face and felt the stubble of a two-day beard. Looking down, Ray saw that his suit was badly wrinkled and concluded he probably looked just as hellish, if not worse.

Barnes initially paid no attention to Ray. His gaze was fixed on the miniscule briefing binders the navy flag officers had brought with them. They were easily one-third the size of the ones he had prepared. Confused, Biff looked up at McConnell, his right hand gesturing toward the remarkably thin binders in front of Schultz with a facial expression that screamed, "Are you serious?!" Ray briefly glanced over at Schultz and immediately understood what Barnes was asking. Looking back, all he could do was offer the air force captain a slight shrug. Biff suppressed the desire to laugh out loud. *This will be a piece of cake,* he gloated to himself.

An aide broke the murmured conversations with the announcement that the chairman would be in shortly; he had been called to the White House earlier in the morning and had just arrived at the Mall entrance. Barnes looked around the room again with confusion. The projectors were off, and no one was at the computer bringing up the two presentations. He knew the chairman's staff personnel weren't idiots. Something wasn't right.

Before Barnes could even ask a question, General Kastner strode quickly into the briefing room, followed immediately by Secretary of Defense Peck. Both were hurrying, and the chairman reached the podium before everyone had even finished coming to attention.

"My apologies for being tardy, gentlemen. Please be seated."

The chairman waited until everyone had sat back down, then cleared his throat. "I know that I asked Admiral Kramer and General Warner yesterday to prepare their positions on the *Defender* issue. The circumstances have changed. Secretary Peck will explain."

Secretary of Defense Everett Peck was a political appointee, with little experience in the government. The balding, professorial lawyer had served as chief of staff for the president's election two years ago. He'd stayed out of trouble by leaving the DoD more or less to the chairman to administer while Peck dealt with Congress.

The secretary spoke with a measured tone that had been perfected in the courtroom; "The chairman and I have just come from a meeting with the president. This follows an earlier meeting last night where General Kastner briefed us on the *Defender* concept."

Peck paused, and tried to look sympathetic. "I understand the purpose of this meeting was to choose a service to run the *Defender* program, but that decision has been taken out of the chairman's hands."

What? Ray looked at the admirals, who were just as shocked and puzzled as he was. In fact, everyone at the conference table was exchanging stunned glances. Ray caught Barnes's eyes. The fighter pilot looked deeply disappointed. Ray knew immediately what he was thinking—*all that work, for nothing!* All Ray could do was wearily nod his agreement as Secretary Peck continued.

"The president has decided to create a new branch of the armed services to manage this new military resource. It will be structured similarly to the Special Operations Command, with assets and personnel assigned to it from the other services on an as-needed basis."

Peck didn't even wait for that to sink in but just kept on going. "This service will be known as the United States Space Force and will be headed by Vice Admiral Schultz. As a new service chief, he will be advanced to the rank of full admiral, effective immediately." Schultz looked completely thunderstruck; Ray thought he'd suddenly turned a little pale.

The secretary looked at Admiral Schultz, who was still trying to recover from the surprise announcement. "Your title will be 'chief, U.S. Space Force.' Your new rank is contingent on approval by the United States Senate. Do you accept?"

Just like that. No warning, no fanfare, just a point-blank question, on behalf of the president of the United States, no less. Schultz quickly regained his composure, swallowing hard. Ray heard the admiral mutter, "Ho boy." Standing, Schultz replied simply, "I accept, sir."

"Good. Admiral, notify your deputy at NAVAIR to take over your duties immediately. You will no longer report to the CNO, but to the chairman, on administrative matters. You will report to me regarding operational matters. You can establish your headquarters wherever you wish, but I assume you will want to be co-located with the construction effort, wherever that is based."

Kramer, suddenly Schultz's former boss, was still in a state of shock, as were most of the officers in the room. Kastner had a big smile on his face and didn't seem like someone who'd had a "decision taken out of his hands."

"I won't congratulate you, Admiral," Peck went on. "You'll probably come to regret this assignment, but I'm also sure you'll give it your best effort. And we are in desperate need of that. You have presidential authority to call on *any* resources of the Department of Defense—indeed, the U.S. government—to get *Defender* built and flying. Your orders are simple: Stop the Chinese from destroying our satellites."

Peck glanced at his notes again. "Now for the bad news. Most of you know that the two spare satellites in orbit are also nonfunctional and presumed destroyed. That means we've lost a total of seven GPS satellites."

Ray's heart sank. He'd heard the rumors but had hoped they weren't true.

"I can also tell you that while we have several satellites waiting to be put in orbit, and contracts have been let for replacement satellites, the president is reluctant to launch any until the threat is contained."

Reasonable, Ray thought. No sense giving the Chinese another half-a-billion-dollar target to shoot down. And even with the order placed, it'll take a long time for those replacements to be built.

Peck continued. "Unfortunately, we probably won't have a choice. The Chinese appear to be able to launch one attack vehicle a week. Given the number of satellites remaining in the constellation, at that rate we'll lose our ability to conduct precision strikes during the nighttime hours in about six weeks, or forty-two days."

Warner's face was grim; he knew exactly where this was going. "Which means any strike we send in will be on a suicide mission, as they'll have to go in during the day. This doesn't completely negate stealth, but it severely reduces our chances of success and increases our potential losses should we have to strike Chinese targets."

"They're attacking our way of war, General," observed Schultz. "As long as we don't get involved in the Vietnam crisis, we won't lose a single soul. And the slick part of all this is that the losses are largely transparent to the average Joe on the street. The majority of our citizens don't need 3D accuracy for their day-to-day living, and those that do are just shifting over to the new Galileo system. The Chinese are being very clever. They're pushing us into a corner that will be very difficult to get out of politically."

"Correct, Admiral," answered Peck. "We can delay this situation by launching the four satellites we have on hand, but that only buys us a few weeks. In seventy days, our ability to stop the Chinese will be severely crippled. That is how much time we have to build *Defender*."

Ray whistled softly. Just over two months to build and deploy an entirely new system, to fight in a new environment—space. Even with proven components and technology, that was an absurdly aggressive timeline.

Suddenly, three hours of sleep seemed like a lot.

Rayburn House Office Building
Washington, D.C.
October 8, 2017

Ben Davis rushed up to meet Rutledge as soon as he burst through the door. The congressman was in a bad mood. The urgent message from his chief of staff had pulled him from his church services, and he would probably have to cancel his golf outing with the House minority leader—nothing could get Rutledge into a tizzy faster than screwing around with his Sunday routine.

"Let's have it," the congressman demanded sourly.

"Here you go, Tom." Davis handed Rutledge an abbreviated transcript of the Chinese announcement. "They're damn gutsy, that's for sure. It's basically an ultimatum, either we . . ."

Rutledge raised his left hand sharply, demanding silence while he read. It took him only a moment to finish the short piece; he then snapped the paper back to Davis. "What has the White House said in response?"

Davis shook his head woefully. "Very little. A State Department spokesman merely reiterated the administration's demand that the Chinese cease their attacks."

An arrogant snicker burst out from the congressman. "Like that will do anything. Has there been any announcement of a press conference?"

"No, sir."

"What is the president thinking?" asked Rutledge incredulously. "Does he truly believe he can just ignore a threat like this and hope the problem will simply go away?"

"Tom, this problem will eventually 'go away' on its own. When we no longer have the ability to deter the Chinese from invading Vietnam. Not without the prospect of taking unacceptable casualties, that is. They're taking the night away from us, plain and simple."

Rutledge started pacing, chewing on a nail as he considered his next move. The complete lack of leadership by President Jackson throughout the current crisis was obvious to the most casual observer. Someone needed to step up to the plate and get the country energized. He could think of no one better than himself.

"All right, call Bill Hamilton in and get started on a press release. It needs to be strongly worded, with some language on what the administration needs to do to respond properly to the Chinese. And where are those statewide poll numbers I asked for over a week ago?"

"We got them in late Friday; the report is in your in-box. But the results are essentially consistent with those taken from your own district. The majority of the people in Nebraska don't see an invasion of Vietnam, or the taking out of our GPS satellites, as justification for war."

"I'm not advocating war, Ben!" Rutledge snapped back. "Lord knows we don't need to become involved in another major conflict. What I'm looking for is some tough words on things we should be doing. Don't provide any details—leave it vague—but get me a couple of plausible options that we can throw out. If the president won't get off the dime and do something, then we should capitalize on this opportunity."

Davis suddenly became hesitant, a look of concern flashing on his face. Rutledge saw it immediately and asked, "What's wrong, Ben?"

"Tom, Rep. Urick stopped by on Friday. He had a message for

you to tone down the rhetoric. Your last missives were viewed as being 'counterproductive' to the president's agenda."

Representative Russell Urick was the Democratic Party's whip, and he was often used to deliver unpleasant messages from the party's leadership to the rank and file. Clearly, the House minority leader had issues with Rutledge's last press release.

"Really?" Rutledge asked with feigned surprise. "Well, we certainly can't ignore a visit by the party's whip. I guess I'll keep my golf date with Thad Preston after all. Perhaps he can enlighten me as to his concerns. But get Bill in here nonetheless, and get started on that press piece. Tell him to throttle back a little, but I want something in the hopper for this evening."

Carlsbad State Beach
San Diego, CA
October 8, 2017

Jenny Oh always enjoyed an early-morning run on one of San Diego's many sunny beaches. With the sun just popping up from behind the hills, she had the luxury of having it all to herself—there wasn't another soul in sight. And that was just fine with her. No need to worry about the traffic, parking, or crowds. There was a slight breeze coming off the ocean, and the only sounds were that of the surf and seagulls. As far as Jenny was concerned, this was the closest thing to heaven on earth.

She was on the back half of a five-mile run when her phone started vibrating. Irritated, she glanced at the display to see who dared to interrupt her much-needed solitude. But when she saw that it was a text message from Ray, she came to a quick stop and touched a button. The message that popped up on the screen was at best vague.

YOU WOULDN'T BELIEVE WHAT JUST HAPPENED. PIGS CAN FLY. CALL ME WHEN YOU GET A CHANCE.

8

Scramble

The Pentagon
October 8, 2017

Secretary Peck left as quickly as he'd arrived, and, after a moment's pause, Ray found himself next to the most popular man in the room. He did his best to get out of the way as the service chiefs surrounded the new four-star admiral. Schultz, still a little glassy-eyed from the surprise promotion, gracefully accepted congratulations and good wishes, deferred all questions, and tried to gather his notes with his one free hand.

Ray was still absorbing the news. A "space force." Well, why not? And if Schultz was going to be in charge, then his baby was in good hands.

Schultz broke free of the scrum and gestured to Ray as he headed for the door. Ray followed, speeding up to match the admiral's fast pace. Once Ray had caught up, Schultz explained, "General Warner's promised us a C-20 for our use." The C-20 was a military version of the Gulfstream executive jet adapted for VIP transport. It was loaded with communications gear and conference facilities.

They were headed back to the admiral's office at a fast walk. Schultz spoke almost as quickly. "It will be ready for takeoff in an hour or so. Where do we fly, Ray? Where's our headquarters going to be?"

Luckily, Ray had asked himself the question already. Prompted by Secretary Peck's comment, he responded quickly, "It has to be Edwards, Admiral. That's where the *VentureStar* prototype is stored, and where the pad is. Building another pad doesn't make sense, and we don't have the time anyway. Besides, this way we don't even have to move the vehicle."

Both understood that Ray meant Edwards Air Force Base in Southern California. The prototype was mothballed there, near the never-used launchpad. Edwards was a major test center. Parts of the base were designated as historical sites because of their role in aviation history.

The admiral nodded. "Edwards will be a good place to set up shop. We'll have NASA's Armstrong Flight Research Center, the Air Force Research Lab's Propulsion Directorate research site—all those test facilities could come in real handy." He grinned. "It's also close to the Skunk Works in Palmdale and, of course, Los Angeles, not that you'll have much time to go there."

A little confused, Ray started to ask what he meant, but they'd reached the door to Schultz's office. As Ray opened it and followed the admiral in, a wave of applause and even a few cheers washed over them. Ray had to stop short as the admiral was again mobbed by well-wishers.

Captain Levin, Schultz's aide, explained. "One of Secretary Peck's aides called and told us the good news, sir."

"Are we ready?" asked a voice behind Ray.

Schultz spun around and saw a gaggle of flag officers pouring into the room. In the lead was the CNO, Admiral Kramer, followed by the vice CNO, the commandant of the Marine Corps, and several others.

"Yes, sir," said Levin.

"Very well. Let's get this man promoted so he can get to work," ordered Kramer.

"Aye, aye, sir," Levin replied, then, turning to a woman nearby, "Dorothy?"

A little breathless, the woman handed the CNO a small box. Levin, raising his voice a little, called "Attention to orders!" There was immediate silence, and those in uniform came to attention. Even Ray braced, his old air force habits kicking in.

Kramer issued the oath of office and then took one side, while Dorothy took the other. They unfastened the three-star insignia from the collar of Schultz's khaki shirt and replaced them with four stars. Flashes from phones and one actual camera recorded the moment.

"Thanks, John." Ray could see Schultz's pleasure. It was a moment most officers could only dream of.

"Congratulations, Bill!" exclaimed Kramer. "However, in light of your new responsibilities, we'll defer the wetting down for now. Note, I said defer, not abrogate, negate, or cancel. You're still on the hook to buy a round or two of drinks."

Schultz snapped his fingers in feigned disappointment. It would be quite the bar tab.

Each of the accompanying flag officers congratulated Schultz, shook his hand, and, with the traditions of the U.S. Navy satisfied, departed.

As Levin shook the admiral's hand, he remarked, "The aide said there was some more news, but that it would be better if I got it from you directly. He sounded very mysterious."

The admiral's smile didn't disappear, but it changed shape. "You're gonna love this. I need you in my office." He turned to Dorothy and said, "Hold all my calls, but tell Admiral Drake I need to see him here, ASAP."

She answered, "He's out at Pax River today for that . . ."

"Whatever he's doing," Schultz interrupted, "this is more important. As quickly as he can, Dorothy."

She nodded, but Schultz was already headed for his office.

Once inside, Schultz filled in Levin, and surprised Ray by telling his aide that Ray would be the project's technical director. Ray protested immediately. "I don't have the seniority for that . . ."

"You will by the end of the day, Ray," Schultz answered quickly.

"Don't worry about bureaucratic limitations. Those are man-made. Our only barrier is the laws of physics, and I want you to bend as many as you can." He paused, then observed, "I never did ask you if you wanted the job or not." He smiled. "There's a nontrivial pay bump, but I hear the hours are brutal."

Ray answered without hesitation. "Yes, Admiral, I want it," eagerly diving into the great unknown.

"Then start drafting a message to Secretary Peck telling him we're picking Edwards and would he please tell the base commander to expect us? And we'll need another from Peck to Lock Mart telling them that their *VentureStar* program's been funded again. Go."

While Ray sat down and began typing, Schultz told Levin, "Anyone from my staff who wants to come with me can come, but will have to move to California. We'll have temporary housing at Edwards." Levin started to speak, and Schultz quickly added, "Of course, you can come, Jeff, but not right away. I need you here to get Admiral Drake settled in, and be my man in Washington."

Ray half-listened as he worked. Schultz's main headquarters was at Patuxent River, in Maryland, about an hour and a half southeast of Washington by car. The Naval Air Systems Command was responsible for everything in the navy that flew: aircraft, missiles, and UAVs. It was a sizable fraction of the service, and Levin quickly made notes as Schultz fired off instructions about people and projects that his deputy, Rear Admiral Drake, would need in order to ensure a relatively smooth turnover.

There were a hundred details, but Schultz remembered ". . . and send someone over to Ray's hotel to pack up his stuff. Send it to Andrews along with my travel bag. Ray, how are those messages coming?"

"Just finished, Admiral. I kept them short."

"Good thinking. Peck's a busy man." Levin took the files and promised they would be sent within minutes.

"All right, then. Let's get over to Andrews," Schultz announced. The plane will be ready by the time we get there."

Even Levin was surprised. "What about Admiral Drake?"

"You take care of the turnover, Jeff. Don't tell him anything about the Space Force or *Defender*—just that I've been promoted and assigned to new duties and he's got the ball. He won't like it, but he's now acting NAVAIR. Get my car over to the south entrance."

Back in the NMCC, Biff watched General Warner congratulate the newly promoted four-star admiral and wish him Godspeed. "Anything the air force can do for you, just ask." As the other service chiefs filed out, he followed the air force group. Nothing was said in the hallway, not only because of security, but because, like the others, Biff couldn't think of what came next.

Warner led them back to the conference room they'd used to prepare their proposal. He ordered, "Take a chair, everyone," and the officers sat down, still silent, at a table littered with papers and coffee cups. Biff could feel the mood, somewhere south of glum, bound for despair. He felt it personally. He'd put everything he could into that proposal, cheered on by the highest-ranking officers in the air force, and it hadn't been enough. Hell, they didn't even get the opportunity to try!

Warner took them in with a glance and said, "Nothing's changed." He let that sink in, then continued, "Does anyone here think that this new Space Force will be able to get a civilian spacecraft out of mothballs, arm it, and launch it on a combat mission in seventy days?"

They were still silent, but there were a few rueful smiles, and almost everyone shook their heads. Not a chance. It was impossible.

The general said, "I want them to succeed, and anything the air force can do to support them, we will. But even with every resource, their chance of success is somewhere between slim and none. It's more likely that the whole thing will quickly implode, and the U.S. will be back at square one."

After another short pause, Warner declared, "The air force belongs in space, and while the Chinese attack on our GPS satellites is a terrible thing, it's a clear demonstration of why we need to be there. As of this moment, we are reorienting the service to meet that need."

He saw the questions forming on some faces and explained. "If and probably when the *Defender* project fails, the air force becomes plan B, so I want a plan in place, not just to stop the Chinese attacks but to establish us in space permanently." He turned to General Ames. "Cliff, get us started. We need to make this happen."

While Ames gathered Warner's staff, the general pulled Biff aside. "We never got our chance at bat. You did well, Clarence, and I'll be sending Major Pierce an endorsement for your performance report."

Barnes winced at the general's use of his given name. He risked saying, "Please, sir, just 'Biff.' "

Smiling, Warner said, "Then 'Biff' it is. I'll be keeping my eye on you, Captain."

Joint Base Andrews
Washington, D.C.
October 8, 2017

As the plane taxied for takeoff, Ray McConnell listened to Admiral Schultz as he argued with the Office of Personnel Management. Technically, as a civil servant, Ray worked for them.

"Of course I understand that you'd want to verify such an unusual order," he said calmly, almost pleasantly. "It's now been verified. And I need you to process it immediately. I know you've spoken to your director." His voice hardened a little. "I'm sure I won't have to speak to the director as well."

Schultz smiled, listening. "Certainly. There will be other personnel requests coming through this same channel, possibly quite a few. I'm certain you'll be able to deal with them all as swiftly as this one."

He turned off the handset and turned to Ray. "Congratulations. Say good-bye to Ray McConnell, SPAWAR engineer, and hello to Ray McConnell, technical director, U.S. Space Force."

It still didn't feel right to Ray. "I'm not senior enough . . ."

The admiral cut him off. "You're as senior as you need to be. You're now a Senior Executive Service, Level 3, according to OPM." Schultz saw Ray's stunned look and smiled. "It's not about the money. You're going to be doing the work of a Technical Director, and you'll need the horsepower of the pay grade. If there was ever a test of the Peter Principle, this will be it."

Schultz leaned forward and spoke softly and intently. "Listen, Ray, you're going to have to grow quickly. I offered you this job not because *Defender* was your idea, but because you had an original idea and put the pieces together to make it happen. Now you're going to have to do a lot more original thinking. You're going to build *Defender* and set speed records doing it."

Schultz leaned even closer. "I'm also going to give you this to think about. This isn't just an engineering problem. You're going to be dealing with people—a lot of them—and you can't expect them all to automatically commit to *Defender* the way you have. There's a transition everyone in charge goes through as they increase in rank, from foot soldier to leader. Foot soldiers only have to know their craft, but leaders have to know their people as well."

He straightened up in his chair. "End of lecture. We're due to land in Edwards in five hours. Your first job is to set up your construction team. Use names if you can, or describe the skills you need and let the database find them. After that—" He paused. "Well, I'll let you figure out what to do next."

Ray had no trouble coming up with plenty of things "to do next." During the flight, he found himself searching thousands of personnel records, balancing the time it took to review the information with the need to fill dozens of billets. Taking a page from his experience in the NMCC, he was careful to take people from all the military services and to look for key phrases like "team player" as well as professional qualifications. He also included people from NASA, the

National Weather Service, and even the Federal Communications Commission.

Then he went outside the government, requesting people from private industry. The government couldn't order them to participate, but if he had to, he'd hire them out from under their employers.

Remembering the JCS meeting and Captain Barnes, he called up the officer's service record. Eyes widening slightly, Ray added the captain to his list. He could find a use for a man with his qualifications.

Then there was Jenny. He needed command, control, and communications specialists, and he'd never have to wonder about her commitment to the project. But there were rules about that sort of thing.

Schultz was scribbling on a notepad, and Ray waited for him to finish his thought before asking, "If I hire Jenny, will there be a problem?"

The admiral responded, almost automatically, "Not unless you two create one." After a pause, he added, "I doubt if you'll find the time. She's smart and a clear thinker. And since you won't be writing her FITREP, most of the rules don't apply. She'd be a good addition, but will having her nearby distract you?"

Ray paused thoughtfully, then answered. "I think it will be less of a distraction than her being far away."

Schultz shook his head, smiling. "You've got it bad, son. Hire the lady and move on."

Ray took five minutes to call Jim Naguchi at work. Ray had decided not to include Jim on the list. Although he was a good friend, he was very much involved with his own project, designing a new naval communications system. Naguchi had never shown up for any of the design sessions, either, although he knew all about *Defender*. Ray had been a little disappointed, but not everyone was as crazy as he was.

It was just before nine in California, and Ray caught the engineer at his desk. "Naguchi here."

"Jim, it's Ray. I need you to clean out my office for me and keep the stuff for a day or two. I'll send someone around to collect it."

"What?" Naguchi sounded surprised and worried at the same time. "I knew Carson was pissed. Did he bar you from the building?"

"No, it's nothing like that, Jim." Ray almost laughed. "I can't tell you much. It's good news, but I'm going to be very busy for a while."

"Okay," Jim agreed. "As long as someone doesn't think I'm ripping you off."

"No, I sent an e-mail to Rudy. He'll know. And don't tell anyone else about this."

"Okay, but later you have to explain what's going on."

"I promise." Ray hung up and sat, holding the phone. He had a hundred things to think about, but Jenny kept on moving to the top of the pile. *Deal with it, Ray,* he said to himself.

He used his phone to send her some flowers, with the message, "You've saved *Defender*."

About an hour into the flight, an air force communications tech reported, "Admiral, I've got the telecom with Edwards set up."

"Good." Schultz got up and called over to Ray. "I want you in this conversation as well."

Major General Elliot Baum was commander of the 412th Test Wing, the biggest of the dozens of units scattered across the desert base. Balding, with sharp features and glasses, he was seated at his desk. Another general within the camera's scope was seated at his side.

"Good morning Admiral Schultz, sir. Welcome to Edwards Air Force Base. May I introduce you to my deputy, General Hayes?"

"Good morning to both of you," Schultz replied warmly. "This is Ray McConnell, technical director for the *Defender* project."

Baum said, "I've just finished a conversation with General Warner and General Hughes, Commander of the Air Force Test Center and my immediate boss. That followed a call from Secretary Peck." Baum looked a little flustered. "I'm still not sure I heard them correctly."

"Is there anyone else present in your office, General?" Schultz asked sharply. "Is this link secure?"

The air force general answered quickly, "Yes, sir." Ray noticed that Schultz's new four stars were already proving their worth.

"The link is encrypted, and only myself and General Hayes were briefed about your . . . project."

Ray made a note on his pad: *"Security Staff."*

"The *Defender* program is intended to stop the Chinese attacks on our GPS constellation. I'm sure both Secretary Peck and General Warner explained that."

Baum straightened up a little in his chair. "Yes, sir, they did, and we're behind you one hundred percent. But how? They said seventy days. I may have misheard. Is that when your command will stand up?"

"No, General, that is when we will launch. I'll be establishing my headquarters on your base, along with the construction effort and the launch-support facilities. The center of the effort will of course be Area 1-54, where the launchpad is located. We will need housing and messing facilities for several hundred people, as well as a large hangar and working spaces, all within a high-security perimeter."

"Several hundred!" Baum exclaimed.

"To start with," Schultz commented. *"Defender* won't build herself. They'll start arriving tomorrow."

Ray made another note: *"Personnel in-processing, orientation."*

"Tomorrow?" Baum repeated.

"And we need them to be productive the minute they get there." Schultz glanced at his watch. "We'll be on the ground in a little over four hours. At thirteen hundred your time, we need to meet with your facility manager and your security officer, as well as your wing's technical director."

General Baum nodded soberly. "They'll be there, along with

General Hayes and myself. Is there an official legend for the facility yet?"

"The cover story is that we are a new joint program, which will explain the different uniforms and civilians at the base. The *VentureStar* prototype is being adapted to serve as a rapid reusable transport for a new generation of survivable GPS satellites, designed to replace the ones shot down by the Chinese."

Ray made another note: *"Intelligence. Misinformation manager."*

"Understood, Admiral. If there's nothing else, we'll start preparing for your arrival."

"Very well, General. We will see you in a few hours." Schultz nodded to the tech aboard the plane, who broke the link.

The admiral shook his head. "We're going to have trouble with those two. We're going to suck up all their scarce resources and mess up their plans. Let's hope you do better with Lockheed Martin."

"Me?" Ray answered.

"They're engineers, just like you; you speak their language. I can't do all the work."

Air Force Plant 42, Site 10
Lockheed Martin Advanced Development Programs
Palmdale, CA
October 8, 2017

George Romans hurriedly turned over his smartphone and tablet to the security guards. One said, "Mr. Weber's already up on the VTC channel," and Romans nodded wordlessly as he signed the clipboard and noted the time.

The other guard punched the door combination and pulled it open. The door was labeled SCIF 3 under a large decal of a cute-looking skunk.

Inside, the room's familiar office furniture clashed with the bare metal walls. Sounds echoed despite the rubber mats on the floor. Surrounded completely by metal, the Sensitive Compartmented Information Facility would prevent any electronic eavesdropping. It was one of many at the Skunk Works site, which made sense considering how many compartmented programs the company was involved in.

While others were spacious enough for a dozen or more offices and workspaces, this room was small and set up for teleconferences. Several chairs at a long table faced two flat-screen monitors on the wall. Another small table held a coffeemaker, but clutter in the room was kept to a minimum. Fewer places to hide eavesdropping devices.

George Romans, the head of Lockheed Martin's Advanced Development Programs, or the famous "Skunk Works," nodded to his boss, Henry Weber, Vice President of Lockheed Martin Aeronautics, at his headquarters in Fort Worth, Texas. "The call's set up for ten hundred central time. They're still in the air," Weber reported.

Romans sat down heavily in one of the chairs, his breathing labored. A little overweight, he'd hurried from another plant after receiving a surprising phone call from the company president.

"Sorry for being late. I was out of the building when I got the call. We were supposed to link up after you arrived. Should I make the connection?" Romans asked.

"Not yet," Weber ordered. "I just want to confirm that you got the same call from President Markwith that I did. New classified DoD program, restarting and arming the *VentureStar* prototype."

Roman nodded and held up a copy of the *Defender* file. "That's what I got, too, along with high priority, and that the DoD had already paid five hundred million this morning to take over the program." He sounded unsure of his facts, as if he'd heard them wrong.

"That more than pays for the money we've invested in the *VentureStar* project," Weber confirmed. "Boom, and it's a major DoD program."

"But is it the same thing that's been circulating on SIPRNET? They can't be serious."

"Five hundred million says they're serious, or crazy. For that kind of money, we make the call and hear what they've got to say."

"Do you have any guidance for me before we call?"

"No, George, you know the drill. Besides, guidance would imply that we knew what was going on. All we can do is avoid the obvious pitfalls and hope for the best."

Romans tapped a key on a laptop computer and spoke into a microphone. "This is Lockheed Martin Skunk Works. We're ready on our end."

The second flat screen came alive, replacing the Lock Mart star logo with the image of two men sitting in an aircraft cabin. An older, balding man wore the uniform of a U.S. Navy full admiral; the other was a civilian, maybe in his early forties.

The civilian said, "I'm Ray McConnell, technical director for the *Defender* project, and this is Admiral Schultz, our commanding officer."

Romans hid his surprise. Technical director? McConnell's name was all over the *Defender* file. It *was* the same idea. While Weber was making the introduction from Fort Worth, Romans tried to mentally shift everything he'd read in the document from the "wacky" drawer to the one labeled "new job." It was difficult.

Ray said, "We were hoping Mr. Hugh Dawson would be with you. He's the most senior name we could find associated with the *Venture-Star* program."

Weber gestured to Romans to field the question. The engineer answered. "That project ended before I became head of the Advanced Development Programs, but personnel found him quickly. He's still with us, and is the director of a compartmented project here at the Palmdale facility."

Weber continued. "They're approaching an important milestone, and I thought we could have this meeting first to see whether he's really needed for this new program."

Ray answered instantly. "It's vital that we have him. Speed is everything, and his knowledge will save us weeks, at least."

"And it will cost us at least that much time if we take him away from the work he's now doing. That means a delayed milestone and an unhappy customer, who is also a part of the DoD. Will your program pay the penalties Lockheed Martin would suffer for a late delivery?"

"The call from Secretary Peck to Mr. Markwith should have included that this program has the highest priority within the DoD," injected Admiral Schultz.

"High-priority programs are a specialty of the Advanced Development Programs," Romans answered smugly. "Maybe you've heard of the F-22, or the F-35? How about the U-2 or the SR-71?"

"Don't patronize us," Ray snapped. "We need Mr. Dawson immediately. We have a meeting at thirteen hundred with General Baum and his people. We'd like you and Mr. Dawson to be there, plus anyone else you think would be helpful in restarting *VentureStar.*"

"That won't be possible," responded Weber. Hugh Dawson is on travel, and we'll have to get him back. The earliest we could meet would be late tomorrow morning, perhaps later. It all depends on when we can get him a flight. But as far as moving him from his current assignment, you haven't explained why his expertise is so necessary."

"As I said earlier," Ray replied carefully, "his knowledge of the program will save time. We need every edge we can get if we're going to launch on schedule."

"That's another thing," Weber said. "This schedule you've sent is completely unrealistic. I'm not sure we can get the vehicle out of mothballs in less than a month."

"We will do it in much less than a month, Mr. Weber," Ray replied. "You are the legendary Skunk Works. Does anyone there still have a copy of Kelly Johnson's rules?"

Romans bristled. "I do, and so do a lot of other people here. But Lockheed Martin officially stopped calling my shop the Skunk Works back in 1999, shortly after the *VentureStar* program was canceled."

"I grew up with those rules," Ray explained, "and you'd better dust them off."

Admiral Schultz saw the defiant looks on the faces of the Lockheed

Martin executives. "Mr. Romans, can you tell me which program Mr. Dawson is working on?"

"As I said, sir, it's a compartmented black project."

"I'm very familiar with them," Schultz replied coldly. "What's the unclassified label?" While the actual code name of the project was itself classified, every "black" program had one or more "white" labels that could be used in administrative documents.

Romans looked at Weber, who returned his gaze and shrugged. Busted. "The unclassified label for the program is Baseboard."

Schultz nodded. "I'll make inquiries about the project and its utility in the current circumstances. I'd think you'd be more eager to stop the Chinese. After all, Lockheed Martin builds the GPS satellites."

"I'm all for stopping the Chinese, Admiral," Weber responded, "but there are rules to follow, people I'm accountable to."

"Rules can be changed or waived," Schultz answered. "Please use all deliberate speed, especially when we're just beginning. Time saved now will be multiplied manyfold in a few weeks."

Schultz gestured to someone off screen, and the display went dark.

Romans let the silence last for almost a minute, since his boss seemed completely self-absorbed. Finally, he asked tentatively, "Should I get Hugh Dawson?"

Weber quickly answered. "Yes, get Dawson back, and make arrangements for a car to take the three of us to Edwards. Under other circumstances, I'd let you and him handle this, but I want to stay close on this, at least for the moment. I'll leave Fort Worth early tomorrow morning and fly directly to Plant 42."

He saw the look on Romans's face and quickly added, "I trust your skills, George, but I don't trust these folks. Do they really think they can bring that"—he slapped the *Defender* document on the table—"to life?"

"What else could it be?"

"I'll tell you what it could be. How about an excuse for the Jackson administration? We know there's not much they can do about the GPS shoot-downs. What if they create a "supersecret program" based on *Defender,* knowing it will fail? After it goes bad, word of the failure will be 'leaked.' It shows that they were trying to do something constructive. Look at McConnell, the guy in charge: the *Defender* hard copy says he's a midlevel supervisor with SPAWAR. He's way too junior to run a major program like this. They're taking his fantasy and turning it into a decoy."

"What about the five hundred million?" Romans asked. "I don't think the check will bounce."

"Political cover at scrap-metal prices," Weber replied. "And who do you think gets blamed if it doesn't work? The government? They'll do their best to shift it to us. That half billion will be chump change compared to the price we will pay then."

Romans was still processing the idea when Weber started firing orders. "Okay, first thing: We write everything down. Document every meeting, every phone call, every scribble they write on a napkin. If they want anything, even doughnuts in the morning, they have to put it in writing. Second thing: If this project fails, it won't be for a lack of us trying. Make sure Dawson is in the car with us, but also get a team over to Area 1-54 and see what we have to do to get the pad ready for use. Get another team over to the storage hangar and have them begin getting the vehicle out of mothballs. Work goes on around the clock."

"Who do I use?" Romans asked.

"Anyone who's free. Tell them it's a treasure hunt and there's a golden rivet somewhere." When Romans laughed, Weber added, "But that's only temporary. Get out an Internal Personnel Requirement right away calling for people willing to transfer to a 'new aerospace project.' Tell personnel I want it out by e-mail to everyone west of the Rockies by early afternoon, to start work tomorrow."

C-20 Flight, Bound for Edwards Air Force Base
October 8, 2017

After the connection broke, Ray saw that Admiral Schultz had also been taking notes. Before Ray could speak, Schultz made a call. "Jeff, I want you to run down a black program. The white label is Baseboard. And find out about someone named Hugh Dawson. He's supposed to be in charge. Okay? Great, soon as you can."

Schultz closed the phone with a small smile on his face. "And that's why I left Captain Levin in Washington. We could certainly use him out here, but I can't be in two places at once." He grinned. "Unless that's what the Baseboard program does."

Air Force Plant 42, Site 10
IT Division, F-35 Project
Lockheed Martin Advanced Development Programs
Palmdale, CA
October 8, 2017

Glenn Chung was logging in a software upgrade when Patty Rivers poked her head in the open door to his office. "Glenn, do you know anything about that new IPR?"

"What new IPR?" Chung asked without moving his eyes from the screen.

"It came out about an hour ago." Patty was one of the biggest grapes on the office grapevine. He'd been too busy to check his e-mail box since lunch. There were messages waiting, though.

He only had a few new messages and quickly spotted the one sent by "LMAERONAUTICS."

INTERNAL PERSONNEL REQUIREMENT

IMMEDIATE OPENINGS AVAILABLE WITH A NEW LOCKHEED MARTIN

AEROSPACE PROGRAM, LOCAL TO PALMDALE AREA. IMMEDIATE

PERSONNEL TRANSFER, WITH PROMOTION POSSIBLE IF REQUIRE-
MENTS ARE MET.

The list of jobs available was extensive, including engineers in several fields, electronics specialists, aviation machinists, even computer
types like himself.

Patty gave him a moment to read it, then asked, "Do you know
what program they mean? They need people now, and a lot of them."

Chung scanned the list. "No hint here about the kind of program
it is."

"Could it be a new classified project?"

He stifled a small laugh. "They wouldn't announce it in the IPR.
When you applied, and didn't have the right clearances, you'd just
be turned down. If it is a new unclassified program, we'll probably
hear about it in a few days by some press release. If it is classified,
we just won't hear at all."

"Unless you get a job there," she offered.

"Are you that curious?" he asked.

She shrugged. "It might be more interesting than what I'm doing
now. I'm ready for a change. See you!" Patty flitted off in search of
more information. She had a sweet personality but thought her job
description included "networking," not "network support."

Chung read through the list of open positions carefully. Nope.
There was no clue what the new project would be, and he did try to
pay attention to what the company was doing. What the heck. He
hit the REPLY link and started typing.

He felt the need for a change as well.

9

Skunk Works

C-20 Flight, Bound for Edwards Air Force Base
October 8, 2017

The list of potential locations for the U.S. Space Force headquarters had been short to begin with. Only a handful of military and civilian facilities met even the minimum requirements. In reality, the massive Edwards Air Force Base complex was the only viable option. The second largest air force base in the United States, it sprawled over slightly more than three hundred thousand acres of the western Mojave Desert. Named in honor of Captain Glen Edwards, a decorated World War II bomber and air force test pilot, it was the home of the 412th Test Wing, along with a host of advanced research and development organizations, many of them space-oriented.

The team's choice of Edwards was also logical from a practical point of view. The full-scale *VentureStar* prototype was stored in an unused hangar on the base, the launch complex at Area 1-54 was virtually complete, and there were plenty of runways available for recovery. The base was also conveniently close to Air Force Plant 42 in Palmdale, thirty-three miles away, where Lockheed Martin's Advanced Development Programs Division was located.

Formerly known as the Skunk Works, the ADP had developed and fielded some of the most advanced aircraft in the U.S. inventory. But more important, the ADP had been the Lockheed Martin lead contractor in the *VentureStar* program, and any residual expertise would be found there.

The problem was that in the Pentagon, politics could easily trump logic. And making a land grab in someone else's backyard was a sure-fire way to get the hackles up on another service chief's neck. In this case, the U.S. Air Force.

During their flight, Schultz made and received a number of phone calls. One was from General Warner, and it was clear from what Ray heard that while the conversation was friendly, there was a hint of strain in the admiral's voice.

"No, Mike," Schultz said patiently, "I don't need or want the whole base. The Space Force will be just another tenant command on Edwards; I have no desire to build a huge empire at your expense. We just need a large hangar with secure office space close by."

Ray could hear the air force general on the other end of the line laugh, and the wrinkles on Schultz's face seemed to ease.

"The old airborne laser hangar will be just fine, Mike. I appreciate your help on this." Schultz jotted the numbers 151 on his notepad. "Yes, of course I'll let you know if we need anything else, but I promise not to be too much of a nuisance. Thanks, we'll need it. Out here."

As he hung up the phone, Schultz let out a heavy sigh. Turning to Ray, he explained. "General Warner is giving us the hangar that was used by the canceled Airborne Laser Program, Building 151. It's big enough to hold a 747, so *Defender* will fit without any problem. And the chemical storage tanks for the laser system are still good. We'll need to get them recertified, of course, but that's a hell of a lot easier than building a new storage system."

"It sounds like the general is being very cooperative," Ray remarked carefully.

Schultz chuckled. "Mike doesn't want to be seen as an obstructionist, not with a presidential mandate staring him in the face, so he's being helpful, for now. He's also a very experienced Pentagon insider, and he knows that it will be easier for him to take over the Space Force's mission if our assets and facilities are already on an air force installation. He's just doubling down on his bet that we'll fail."

Ray felt a sudden chill. "Nice to know we engender such confidence," he said sarcastically.

"Get used to it, son. We have a tremendous task ahead of us, and the odds aren't exactly in our favor. I can't fault General Warner for being pragmatic. At least he's cooperating. There will be others who will do everything in their power to ensure we fall flat on our faces."

Disturbed by Schultz's blunt prediction, Ray leaned back in his seat and wondered whether he'd made the right decision to sign on. It was one thing to fall short due to insurmountable technical issues, but quite another to fail because of political infighting and backstabbing.

Glancing over at Schultz, Ray saw the admiral staring at the impressive to-do list on his tablet PC. He looked calm and composed. Well, if the boss could be at peace with their situation, then Ray needed to at least try. Looking out his window, Ray watched as white puffy cumulus clouds passed slowly by, piled up into fantastic shapes. The peaceful scene, combined with an adrenaline letdown and sheer exhaustion, caused Ray's eyelids to drift downward. Within moments, he fell into a deep sleep.

It was early afternoon when they landed. The skies were clear, and the temperature was on the warm side. Even in autumn the Mojave Desert can get into the mideighties. The bright sun tormented Ray's eyes as he stepped out of the plane and onto the tarmac. He'd been to Edwards once before, years ago on a space shuttle–orientation trip sponsored by NASA. From what he remembered, it looked like nothing had changed.

Major General Baum and his deputy were waiting as the two new space force executives disembarked. After a quick exchange of salutes and handshakes, Ray and Schultz were whisked to the High Desert Inn to check in and dump their bags. Baum had offered to let the two get some rest, but both Schultz and Ray were insistent that they get to work immediately. They'd both had a few hours of sleep and were once again on an adrenaline high. After a quick lunch, Baum took them to Building 151—the new U.S. Space Force Headquarters. Ray liked what he saw.

Although he'd expected the hangar to be large, it still impressed him: It was over seven stories tall and wide enough not only to hold a jumbo jet but also to allow enough room to take it apart, if needed. Sounds echoed off the metal surfaces and the concrete floor. It was hot and humid inside, with the ventilation systems still turned off. Ray half-expected to see a local thunderstorm building at the apex of the domed roof.

A four-story office structure was grafted onto one side of the structure. That looked good to him. People wouldn't have to waste time traveling from one building to another. It was still dusty—much of the building had been unused for years—but Baum promised to have people there within the hour to begin cleaning.

The day flew by in a blur, and, after a late dinner, Schultz turned in for the night. Ray sat in his room fidgeting. He tried reading, but his mind whirled with future tasks and potential difficulties. He tried making to-do lists, but, instead of clearing his mind, the now-organized tasks accused him of inaction.

Unable to sleep, he grabbed his jacket and went for a walk down to the massive Rogers Dry Lake. For most of the year, the lake bed was a bone-dry salt flat, although during the short rainy season some water would accumulate in its basin. This made the lake bed perfect for flight operations and a dozen of Edwards's runways were little more than black lines painted on the hard ground.

With the sun down and the wind picking up, Ray headed back to his temporary quarters, zipping his jacket up as he went. The past forty-eight hours had been one hell of a roller-coaster ride, and he still had trouble wrapping his mind around everything that had occurred.

He felt numb, unable to put into words the hodgepodge of emotions bouncing around in his head. Either that or the desert cold and fatigue were finally setting in.

But as he contemplated the enormity of their assignment, doubt crept back into his thoughts. Could they really pull this off? Or were the technical and political cards so stacked against them that failure was inevitable? He shook off the nagging worries as he got ready for bed. They might fail, but it wouldn't be for a lack of trying. Come what may, Ray intended to give it his best shot. Satisfied, he laid down. He wouldn't remember his head hitting the pillow.

Edwards AFB
October 9, 2017

The next morning marked their first full day at "Space HQ," which had taught Ray more about logistics and people than he'd ever thought there was to learn.

A hot breakfast at zero six-thirty had been a good start, but it was constantly interrupted by phone calls or urgent e-mails. It seemed to Ray that he had to answer either his cell phone or tablet PC, or both, after every bite. Schultz actually turned his off to "finish his meal in peace." The arrival of their car found them dashing off after taking one last hurried bite. Waiting for them at the inn's entrance was the base operations officer and a tech sergeant. As the car turned onto the road, the ops officer gave Schultz a quick rundown.

"We've gotten most of the current occupants out of the hangar. The stragglers will be gone by noon. We've pulled in as many of the custodial service people as we can to do a thorough cleaning. Oh, that reminds me, sir. I'll need your signature to authorize the overtime if we're to get the building cleaned by tonight."

Schultz reached for the clipboard, scanned the form, and signed it. Handing the clipboard back, he said, "I appreciate you efforts, Colonel. Thank you. And while a clean building is a nice start, I'm more concerned with how we're going to take care of my people. The first batch should be arriving by this afternoon, and they'll already be confused after being summarily summoned on extremely short notice. I need help in getting them corralled, lodged, and processed as quickly as possible and with minimal chain jerking."

"Yes, sir. Tech Sergeant Klein will see to getting your personnel checked in and shown their accommodations. Unfortunately, we had to go with double occupancy in all the rooms. We just don't have space."

"That'll work for now, Colonel. Next subject. What about the SCIF?"

Ray watched as Schultz quickly nailed all the big-ticket items during the short ride to Building 151. He was certainly efficient, but what struck Ray as odd, as well as refreshing, was the admiral's focus on his people. They hadn't even shown up, and already he was intent on easing their transition into his command. It was unusual for such a senior officer to be so concerned about his subordinates' well-being. Ray didn't need all the fingers on one hand to count the number of flag officers he served under at SPAWAR who shared Schultz's philosophy. No wonder Jenny thought highly of the man.

The morning blew by in a frenzy of activity. Movers, cleaners, and building-management personnel swarmed about the office spaces. Ray surveyed every nook and cranny, marking possible functional areas on a digital copy of the plans. Schultz had directed him to "put the organizational spaces together" while the admiral tackled the higher-level stuff that required his four stars.

Dodging in and out of the organized chaos, Ray frowned as he saw unassembled cubicle sections lining the walls. Disdainful of the traditional Dilbert "cube village," Ray drew out a notional plan, based on the same arrangement as the functional *Defender* design teams back in his house. If there was a secret to their initial success, it was collaboration, the effective melding of a lot of smart people's efforts toward a common goal. He'd have to kick that collaboration up a notch if they were to get *Defender* into orbit in sixty-nine days.

Ray firmly believed that old-fashioned face-to-face interaction was severely underappreciated. Most business gurus pushed the concept of lean, dispersed working groups that linked together "virtually" through e-mail and videoconferencing. While this did have some fiscal advantages, Ray was convinced that face-to-face collaboration was more effective at sharing knowledge and creating an atmosphere that encouraged rapid innovation—qualities they'd need in abundance.

He also knew the command would have to provide some amenities if they were to keep the soon-to-be overstressed workforce sane. Ray wrote down a quick note to talk to Schultz about a "morale officer." Armed with his crude workplace strategy, Ray set off in search of the base facility manager.

The office looked like it had been a storage closet in a former life and was filled with a couple of portable tables and folding chairs. Detailed building plans were stacked on one table, while a laptop, briefcase, and an open jar of peanut butter adorned the other. Curious, Ray stepped in and took a closer look at the well-worn briefcase; it was covered with scratches and scuff marks along with two slightly faded stickers. One said USAF RETIRED. The other had a cartoon of a collapsing building with the phrase FIRST LAW OF CIVIL ENGINEERING: IF IT MOVES, IT'S BROKE. Ray chuckled quietly; the facility manager seemed to have a decent sense of humor—that was a good omen.

"Excuse me," came a voice from behind him. "I was looking for the facility manager's office."

Ray turned and saw a tall, lean man standing in the doorway. He was wearing a hard hat and carrying a tablet PC and what looked like a laser distance measurer.

"I'm sorry," said Ray as he scooted over to make way. "This is the place, but I don't know where the facility manager is."

"Well, it's good to know I'm not lost," replied the man as he pushed his way by and placed the hard hat, tablet, and laser measurer on the plans. Turning back toward Ray, he asked, "So what can I do for you, Mister . . . ?"

It suddenly dawned on Ray that the man in front of him *was* the Edwards AFB facility manager. Embarrassed, Ray offered his hand and replied, "Ray McConnell. I'm the technical director for the new U.S. Space Force."

"Robert Ardery, at your service. So how can I assist you in your struggle for excellence, Mr. Technical Director?"

What the . . . ? thought Ray. Ardery's introduction was certainly bizarre, but while the man may have been a tad eccentric, he did seem willing to help. Ray mentally shrugged past the strangeness and began his pitch. "I need some help in laying out the office arrangement to make efficient use of what space we have and to maximize personal interaction."

"All right," Ardery responded. "Show me what you have in mind and I'll see what I can do."

Ray put his tablet on the desk and started explaining his roughed-out plan, pointing toward the display screen as needed to emphasize a particular point. Ardery stood silently, his arms crossed, cradling his chin in one hand. Occasionally he would mumble a low, "Uh-huh," but more often than not he would just nod.

As Ray wrapped up his explanation, Ardery silently reached for the jar of peanut butter, scooped up a large spoonful, and placed it in his mouth. Taken aback, Ray's voice trailed off, his expression one of confusion. Ardery looked up, the spoon still protruding from his lips, waiting for Ray to finish his train of thought. But as the pause continued, the civil engineer caught on, rolled his eyes, and pulled the utensil form his mouth. Raising the peanut butter jar, Ardery grumbled, "It's either this or doughnuts, Mr. McConnell, and I don't see any doughnuts! So, is that it?"

Still a bit off balance from Ardery's unorthodox behavior, Ray uttered, "Uh, yeah."

"Then let me summarize your requirements," said Ardery curtly. "You want to bring about two hundred and fifty people into this building, provide them with full connectivity, across all classification levels—you do realize that means three separate networks— heavy-duty engineering computing capability, and at the same time reserve room for interactive spaces and basic amenities, correct?"

"Yes, exactly, Mr. Ardery. You got it."

"Well, I might be able to accommodate you if you give me a year and several million dollars to reconfigure the building."

Stunned by the facility manager's blunt response, Ray started to argue. "There's plenty of space. I've gone over the plans myself!"

Rolling his eyes again, Ardery shot back. "Why does everyone think volume is the be-all, end-all of a building's capacity? Yes, Mr. McConnell, the building has the physical volume to contain that many people, if you think a gerbil cage provides an adequate work area."

"I admit it's a bit tight . . ."

"Tight!?! A submarine offers more room per person! Regardless, space is not the only consideration!" snapped Ardery. "First off, three networks and engineering-level processing power means almost a thousand workstations, then add upgraded lighting, copiers, secure and open phones, and God knows what in the galley. Where do you think you're going to get all the electrons to run this gear? As Scotty so quaintly put it, 'Ye canna' do it, Captain, ye donna' have the power!'

"And even if I could somehow route that kind of electrical power throughout the building, the air-conditioning and ventilation system would choke on the heat generated by all those bodies, computers, and the other pieces of equipment, probably including several dozen coffeepots. This place will be hot and muggy even in winter, and come summer it will be completely uninhabitable. And then there's this minor detail called restrooms—you're not even close to having enough for that many people. I can go on if you're feeling masochistic, but I think you get my point."

Ray stood wide-eyed and shocked, feeling like a student that had just been chewed out by a professor for not thinking through a problem clearly enough. He knew there would be some problems with the electrical requirements, but the air-conditioning overload and the insufficient number of bathrooms had completely escaped him.

Ardery sensed that he had Ray's undivided attention. "I'll do what I can, Mr. McConnell, but I wouldn't get my hopes too high if I were you. I might be able to squeeze in most of your people, perhaps a hundred and seventy-five, but I'll have to bend some rules to even get that many. If your workforce is going to be larger than that, then I'd strongly recommend that you find some additional space."

A vibrating smartphone with a text from Schultz was just the distraction Ray needed to disengage from Ardery's scathing evaluation of his office plan. After promising to get back to the civil engineer, Ray bolted for the stairwell. As he wound down the stairs, Ray realized that he had just come away easy from a hard lesson. Yes, they were under a severe time constraint, but that was no excuse to rush things and do a sloppy job. This time it was only his ego that was bruised.

Air Force Plant 42, Site 10
Lockheed Martin, Advanced Development Programs
Palmdale, CA
October 9, 2017

Hugh Dawson stared at the e-mail in disbelief; the Baseboard program had been suspended. Until further notice, funding authorization would be withheld, and all work was to cease immediately. Only maintenance and other caretaker activity would be allowed for the foreseeable future. *But I was on schedule, on budget, and the Milestone C review is in six months.* Dawson groaned to himself. A sharp knock on the door broke his depressed train of thought.

George Romans burst into Dawson's office. "I just got off the phone with Hank Weber. He's en route from Fort Worth! He confirmed the e-mail is valid. As of last night, Baseboard is formally on hold!"

"But why, George?" lamented Dawson. "We are smack on the glide path—we'll be ready for the Defense Acquisition Board review in March!"

"It must have been Schultz," fumed Romans. "He wanted you badly for this *Defender* program, but Hank and I wouldn't give in. We told him you were critical for Baseboard's upcoming milestone review and couldn't be spared. It appears Admiral Schultz doesn't take no for an answer. The man has serious stones, as well as significant top cover. You'd better find all those old *VentureStar* design files, Hugh. We leave for Edwards as soon as Hank gets here."

Edwards Air Force Base
412th Test Wing Headquarters Building
October 9, 2017

Weber, Romans, and Dawson were escorted to the wing's main conference room by a pair of air force security guards. Already seated at the table were Schultz, Ray, and the two air force generals. No one else was in the room. As the trio approached the table, Schultz rose from his chair.

"Good morning, gentlemen. I'm pleased to see you made it." Schultz offered his hand to Weber, who accepted it hesitantly, his face still hard from the morning's unpleasant news.

"That was dirty pool, Admiral, turning off Baseboard's funding like that." Weber's voice was measured, but Ray heard the underlying anger. No doubt about it, the man was severely pissed off.

"Was it, Mr. Weber?" replied Schultz just as forcefully. "You made it clear during yesterday's VTC that Mr. Dawson could not be made available due to contractual responsibilities your company had with DoD. I simply had Lockheed Martin relieved, temporarily, of those responsibilities. I told you, *Defender* is currently the Department of Defense's number one priority. I trust that I've provided ample proof of that claim."

Resigned, Weber nodded curtly and then introduced Dawson to Ray and the others. After taking their seats, coffee was served and the meeting began in earnest. Schultz wasted little time and went straight to the heart of the matter.

"Mr. Dawson, I'm assuming you've read the *Defender* concept paper that was e-mailed to your company?"

"I read it just a few hours ago, Admiral, but you can't be serious. This is the same thing that was circulating on the SIPRNET. I thought it was just another cover story."

Schultz said calmly, "It's not a cover story, and, yes, we're serious. Dead serious."

Dawson's face went blank with confusion. Schultz didn't give him any time to respond.

"Mr. Ray McConnell here is the technical director for the project, and for the U.S. Space Force. He led the team that did the initial *Defender* design."

Dawson looked at Ray, but he was still reacting to Schultz's words. "There's a U.S. Space Force?"

Schultz smiled proudly. "As of yesterday morning there is, and you and *VentureStar* are going to be a big part of it. Did you start the preparations to move her?"

Dawson nodded, replying mechanically. "Yes, we've started. I understand you're in a hurry. My engineers are inspecting the landing gear, tires, and brakes as we speak. The rest of the preps will be done by the time the carrier plane arrives. Figure two days to make her safe and preflight the carrier and a day to mate the two . . ."

Ray abruptly interrupted, cutting Dawson off. "What's this about a carrier aircraft? Where are you expecting to move *VentureStar* to?"

Puzzled, Dawson froze. Romans jumped in and answered. "We assumed we'd be moving the vehicle to the Space Shuttle Refurbishment Facility over at Plant 42. It's the best location to finish assembly and conduct the initial tests."

"And how long will it take to get her into the refurbishment building?" asked Ray.

"About a week. We'll need to rebuild the mating-demating gantry, and it will take a couple of days to get one of the shuttle-capable 747s out here."

Ray shook his head vigorously. "Too long. We need to begin work sooner. We'll tow her to Building 151, the old ABL hangar. It has most of the equipment you'll need. The rest can be trucked over from Plant 42."

"What if we need to manufacture components? Or make adjustments to existing ones? We won't have that type of production capability in a hangar," pleaded Dawson.

"Any component that requires precision machining can be done at Plant 42 and shipped here. It'll be faster."

"I just don't see how this is even possible." Dawson was almost groaning.

"Mr. Dawson, the design is sound. We're going to improvise and find new approaches." Ray pushed. "The Joint Chiefs, even the president, have signed off on this. I know it can work."

Dawson sat, impassive. He still wasn't convinced.

Damn it, Ray realized he knew nothing about this man. What did he care about? There had to be one thing.

He tried again. "The Chinese are shooting down our GPS satellites, Mr. Dawson. *VentureStar* can stop that. She's the only platform with the space and payload to carry all the equipment we need. In sixty-eight days, we'll have her flying and doing things nobody ever imagined her doing when she was designed, and you'll be the one making the changes. She'll still be your baby."

Dawson responded angrily. "But the time, sixty-eight days! We can't possibly do it!"

"We can if we decide we can, Hugh." Ray was getting motivated himself. "No paperwork, no bureaucracy, no congressional briefings. Just results."

"Some of that paperwork is necessary," Dawson reminded him. "They laid out the P-51 Mustang on the floor of a barn, but that doesn't work anymore."

"We'll keep some, of course, but how much of that paper is needed to do the actual work? The vast majority is to meet government reporting requirements on how you're doing, how you're spending the money, and that you are properly dotting the i's and crossing the t's on all the forms. A lot of it takes the place of good supervision. I'm not here to document a failure."

Ray sensed he was getting through and he pressed his point. "The rules will be different here. We're going back to the Kelly Johnson basics. We're going to keep this group small. And I'm the government, as far as *Defender* goes. You won't have to write a memo to me because I'll be there on the floor with you."

Dawson sat, considering for a moment. "Marilyn's going to think I've taken up with another woman," he observed, smiling. "What about security?" Dawson asked. "Our PR people will want to know . . ."

Ray smiled. One down.

Edwards Air Force Base
Building 151
October 10, 2017

By late afternoon, enough people had arrived and been settled in so that they could start preparations to receive the vehicle. Or rather, to prepare to prepare.

The hangar at Building 151 was big enough but required modifications to finish assembling the *VentureStar* prototype. The launchpad at Area 1-54 had to be inspected and brought back to life. A new computer hub, independent from the Internet, needed to be installed, and the building hadn't been wired for all the classified networks. They still had to decide where to put launch control. Housing on Edwards was insufficient for the number of semipermanent residents that were arriving and needed to be expanded. The galley had to be built from scratch. And what about recreation?

Ray's "to do" list made him wish for a tablet with a bigger screen. He had one idea and ran it past Schultz. "I love it," the admiral said. "I'll have one of my staff get right on it."

At Ray's suggestion, the evening meal was held outside. Even in the fall, the weather was excellent, warm and dry, and the people at the Edwards AFB Oasis Community Center fixed an impromptu barbecue.

It was an important occasion. Almost everyone was a stranger to each other, and a lot of ice needed to be broken. Doubts about the feasibility of the mission, combined with being thrown together on very short notice, had ramped up the stress level throughout the last two days. Ray realized he needed to get these people together, make them one team, with one mission. Schultz wholeheartedly agreed.

Ray waited just long enough for everyone to be served. It was nothing special, just burgers, fries, mixed salad greens, and soft drinks. Ray himself was too nervous to eat. He'd tried to eat something, at Schultz's urging, but the first two bites started circling each other in his stomach, like angry roosters squaring off.

The time had finally come, though, and Ray had climbed up on an improvised stage. The portable amplifier gave its customary squeal as he adjusted the volume, and suddenly everyone's eyes were on him.

"Welcome to the United States Space Force HQ." He paused for a moment and heard a few snickers, mostly from the civilians. He smiled broadly, so he could be seen in the back. "I like the sound of it. The good news is you are all founding members of America's newest and most modern military service."

He made the smile go away. "The bad news is, we're at war. The

Chinese are taking out our satellites, denying us the use of space, for both military and civilian use. *Defender* is going to regain control of space for us, for our use.

"You all understand the danger we face. They aren't on our shores, or bombing our cities, but they are overhead. And we all know about the value of holding the high ground.

"I'm expecting each of you, once you're settled, to take your job and run with it. More than that, though, if you see something that needs doing, don't wait for someone else to notice.

"There are going to be a lot more people coming in over the next few weeks. By the time the last of them arrives, you'll be the old hands, and I want you to tell them what I'm telling you now.

"You'll soon wish we were twice as big. It's not for lack of resources. We've got a blank check from the president himself for anything or anyone we need. You're here because you're some of the best. I could have asked for more, but I didn't. A small organization can think faster and move faster.

"Some of you may think that this is an impossible task, or that even if it's possible, we don't have enough time to do it. It's just a matter of adjusting your thinking. The question to ask is not 'Can this be done in time?' but 'What needs to be done to finish in time?'"

Ray got down quickly, to a gratifying applause. Schultz nodded approvingly, and Ray noticed someone standing next to him, still holding an overnight bag. Jenny's faced beamed with excitement.

Staybridge Suites
Palmdale, CA
October 10, 2017

The outside line rang, and Geoffrey picked up the phone. "Good Morning, Staybridge Suites concierge desk. Geoffrey Lewes speaking."

"Mr. Lewes? This is Captain Munson, United States Navy. I'm

sorry to call you at work, but we couldn't reach you before you left your home."

"The navy?" Lewes was a little confused. He'd served in the navy ten years earlier, as a storekeeper. That was before he'd gotten his hotel-management degree, before he started working in the accommodations and food-services industry.

"I'll be brief, Mr. Lewes. I need someone to take care of a large group of people. They're very busy and have little time for the basic amenities. You will manage a staff that will see to their needs while they work on other matters."

"Captain Munson, I'm not sure I understand. I'm quite happy . . ."

Munson interrupted and named a salary figure over twice what Lewes made as a junior concierge. He wasn't sure a senior concierge made that much.

"The position is a temporary one, at least six months, but there is a very good chance it will become permanent. You'll work hard for that money, and you'll have to live on site."

"And where is that site, exactly?" Lewes asked. The mystery of it was as intriguing as the generous salary.

"Not too far," answered Munson carefully. "Your quarters will be quite comfortable. What's your decision?"

"Just like that?"

"Just like that," replied Munson. "I apologize for the hard sales pitch, but we're a little pressed for time."

"The money's good," Lewes admitted. "But you don't know enough about me."

"We know quite a bit about you, Mr. Lewes. Please, if you don't want the job, I have other calls to make."

Lewes looked at the next thing on his list—tickets to the Palmdale Playhouse for a couple from Kansas. Whoopee.

10

Circus

The air force C-141 transport left Joint Base Andrews at 0800. Biff had spent most of the evening before at the office with Major Pierce, then hurried home to pack. He'd managed to grab a few hours' sleep before heading to the air terminal. While he'd gotten some sleep during the five-hour trip, the metal-framed canvas seats were not designed for comfort. His mood had only worsened as the flight progressed.

They'd gained three hours flying west, so it was still bright morning sunshine that almost blinded him as the rear ramp opened. Waiting his turn while the passengers in front of him found their bags, he finally retrieved his deployment bag and backpack from the pallet and walked down the ramp.

Sunglasses provided partial protection, and he remained near the rear of the aircraft, in the shade. As the knot of passengers dispersed, he spotted a Marine corporal with a sign saying CAPTAIN BARNES. It also listed several other names, and Biff recognized others he'd seen on the flight from Washington.

There were five of them altogether, and Corporal Sims, according to the name tag on his uniform, led them over to an air force blue minivan. The other four passengers were two civilians, a navy petty officer, and an army second lieutenant, so, as the ranking officer, Barnes got the best seat—in front, next to the driver.

Sims asked a question as they got in and buckled up. "Is there anyone here who is not going to Building 151?" When nobody spoke up, he started the engine and began what had to be a well-practiced spiel.

"Welcome to Edwards Air Force Base. I'll be taking you to Building 151 on the South Base complex. After we get to the headquarters building, I'll take you to security for a fifteen-minute orientation brief by someone from Colonel Evans's security staff. Packets are waiting for you there with your housing and work assignments. We're having typical weather today, with temperatures in the low eighties and lows tomorrow morning in the midfifties. There's no chance of rain."

I can believe that, Biff thought. The flat landscape was dotted with short scrubby plants, almost as brown as the bare dirt they grew on. How they found enough moisture to live was a mystery. Blacktop roads crossed the surface, connecting the scattered buildings.

Edward's desert terrain, especially Rogers Dry Lake, made it perfect for the air force's needs. Biff had visited Edwards before, when he was still in the astronaut program, and passed through a few times while serving with the 301st out of Holloman.

". . . and there are regular shuttles, like this one, to the local exchange, as well as housing."

After Sims had ended his speech, Biff asked him, "How many trips have you made today, Corporal?"

"This is my third, sir. Lots of folks coming in. Most of them arrive here, some at Palmdale's airport, even some at LAX, and that's a two-hour drive to get up here. I was driving most of the day yesterday, and I expect I'll be doing that today, and likely tomorrow as well."

"I didn't know there were Marines here," Barnes commented.

"There aren't normally, sir. I'm from Camp Pendleton, down near San Clemente. Two days ago, my company got the word to send everybody fit to work up here, and we've been busting our humps ever since."

The van pulled up to a sandbagged strongpoint manned by army military police. "Everyone has to get off here," Sims announced. While the MPs checked everyone's ID cards and orders, their luggage was spot-checked and the minivan searched. Two men searched the underside with mirrors, while a canine unit sniffed its way around. Once the security check was completed, the occupants got back on board and headed down a short taxiway.

Barnes spotted several crews at work in the area. One was erecting a chain-link fence, another was laying some kind of cable, and he could see a trailer being added to a row of similar trailers just a hundred yards to the northwest of a huge building. Another trailer was waiting its turn on the tarmac.

Once inside the gate, the bus dropped them off in the shadow of the towering, weathered hangar. Biff was used to structures that could house two or three fighters, but this monster could easily hold a jumbo jet. A multistory office building was attached to one side.

A freshly painted sign reading SECURITY ENTRANCE contrasted with the faded black building number, 151. A pair of army MPs checked their IDs carefully, and a civilian with a clipboard checked their names off an access list as they went inside. There was an open area for them to leave their bags, and they were directed down a hall toward a classroom.

A young Asian woman in navy khakis was waiting just outside the classroom and approached him. "Captain Barnes? I'm Lieutenant Commander Jennifer Oh, C3 team lead for Project *Defender*. You don't need to attend the briefing. I'm here to take you to Mr. McConnell; he's waiting for you." She handed him an envelope and a loop with a photo-ID badge attached.

"Your military ID will let you go anywhere on Edwards," she explained. "This badge is for our areas only and is not to be displayed outside of the compound." It was simply labeled VENTURESTAR, along with his name and photo.

"The orientation just tells new personnel about the *Defender* project and reviews the classification requirements. You don't need to waste time with that; you're already fully briefed. The envelope has information about your housing, and Mr. McConnell will tell you about what you'll be doing."

She started to lead Biff down a hall, but a civilian stopped her, explaining, "He still needs to sign the security form." He handed Biff a clipboard. LCDR Oh seemed impatient to leave, but Biff took his time, carefully reading the form, then filling it out and signing it. It was a standard form. He'd seen and signed many of them before, but Barnes was careful about reading anything he signed.

At least that was his excuse. Actually, hearing McConnell's name had crystallized his bad mood into something less than anger, but more than irritation. It gave him some small satisfaction to make her and McConnell wait, even as he realized how petty that was. He handed the clipboard back, then said, "All right, let's get this over with."

Oh shot him a puzzled look, then shrugged and gestured toward the door. She said, "Security will watch your bags until you get time to settle in." Biff was hoping he wouldn't even have to unpack.

The office annex of Building 151 was four stories high, and, after they left the security area, she led him up two floors. The stairwell opened out to a long passageway that was more than bustling. With LCDR Oh in the lead, they threaded their way around a knot of workmen and people discussing a circuit diagram they'd taped to the wall. The noise level was enough to make casual conversation challenging.

A stack of office furniture created a choke point, narrowing the corridor and forcing traffic into two opposing lanes. As they finally reached a door with a sign taped on it marked TECHNICAL DIREC-TOR, Oh mentioned something about "getting better," but he wasn't sure if she meant the traffic would get better or that the traffic was better than it had been. She knocked twice, but, given the background noise, she didn't bother waiting for a reply before opening the door.

McConnell's office was large, which was good, because there were a lot of people in it. A navy lieutenant was seated next to his desk, speaking with him about something, while a trio of civilians was bent over a diagram at a large table in one corner. Barnes spotted another smaller table with the obligatory coffeepot and a toilet kit sitting next to it.

Ray looked up from his discussion as Jenny and Barnes came in. He nodded to Barnes and shot a quick smile to Jenny, who said to Barnes, "I'll leave you here," and then left. Ray raised a finger and said, "Give me one moment, please," quickly finishing his business with the lieutenant. As the officer stood to leave, Ray called to the other group, "I need the room now, Hugh. I'll find you in fifteen minutes."

They quickly rolled up the large diagram and left, leaving only the background noise in the hall as a reminder of the furious activity. McConnell came around from behind the desk to shake Biff's hand, greeting him warmly.

"Captain Barnes, you don't know how pleased I am to have you as part of the program."

Biff didn't feel particularly a part of anything, automatically shaking Ray's hand, but definitely not smiling, and biting back the first harsh question that came to mind. He settled for a milder version, one that wouldn't start a fistfight. "Why have you brought me out here? How do you think I can help with this—circus?" Barnes's tone was hostile, almost angry, and his expression matched his tone.

Ray paused, then shrugged and went back to sit behind his desk. He motioned to a nearby chair, and Barnes sat as well. "Captain, after seeing your brief, I knew you believed in the *Defender* concept as much as I did, and then I examined your background and experience. I believe you'd make a valuable addition to the project team. Your brief on *Defender* was impressive, and you made some changes to the design that I wanted to discuss with you." He stood and went over to the coffeemaker and brought back two cups.

As Barnes accepted one, he frowned and shook his head. "I believed in turning *Defender* into an air force program. Or a navy program," he quickly added. "But creating a separate service for it? And then giving you a little over two months to fly? That's nuts. You have no resources, no infrastructure, and an impossible task. It's possible *Defender* might eventually lead to a separate Space Force. After all, that's how the air force was created. But not right off the bat."

"It wasn't exactly my idea, either. If you remember, Captain, I was just as surprised as you were," Ray responded. "But since the president made that decision, he's also given us permission to use any resource in the federal government, and that 'infrastructure' would only slow us down. Consider carefully, Captain. Would either service be able to get *Defender* launched in seventy days?"

"No way," Barnes answered firmly.

"Then there's no harm in us being on our own and trying something new. The services have their own ways of doing things, and they take too long. Even a fast-track program takes too long because of the massive bureaucracy. A small group can think, decide, and move faster than a large one. That's my mantra for this project."

"It still doesn't make sense," Barnes protested. "We researched your background while we were studying *Defender*. No disrespect, but you're not qualified to be the technical director of this project."

"I agree," Ray replied honestly. "I'm also not qualified to build a house, either, but I can get it done by hiring the right people. One of which I want to be you."

"What do you need me for?" Barnes demanded. Frankly, he was curious about what this madman wanted him to do.

"Doing what you already did, but more so. You're assigned to the Rapid Capabilities Office; you're familiar with advanced technology for spacecraft, both in the civilian and the classified worlds. Your first job is scouring the aerospace industry and the black compartments for anything that will help *Defender* fly and fight."

"Oh, is that all?" Barnes was amused and horrified at the same time. "That's a tall order. I assume I don't have the several months to a year such a task would normally take."

"The timeline calls for locking down all the technology in a week."

He almost laughed. "A week?" Barnes couldn't believe what he'd heard. McConnell obviously had no clue as to how the Department of Defense operated.

"You included several new technology programs in your brief to the JCS. Start with them and build on that."

Barnes sighed. McConnell sounded so positive. "I'm briefed into three black programs, none of which were relevant to *Defender*. And you're right—I was able to get sanitized information on a couple of others for the brief. It would take weeks to get clearance for just those programs. I can't imagine how long it will take to get cleared into every black program, or whether they will even give me clearance." He looked thoughtful. "I have no idea how many black programs there actually are, which is sort of the idea, I guess."

"You'll have blanket access tomorrow," Ray stated flatly. "Every program."

Barnes stared at Ray with stark disbelief. "I've never heard of such a thing!" he exclaimed.

"Nobody had ever heard of the Chinese shooting down GPS satellites before, either. It's just a bunch of rules people made up. Rules can be changed," he said with intensity.

"Admiral Schultz has promised both you and me universal access to all compartmented programs by zero eight-hundred our time tomorrow. You, so you can make the search. And me, so you can tell me what you found. Anything that could be of use will be moved out of its compartment. That happens in week two, by the way."

Barnes sat thoughtfully for a moment. "I came in here intending to tell you that I wanted nothing to do with the program—that I wouldn't work on it. General Warner as much as promised me a command billet, ops officer in a fighter squadron, when I finished my tour at the Pentagon, which is fifty-three days from now, but who's counting?"

"So you've changed your mind?" Ray asked hopefully.

"No, I still think you are bound for a failure of biblical proportions, and I don't want to be anywhere in the vicinity when this program implodes. But my curiosity is piqued. I'll stay at least long enough to do your survey. Maybe when you see the enormity of just this one task, you'll understand how hopeless all this is."

Ray smiled. "Maybe when you see how much can be done in just a week, you'll change your mind. We are recertifying the SCIF. Once that happens, your office will be here on the third floor, a few doors down from me. Until then, you'll work out of the C-20 parked in the hangar. It's got secure communications, and we're running it on ground power. It's unconventional, but it works."

"Where do I sleep?" Barnes asked. "Assuming I get time to sleep, that is."

"Did you see that row of trailers being brought in? One of those is yours."

"I'm living in a trailer?"

"Courtesy of FEMA. It has more room than what you'd get in the BOQ, and the commute is a lot shorter."

"Thus saving time," Barnes concluded.

"My other mantra." Ray answered. "I suspect a lot of the classified programs we're interested in will have offices here in Southern California. If you have to travel, the air force has loaned us a helicopter, and I want you to use it."

"Who is paying for all this?" Biff asked.

"Admiral Schultz has a big barrel of money next to his desk. We give him the receipts."

"Seriously," Biff persisted. "Congress would have a field day if you start spending money like that."

"Compared to the cost of a GPS satellite, jet fuel is peanuts. Every week we shave off the launch date saves the government a half-billion-dollar satellite, which works out to just under fifty thousand dollars a minute. Time is as much an enemy as the Chinese."

"Then I guess I'd better get going."

National Aeronautics and Space Administration
Washington, D.C.
October 12, 2017

Dr. Harold Matheson was irritated by the knock on the door. His assistant, Helen, opened the door a little. "Doctor, I know you're in an important meeting, but John Alvarez is calling from Houston. He says it's urgent, and a classified matter."

Matheson harrumphed a little, which he was quite good at. "It must be the day for it. Barbara Alwyn and I are discussing an 'urgent, classified matter' as well."

Helen said, "He's ready to teleconference, if you want."

"Then it must be serious," Matheson remarked. He turned to the woman seated across from his desk. "Please excuse me, Barbara. Let me find out what this is about."

She started to get up, but Matheson said, "No, please stay. You've got the same clearances I do, and this will just take a moment. Whatever his problem is, yours is more important. He can wait. I'll just set up a time for him to call back."

The flat screen came on with the image of a middle-aged man with thinning hair and a neatly trimmed beard. The camera was looking up, which distorted the image a little, and was centered on the bolo tie he wore. His expression of concern matched his tone. "Dr. Matheson, we've got to do something about this *VentureStar* project."

Matheson began to tease him, "Hello, John, it's good to see you, too . . . ," but then stopped in midsentence. "*VentureStar*," he repeated, looking over at Barbara Alwyn, and then turning back to the screen. "Is this regarding a request for personnel and equipment to be shipped to Edwards Air Force Base?"

"It's not a request, more like a requisition. They want my best people, and two of my simulators. I was told crews and aircraft are already en route to remove the simulators and take them to California!"

Matheson absorbed the news calmly. "John, you remember Barbara Alwyn, don't you?" She shifted her chair a bit so she was within the camera's field of view. "Barbara and I were just discussing a similar issue. She's head of the Software Assurance Technology Center. The *VentureStar* people are asking—no, requiring—her to send her best four people to Edwards—immediately! They've gone home to pack and they're on a morning flight. Not even enough time for a proper turnover to their supervisors."

Alvarez nodded sadly. "And it's probably doing to her schedule what this is going to do to mine. We received no warning. Did you know about this?"

"I did, and thought I'd put a stop to it," Matheson replied. "I received information about the program last night, and a list this morning of all the resources that NASA was directed to send to this new program. It was flagged as highest priority, and I responded immediately with questions about how were we supposed to complete our programs on time and how we were to be compensated for the transfer of all this equipment from one federal agency to another."

"We got our list this morning as well," Alvarez commented. Alwyn nodded agreement. "It treated the requisitions as an established fact. The division managers here involved received messages as well."

"They're completely ignoring the chain of command," Matheson fumed. "I can't manage NASA if I can't control what's going on."

"When do you expect a response?" Alvarez asked.

"The orders came from Secretary of Defense Peck's office. They haven't responded to my queries yet. Since we're an independent federal agency, we don't take orders from any of the cabinet secretaries. On the other hand, since both NASA and the DoD are in the executive branch, I'm pretty sure Peck will have cleared this with the president before sending it. But NASA is not some aerospace warehouse that other agencies can raid at will. If Peck can't or won't answer my questions, then I'll make an appointment to see the president."

Matheson seemed to sit up a little straighter as he spoke. "John,

Barbara, on my authority, refuse any requests for personnel or equipment from within NASA until you hear from me, via the chain of command. After all, that's the way this should have been done in the first place. I'll have a NASA-wide directive ready shortly for Helen to distribute that will say the same thing."

"What about the people coming to remove my simulators?" Alvarez asked.

"They can go back to Edwards or wait, hopefully the former. They don't belong to me. It's *VentureStar*'s problem for sending them out half-cocked. Like I said, if they want to complain, they can call here. I may even take the call. I'm curious to see what these empire builders in California are up to."

Space Force Headquarters
Edwards Air Force Base
October 12, 2017

General Carl Norman found Ray McConnell that evening at dinner. For the moment, meals were being served in the hangar, still awaiting *VentureStar*'s arrival. A buffet line had been arranged along one side, with the diners seated at what looked like brand-new patio furniture. Although there were dozens of tables, the dining area didn't fill a fifth of the cavernous hangar floor. The evening was still pleasantly warm, but the doors at one end of the hangar had been closed to block a chilling breeze.

As Norman's guide, an army colonel named Evans, pointed out Ray McConnell, Ray spotted the pair and hurried over. "General Norman, welcome to the U.S. Space Force headquarters. I'm Ray McConnell, technical director."

As he shook McConnell's hand, Norman replied, "I wanted to speak with the ranking officer, but Colonel Evans here says you're the man I should be talking to."

"About your Marines?" Ray guessed.

"Exactly," the general answered. The man didn't waste time.

Ray nodded and pointed to the buffet. "Will you join us for dinner, General? They just started serving, and if you've come up from Pendleton, you haven't had time to eat."

The colonel added, "By the way, General, this is what your men assigned here are eating tonight."

Norman smiled. "Well, that almost makes it mandatory. By all means," he said, gesturing for them to lead the way.

As they got into the line and waited for their turn, Ray explained, "We're using the base kitchens at Edwards, and the food is brought over here. We've hired a civilian chef to make sure the food's top quality. He supervises a staff that handles all the purchases, the cooking, and the transportation."

Norman was favorably impressed. Although it was obviously improvised, it looked more like a hotel's buffet than a cafeteria-style serving line. There were three main dishes, one meatless, sides, and condiments. He saw other small details: flowers in bare spots on the table and a rope barrier that provided some separation from the rest of the hangar, even if it was just psychological.

McConnell continued. "We serve dinner from sixteen hundred until twenty hundred, and there are sandwiches and fruit available from then until breakfast."

Norman loaded his plate with as many different selections as possible. He took his responsibilities seriously and wanted to see how the food matched what his Marines got back at Pendleton.

A civilian at the end of the line was supervising the servers. Ray introduced him to Norman. "This is Geoffrey Lewes. He handles morale and welfare for the project." Lewes was a sandy-haired man in his midthirties. Large glasses on his round face made his head seem large for the rest of his spare frame. While most of the civilians wore jeans and polo shirts, Lewes was dressed in khakis and a sport coat. As he shook the general's hand, Norman thought he caught a whiff of cologne.

"I love what you've done with the place," Norman joked.

Lewes beamed. "Thank you, General. By tomorrow, I'll have screens along one side"—he gestured—"and a sound system for music. I've got volunteers organizing playlists . . ."

Ray said, "Geoffrey and his staff take care of the people here. Run errands, provide basic amenities, reduce their distractions. A laundry service, for example. This lets the engineering staff focus all their time on the mission."

"I've never had to sign a top secret security form to be a concierge before," Lewes joked.

Ray grinned. "And you've never had army quartermasters as your staff. But our people have all had their lives and jobs interrupted to work here. Do as much as you can to take care of their personal needs."

Lewes smiled. "I've got plenty of ideas . . ."

Ray broke in: "Gotta go, Geoffrey. It's great work." And they headed for an empty table.

As the group sat down, Norman explained. "When I got the call three days ago asking for a company of Marines to be assigned to 'temporary security duty' up here at Edwards, I approved it automatically. We've done such things in the past, and while this China business is keeping us busy, I can spare the men. Then, yesterday, you folks asked for another company, which I approved, but if I hadn't been in the field, I would have come down with them right then. What are you doing with my Marines, and how long do you need them?"

Ray was chewing and looked to Evans, who answered. "You saw them manning the gate jointly with my MPs. They're also patrolling the area until we can get the security fences up. Edwards barely has the personnel to handle their own security requirements. There was no way they could give us the support we needed."

"That much is obvious," Norman agreed. He'd finished the baked chicken and tried the fish. Both were quite good. "I also heard they're acting as drivers and messengers. Which is fine. But what are they guarding?"

This time Ray answered. "We're restarting the *VentureStar* program, General. We're going to equip it to lift a new generation of replacement GPS satellites into orbit. There will be a lot of them to lift, so it's cheaper and quicker to use *VentureStar* than a lot of expendable boosters."

"How long will you need them for?"

"At least seventy days. We'll stand up our own security force as soon as we can." Evans nodded agreement as Ray spoke.

"And what areas are they responsible for?"

"Here, the launchpad at Area 1-54, and a hangar at the north end of Edwards where *VentureStar*'s being reactivated. We've got over two hundred people working at all three sites, round the clock. There are more coming in every day."

Norman was incredulous. "Around the clock? With two companies of Marines? That's not nearly enough, even if you stop using them as drivers and such. You need twice that many, which is a battalion, which would be good because then you'd have the headquarters platoon to manage them. Who's doing it now?" Norman asked.

Ray answered, "Colonel Evans is running them out of his security office."

Norman frowned. "Colonel, I'm sure you're doing your best, but that's simply not enough men to establish a secure perimeter around so many dispersed facilities."

Evans looked unhappy but nodded his agreement. "They're stretched pretty thin, sir."

During the conversation, Norman almost finished his meal. All that was left was some eggplant parmigiana. He studied it carefully, measuring his dislike of eggplant against his dedication to the Corps.

Someone approached the table, and, out of the corner of his eye, Norman saw a khaki uniform and four stars. Happy to abandon the eggplant, he stood and turned to greet the new arrival.

They were both inside and uncovered, so he didn't salute, but the newcomer offered his hand, and Norman took it. "General Norman, welcome. I'm Bill Schultz." He turned to McConnell. "Thanks for the message, Ray." Schultz also shot a look to the colonel, and Norman knew that the security chief had slipped up.

As they both sat, Ray explained about the general's visit and their discussion about the need for an increased number of Marines. "I'd agree with the general's assessment, Ray."

He turned to Norman. "I'll put in a request for that battalion. It will be on your desk by tomorrow morning."

Norman immediately shook his head. "I'm sorry, sir, but I've got operational commitments. We're glad to help, but it can't conflict."

"This would be an operational request."

"Refurbishing a space-launch vehicle? No disrespect, sir, but I don't see how."

Schultz nodded. "In that case, I think it's only fair that we brief you into the full program. Mr. McConnell only has the authority to tell you our cover story. You'll have to sign some security forms."

"Of course," Norman answered, now intrigued. Schultz glanced over to Evans, but he was already leaving.

As Schultz explained the *Defender* project and its goal, Norman sat quietly, absorbing and processing the information and its implications. Once Schultz had finished, Norman said, "Sir, if you'll let me use your secure communications before I leave here, I'll get the rest of the battalion spooling up tonight. They'll be on the road tomorrow morning. Norman added, "Most of my commitments are contingencies. If one of them becomes real, I'll figure out what to do then. But I'll still need your operational order."

"You'll have it, General," Schultz assured him. "We're not a rogue operation."

Evans reappeared with a clipboard, and Norman studied the form long enough to make sure he wasn't signing a bar bill. As he signed his name, the possibilities began to form in his mind.

"We can make this work," Norman said, with growing enthusiasm. "We'll rotate my battalions through two weeks at a time and treat this as a force-protection exercise."

"We'll have to scramble to find housing for them," Schultz cautioned.

"Not a problem. There's lots of open area for the tents, although my battalion commanders should set up with Colonel Evans to ensure close coordination. We'll take care of mess arrangements, although we might use visits to your 'restaurant' as an incentive."

Ray smiled. "That's high praise, General. I'll make sure the staff hears about it."

Beginning

U.S. Space Force Headquarters
Edwards Air Force Base
Hangar
October 12, 2017, 0430 hours

They'd scheduled the arrival carefully. You couldn't count on cloud cover, especially in the California desert, so they'd chosen a satellite-free window well before dawn.

They all got up early. Ray, standing by the end of the runway with a cup of coffee, saw them show up in ones and twos, walking slowly over to the tarmac. Lewes had set up his customary table with coffee and breakfast, but this time outside the hangar. For the moment, he was using a big tent borrowed from the Marines, but there was a hand-lettered sign over the entrance: THE HANGAR.

Since this was a special occasion, Ray had decided it was a doughnut morning. Now, while he waited, he alternately brushed colored sprinkles off his jacket and warmed his hands with a mug of coffee.

The handling crews were ready, and General Norman had arranged for a nighttime base-security exercise that filled the area with patrols, as well as kept the route clear. The base fire department had also sent their equipment. Ray approved, but thinking about them made a small knot in his stomach.

A voice behind him said, "Thanks for the flowers, Ray." He could hear the smile in her tone, and he turned to see Jenny walking toward him.

He automatically answered, "You're welcome." Some of the fatigue left him, and he kissed her good morning. Then the two stood silently together for a moment. They'd been so busy since coming to Edwards that they'd barely spoken, much less had any time together. He was content to simply enjoy her presence and didn't want to do anything that would end the moment.

Finally, after they'd both stood for a minute, she asked, "Is it going well?"

Ray nodded. "They left the north hangar seven minutes late because someone spotted what looked like a problem with one of the tow bars. It's okay, though. They'll make up the lost time along the way."

"How big is the window?"

He laughed. "Not very large. By the time you factor in the Russians, the Chinese, and the commercial satellites, we get forty-two minutes with nobody overhead. Which is why we're letting the tractors go up to five miles an hour. It's one point two miles, and the route's surface has been inspected three times by three different groups of people. And there's virtually no traffic this time of day, so . . ." He shrugged. "We plan for disaster, and hope for the best."

Jenny almost sparkled with excitement. "I never had time to go to the north hangar to see her."

"Well, it's good you waited. She looks better than she did just a few days ago. She wasn't pretty, covered in plastic and surrounded by crates and dust."

Hugh Dawson came up, a walkie-talkie in one hand. "She made the first turn just fine. They slowed during the turn, of course, but she took it smoothly. Peters wants permission to raise the speed to five and a half miles an hour."

Ray answered thoughtfully, "We'd talked about it." He considered the request for only a moment, then said firmly, "Yes, go to five and a half. It will help make up those seven minutes."

Schultz, approaching the group, heard Ray's order. "Then it's going smoothly?" he asked. Jenny turned and snapped off a sharp salute, which Schultz returned. She wore the alternate working uniform this morning, the blue-and-gray digital camouflaged battle dress. Ray still hadn't gotten used to her wearing it. She looked much better in khakis or dress blues, but battle dress was warmer in the desert predawn chill.

"As well as moving something that weighs two million pounds can go," Ray answered. "Thank heaven for Edwards's flat landscape." He turned to Dawson. "Remind them to allow extra distance to slow down before the turns."

Dawson nodded and said, "Understood," and he relayed the order.

Schultz turned to Jenny. "And good morning, Commander Oh, Mr. Dawson." The admiral asked Jenny, "Are you settling into your assignment?"

"Setting up the command and control infrastructure for an entire space program?" She laughed. "I could have waited ten years for that kind of job, if I ever got it at all." She knew what he really wanted to know, and told him before he could ask. "I can do this, sir. I've had to expand my consciousness a little, but I can see what needs to be done."

Dawson's walkie-talkie chirped, and a minute later he reported, "They've made the second turn. We should be able to see it soon."

"Another benefit of Edwards's flat landscape," Ray observed.

As they waited in the predawn darkness, Dawson would get periodic reports as they passed landmarks. He compared the planned arrival time with their real progress. They'd made up a few minutes. Ray had helped create that schedule and knew it by heart.

"A tire's blown on the lead tractor," Dawson relayed abruptly, concern on his face. "A piece of rubber clipped one of the ground guides.

The medics are with him. He's okay, but they're going to x-ray his arm."

Ray grimaced. "I should have had them check the tractors more carefully. I didn't give them any guidance about the tires."

Schultz saw Ray's expression. "They can disengage the lead tractor, and we can still pull the vehicle with only two. It'll take longer, but that's why we built in the extra time," Schultz reminded him. "The crews probably did the routine tire check. It just wasn't enough in this case. Take it from someone who's been there. You can't think of everything. That's why you have to have good people working for you."

"I just don't like the idea of slowing down," Ray answered emphatically, looking at his watch. "But we'll still get her into the hangar before sunrise."

Dawson asked Peters for their status. Ray could hear his voice over the radio: "The tractor has been disengaged and is clear, starting back up again."

Ray waited impatiently. They'd lost more time, and it couldn't be made up.

"They're building up to three miles per hour," Dawson announced.

The eastern horizon was just beginning to show color, which caused Ray to pace nervously.

"Here she comes," said Schultz softly.

Ray turned as Schultz spoke, his attention drawn by the flashing lights of the escort vehicles as the convoy came into view. A base-police vehicle, red and blue lights flashing, was a hundred feet in front of the tractor. Two gray pushback tractors, each capable of towing a C-5, had been ganged together. Immense as it was, a fully loaded C-5 only weighed 385 tons, while *VentureStar* was almost one thousand tons empty.

VentureStar was the prototype for a fleet of commercial single-stage-to-orbit space vehicles. In development since the early 1990s, an experimental small-scale version, the X-33, had successfully completed testing just after the turn of the century.

Like the space shuttle, *VentureStar* carried its payload in a big cargo bay, fifteen feet wide by fifty feet long. It used the same fuel as well: liquid hydrogen and liquid oxygen. But the shuttle took months to prepare for a launch and used expendable boosters that had to be reconditioned after each launch. *VentureStar* launched using only her own Aerospike engines and landed conventionally, like the shuttle. She could take fifty tons to low Earth orbit after a two-week turn-around.

Two Marine HMMWVs, or Humvees, flanked the convoy on either side, keeping a sharp watch out for trouble coming from the dark landscape. They were well clear of the spacecraft, but close enough to sing out and move in if they spotted something wrong.

Jerry Peters, in charge of the evolution, was actually bringing up the rear. Followed by a truck, Peters was alternately walking and trotting right behind *VentureStar,* watching the gear, the underside of the spacecraft, even checking the road surface for signs that the tires were breaking through.

At the final brief last night, one joker had given Peters a broom and a bucket, "to retrieve anything that fell off." Peters had put them in the truck, just in case.

Lights mounted on the tractors and escort vehicles shone on *VentureStar*'s landing gear, but the black heat shield on her underside absorbed every bit of illumination. From the side, the vehicle's white sides and top reflected the quarter moon well enough to show the overall shape and size, but the bottom half was invisible and had to be filled in mentally.

With a clear side view of the spacecraft, Jenny exclaimed, "My God, it's huge."

"As long as the shuttle and wider at her base than the shuttle with the SRBs attached," Dawson said proudly. It was a smooth, blended wedge shape, and two short wings jutted out from the back, angling up. It had twin tails almost as large as the wings, or maybe the wings weren't much bigger than the tail fins.

Despite all his engineering experience, Ray still had problems watching as *VentureStar* was towed on her landing gear. It just looked wrong. Those gear struts were strong enough to take the shock of the spacecraft landing at over two hundred knots, but to him they looked fragile and completely inadequate to bear its weight.

Schultz added, "I'm amazed the thing can be moved, much less fly."

"That's what I like, a positive attitude," McConnell groused.

Dawson announced, "Next turn coming up," and Jerry watched the procession slow. Then the moonlit shape of the vehicle changed as the nose swung toward them. Finally, a snowy white wedge was pointed straight down the road, slowly growing in size.

Ray was suddenly afraid, and his insides tightened at the thought of its going off the road surface to either side, but he fought the idea and focused on its smooth progress.

A few cameras flashed, and Jerry hoped Evans's security people were on the ball. He'd authorized two staff members to serve as official photographers for the move, but the images would be classified until after the launch. At his direction, Evans had drilled everyone on the "no photos" rule.

He could smell the diesel exhaust now, and the convoy, as planned, shifted. The Humvees formed a protective circle around the hangar as the tractors maneuvered *VentureStar* to face away from the hangar, and then they began backing her in.

The vehicle came to a stop, and the tractors began unhooking from the landing gear. Scattered cheers and applause continued until the hangar doors began closing. The sky was glowing brightly, and when Ray glanced at his watch, they still had four minutes in the window.

Schultz saw him checking the time. "We've got a lot of people out here. Why don't we form letters they can see from space and spell out something rude? Of course, it would have to be in Chinese."

Ray began to laugh so hard he had to fight for air. He could relax a little now. It was an important milestone, but only the first.

Jenny looked at the huge spacecraft and watched as the hangar doors came together. "This makes it real, doesn't it?" Her tone was half pride, half awe.

Ray caught himself about to say something stupid, about his idea coming to life. But that was bragging. It only took one man to have an idea. It had taken many more to get it going and would take considerably more than that to finish it.

"It's starting to be real, Jenny." He wanted to stay, and talk, and he could see she would if he wanted to, but that wasn't why they were here.

Wishing each other good luck, they went back to work.

U.S. Space Force Headquarters
Edwards Air Force Base
Office Annex
October 12, 2017

Biff Barnes was now out of the C-20 and working in his office. As much of the *Defender* program was classified, the upper two floors of the Building 151 office annex were certified as a SCIF, electronically isolated from the rest of the building, and the base for that matter. Without the shielding, not only were they vulnerable to network-style spying, but eavesdropping equipment nearby might be able to record the keystrokes as everyone typed.

And in spite of the certification, a large part of Evans's staff would continue to monitor the area for unusual transmissions or electrical activity where there shouldn't be any.

Barnes's small office was almost barren. He sat at a desk occupied by three tower computers, a shared flat-screen display, and several neatly organized stacks of documents. A printer and boxes of paper sat in a corner, and there was almost nothing else in the room. He'd been too busy to decorate the walls.

He saw Ray come in and pushed an office chair toward him.

"Thanks for coming by. I sent you that message because, although I've just started, I've already found something useful. I don't think it can wait."

"More useful than the improved fuel cells and the radar encoding?"

"Definitely," the pilot responded. "If you're going to use this, and I think you should, we need to move on it right away." He handed Ray a brightly marked folder. "This is the only copy of this information. I'm keeping everything on paper, or up here." He tapped his forehead. "Nothing goes on even the classified server."

Ray was surprised. The whole point of having a classified server was to store information like this. "You're being a little extreme, aren't you?"

"I've already been through more compartmented programs than most people see in their entire careers. I'm going to have to burn my brain after this is over."

"Can I help?" Ray asked cheerfully.

"Ha." Barnes responded flatly.

Ray opened the folder and began reading. His eyes narrowed. "'Conformal AESA antennas? I knew it was theoretically possible. They can do that now?"

"They're not ready for mass production, but it looks like they can hand fabricate skin sections that will be functional radar antennas."

"No deploying a mechanical antenna, less weight, no blind spots. I like it." Ray was getting excited. "But it means changes to the skin, where we weren't going to make any before."

"But now you don't have to design and build that mount that was going to lift the radar antenna clear of the cargo bay."

"What about heat on reentry?"

"The materials they list are almost as heat-tolerant as the skin. We can mount them on the vehicle's sides and top and leave the bottom of the wings as they are. We may have to modify the cooling systems to cover the antennas, and we need to verify all the components are heat-resistant." Besides, by the time *VentureStar* reenters the atmosphere, the mission is over. You won't need the radar anymore."

"What about navigation on the way back?" Ray asked sharply.

"Use GPS, like the shuttle, of course," Barnes replied whimsically.

"You mean the same GPS that the Chinese are shooting down?"

"Details. Do you want this or not?"

"Definitely want!" Ray answered. "I'll tell the admiral immediately." He paused for a moment. "This is good work, Clarence. Thank you."

Barnes winced. "Please, just 'Biff.'"

"Sorry. You hate 'Clarence' that much?"

"I was named for my grandfather, and I couldn't stand the man. He got a charge out of scaring us kids to death every time he saw us. I was so eager to get a call sign I took the first one the squadron committee offered me. They were joking, but I was too new and too desperate to care."

Ray nodded. "I understand. 'Biff' it is." He motioned to the folder. "I'll ask Admiral Schultz to come down here ASAP, along with Gina Morales, our sensors-systems director. How many programs did you have to go through to find this?"

"A fair number. But you were right. Most are obviously irrelevant, and thanks to that blanket access, I didn't waste time finding that out." He answered the next question without asking. "I should be done this week." After a moment, Biff announced, "I'm beginning to think there is a slim chance that this won't be a cosmic disaster."

"Really," answered Ray carefully. "So you think *Defender* will fly, then?"

"Not a chance," Barnes answered. I'm going to finish doing this, and then I want to get out of this crazy place."

"We'll see,' " Ray replied.

U.S. Space Force Headquarters
Edwards Air Force Base
Office Annex, Fourth Floor
October 12, 2017

Glenn Chung spent the day running cables for the secure network. He was supervising three other techs but did as much hands-on work as the others. Not only did it get the work done faster, it allowed him to make the special modifications he needed. Crouched over the bottom of a server cabinet, he was making cable connections, but one cable went to a small USB recording device. Given the nest of identical cables it was hidden inside, there was no chance of it being detected without a deliberate search.

He moved quickly, because there were already people waiting to use the network. He didn't want to delay them.

U.S. Space Force Headquarters
Edwards Air Force Base
Office Annex
October 12, 2017

After Ray told Admiral Schultz and Gina Morales about Barnes's discovery, he didn't go directly back to his office.

The Building 151 office annex was laid out as a long, narrow structure attached to one side of the hangar. A single hall ran the length of each floor, with rooms on each side. Most would hold a few desks, but some were large enough for a meeting or a work group. The offices on the lower two floors on the exterior side had windows. On the interior side, only offices on the second floor had windows, which gave a view of the hangar.

There were no functioning windows on the third and fourth floors because of the security requirements. There's no point in electronically shielding a room if someone can just open a window and toss something out. Armed sentries guarded the stairwells, and anyone who entered or left was electronically logged.

Admiral Schultz, Ray, and the division directors had offices on the fourth floor. Instead of turning right and heading back to his office, Ray turned left and walked the length of the fourth-floor hall, just listening and watching. There were stairwells at each end, as well as in the middle, and he'd picked an office right next to one of the ends. He'd walk the length of the building, then go down to the third floor and walk back, then take the stairs up to his office.

All the spaces weren't occupied yet, but the floor still hummed with activity. He walked by, trying not to attract attention, just listening and watching. It wasn't eavesdropping, but he didn't like to think of it as managing anyone, either. He couldn't remember if it was one of Kelly Johnson's rules or not, but he didn't believe in sitting in his office, waiting for people to come to him with problems. And there were some folks who didn't know when to ask for help.

His walk seemed justified when someone in the propulsion group spotted him and asked a question, and he was able to answer it immediately. *That's one less e-mail to deal with,* he thought. But there were plenty more waiting in his in-box. Still, he pressed on to the end of the hall, then went down to the third floor.

This floor had the same hectic atmosphere. It took several minutes to walk the long corridor, even at a fast pace, and he walked slowly, almost strolling.

He'd only walked past a few open doors when he heard a fragment of a conversation, ". . . not my problem." The two voices were raised a little, not unusually so, but he stopped several feet from the open doorway, listening. Okay. Now he was eavesdropping.

The handwritten sign taped to the door listed a name under the title "Laser"—Bert Anderson. He remembered Anderson's name from his research. Ray had recruited him because he was one of the veterans from the discontinued Northrop-Grumman Airborne Laser Program.

"We need to work with your people, but they say everything has to go through you."

Ray inched a little closer to the door frame and tried to look like he wasn't listening. He checked his watch, as if he were waiting for whoever was inside.

"Well, that's simply not correct. Of course our people can coordinate at lower levels, once I've signed off on what they're doing. After all, I'm responsible for everything that comes out of this division. How do I know what someone's committing us to?"

"But that's just too slow. My people are planning where to lay out power cables, and your people say they won't tell us anything about the laser's requirements until they've cleared it with you, and when they go off to do that, nothing comes back."

Ray identified the other speaker as Ethan Kirsch. He was head of the Power Systems Division. He was responsible for the fuel cells that were *Defender*'s main power source and the equipment that supplied power to all of the spacecraft's systems.

Anderson said, "I remember that e-mail." After a pause, he added, "Here it is. I can't give you an answer on this because the ABL hasn't arrived yet. There's also some new technology that hasn't been incorporated. Once we know if it works, we'll be able to give you a good number."

Kirsch asked, "And when will the laser arrive?"

"They're moving heaven and earth, I hear. It's coming from Davis-Monthan in Arizona. They're sure they'll have it here by Thursday—then add a week, maybe only five days, for the modifications . . ."

"That's simply too long," Kirsch protested. "We need those cable layouts now, because when you're done with those modifications, the laser will have to be dropped in with the cables already installed."

"Like I said, that's your problem. My job is to get the laser functioning and installed."

"We don't have the time for this. We can plan for a higher requirement. Just give us your best estimate; then we'll add ten percent and move on." Kirsch was almost pleading.

"And when the final requirement's higher than that? Who's going to look bad? You, or me?" Anderson was defensive, almost belligerent. "Everybody wants us to hurry. Fire control wants the control interfaces. Space frame wants weights and attachment points. This is my division. Nobody gets anything until the information is locked down."

Ray had been listening with concern, then alarm. He remembered his interview with Anderson. The man was technically brilliant, and his boss's evaluation had described him as a "great organizer." Of course they'd said the same thing about General George McClellan during the Civil War.

The large laser system they had chosen to arm *Defender* had been developed by Northrop-Grumman as part of the Airborne Laser Program back in 1996. The original idea was to mount a laser in a Boeing 747 and have it orbit near hostile territory. If the enemy launched ballistic missiles, a chemical laser would shoot them down while they were still climbing. Initial tests were successful, but the program had been shelved in 2012 because of cost, as well as concerns that the laser wasn't powerful enough. Lasers work better without an atmosphere, and the laser's six modules would fit in *VentureStar*'s bay with room to spare.

Ray fought his first urge, to just go in and overrule Anderson. But as he listened, his worries became concern, verging on outright distress.

This was not a technical problem, and Ray tried to understand Anderson's thinking. The director didn't want his division to look bad. *His* division. He took it personally. Keeping tight control over his subordinates and refusing to act until the answer was clear-cut meant he was afraid of making a mistake. So he doesn't trust his own judgment, and it sounded like he didn't trust his people's judgment, either.

So, should Ray sit down with Anderson, try to change his attitude? It wasn't simply a matter of telling him that they were pressed for time. He might be able to get Anderson to change his policies, but would it stick? He started typing a message on his tablet almost without realizing it, and, as he typed, the decision crystallized.

They were still arguing, or, rather, Kirsch was still trying to pry information from the director of the laser division, without success. There was no future in this. Ray stood close enough to be seen standing by the edge of the door and waited to be noticed.

Kirsch was facing away from the door, but Anderson noticed after just a few moments. "Mr. McConnell. Is there something I can do for you?"

"Yes, Bert." Kirsch started to leave, but Ray said to him, "Ethan, can you come by my office in fifteen minutes?"

Kirsch, still looking unhappy, replied, "Of course," and quickly left.

As Ray closed the door, Anderson started to explain. "Ethan Kirsch wants data on power requirements. I should have it for him . . ."

"Bert, I'm replacing you as head of the Laser Division. Amy will take over immediately."

"What?" Anderson looked at him, unbelieving, almost stunned.

"I've decided that you're not a good fit for this position. For the good of the program, I want you to turn over your files to Amy. She's on her way here now."

"Just like that? Wait. Did we make some mistake I haven't heard about?"

Ray shook his head. "No, Bert, it's more an aversion to making mistakes. We don't have the time to get everything right. I'd rather have you take a best guess than wait for the perfect answer."

"I've never done that!" Anderson exclaimed.

"And now is not the time for you to learn," Ray answered.

Anderson started to protest again, but someone knocked twice, then opened the door partway. A small woman with short black hair peered inside. Amy Sloan was Anderson's number two, a specialist in chemical lasers.

"Come in, Amy, and close the door." Ray's instructions and Anderson's expression both confused her, but Ray didn't take time for explanations. "I'm putting you in charge of the Laser Division. Do you want the job?"

She took a moment, processing the unexpected question. "What about Mr. Anderson?"

"You'll be replacing him. I need you running things in this division. Will you take the assignment?"

She drew a deep breath and said, "Yes."

Ray turned to Anderson. "The *Defender* program can still use your skills, Bert. Do you want to remain in the division?"

"With a demotion, you mean."

"You wouldn't be supervising anyone. It would still be useful work. Valuable work."

Anderson shook his head. "No." His answer sounded very final.

"Then turn over everything to Ms. Sloan and report to Colonel Evans for out processing. I'll make sure Northrop-Grumman gets a positive review of the time you spent here."

"I barely had time to unpack," Anderson mused.

"So it was good that we found out early."

Ray told Sloan, "After you finish the turnover, see me right away."

She nodded wordlessly, and Ray got out of Anderson's office. There was more that he could say, but it wouldn't help. Sometimes the best way to manage was to shut up.

As he headed back to his office, he realized his to-do list was more about people than spacecraft. Kirsch was probably waiting for him, and, after that, Sloan would be coming. She needed to make changes in the Laser Division, and Ray had to tell her how he wanted her to run things.

It was a radical change, and he'd virtually ignored Bert Anderson's feelings, but there wasn't time for a soft letdown. It felt like the right decision, but Ray still kicked himself for hiring Anderson in the first place.

He needed to know more about his division heads, spend more time with them, learn about them, and understand the person better, not just the résumé. Not at structured meetings but informally, at meals and such. The technical issues would be solved. After all, most of the people on his team were more qualified than he was. He imagined a new organizational chart, with the division heads interacting directly while he, not acting unless there was a problem, watched.

Surprised, Ray remembered Schultz's counsel about knowing his people. He wasn't surprised that Schultz was right, just at how right Schultz was.

National Aeronautics and Space Administration
Washington, D.C.
October 13, 2017

The timing hadn't been his idea. It was later than he'd like. Usually by five o'clock, he was headed home or to dinner in town. But this couldn't wait until tomorrow. He had to get to the bottom of this business, and Admiral Schultz was the man to talk to. The admiral's staff had set up a 2:00 call. Of course, that was California time.

A balding four-star admiral in navy khakis appeared. It had to be Schultz. Dr. Harold Matheson didn't waste time on introductions. "Admiral, I'd like to know why you think you can raid NASA at will."

"Dr. Matheson, I presume," Schultz remarked casually. His tone irritated Matheson even more than the latest e-mail from Peck. The admiral continued. "This isn't a raid, Doctor. The federal government is transferring people and property from one agency to another. I assume you've received Secretary Peck's confirmation of the original message. You'll note President Jackson's comment."

"I see one short sentence from the president's office, stating that NASA is to provide the requested material as soon as possible."

Schultz didn't back down. "I would think messages from the president's office would be taken as instructions, not simple statements."

"Those instructions will disrupt over a dozen NASA programs,

Admiral. And the equipment being transferred was bought with NASA money . . ."

"It's the U.S. government's money, and it's U.S. government equipment, even if NASA's using it." Schultz added, "The confirmation this morning made clear that NASA will receive funds to replace the equipment and personnel."

"Then use the money yourself to buy what you need. Don't tear my programs apart."

"There's no time for that, Doctor."

Matheson paused for a moment and studied Schultz. He obviously had no respect for NASA or Matheson's position. Time for a change in strategy.

Matheson smiled and spoke less forcefully. "Admiral, I understand that we both work for the federal government, but your 'space force' is making unreasonable demands on almost every part of NASA. If I knew more about your exact needs, I'm sure we could work out arrangements to share facilities. And maybe you don't need to take all the key people from a program."

"You know what we're doing—reactivating the *VentureStar* to lift GPS satellites into orbit. We're on a *very* tight schedule."

"Not a bad idea," Matheson agreed. "The technology may have advanced to the point where we can finally field a single-stage-to-orbit vehicle. But I have to wonder why it wasn't made a NASA program, or why a new 'space force' was created to operate it."

Matheson shrugged, then continued. "The government could have even left it as a private venture, just given Lockheed Martin the money to finish it. I wonder if it has anything to do with this." The director held up a hard copy of the *Defender* document. He was looking for a reaction from Schultz, but the only response was a deeper frown.

"It's been all over the SIPRNET for weeks, and there's been a lot of talk, but nobody took it seriously." His voice hardened. "I'm not a fool, Admiral. Brief me on the program."

"Not possible, Doctor. We have our reasons for what we are doing. Whether your guesses are right or wrong, you're aware we're in a crisis. My people are going to deal with the Chinese threat, and my mandate is to draw on any part of the federal government that has what we need."

Matheson argued. "I can find ways for NASA to help you."

"The best way for NASA to help is to tell your people to expedite our requests. I have to report my progress to Secretary Peck every night, and I'll urge him to speed up the transfer of that special funding to NASA."

Oh, he's good, thought Matheson. Schultz didn't have to mention that he would also report on NASA's cooperation or lack of it. But Matheson wasn't going to be bullied. Matheson didn't report to Peck but to the president.

"I'd appreciate that, and perhaps the secretary could speak to the president about my request to meet with him. Once I've made my case to the president, we'll see how many NASA resources are actually transferred to your 'space force.'"

"I think you should understand that the president is briefed by Secretary Peck daily on the progress of our program . . ."

"Which means it's certainly about more than just lifting GPS satellites into orbit," Matheson interrupted.

"I expect you to keep any speculation regarding our program to yourself," Schultz responded harshly. Then he added, "The secretary's meeting with the president this evening will include our next round of transfer requests. In anticipation of that, I think you'd like to contact Ms. Garvey and give her as much warning as possible."

"You mean Anne Garvey—the administrator at Dryden?" Matheson asked. "Well, at least you're telling me before you tell her. What are you asking for? One of the test rigs at the Flight Loads Laboratory? Maybe the whole Fabrication and Repair Facility?" He tried to make it sound facetious, silly, but some of his anger was there as well.

"Actually, we're taking over the entire facility. There are at least five resources at Dryden that the program can use immediately, and it's less disruptive to leave the personnel and equipment in place, since it's right there at Edwards. It's also quicker, since NASA's being so slow about the transfers."

Matheson sat quietly through Schultz's explanation and remained quiet for another moment but finally responded, almost automatically. "You can't possibly think they'll allow you to . . ."

"They've already approved it. I wanted to invite Anne Garvey to dinner tonight so we could get started, but I thought you'd want to call first. Of course, if she wants to stay with NASA, we'll have to work on her replacement."

"This is not . . ."

"I'm sure you'll want to speak to the president about this issue, as well as the earlier ones. I'll make my daily report to the secretary early and tell him about your concerns. He may be able to arrange a quick videoconference with the president. Can you stay there while I make the call?"

Matheson could barely speak. He finally managed an, "I'll be here," and Schultz broke the connection.

CNN News
October 13, 2017

Mark Markin's backdrop for his scoop was an artist's animation of the Chinese ASAT weapon, the "Dragon Gun" as it had been dubbed in the Western press. The artist had added a one-hundred-foot-long tongue of flame emerging from the barrel as a projectile spewed from the muzzle. Markin didn't know if it was accurate or not, and it really didn't matter. It looked dramatic and would get his audience's attention.

"With the crisis now into its second month and six GPS satellites destroyed, continued inaction by the United States has been taken as proof of their helplessness. Their refusal to act to protect their vital space assets has been puzzling.

"But the situation may not be as it seems. Presuming that the administration would not stand idle, my CNN team has been running to ground numerous rumors that the U.S. military is acting after all. Residents near the massive Edwards Air Force Base have reported heavy truck traffic at the front gate, and air force cargo aircraft have been arriving at all hours."

The image shifted to a picture of Edwards's front gate. "On a visit to the base yesterday, we noticed increased security, and we were not allowed to take any photographs while on the base. There are also portions of the base we were not allowed to visit at all. All these provisions were blamed on an increased terrorist threat, but the air force spokesman could not tell me the source of that threat.

"There have also been stories of hurried requests at defense contractors for personnel and equipment, but these could not be verified.

"All this could be attributed to the activities of the air force's new Aerospace Defense Organization; the timing of the activity closely correlates with the recent announcement of the ADO."

12

Rumors

Gongga Shan
Sichuan Province, China
October 13, 2017

The smoke was still swirling out of the muzzle when they left the command bunker. The party was small, just General Shen and President Pan. Their aides followed at a discrete distance.

Pan Yunfeng was the President of the People's Republic of China and the Chinese Communist Party General Secretary, a point General Shen continually reminded himself of as he answered the same questions he'd answered dozens of times before.

It was impossible to speed up the large cannon's firing rate. The ablative lining inside the barrel had to be replaced after each launch. During tests, two-thirds of the projectiles had been damaged when the lining was reused, and there had been one near burn-through. Better lining would be more durable but required exotic materials that were unavailable in sufficient quantity.

No, assigning more men would not get the barrel relined more quickly. Although a kilometer long, it was just three meters in diameter, so only a limited number of men could work inside. Furthermore, all the old lining had to be removed and the barrel surface cleaned before each section of new lining could be installed. To ensure a good seal between the ablative panels, one section had to be completed and inspected before the next could be added.

Unlike many of China's leaders, Pan was relatively young, in his late fifties. His hair was jet-black, and there was an energy about him that had been missing from some of the other men Shen had dealt with. His impatience personified the feeling of the entire Chinese Military Commission's leadership. Why was it taking so long?

Now Pan stood on the side of the mountain, nudging one of the used liners with his shoe. The ten-square-meter section was one quarter of a circle, and several centimeters thick. The outside was smooth, marked with attachment points and dimples, which Shen explained allowed for some flexing as the projectile passed.

The inside curve of the liner told the real story. The concave metal surface showed hints of the former mirror polish, but the heat and corrosive propellant gases had pitted the lining. Some of the pits were deep enough that a man's fingertip could easily fit in them. The different layers that made up the lining were visible, a mix of metal and ceramic and advanced fibers.

"Dr. Bull came up with this solution," Shen had explained. "The best steel in the world can't withstand the forces generated inside such a barrel when it fires. Instead, we just replace the liner after each launch."

"Which takes a week," the president remarked with a sour face.

"It's not wasted time, Comrade President. We use the necessary pause to do maintenance on the control system, test the breech, even improve the antiaircraft defenses." He pointed to a nearby hilltop, a new excavation on the side holding a massive billboard radar antenna.

"That radar is part of a new bistatic system designed to detect stealthy aircraft. We've also increased the depth of the surface-to-air missile belt and added more standing fighter patrols."

———

Later, in the general's office, Pan had questioned Shen even more, looking for any way to shave even a day off the interval between launches.

"We're concerned about the time it's taking, General. In any long-term campaign plan, we have to assume the enemy will take some action to counter ours. So far, the Americans have reacted as we expected. But I'm still concerned that the longer this goes on, the more likely they will depart from our expectations."

Shen listened respectfully. "I've seen the intelligence reports. I'm expecting that the Americans will do something eventually, of course, but by then we will have already won the first battle. In a few months, we will have our upgraded version of the *Tien Lung* ready. And when you approve the construction of the second Dragon Gun, we will be considerably less vulnerable."

"But what measures have you taken in the meantime?"

"You know about the Long March booster modifications to lift a more traditional antisatellite kill vehicle. And our intelligence services are blanketing the Americans and their allies." Shen tried to reassure the official. "All we have to do is deny them the use of space. It's easier to shoot spacecraft down than it is to put them up. Have the Americans tried to replace any of the lost satellites? Have they launched any satellites at all since we started our campaign?"

Pan didn't answer, but Shen knew they both saw the same information from the Ministry of State Security's Second Bureau, China's primary intelligence organization.

Shen pressed his point but was careful to keep his tone respectful. It didn't pay to argue the party's top official into a corner. "The Americans don't have any good choices. They'll either lose their valuable satellites or publicly acknowledge our rights as the regional power in East Asia. I think they'll wait until the last possible minute to do so, but they'll refuse to accept the inevitable for as long as they possibly can. When they do realize they're backed into a corner, they'll give in. Either way, America is weaker, and we become the ascendant power in this part of the world. No, Comrade President, time is on our side."

U.S. Space Force Headquarters
Edwards Air Force Base
Hangar
October 13, 2017

The call came while Ray was inspecting the hangar. He'd been walking around *Defender,* née *VentureStar,* watching the small army of engineers and technicians as they labored to finish assembling the vehicle. The shift supervisor flagged him over to his office, lifting the phone handset high. It was Schultz's voice, sounding resigned. "They've done it again. Check CNN."

Ray brought up the CNN Web site on the shift supervisor's unclassified computer. ". . . have confirmed the latest Chinese claim, made less than fifteen minutes ago. Another 'American targeting satellite' has been destroyed, and the Chinese renewed their promise to do the same to every American satellite unless they 'acknowledge China's regional interests.'"

The correspondent's face was replaced by a press conference, while his voice added, "In response to growing pressure to act, U.S. defense officials today announced a new program."

Ray's heart sank to the floor. Had some fool decided to take them public? Automatically, without thinking, he started pacing, while still watching the display.

The official at the podium spoke. "To deal with this new threat to American commerce and security, an Aerospace Defense Organization has been established under the direct command of General Michael Warner, Chief of Staff of the Air Force. The other services will also take part. Its mission will be to defend American space assets against any aggression. Here is General Warner, who will take a few questions."

By now Ray was walking quickly, almost jogging, making a bee-line to Schultz's office. In the background Ray heard Warner assuring the press that he had no intention of taking over NASA.

The admiral saw Ray and waved him in, with one eye still on the screen. The rest of the admiral's attention was on the phone. "I appreciate the need for security, Mr. Secretary, but the effects on staff morale should have been considered. A little warning would have let us brief them. And I must have your assurance this will not affect our resources. Thank you. I'll call tonight, as always, sir. Good day."

Schultz hung up, almost breaking the little handset as he slammed it into its cradle. "Peck assures me this new organization is a blind, designed to distract attention away from us."

"And reduce some of the heat DoD's been taking," Ray added cynically.

"For about one week, I'll bet." Schultz agreed. "As soon as the Chinese shoot down another satellite, they'll be all over the good general, asking him why he hasn't done something."

"And what about resources?" Ray asked, concerned.

"Well, he's going to need people, and money, and I have a hunch Warner's going to take his charge seriously. I'd have to agree with him, too. I'm a belt-and-suspenders kind of a guy. So he might get people or gear we need."

Ray asked, "Well, can we draw on his program? Use it as a resource?"

Schultz sharply disagreed. "No way. We don't want any links with them at all. It's bad enough they went public with this so soon. We might be able to hang the inevitable rumors concerning *Defender* on this new organization, but any contact between the two organizations carries the risk of being traced back to us. And if we start poaching, we'll make enemies. We may have the highest possible priority, but we can't throw our weight around with impunity. We've already used a two-by-four on Matheson; it's not wise to smack everyone who pushes back with a sledgehammer. There are people in every branch of the government who would love to see us fail, if they knew what we were really trying to do."

Ray sighed. "I'll put a notice on the splash page, and I'll speak personally to every department head, especially security."

Schultz's attention was drawn to the wall display. A new piece, labeled "Reaction," was on. A congressman was speaking on the Capitol steps to a cluster of reporters. Schultz turned up the volume. ". . . done the math, this new Aerospace Defense Organization will have to act quickly or we'll have nothing left to defend."

U.S. Space Force Headquarters
Edwards Air Force Base
Office Annex
October 13, 2017

The classroom was chock-full of new people, most of them Geoffrey Lewes's civilian support personnel. He stood in the back, leaning up against the wall, anxiously waiting for the security brief to be over and done with so he could get them started on their duties. For the past two days, Lewes had only had sixteen army quartermasters assigned to him, and while they were fantastic workers, there just weren't enough of them to meet all the growing requirements being placed on his department.

The *Defender* project workforce had expanded greatly during the last two days, to nearly one hundred and fifty engineers, technicians, and administrative personnel, and Mr. McConnell estimated it would be twice as large by the end of the following week. Add in the army and Marine security detachments and Lewes was looking at feeding and providing other services for almost fifteen hundred people when all was said and done. Even with a full staff of seventy-five civilian and military personnel, they were still going to be bustin' their rumps to keep up.

The former concierge smiled as he surveyed the class; he had some awesome plans for these new people. At first, the job had seemed daunting, but once he got started, his old habits as a first class petty officer kicked in, and he started delegating responsibilities to the army NCOs. They were good people and had risen to the occasion, allowing Lewes to do some long-range planning. Now, he had the manpower to bring some of those plans to fruition.

Lewes saw that the security presentation was starting to wind down. He knew he'd be up soon, and he started thumbing through the papers on his clipboard. A whispered, frustrating sigh escaped his lips; he'd left the duty roster back in his office. *Brilliant, Geoff,* he thought. *That's what I get for only having three cups of coffee.* Lewes signaled the briefer that he had to leave and would be back in five minutes. A quick nod from the security officer had Lewes bolting from the classroom.

Arriving at his office, Lewes found a young man inside, rummaging around his desk, looking for something. Irritated by the intrusion, Lewes challenged the individual. "Excuse me, but is there a reason why you're trashing my desk?"

The young man looked up, startled by Lewes's appearance, but he recovered quickly and explained. "My apologies, Mr. Lewes. I'm Glenn Chung. I'm with IT support conducting the system install. I was looking for your installation order to see what network access you're to have here."

"Network access?" questioned Lewes, his ire subsiding. "To my understanding, Mr. Chung, I'm only to have NIPRNET access, since I'm outside of the SCIF."

"Agreed, sir. But my work plan says I need to install a SIPRNET machine as well. Since that didn't make a whole hell of a lot of sense, I started looking for the install order to see what it had down."

Pressed for time, and with the conversation fueling his impatience, Lewes walked over to his computer terminal and grabbed a sheet of paper taped to the tower. "Is this what you're looking for?" he asked tersely, offering the paper to the young man.

Chung took the paper, scanned it briefly, and, as his face turned a nice shade of red, he said, "Yes, sir. That's it." He scanned it quickly. "And it doesn't mention a SIPRNET machine, which is good. Now that that's cleared up, I can have your unclassified machine hooked up and running in about thirty minutes."

"That's fine," replied Lewes as he grabbed the duty roster from the jumbled piles. "I'll be meeting with my new personnel for the next half hour, so I won't need my office. Just do me a favor and don't destroy the rest of it, please!"

Rayburn House Office Building
Washington, D.C.
October 13, 2017

Rutledge walked into his office wearing a huge smile. Not only did he get some face time on national television, the president had actually adopted one of his proposals. It didn't matter that he had shotgunned numerous vague ideas out to the public in his press statements. When all was said and done, he only had to point to the one that had been adopted. Yes, Congressman Rutledge was in a fine mood.

"That went better than I expected," Davis observed, pleased with his boss's performance. "Your tone was spot-on, and I loved that you didn't take credit for the idea on TV, gives the president a little room to maneuver, while at the same time the Washington insiders know who came up with it first."

"Yes, it did go well. But we can't rest on our laurels, Ben," stressed Rutledge. "I'll want a concept-of-operations brief for this new Aerospace Defense Organization from the air force as soon as possible. They probably don't have one fleshed out yet, so give them until Wednesday; then you can start nagging them."

Davis wrote down the date in his day timer, circling it with red marker. He'd give the Air Force Congressional Liaison Office a call once he and Rutledge were through.

"In the meantime, we must continue to go about the people's work.

What's on the docket for the rest of the day?" asked Rutledge, still quite pleased with himself.

"Since I didn't have a firm time for the news release, I kept the afternoon pretty light," Davis said as he glanced at his copy of the daily schedule. "The only item left is the Regal Composites issue. And before we start, I received yet another e-mail from Tony Partlow, the company's president. He's demanding that you look into why his air force contract has been suspended. He claims the lead contractor, Lockheed Martin, is refusing to take delivery of the first shipment of components and, more importantly, won't pay him for work completed. Partlow said he had to buy new equipment and hired on more people to fulfill the order, and he still has those bills to pay."

Rutledge frowned; he was easily aggravated when a large corporation like Lockheed Martin bullied a much smaller company in his district. This was especially true of DoD-related contracts, as there were only a few companies in the 3rd district that had successfully broken into that market.

"Did Lock Mart provide any rationale for their actions?" demanded the congressman.

"Not really. All Partlow was told was that the air force had suspended the contract, and everything was on hold until further notice."

"That's damn odd. Are there any air force programs in that much trouble to warrant suspension?"

Davis shook his head. "Not that I know of, Tom."

"How much is the contract with Regal Composites worth?"

"According to air force records, Regal has a ten-million-dollar contract to supply small composite components to Lockheed Martin for a classified program."

"Ten million dollars!?" howled Rutledge. "That's decimal dust!"

"That may be true in the grand scheme of things," remarked Davis sternly. "But in Kearney County, it is one of the largest DoD contracts, and to your constituents, it is certainly not a trivial matter."

Rutledge acknowledged his aide's reproach with a simple nod.

Davis was, of course, quite correct. The congressman had to look at this issue from the perspective of the people he represented, not from the overall national level. Sighing, Rutledge faced Davis and said, "All right, Ben, get with the Air Force Congressional Liaison Office and find out what program got suspended and why."

"Yes, sir. Immediately," Davis replied and turned to leave.

"Ah, Ben, one more thing. When did this suspension occur?"

Davis paused to think. "Three or four days ago, I believe. I can verify the date after I look at Partlow's e-mail trail."

"Please do so," ordered Rutledge. "If it is only a few days ago, then also ask the air force if the suspension had anything to do with the stand up of this Aerospace Defense Organization. The money to fund this new entity has to come from somewhere, and I have a sneaking suspicion General Warner is scouring the programmatic country-side for low-hanging fruit to get his new command started."

Davis's eyes widened as Rutledge laid out his argument. "Yes, of course! The two events are too close together for it to be just a coincidence!"

"I don't believe in coincidences when it comes to politics, Ben," responded Rutledge coldly. "These events must be connected. I need you to find me some proof they are. Follow the money, Ben."

U.S. Space Force Headquarters
Edwards Air Force Base
Housing Trailer Park
October 13, 2017

Glenn Chung yawned and stretched his weary body. It had been a very long day, and he was dog-tired. He would have normally been asleep by now, but he still had some work to do. He waited patiently as his roommate finished his snack, gathered his tools, and left for his shift. It had been a simple task to adjust the master list to get the two of them on alternate work schedules. Chung now had eight hours of uninterrupted time to finish his report and send it off to his "other" boss.

As soon as the trailer door to their room had closed, Chung jumped from his chair and carefully peered out the window. He waited till his roommate was out of sight, then locked the door and turned off most of the lights. Walking over to his dresser, he retrieved a small lockbox and opened it. Inside were half a dozen four-gigabyte secure flash drives. Grabbing one, Chung made a mental note to put in a request for more. He also picked up an envelope that contained a single piece of paper with Vietnamese characters on it. Returning to his desk, he plugged in the flash drive, entered the next password on the sheet, and began writing his report.

Shortly after the Edward Snowden revelation in 2013 that the NSA had successfully managed to monitor massive amounts of e-mail traffic, the Chinese intelligence service forbade its deep moles from using electronic means to deliver the fruits of their collection activities. Even encrypted e-mails, over a period of time, would have drawn unwanted attention to their operatives. So, the Ministry of State Security's Second Bureau fell back on the old Cold War tactic of using dead drops to transfer the data back to mainland China.

While this method had its own risks, they were judged to be less risky than any form of digital transmission. The risks were also mitigated by the use of encrypted, secure flash drives and languages other than English or Mandarin, in this case Vietnamese. So even if the flash drive were intercepted, determining its contents would be extremely difficult.

Chung brought up the Vietnamese character list and started typing, grimacing as he began his report. Even though he was fluent in the Vietnamese language, it was still slowgoing using a Western QWERTY-style keyboard with an on-screen overlay. But once he got started, it became easier, and his speed increased. He had to go through this mental recalibration every time he wrote in Vietnamese, which he usually did when writing letters to his father. Even though Chung's family originally hailed from Vietnam, they were of Hoa descent, a Chinese ethnic minority despised by the indigenous population.

His family had been driven out of Vietnam during the short and bloody border war with the People's Republic of China in 1979. Like hundreds of thousands of others, the Chungs were "encouraged," at gunpoint, to migrate back to China. Many of his father's family didn't survive the forced relocation, and the bitterness of the father had been handed down to the son. The younger Chung became fascinated with his ancestral past and developed a passion for all things Chinese. He dove into his studies of the history and culture of China with the same enthusiasm that he had for computers. When the Chinese intelligence service contacted him with a job offer, he was a willing recruit.

Chung summarized the movement of the *VentureStar* from its storage hangar on the Edwards main base to Building 151. The security personnel had taken extreme measures to hide the transfer, and Chung was confident that it was done during a gap in Chinese overhead-imagery passes. The last line was a bit gratuitous, but Chung was well aware that marketing one's abilities was a necessary evil, even in espionage.

He then provided an overview of the personnel roster, stating that of the 148 people involved with the project, approximately 105 were engineers and technicians—mostly senior ones. Furthermore, it was expected this number would double within the week. The security forces were growing even more rapidly, with at least two company equivalents providing physical security. A USMC general, last name Norman, had recently visited the facility and held discussions with the U.S. Space Force commander to enlarge the security contingent even further.

Chung then described the two main rumors as to *VentureStar*'s mission. The first was that the vehicle was needed because of its lift capacity. Supposedly a new GPS satellite was being designed at Air Force Plant 42 to incorporate stealth features and possibly armor. Supposedly this made the satellite too heavy for current U.S. space-lift vehicles to put more than one in orbit at a time. *VentureStar* was to carry multiple satellites to rapidly reconstitute their constellation. Since this mission was openly and freely discussed, Chung didn't think it was likely. Furthermore, as he had just left the Skunk Works, there had been no discussion at all of a heavily modified GPS satellite to make it more survivable.

The other rumor, and in Chung's opinion the more likely one, was that the *VentureStar* was being modified to become an armed space vehicle. The presence of a large number of laser engineers, and the fact that the *VentureStar* was placed in the hangar formerly used by the Airborne Laser Program, strongly suggested a laser-based armament. The new name of the vehicle, *Defender,* was also highly suggestive. He closed by adding that more definite information should be available in a few days.

After adding some scanned images of the U.S. Space Force's organization charts and an annotated Google Earth image outlining the facilities, Chung closed the flash drive. Double-checking to see that the data had been properly encrypted, he placed the flash drive in a small plastic faux rock and e-mailed his handler that a pickup would be waiting at the new primary drop point on the fifteenth hole of the Muroc Lake Golf Course. Even though the golf course was on Edwards AFB, it had been opened to the public in 2011. All one needed to do to gain access to the base was to schedule a tee time; a pass would be waiting for you at the main base entrance. It was very convenient for Chung and his associates.

13

Working the Problem

U.S. Space Force Headquarters
Edwards Air Force Base
Office Annex
October 24, 2017

"They're gouging us," complained Hank Nichols, the *Defender* project contracting officer. It was a critical position in a program that had to move fast with a minimum of paper shuffling. Ray had been lucky to find Nichols available, having just handed over an air force ordnance development program—on time and under budget.

Ray had worked with contracting officers at SPAWAR, of course, but Nichols was the best he had ever worked with, and he trusted Nichols's judgment without question. "I see your point, Hank, but is there anything we can do about it?"

Nichols's dark features were compressed in a scowl that had some anger in it as well as frustration. "It's the classic problem. They know we have to come to them because of the time and classification constraints. The stuff we're ordering now isn't that special. It's electronic components, aerospace materials, tools—things we might be able to get elsewhere once we'd read that company into the program and were prepared to pay the charges for rush delivery."

"Which would be almost as bad as the charges Lock Mart is slapping on us for rush delivery," Ray added. "Along with the lost time, because with two suppliers, we'd have to go through a bidding process."

Nichols nodded sadly. "And while I can't see anything illegal going on, they're making sure to bill us for any and every conceivable expense, and then multiplying it all by that 'rush' factor."

"So the Grand Unified Theory isn't about time and energy, it's about time and money," Ray joked.

"I know that money isn't supposed to be a constraint, not with us losing a half-billion-dollar satellite once a week, but Lockheed Martin is getting away with legalized bank robbery," Nichols growled.

Ray shook his head ruefully. "Nope. Banks have less money in them." He paused and considered his options. There weren't many. *Time to kick this one upstairs.* Rising, he said, "Let's tell the admiral about it. He should know what's going on, even if there's nothing we can do." McConnell didn't believe in passing problems up the chain if he could fix them himself, but he also liked to keep his boss in the loop.

With Nichols in tow, Ray walked the dozen steps to Admiral Schultz's office and knocked on the door frame. It was open, and Schultz was alone. He smiled and waved them in. "You look serious, Ray. You never look that unhappy when it's a technical problem."

"Sir, Hank came to see me about the charges Lock Mart's putting on their invoices. I don't think there's much we can do about it." He passed Schultz a single page. "That's a summary of their billing to the program so far."

"And we've only been running a few weeks," Schultz observed as he studied the figures. After a quick examination, he turned to the contracting officer. "Hank, this is good work. It shows we picked the right man for the job."

Schultz sat back for a moment and finally said, "You're right. It's beyond our power to solve—for those materials. But have you seen this?" He handed Nichols a thick document. While the contracting officer paged through it, Schultz explained to Ray that the conformal radar antennas Biff had discovered were being produced by a specialist contractor in Cincinnati as part of a compartmented air force program. After being contacted, the contractor had already begun the steps needed to fabricate the antennas for *Defender,* but they couldn't simply be mounted on the spacecraft's sides. They had to be "integrated," or connected to the existing sensor suite, requiring modifications to the radar's hardware and software. There were also changes that had to be made to the space frame and the cooling system to accommodate the antennas. Making sure the companies involved were working off the same plan was called "systems integration." It was always expensive, and when the plans were incomplete and the work had to be done quickly, it was doubly so—literally, in this case.

"It's their estimate for the materials and services to integrate those conformal radar arrays into *Defender.*" He turned to Nichols. "The figure you're interested in is on page ten."

Nichols nodded. "It was easy to find, since you circled it in red. I've just been trying to see if there's any justification for a figure that high—or a math error."

"We should be so lucky," Schultz grumbled. "But since you're here, and this is on my to-do list, you'll want to be here while I discuss this estimate with Mr. Weber."

Ray and Nichols shifted their chairs over to the side, while Schultz's assistant placed the call.

Henry Weber's face appeared almost immediately, smiling broadly. "Admiral Schultz! It's a pleasure."

"Henry, likewise," Schultz answered briskly. "I want to discuss the radar array-integration proposal."

"Understood, sir. We're ready to send engineers out to Ohio within hours of you giving us the go-ahead. We can get the paperwork sorted out once things are moving forward."

"Henry, I like your attitude, which is why I wanted to give you the news as soon as we decided ourselves. It turns out that we can do the integration in-house. There are some engineers at the Air Force

Research Lab that have done a lot of work with the conformal array on the B-2. We're bringing them on board, so we'll be scaling our requirement to you way back—just some materials, most likely."

Weber frowned. "Are you sure that's the best course? I can't speak to the people you're bringing in, but I can guarantee top-notch work, and we'll be there round the clock to make it come together."

"And bill us time and a half for all the overtime," Ray whispered to Nichols.

"Nope, Henry, this time we decided to do it ourselves. Why should we pay for your expertise when we have equally qualified people already drawing a government paycheck? We will be working closely with Lockheed Martin throughout this program, and I'll probably be calling you tomorrow about some new issue."

Weber could recognize a send-off and reluctantly said good-bye. The instant the screen went dark, Schultz smiled broadly, then turned to face Ray and Nichols. "Ray, I was going to find you and tell you about this, but I didn't think you'd have any objections. I had Captain Barnes do the legwork. I hope you're not upset."

"Not at all," Ray answered, surprised.

"It's my fault we even asked Lock Mart to do the work. Old habits die hard, and I was in a hurry. Too much stuff gets contracted out, and the contractors are more than happy to oblige our requests. I'm not out to punish Lock Mart for overcharging us, but from now on they'll have to think about what they're charging us for."

"Not that I'm against it, but this means more people for us to manage," Ray cautioned.

"It's more government people or more Lock Mart people. They'd still be part of the program. We can do just as good a job, and I believe in the end it will mean less administrative overhead by us, and less work for you, Hank."

"I can accept that," Nichols said, smiling.

U.S. Space Force Headquarters
Edwards Air Force Base
Office Annex
October 27, 2017

They all looked at the wall display in Schultz's office. It showed a spiderweb of lines linking boxes. One box at the left was labeled BE-GIN CONSTRUCTION, and a dozen lines angled out of it. All the lines eventually led to a single box at the end labeled LAUNCH. A dotted line with today's date ran vertically across the diagram. Colors indicated the status of a task, ranging from deep red to grass green. Over half the chart was red, and a lot of the red was on the wrong side of the line.

Ray McConnell had asked for the meeting, officially to "brief" Schultz, unofficially to ask him to make a decision Ray couldn't.

"We've made tremendous progress." Ray hated those words as soon as he'd said them. *Trite, Ray. Be specific.* Using his tablet, he started to highlight boxes on the chart.

"The kinetic weapon rack will be installed this week, and the mounts for the laser are being installed right now. Sensor integration is time-consuming, but we've got good people on it."

He came to one box labeled FABRICATE LASER PROPELLANT TANKS. "It's the one thing we couldn't plan for. Palmdale only had two fabrication units, and one has gone down. The parts to fix it will take two weeks to obtain and install."

Ray nodded in the direction of Hugh Dawson, who had become a de facto department head at Space Force HQ. "Weber has moved heaven and earth, but we've only got one fabricator and two tanks to make. This is what happens to the plan."

He tapped the data pad and the boxes on the chart shifted position. Lines stretched. One line, darker and thicker than the others, the critical path, changed to run through the PROPELLANT box.

"At least the heat's off the software," someone muttered.

The change added three weeks to the construction schedule. Luckily, Ray didn't have to say anything, because he couldn't think of anything to say. They'd struggled to cut corners, blown through bureaucratic roadblocks, invented new procedures. They'd carried positive attitudes around like armor against the difficulty of their task. Suddenly, he didn't feel very positive.

Schultz stared at the diagram, then used his own tablet to select the PROPELLANT TANK task. It opened up, filling the screen with tables of data and a three-dimensional rendering of the two tanks in the cargo bay of *Defender*.

Defender's laser needed fuel to fire, hypergolic chemicals stored as liquids and mixed to "pump" the weapon. The ABL-1 aircraft carried fuel for fifty shots, an extended battle. The current *Defender* design requirement was to carry fuel for twenty-five shots, enough for four engagements.

While the laser and its mirror could be taken out of its 747 carrier aircraft and used almost as is, the laser's fuel tanks had been built into the aircraft's structure. They were also the wrong size and shape for *Defender*'s bay. New ones had to be made.

Schultz grunted and selected the 3D CAD diagram. It was replaced by a schematic of the cylindrical tank that was not as neat and showed signs of being hurriedly drawn. The date on the drawing indicated that it was a month old. The multilayered tanks were built up in sections; then the end caps were attached.

"Reduce the number of sections in each tank," remarked the admiral. "That reduces the number of welds to be made."

"We can't make the individual sections larger," answered Dawson. "They come prefabricated from the manufacturer, and they're limited by the size of their fabrication jig."

"Then we reduce the number of sections," Schultz replied. "What if we cut the number of shots in half, three sections per tank instead of six?"

Ray heard an inrush of breath in the room. The laser was *Defender*'s main battery. Halving its firepower was a drastic step.

Schultz pushed his point. "Better a functional laser on time than a better laser too late. We can replace the small tanks with larger ones later."

McConnell nodded his head and started working. He ticked off points as he worked. "We'll save weight by carrying less laser fuel, but we'll need more structure surrounding the tanks. It's less weight overall, but it changes all the center-of-gravity calculations." He paused. "And we only carry enough reactants for two engagements."

While Ray worked on the design, he saw Dawson recalculating the fabrication time. The executive finished first, and Ray watched him send the figures to the main display.

The chart shifted again, shrinking the timeline, but not enough. They were still a week late.

Ray spoke up this time. "We need more time. If we can't raise the dam, let's lower the water. Launch another GPS satellite. That gets us a week. The SECDEF already knows we'll have to do this. We just need to do it sooner than we thought." That was a decision Ray knew he couldn't make. Would Admiral Schultz?

"At five hundred million a bird, that's a pretty expensive week," Biff Barnes remarked.

Schultz nodded, agreeing with Barnes. "There are political costs as well. The public won't know why. Even the people launching the satellite won't know they're buying time for us."

Ray persisted. "I know this will be a tough sell, but the bottom line is that there aren't any more corners that we can cut. We simply need more time." He hated sounding desperate, but he was.

The admiral sat silently for a minute. Ray prayed for everyone to be silent. Schultz knew the situation as well as anyone in the room. He didn't look pleased, but it wasn't a pleasant situation.

"This is where I start earning my pay, I guess," Schultz announced. "All right. I'll pass this up the line." He looked over the assembled group. "And I'll make it happen. But you should all understand the political capital that will be spent here. Even though the powers

that be knew we'd have to put more birds in orbit, doing this
again will be even more difficult. You'll get another week. Don't
waste it."

U.S. Space Force Headquarters,
Edwards Air Force Base
Office Annex
October 27, 2017

Glenn Chung's work took him all over Building 151, and indeed the
entire complex. New structures were being built to house work spaces,
although most were "open." Chung had classified the *Defender* program areas into two types. His badge would get him into "open" areas without any problem. This included all the new housing, the mess
and recreational areas, and the lower two floors of the annex. He could
move through them at will. He still needed his clearance to be there,
but they didn't have what he was looking for.

The hangar and the two floors of the office annex were "secure,"
and if he wanted to go in there, he needed a written order from Ms.
Crane, his division chief, and an escort. Still, he was now one of the
senior network techs. Not only was he skilled, he had the advantage
of having set up many of the network nodes, so when something
wasn't working, he was usually the one called on to fix it. In fact, he
made it his business to be available.

Like he was doing now, tracing a fault on the third floor. This gear
was still new enough that they had more than a few cases of "infant
mortality": new components that broke down shortly after they were
put into service. The rule of thumb was that if it lasted thirty days,
it would probably last years without failure. Not that it did him any
good, he grumbled.

The one bright spot was his "escort," June. While she might prevent him from physically stealing any classified material, she didn't
appear to understand what he was doing at all. She'd asked a few

friendly questions, but his answers had only confused her further. Finally, she stopped asking and retreated to a nearby chair, where she could make sure he didn't stuff something under his shirt.

Chung had the server cabinet open and was using his test gear. At the same time, he checked on the well-being of one of his special network "upgrades." The occupants had carefully removed anything classified and locked it away before letting him in the room, but his little silicon eavesdropper had been faithfully recording everything that passed through the server. But there was a problem. According to his test gear, it was connected to the hub that had failed.

A bad hub wasn't an unexpected problem, and he'd brought a spare. The question was, did he reconnect his small friend to the replacement hub? His original plan had been to wait a while longer before removing it at some convenient opportunity. But he hadn't expected the opportunity to come so quickly, and he certainly hadn't intended to attach it to a bad hub.

He couldn't leave the device in place indefinitely. Chung wasn't the only network tech anymore, and if it was found by someone else, he was done for.

They said the network had been "flaky" for a few days. His special attachment had been there for almost a week. Was that enough? Possibly, but he wouldn't know for certain. Would he get another chance? Possibly, but then again maybe not. He weighed the probabilities as he replaced the faulty hub. The only thing he could be sure of was that his special device had not caused the breakdown. His test equipment confirmed a genuine hardware failure—a bad switch in the hub.

Finally, he decided, and disconnected the cable with the eavesdropper. Coiling the cable and palming the device, he made sure June was looking away and stowed it in his toolbox with other electronic clutter. A small part of him was ashamed and condemned his cowardice, but a much larger part reminded him that, to succeed, he had to remain undetected.

He would hope that what was already recorded would be enough.

U.S. Space Force Headquarters
Edwards Air Force Base
Office Annex
October 27, 2017

Barnes knocked on McConnell's open door, then stepped in almost without pausing. Everything was done quickly, Barnes thought, with the formalities honored, but only barely.

Ray, in the middle of a phone call, waved him in and pointed to a folding chair, then said into the phone, "I'll call you back." He hung up and turned to face Barnes.

Expecting to be questioned about the technology survey, Barnes started to offer his tablet, but Ray waved it back.

"You're close to done, aren't you?"

"Yes," agreed Biff. "We've already started to receive some material. But there's a lot of follow-up work to be done."

"That's old business, Biff. I need you to turn it over to someone else as soon as you can." Ray paused but kept looking at him. "We need you to be the mission commander for the flight."

Biff didn't say anything. He absorbed the information slowly. Although he'd wondered in his few spare moments who would get to fly the mission, he'd assumed NASA would supply rated astronauts.

Did he want the job? Well, hell yes. Biff suddenly realized how much he wanted to fly in space again, and on what would be a combat mission. He knew he could do it. He was a fighter pilot, after all.

Ray pressed a key on his tablet. "Here's a list of the prospective flight crew candidates." Biff heard his tablet chirp and saw the file appear. He opened it and scanned the list as Ray explained.

"Most are already here, a few are not, but all met the criteria Admiral Schultz and I came up with. You'll need six: a mission commander, a pilot, a copilot and navigator, a weapons officer, a sensor officer, and an engineer. We listed all our requirements. If you disagree with any . . ."

"Your name isn't here," Biff interrupted.

"What? Of course not. It's not the whole team, just the . . ."

"No," Barnes insisted. "You should be the engineer. You're the guy who's overseeing *Defender*'s construction. You know her better than anyone else."

Ray was as surprised as Barnes had been. "What?"

"Articulate answer, Ray." Barnes grinned. "Look at it this way. It's the ultimate vote of confidence. You build it; you fly in it."

He couldn't say no. "This only fulfills one of my lifelong ambitions," Ray answered, a little lightheaded.

"One of mine, too. I get to boss you around."

U.S. Space Force Headquarters
Edwards Air Force Base
Office Annex
October 27, 2017

Ray stayed late that evening, even later than usual. Biff's training schedule was going to tear a huge chunk out of each day. Not only were there obvious things like joint training sessions with the other crew members, but Barnes had insisted on a physical training schedule. Ray was in pretty good shape, but the new mission commander insisted on a higher standard.

So Ray was trying to find more work he could delegate, trying to look ahead now that many of the critical design decisions . . .

A knock on the door frame sounded unusually loud. At this hour, the annex was relatively quiet, and he wasn't expecting visitors. Startled, he looked up to see Jenny. She was holding a small bottle of champagne and two glasses. Her expression was hard to read. She wasn't smiling. In fact, her face was almost a mask, completely impassive.

"So I heard you've been added to the crew. I think a celebration is in order."

"So Biff made the announcement?" Ray asked.

She shrugged, and walked toward the desk and sat down. "He really didn't have to. He told the individual crew members first, and the grapevine picked it up instantly. By the time they made the general announcement, everyone knew who was flying and who wasn't."

By now, she'd set the two glasses on his desk and was removing the wire over the cork. It came out neatly, with a small pop. As she filled the glasses, she continued. "I found out from Trudy and Van in my section, when they congratulated me and asked if I was worried about my boyfriend going into space like that. I told them I really hadn't thought about it very much. What else could I say? That was the first I'd heard."

Having filled the second glass, Jenny reached over the desk and poured the rest of the bottle over Ray's head.

Ray was so surprised he didn't move until the bottle was almost empty. Spluttering, he pushed back in his chair, out of range. He looked at Jenny, who had a faint smile on her face. After a short pause, he said, "I think I've made a huge mistake."

Her annoyed expression spoke louder than words. Quickly, he added, "No, I'm sure I have. In my preoccupation with my new role, I've totally neglected my personal relationships, which are far more important than flying in space."

She set the bottle on his desk and sat back down. Smiling, Jenny spoke firmly. "You just need to remember your priorities, Ray." Ray concentrated on listening while he blotted his head with some paper towels. "I want *Defender* to succeed, and I understand how important she is to you." Her voice hardened. "But I won't let her take my place."

"I wouldn't let that happen," Ray protested.

"It did today," she insisted. "Just a little," she said, tapping the empty bottle. "I should warn you, I have a jealous streak."

"I promise. I'll do better. You're worth it."

She picked up the glasses and handed one to him. "Then let's drink to a successful flight and your safe return."

14

Escalation

CNN News
November 3, 2017

Mark Markin stood in front of a large flat-panel display with a digital depiction of the earth and the U.S. GPS satellite constellation; there were now eleven glowing red *X*s on the screen. The reporter pointed his finger toward the newest *X*.

"At eleven forty-five A.M. Eastern Standard Time, the Chinese Dragon Gun claimed yet another victim. A GPS satellite, space vehicle number fifty-five, was destroyed when a *Tien Lung* projectile detonated near the satellite as it passed over the Pacific basin. This would have been the ninth satellite neutralized by the Chinese supergun, but a source close to the GPS program has told CNN that, in reality, the U.S. has lost eleven satellites. According to our source, who spoke on the condition of anonymity because they weren't authorized to speak to the press, the two reserve satellites were probably destroyed early on in China's space antiaccess campaign."

The graphic on the display changed behind the reporter, showing the periods during the day when U.S. precision-guided munitions that depended on GPS would be degraded due to a lack of satellites. There were now two four-hour windows over China during which an airborne GPS receiver would lack 3D coverage, resulting in navigation errors that could throw off a weapon's accuracy by hundreds of meters. One window covered half of the nighttime hours.

"The gap in GPS coverage during the night has had a significant impact on U.S. contingency planning," continued Markin. "Without their ability to use GPS-directed precision-strike cruise missiles or other weapons from stealth aircraft, the U.S. Air Force and Navy are effectively hamstrung. Even with the formation of the U.S. Air Force's Aerospace Defense Organization, the U.S. continues to experience a rapid decline in its ability to deter China from invading Vietnam.

"However, last week the appearance of a name— *Defender*—caused the security dam to burst. We go to our Holly Moore in Washington, D.C., for more on this remarkable revelation. Holly?"

Holly Moore, CNN's White House correspondent, handled this piece, rather than Markin, since it covered the political implications more than the military ones. She stood on the wind-whipped U.S. Capitol steps. The image lasted only seconds, though, before being replaced by the cover of the *Defender* document.

"Late last week, CNN obtained a copy of a detailed design for an armed spacecraft reportedly intended to attack targets in space and on the ground. According to the unidentified source who posted it on the Web, it was widely distributed in classified DoD circles."

"Based on the aborted *VentureStar* spacecraft, the design is reportedly equipped with advanced radar and laser sensors, guided-ground-attack weapons, and a high-power laser from the air force's canceled Airborne Laser Program.

"No one in the defense department would comment on the document, and everyone referred us to the new Aerospace Defense Organization. We also tried to contact Mr. Ray McConnell, listed on the cover as the lead designer, but all attempts to locate him have failed. There is another list of names on the inside, all described as contributors to the document. The few CNN has been able to locate have either denied knowledge of *Defender* or refused to comment.

"Some sources have linked *Defender* with the mysterious activity at the South Base complex on the gigantic Edwards Air Force Base. Since the initial report broke last week, security at the South Base complex has been described as tightened to extraordinary lengths. Our repeated requests to visit the complex have been denied.

"Opposition to *Defender* appeared immediately after the report of its existence was aired. Some individuals are opposed to the blatant militarization of space. Others don't believe the spaceship can be built in time to do any good, and others claim it can't be completed at all due to insurmountable technological problems. All are asking for an accounting of the undoubtedly high costs. Links to Web sites opposing *Defender,* as well as the original design document, are available on our Web site.

"Congressman Tom Rutledge, Democratic representative from Nebraska, spoke on the Capitol steps moments ago."

The image changed to show a tall, photogenic man with a cloud of salt-and-pepper hair fluttering in the fall wind. "As a member of the House Armed Services Committee, I intend to find out why Congress was not consulted on this wasteful and extremely risky project. The investigation will also deal with the administration's continued inability to cope with this crisis. In a little over a month, our *expensive* and *valuable* GPS satellites will be unable to provide our military with the navigation information the 'American way of war' demands. That means we either back off—and need I remind everyone we don't have a formal defense treaty with Vietnam—or we foolishly press on at the expense of many of our young people's lives."

Moore's face reappeared on the screen. "Ominous words, indeed, from Congressman Rutledge. Now back to Mark with a related piece on the congressman's comments. Mark, over to you."

Markin came back into view with the famous Dragon Gun animation sequence running in the background. "Thank you, Holly. Not long ago, I interviewed Mr. Michael Baldwin, an acknowledged expert on the NAVSTAR GPS system. I asked him how long the system would be able to function under continued Chinese attacks."

Baldwin was a slim, long-faced man in his fifties with a short gray haircut and a neatly trimmed beard. He sat against a backdrop of jumbled electronic equipment and computer screens. He spoke with ease, secure in his knowledge. "The constellation's been severely affected. There are few places on Earth now where the military can't reliably get the kind of three-dimensional fix it needs for precision-guided munitions or even accurate navigation for any airborne vehicle. For the most part, civilian users are largely unaffected, as they don't require such accuracy. However, people who travel in mountainous areas and the airline industry have seen significant degradation in the navigation data.

"In the past, this would be more than a mere inconvenience. We've come to expect that GPS service will always be there, like the telephone or electricity, but, as with these industries, there is now more than one provider, and the European Galileo system has taken up the slack caused by the loss of GPS satellites."

"Then why can't the U.S. military use the European system if it is still healthy?"

Baldwin shook his head. "It doesn't work that way, Mark. The U.S. weapons don't have the ability to receive the signals from the Galileo satellites. They could be modified, but that would probably take more time than we have. And besides, the Galileo system is far more prone to jamming than the GPS military channels. So, even if we did modify our weapons, it wouldn't change the situation."

"How long before the GPS network ceases to be any use at all?"

"If the Chinese continue shooting down satellites at the rate of one a week, by early to mid-December, the U.S. military will not have any 3D coverage during the nighttime hours, and for a significant portion of the daytime as well. This would all but cripple our precision-engagement capability."

Markin's face became stern; his next question was a loaded one. "Some pundits are saying that if we can't destroy the gun with Tomahawk missiles or air strikes, we should use nuclear weapons. What do you think of that?"

Baldwin seemed surprised by the question but answered it quickly. "No U.S. citizen has been harmed, and the degradation in the GPS system hasn't really impacted our economy. It's only affected our military's ability to fight. In my opinion, it's almost impossible to justify the use of nuclear weapons in this situation. Unfortunately, the Dragon Gun is too deep inside Chinese territory for anything but a ballistic missile or a stealth bomber to reach, and without accurate navigation data, it would be extremely difficult to get a hit. I'm personally against the use of nuclear weapons. I don't know anyone who is even seriously suggesting it." He grinned. "But, in the final analysis, we have precious few options other than walking away from this crisis. I'm hoping this *Defender* is for real."

Markin asked, "Can we do anything to reconstitute the constellation?"

"Not until they can protect the satellites somehow," Baldwin replied firmly.

"So we shouldn't launch any replacement satellites right now?"

The expert shook his head vehemently. "Adding more sitting ducks to the barrel won't solve anything. It would be lunacy to even consider the idea."

U.S. Space Force Headquarters
Edwards Air Force Base
Office Annex
November 4, 2017

"I'm glad you're such a cautious, anal-retentive individual, Ray." The security director's face was grim, but his tone was light and triumphant. "What you meant as a configuration-control mechanism has enabled us to track this document as it wormed its way through the SIPRNET."

He stood before McConnell's wall display, which held a diagram. It repeated the same symbol, an icon-sized image of the *Defender* document file. Starting at the left, it was labeled MCCONNELL. Line segments connected it to other nodes, each labeled with a name and sometimes a date.

"CNN either took off the version number, trying to hide the source, or it was removed before it was posted. But the design-data tables are so full of numbers, the poster missed the version number embedded in said tables. We were able to determine which version had been compromised and its creation date in half a day. Checking your SIPRNET e-mail records, we were able to find out who initially received this version of the design and when they received it. We know when it was posted on the Space News blog, and we started running down the e-mail trail with the help of NSA. We got a lot of cooperation from some of the addresses, and not much from others, which in itself helped us focus our search."

Ray had listened to the presentation with both anger and fear. CNN's scoop had devastated morale. Secrecy had been part of their strength. It allowed them to move quickly, unhindered. Now friend and enemy alike could interfere with a timetable that had no room for delay.

He knew *Defender* was a long shot. The Chinese now knew where they were. Could they take some sort of counteraction? Even well-meaning friends now could derail the project.

The army colonel handed Ray his tablet PC. "Here's the report. I've found two individuals, one at SPAWAR and the other at NASA. Both received copies of this version, third- or fourth-hand, and according to the investigators I sent out, both have openly criticized *Defender*. One, at NASA, was quoted saying, '*Defender* had to be stopped. It could cripple NASA's plans for developing spacecraft technology and would lead to the militarization of space.'"

Ray nodded, acknowledging the information but not responding immediately. The colonel respected his silence, but obviously waited for a reply. Ray knew who leaked the design document; it didn't take Sherlock Holmes to solve this case. He wanted to strike out at the individual, but there was little he could do.

Ray stated flatly, "I think you'll find that Matheson, the NASA director, is the one who compromised our little project. He was more than angry about the demands we put on NASA. My understanding is that he was absolutely livid when the president told him to sit down, shut up, and play ball. Since the original *Defender* document was never classified, it's not a crime to release it."

"Dr. Harold Matheson is one of the two people I referred to. But anyone who slipped the document to the press certainly isn't our friend," countered Evans. "By exposing us, they've hurt our chances of stopping the Chinese. I'd say that's acting against the best interests of national security."

"By the time we indicted him, it would be moot. Our best revenge will be to succeed." Part of Ray didn't agree with what he was saying, but he was trying to think with his head, not his emotions.

"I could leak his identity to the press. It wouldn't be hard to cast Dr. Matheson as a disgruntled federal employee who disobeyed a direct order from the president and took matters into his own hands. Fight one leak with another," suggested the colonel.

Ray shook his head slowly. "Tempting, but that would open the door to more accusations and counteraccusations—in other words, more attention. I need you for other things now. All our energy has to be devoted to getting *Defender* in space. We need to let this incident die down and buy us a few weeks, if we can. In the meantime, we mustn't provide anything that corroborates this story. No sense pushing the cover story anymore; it's been totally discredited. Complete silence is probably our best defense."

Evans wasn't convinced. "That may work on the home front. But we have to assume the Chinese now know of *Defender*'s existence and where she's parked. They may try to sabotage or even attack us at this location."

"Then we increase our defenses accordingly," Ray declared. "If we need to bring in a Patriot battery or a division of Marines, then that's what we'll do."

Evans nodded. "I'll increase our patrols immediately. I'd appreciate it if you'd have Admiral Schultz request additional support form General Norman. I'll do the same up the army side."

"Thanks, Jack. I'll pass on the request when I report to the admiral." Ray was certain Schultz wouldn't be thrilled with his decision, but he knew it was the best they could do given the circumstances.

As the colonel left, Ray started to get up; he had to report the unpleasant results of their investigation to his boss. But Schultz would want to know what they were going to do about the exposure, and Ray knew that merely increasing their security wasn't the full answer.

Opposition to *Defender* was forming incredibly fast—anti-*Defender* Web pages already? Ray had implicitly assumed that there wouldn't be a lot of resistance, but that view was based on his perception of the power of a presidential order and secrecy. With the project now fully out in the open, all bets were off. The president could only do so much, particularly if Congress got directly involved. A congressmen or senator could demand the program be stopped or delayed for review. Or, worse, if both houses were sufficiently angry enough, they could withdraw funding.

Only then did he recall Schultz's cynical warning during their flight out to Edwards. Ray had been so focused on standing up the U.S. Space Force and getting *Defender* ready that he hadn't thought about the implications of a leak objectively. Ray's single-mindedness to get his dream into space had given him a bad case of tunnel vision; nothing else mattered but the technical challenge. Now the entire command had to hustle to play catch up due to his lack of foresight.

The war in space against a hostile nation had morphed into an information war at home. Anyone who'd seen the news knew the media would pick up and report anything that was fed to them. They were like sharks in a feeding frenzy. Well, it was time for him to do some feeding of his own. Ray remained convinced that people formally associated with the project had to lay low and stay quiet, but that didn't preclude him from using proxies, sympathetic to their cause, from speaking up for them. It wasn't his preferred method of debate, but the lack of any other option left him with few choices.

He opened the e-mail address book on his unclassified computer. Ray had contacts all over the defense, space, and computer communities. They'd helped him get *Defender* started. Now he needed their assistance to fend off the detractors. *Defender* needed some defending.

Pulling up a new e-mail, he started typing in the subject box. "*Defender* needs your help . . ."

Gongga Shan
Sichuan Province, China
November 4, 2017

Shen had insisted on having the Central Military Commission meeting here, in the shadow of the mountain. Ignoring the recall order to Beijing had seemed suicidal to his staff, but the general knew that, once away from the mountain, any flaw or error here could be blamed on his neglect. So far, the *Lung Mu* had worked flawlessly, but that had just made him a more important target to his adversaries within the party.

Friends in Beijing had kept him informed. There were those who resented his success, even if it helped China against the United States. There were those who wanted to discredit him, weaken him, and then take over the gun for their own political agendas. Some party members simply thought he had too much power. Others complained the president was just echoing Shen's words. Most thought he had undue influence on China's direction during the current crisis.

He'd been able to fabricate a reasonable excuse for remaining on the mountain, and to his relief Dong Zhi had backed him up. Shen had expected his chief scientist to do so, but the first rule of Chinese politics was that trust was like smoke. When it was there, it blocked your vision. And it would disappear with the first puff of wind.

Instead, Dr. Dong and the rest of the CMC members now sat in the main observation gallery, while an intelligence officer briefed them on the new American spacecraft.

The army colonel had passed out edited copies of the original design document, annotated in Chinese with an engineering analysis attached. He'd reviewed the systems—the laser, the projectiles, and the advanced sensors. Shen, Dong, and the other technical people present were fascinated by the vehicle's complexity, as well as the Americans' audacity. It was a potentially dangerous craft. Shen noticed that the politicians spent more time gazing out the window than watching the presentation. Had they already heard it? Or were the exact details too mundane, unimportant?

The colonel finished his briefing, but the CMC members wanted definite answers. Was the design real, or fiction? Was it merely an attempt at disinformation to buy time? When would it be ready? Would it interfere with the overall Vietnam campaign? How could it be countered?

The colonel declined to make any definite conclusions. "I apologize that I can't be more specific at this time. We're still analyzing the information we've collected. As you can see, it is a very complex topic, and we've only had a week to review the leaked document."

"It looks like pure fantasy to me," blurted General Jing, Commander of the People's Liberation Army Air Force. "It would have taken years of effort to get to a point where a launch would be possible in only a couple of months. We've heard *nothing* about this vehicle until recently." The tone of the general's voice highlighted his irritation.

"That's not entirely true, General," countered General Zheng, Director of the Armaments Department. "The General Staff's intelligence arm has kept an eye on the *VentureStar,* and everything indicates it was laid up in storage." Turning back to the briefer, Zheng asked, "Colonel, how confident are you that this vehicle is actively being worked on?"

"Comrade General, four days before this document appeared on the Internet, the Ministry of State Security's Second Bureau received an intelligence report from one of our deep operatives in the American Lockheed Martin Corporation. This operative recently took a new position in a top-secret contract that, fortuitously, turned out to be the reanimated *VentureStar* program."

Shen's ears perked up. He knew exactly whom the colonel was referring to, a capable young man of Chinese heritage who had provided a large quantity of information on the U.S. GPS satellites. The revelation annoyed Shen, since he was completely unaware of this latest report, or that the source had even changed jobs. He listened carefully as the intelligence officer continued.

"The operative reported that the United States has formed a new branch of their military, the U.S. Space Force, which was created secretly less than a month ago. This new military arm is being rapidly stood up and its headquarters is located on the South Base complex at Edwards Air Force Base.

"Our source hasn't had much of an opportunity to collect any detailed data since the headquarters building is being reconstructed. However, he has confirmed that the *VentureStar* has been moved to the large hangar in Building 151 and that the technical director is the same Ray McConnell identified as the lead designer on the leaked document. Based on records from the personnel office, hundreds of engineers and technicians are being brought in to work on this vehicle. The large cadre of specialists associated with the canceled Airborne Laser Program supports the conclusion that the *VentureStar,* or this *Defender,* will be an armed military spacecraft."

Zheng nodded. "Much of what you are telling us, Colonel, is consistent with the American press reports of mysterious activity on the Edwards base. Given the presence of this McConnell individual and what appears to be some internal friction between the U.S. space agencies, I believe you have sufficient grounds for your conclusions."

Jing remained unimpressed. "I agree with you, Comrade General, but I still haven't heard how the Americans can possibly get this vehicle into space within a month. And even if they can, what is the risk to our campaign in Vietnam?"

Shen finally spoke up; there was no risk in stating the obvious. "If the American design works as described, it will have the capability to interfere with our antisatellite attacks."

"And the chance of that happening?" Pan demanded abruptly. As the president of China, and first secretary of the Chinese communist party, Pan Yunfeng also held the position as chairman of the CMC and led all the meetings of this important conclave.

"Impossible to say, Comrade President. However, this is not something they can build in just a few months. While the *VentureStar* space vehicle is largely complete, it had not been fully certified for service and has been in storage for almost a decade. It will have to be adapted to this new role, and a number of the systems discussed in the document have yet to be fielded."

"Is it possible that this is a disinformation campaign?" a skeptical Pan asked the briefer.

The colonel shook his head vehemently. "Very unlikely, sir. The American administration is suffering intense criticism because of this now-exposed 'secret project.' The fact that the leak appears to have come from another entity of the American government has only compounded their embarrassment. They've gained nothing from the revelation. Combining this with the report from our operative convinces us that this *Defender* program is real. Whether or not the Americans will be able to field it when they say they will is a matter of conjecture."

"Then what do they hope to gain by doing this?" demanded a frustrated Pan.

Shen replied, his tone light, almost casual. "Oh, they're building this *Defender*, all right, but there will be very little to defend once it is operational, perhaps within a year. By that time, the new *Tien Lung II* projectile will also be ready. It has stealth features, a more energetic warhead, armor, and it's semiautonomous." Shen smiled. "We'll use the Dragon's Mother to keep them on the ground. We can destroy anything they launch."

"General Shen!" shouted Pan angrily. "I don't think I need to remind everyone here that the Americans have an annoying habit of doing what people say is impossible!"

Shen was taken aback by the president's sharp remark. He had badly misjudged the president's tolerance for risk; someone had gotten to him and fueled his doubts.

"Comrade Generals, I keep hearing why you believe the Americans can't do this. What I'm not hearing is what could happen to our plans if they surprise us and do the impossible."

There was an awkward silence as a number of the senior officers looked down at the table; Shen struggled to find a response.

"Comrade President, if I may?" spoke up General Li, the Chief of the General Staff and Commander of the People's Liberation Army.

"Yes, General Li."

"Sir, I agree with General Shen's overall technical assessment. If the Americans successfully build and launch the *Defender* vehicle, it will interfere with our attacks on their GPS satellites and they will be able to repair their constellation. Perhaps not to full capability, but enough to cause us considerable hardship with their stealth aircraft and precision-guided weapons."

Shen stared intently at the chief of staff. Where was the man going with this?

"More importantly, if they can reduce the effectiveness of our antisatellite campaign, it will be a huge psychological boost to the Americans' psyche; they will dig in their heels and fight. The impact on the Vietnam campaign would not be in our favor."

Shen saw the president, vice president, and minister of defense all nodding. A number of his senior officer colleagues also seemed to be weighing Li's words carefully.

"And your recommendation, General?" inquired Pan.

"We give the Americans another shock, before they are even ready to attempt to counter General Shen's excellent efforts. By striking them before they can react to our last move, we deal another blow to their psyche. At the very least, it will plunge them into confusion and doubt; at best, it may even break them."

"And how do you propose we deal this shocking blow, General?" Zheng asked.

"By moving up our invasion of Vietnam."

The meeting broke into a chaotic rumble as the CMC members rapidly debated the idea with their neighbors. Pan had to shout to be heard above the noise.

"Comrades! Silence, please!" Once the din had subsided, he looked toward General Li. "I appreciate the boldness of your suggestion, General, but are we ready to do that?"

Li shrugged slightly. "There is some risk, of course, Comrade President, but I believe it is minimal. Four out of the five group armies are fully deployed and in position. The South Sea Fleet has the equipment for its marine division already loaded on their amphibious assault ships, and the air force and Second Artillery have the vast majority of their forces in place. The rest can be moved up in a matter of days, perhaps a week at most. We could launch the initial strikes as early as tomorrow."

"No!" shouted Shen, jumping to his feet. "The Americans still have nearly half the day with adequate 3D coverage. By attacking now, our losses will be increased! Everything is going according to plan. This response by the Americans isn't sufficient justification to abandon it!"

There were shocked expressions on many of the generals' faces. Pan scowled with anger at Shen's outburst. But it was the deadpanned Li who delivered the decisive blow. "I do not recall General Shen being a member of this commission."

Immediately, Shen knew he had been outmaneuvered by the army commander, the most powerful military member on the CMC. Quietly, Shen sat back down. Nothing he could say would make the situation any better.

"Does any *member* have additional comments or questions?" asked

Pan. No one spoke. Even the hesitant Jing remained silent. The die had been cast.

"Very well. Generals, have your staffs issue the orders to begin the invasion of Vietnam at the earliest possible time. We need to move quickly if we are to succeed."

15

Invasion

National Aeronautics and Space Administration
Washington, D.C.
November 6, 2017

Harold Matheson watched with smug satisfaction C-SPAN's coverage of the House of Representatives debate on the U.S. Space Force. Many of the representatives were visibly angry. Even the president's allies were upset by his unilateral and secret establishment of a new branch of the armed forces. But by far and away the most vocal opponent of the president's "unprecedented" move was Congressman Thomas Rutledge from Nebraska.

"Mr. Speaker, while I'm sympathetic to the president's desire to deal proactively with China's unwarranted attack on our GPS satellites, this is by no means sufficient justification for his actions. The U.S. Space Force was established without consultation with my colleagues in either the House or Senate.

"Furthermore, this new branch of the armed forces has been funded without the direct involvement of Congress, which is completely unconstitutional! The framers of the Constitution invested in the representatives of the people the 'power of the purse,' the power to tax and spend public money for the national government. The president and the executive agencies are only empowered to make suggestions or requests." A sharp round of applause forced Rutledge to pause. He raised his hand, asking for silence.

"The president may be entirely correct that the time has indeed come for a space force to defend our interests in the heavens, but the way in which he went about doing it is entirely incorrect. Now, I've heard excuses from the president's supporters that speed and secrecy are absolutely critical in this case. Again, that may in fact be true; however, they do not excuse the absence of a proper discussion with the U.S. Congress. The ends do not justify the means!"

Matheson clapped his hands along with many of the other representatives on the screen as Rutledge stepped down from the podium. *The man has hit the nail squarely on the head,* thought the NASA director. Maybe now the president will listen to reason and rein in Schultz and his fanatical minions.

The buzzing of his phone interrupted Matheson's quiet gloating. Irritated, he hastily grabbed the handset and said, "Helen, I specifically asked not to be . . ."

"I'm sorry, Dr. Matheson," said the secretary rapidly, cutting her boss off, "but the president is on the line for you."

Matheson was surprised. He expected a call from the White House, just not so soon. Had the president had a change of heart overnight? Did he see the handwriting on the wall and was now trying to shore up support?

"Dr. Matheson, did you hear me? The president is on the line for you," repeated the secretary.

"Yes, Helen, I heard you. Please connect me. Thank you."

"Yes, sir, you're now connected."

"Good morning, Mr. President," greeted Matheson.

"Is it, Doctor? I trust you're watching the debate going on in the House of Representatives?"

"Yes, Mr. President," Matheson replied with fake sincerity, "a most unfortunate turn of events."

"Really?" Jackson answered sharply. "Then perhaps you should have thought of this 'unfortunate turn of events' before you leaked the *Defender* design document and the existence of the Space Force."

Matheson felt the cold chill of fear go up his back. "I . . . I don't understand what you're talking about, Mr. President."

"Well, then, let me jog your memory. We know the version of the design document posted on the Space News Web site was the same one you had in your possession. We know the Starbucks you went to in an attempt to hide your activities. The IP address was tracked down by the NSA, and we have security-camera footage of you at that establishment at the proper time. This entire mess was due to your incredibly childish behavior."

The NASA director sat frozen, unable to speak.

"I'm very busy, Dr. Matheson, so let me cut to the chase. Your services as the director of NASA are no longer required. Obviously, all of your security clearances have been revoked. Clean out your office of any personal items and turn in your badge immediately.

"There are two FBI agents in your office foyer; they will escort you off the premises. The attorney general will be bringing formal charges against you in the near future, but since your actions were due to petty jealousy and not traitorous intentions, it will take a little time to accurately determine what goes into the indictment. Therefore, out of deference to your past service, for the moment you'll be allowed to stay in your home rather than a jail cell.

"You will be fitted with a tracking device to ensure you stay put, and a warrant has been obtained to monitor all your communications. Good day, Dr. Matheson."

The click over the phone signaled the end of the call, but Matheson continued to hold the handset against his ear, staring blankly at the wall. A moment later, the door to his office opened and a large man walked in.

"Dr. Matheson, I'm Special Agent Romano. I'm here to assist you in moving your personal items out of this office. I have several boxes here, should you need them."

Kunming Air Base
Sichuan Province, China
November 7, 2017

The Il-76 transport lumbered off the taxiway and stopped. A cluster of uniformed Chinese military personnel waited on the tarmac as the large aircraft's engines whined to a stop. The instant the rear ramp touched the surface, a Russian army officer sauntered down and directed the Chinese to come aboard. A short few minutes later, the first huge BAZ missile transporter-erector-launcher rolled out of the aircraft's cavernous bay.

The forty-five-foot, six-wheeled truck inched out of the transport and down the ramp. Four canisters took up two-thirds' the length of the vehicle, overhanging the end of the chassis.

The command and radar vehicles were already on the ground and had moved off to a clear area to one side of the hangars. Technicians swarmed over the two vehicles, checking them quickly before letting them proceed. Railcars and loading equipment stood ready.

An S-400 surface-to-air missile battery, consisting of the command and radar vehicle and four TELs, was already emplaced around the base. It would protect the airfield while the rest of the equipment arrived.

National Military Command Center
The Pentagon
November 7, 2017

"At least three batteries of S-400 SAMs have arrived so far. The first was used to cover the airfield, while the second was sent by rail to the Gongga Shan launch site. We believe the third will be used to cover the Xichang control center."

The news wasn't pretty, but Admiral Overton had more to tell.

He displayed a list of Russian military units, along with their strengths and their locations.

"The Russians have also withdrawn some of their forces, including strike aircraft and ballistic missile units, from the Chinese border. They haven't moved out of theater, but they've moved far enough away to send a clear message.

"The reduced Russian offensive presence on the northern frontier will allow China to move PLA units south as necessary. While disturbing, the latest Russian action is consistent with the growing diplomatic ties between the two countries. Russian official statements have supported the Chinese in the Vietnam crisis, and they've been quiet about Chinese attacks on our GPS satellites. These movements indicate that they've decided to take sides, but in a subtle fashion. The Russians won't become directly involved militarily, but they'll support China's campaign by supplying arms and easing the border situation."

Overton saw their reaction and mentally threw the rest of his presentation over his shoulder, just summarizing the key points. "North Korean air assets have been placed on high alert, and some MiG-29s have dispersed to staging fields near the DMZ. While North Korean army units are mobilizing, we haven't seen any significant movement south."

He put a new list on the display. "Taiwan has put her military on full-scale alert, for obvious reasons. But India, Laos, Cambodia, and Thailand armed forces have also begun mobilizing. Our suspicion is that they fear China won't stop with Vietnam and will keep on going."

"We've only seen the early signs of mobilization in these countries, but if they continue, other powers like Japan, Indonesia, South Korea, and Malaysia will be compelled to follow suit. With tensions running high and virtually every country in East Asia going to high alert, the chances of something going horribly wrong is getting higher with each passing day. In short, no good will come of this."

General Kastner looked thinner after almost two months of crisis. He listened to Overton's brief quietly, then asked, "And the Chinese are still completely ready?"

"All the deployed units are still in place, sir, and they've begun mobilizing reserve units throughout the country. Half their fleet is at sea or ready for immediate steaming. Stockpiles at staging areas near the Vietnamese border have actually increased, and thanks to the Russians, the Chinese will probably be able to protect them better. Given their current posture, China could attack the Vietnamese with less than twenty-four hours warning."

"They certainly know about the congressional resolution," fumed Kastner. Opposition congressmen from the House had started a resolution calling for the cutting of funding for troops in Japan and South Korea. "With Russia and North Korea watching her flanks, China may now feel free to act."

Kastner looked at the assembled service chiefs. Everyone looked tired and discouraged. "Are there any other comments?" Only the Marine commandant spoke. "The Chinese believe they have a free hand against Vietnam, and perhaps even Taiwan. It's possible they may decide to resolve all their territorial issues in one swift campaign. As long as we're perceived as having one hand tied behind our back, we don't represent much of a deterrent."

The chairman sighed with frustration; the situation was crumbling around them, and there seemed to be precious little they could do about it. Picking up a copy of Schultz's request, he waved it about as he spoke. "Gentlemen, we have another difficult issue to address. We all know about the status of *Defender,* and their request for more time. Do we recommend for or against the replacement satellite launch? General Warner?"

The air force chief of staff controlled the GPS constellation, although it was used by all the services. "We knew we'd come to this point, sir, and while I'd hate to waste another satellite, I really don't see us having a lot of other options. We've contracted for new birds, but it will be a while before they're ready. My preference would be to hold out as long as possible and launch when we have a better picture of China's intentions."

"China could go to war tomorrow, Mike. You heard Frank's assessment. By the time you get your 'better picture,' it may be too late. This will be a 'come as you are' conflict, and we'll need whatever GPS capability we can get, for as long as we can get it." General Forest, the Army's Chief of Staff, wasn't shy. "Even if we can't get full coverage, more partial 3D coverage is better than less partial 3D coverage. "

"Trust me, Ted, I'm well aware of the problem," snapped Warner. "My guys and the navy need the 3D coverage more than the army. But we only have a few spare birds," the air force general reminded him. "Once we lose those satellites, we're back to pre–Desert Storm dumb bombs."

"The Chinese will shoot down one GPS satellite a week whether we launch a replacement bird or not, Mike," Kastner injected. "This buys us some time. Putting it in my terms: We're fighting a rearguard action, trading casualties for time." The soldier looked grim but determined.

Warner nodded his head in defeat. He really didn't want to say what he was about to say. "If that's the consensus of the joint staff, then I propose we launch two satellites, not just one. I have one bird each at Cape Canaveral and Vandenberg that could be ready to go within three days. It will buy us a little more time and, hopefully, give the Chinese a bit of a shock, maybe enough to throw them off a little. We need to seize the initiative, and this is one way, albeit an expensive one, for us to do so. But this leaves us with only one, maybe two, satellites left in the barn. After that, we're done."

"Then we have to hope the cavalry arrives as promised," Kastner concluded. "I'll make the recommendation to the SECDEF."

CNN News
November 8, 2017

"With the crisis in East Asia at a boiling point and China on the verge of invading Vietnam, the world waits for China's next move. Will it be just another strike against the U.S. GPS satellite this coming Friday? Or something larger and more menacing?" inquired the CNN anchor. "And yet there have been unsubstantiated rumors of intense activity at the U.S. Vandenberg Air Force Base. Our Mark Markin has traveled to the remote California facility to investigate these rumors. Mark, tell us what you've found so far."

The screen transitioned to Markin standing in front of a beige granite wall, on which the words VANDENBERG AIR FORCE BASE were displayed in bold letters.

"Robert, I'm standing at the main gate of Vandenberg Air Force Base in Southern California, where the rumors of an impending launch are running rampant. Vandenberg is the air force's Pacific space-launch facility and is the installation of choice when classified payloads are put into orbit. According to anonymous sources, a Delta II rocket with an undisclosed payload has been moved to Space Launch Complex 2 and is being prepared for immediate launch. SLC-2 is one of six active launch facilities at Vandenberg and has two launchpads."

"Mark, do you have any leads on what the payload is?" The screen was now split, with both Markin and the news anchor shown side by side.

"No, Robert. No one seems willing to discuss the payload, and our requests to visit SLC-2 have been denied by the air force. The best I can do is give you my informed speculation, but it doesn't take a rocket scientist to conclude it has something to do with the Chinese assault on the GPS constellation. The most likely option is the mystery payload is a GPS replacement satellite, but that makes little sense to me unless the air force has found a way to defend a satellite from attack.

"The rumors of the launch have only added to the fury of speculation on the Internet about *Defender*. Fantastic stories about exotic weaponry or orbital-deployed nuclear weapons are most common. A recent post on a space-enthusiast Web page early this morning said the rocket's payload is an armed defensive satellite that could protect the GPS constellation and that *Defender* could also control it once both were in orbit. All these theories sound pretty far-fetched, but at this point anything is possible."

"But even if we don't know what the payload is, I think it's safe to say that the United States is finally responding to China's attacks. Don't you agree?"

"Absolutely, Robert, and after eleven destroyed satellites, this response is long overdue."

The news anchor frowned; he seemed displeased. "But, Mark, this doesn't sound like much of a response, particularly if it's just a replacement satellite."

"Normally I would agree with you, but there are also rumors of activity at Cape Canaveral as well. These rumors are considerably more vague than what I've been able to find out here at Vandenberg, but, if true, this would suggest multiple launches. And while not unprecedented, it is very unusual. But everything depends on the payload, Robert. Until we know what these space-launch vehicles are carrying, we won't be able to say one way or the other if this response will be effective or not. And since the U.S. government is reluctant to say anything meaningful about this space war, we'll just have to wait until we have better information.

"But there is one thing I can say. If the technical details about *Defender* are accurate, we are looking at a historically unique situation. For the first time, a manned, armed vehicle is being built to wage war in space. This is not even remotely similar to military reconnaissance satellites or even a missile's reentry vehicle. This is a dedicated, reusable spacecraft with weaponry on board to defend U.S. space assets or to attack an adversary's—both in space and on Earth. *Defender,* if it works as advertised, will change forever how space is used. Back to you."

Ba Dinh District
Hanoi, Vietnam
November 9, 2017

The door opened as soon as the bus came to a complete stop. A sudden burst of people rushed out, impatient to get where they wanted to go. After the crowd had exited, a grandmotherly figure slowly climbed down the steps to the pavement. At sixty-two, Vinh Thi Nhung was still quite mobile, but steps, particularly steps down, greatly aggravated her arthritis. Since her glacial pace didn't sit well with the younger people, who always seemed to be in such a hurry, she made it a habit of being the last one out. Once clear, she waved to the driver and thanked him. Vinh still believed in old-fashioned politeness.

She walked along the sidewalk with a throng of other people toward a major intersection four blocks away. The bus stop she chose wasn't the closest one to her destination, but it was closest to an intersection with a policewoman who directed traffic. Even though Vietnamese traffic laws are very strict, the ever-growing number of cars and motorbikes that crammed the streets largely ignored them. Traffic lights, stop signs, and pedestrian crosswalks were often completely disregarded, resulting in serious accidents and injury. After being nearly hit two years ago in a crosswalk, Vinh now only crossed the busy streets where a police officer directed traffic. She also preferred the women police officers, as they were tougher on traffic violators than the men.

Vinh was becoming less and less enamored with Hanoi with each visit; it always seemed to be more crowded than the last time, and the chaotic hustle and bustle of city life chaffed badly against her quiet suburban upbringing. But Vinh's daughter had insisted that she meet her and the grandchildren at the Ho Chi Minh Mausoleum for a family outing. The children had just started their lessons on the great war with America, and her daughter thought it was important for the children to hear the stories from their grandmother, who lived during that "titanic struggle." Vinh smirked as she walked—only the elderly could appreciate the irony of their situation. During that war, the United States was the enemy, and China was an ally. Now, some forty-odd years later, the roles had reversed: China was now the enemy, and the United States the ally.

The crowd had thinned as she walked past the government offices along Hung Vuong Street, and she paused to appreciate the well-planned gardens that surrounded many of the buildings. Abruptly, a loud wailing sound started winding up, filling the streets. Many passersby looked around for the source with curiosity.

Vinh froze. She knew exactly what it was, even though she hadn't heard that sound since she was a young woman. Frantically, she looked for shelter, her reactions driven by embedded training. She started walking as fast as she could. The mausoleum was the closest and the sturdiest building that the general public had access to. The nearest underground metro station was blocks away. As the air raid siren continued to blare, the rest of the pedestrians finally figured out its meaning, and the people began to panic—screaming and running in all directions.

She was still a block away from the mausoleum when the first government office building was struck. The explosion was deafening. The missile's warhead tore huge chunks out of the building's façade and threw the debris high into the air. Shards of glass and shattered bricks rained down around Vinh, but she covered her head with her arms and kept moving, all the while praying that her daughter and grandchildren were already safely inside the mausoleum's thick stone walls. The next missile hit a nearby building across the street, and the blast knocked Vinh down behind a collection of large earthenware planters. Pieces of broken pottery, clumps of dirt, and uprooted flowers poured down around her as the shrapnel disintegrated the planters.

Rising slowly, Vinh cleared her eyes of dirt and plant fragments only to see the mangled body of a young woman a mere two meters away. The shock brought back the nightmare memories of that hideous month in late 1972, when bombs fell on Hanoi like rain.

"It's happening again!" she groaned out load. Vinh then shook her head to clear her thoughts. "Keep moving; get to shelter." She could still hear her mother's words so clearly. Vinh tried to walk but only managed a single step before falling back to the ground, a stabbing sharp pain in her left leg. Looking down, she could see blood on the sidewalk, her blood. Grabbing a piece of a torn window frame and using it as a crutch, she stood back up and began hobbling toward the mausoleum.

Vinh managed to keep walking, but at an agonizingly slow pace. She wanted to rest, but the exploding missiles far behind her spurred her on. As she worked her way in front of the Ministry of Finance building, a Chinese missile targeting it fell short—Vinh never heard the warhead explode.

Cape Canaveral Air Force Station
Space Launch Complex 17B
Cape Canaveral, FL
November 10, 2017

"We have liftoff," squawked the announcing system as the Delta II's main engine and strap-on solid rocket boosters began pushing the space launch vehicle upward. Unlike the space shuttle that seemed to rise slowly at first, the much-smaller Delta II rocket leapt from its launchpad and quickly picked up speed as it cleared the gantry. The initial stage of the launch had been oddly silent, but ten seconds after ignition, the deep rattling roar of the main engine and the solid boosters shook the area near the launch complex.

As the rocket's altitude increased, the noise dropped to a low rumble. Now only the rocket's exhaust could be clearly seen. A little over a minute after launch, the three air-start solid-rocket boosters kicked in, maintaining the vehicle's acceleration. Seconds later, the six strap-on boosters that had fired earlier began to peel away from the rocket's first stage. Their fuel spent, the casings were now just dead weight that had to be jettisoned. A minute later, the air-start rocket boosters also fell away.

Well downrange, the Delta II was now over thirty miles above Earth's surface. Far beyond the thicker portions of the atmosphere, the atmospheric pressure was one-thousandth that at sea level. The first-stage main engine generated sufficient thrust to keep the rocket on its desired trajectory. Two minutes later, a little over four minutes after launch, with the first stage's fuel depleted, the main engine cut off and the first stage separated from the rocket; moments later, the second-stage engine ignited, continuing the climb.

The first firing by the second-stage engine ended some seven minutes later. The rocket would now coast for nearly an hour in a preplanned parking orbit over one hundred miles high. By this time, the vehicle was on the far side of the planet, and the Guam tracking station picked up the telemetry data and began feeding it back to Cape Canaveral. Everything was proceeding according to the flight plan, and the operators saw that the second-stage engine had restarted for a short forty-second burn to boost the rocket into a transfer orbit. There, the second stage separated and the third stage fired, lifting the satellite to its final orbit. Seventy minutes after launch, the Cape Canaveral flight control team confirmed the GPS satellite had successfully separated from the Delta II third stage and had begun deploying its solar panels. After a quick checkout by the Fiftieth Space Operations Wing in Colorado, the satellite was declared fit for service and was brought online. Her sister from Vandenberg would join her three hours later.

16

Setbacks

U.S. Space Force Headquarters
Edwards Air Force Base
Office Annex
0650 hours
November 13, 2017

Ray usually met Biff Barnes about fifteen minutes before the crew training sessions began. There was always business to go over, and they both liked to get it cleared away so they could focus on training.

When Biff didn't show up as usual, Ray went looking for him, first in his trailer, then his office. He found Biff slouched in front of his computer screen, watching a grainy black-and-green video. When Ray knocked on the door frame, Barnes looked up, surprised. His face was puffy, and he hadn't shaved.

"You look like hell," Ray observed. "Were you here all night?"

Barnes didn't bother answering but gestured at the screen. "Results from the first strikes near Lang Son."

"How does it look?"

"It could look a lot better," Biff answered grimly. "I'm seeing way too many misses. This area is a nightmare for an attacker—mountain valleys with only one road. We should be clobbering them. The Vietnamese are doing their best to hold them south of the river, but we were supposed to be attacking the Chinese rear areas. It's the obvious move, though, and they've brought in enough antiaircraft guns and SAMs to shoot down Wonder Woman."

Barnes clicked on a video. "This is a reconstruction of a strike on a SAM nest near the Khon Pat Bridge. They've got HQ-9 long-range SAMs, with HQ-7 and HQ-17 shorter-range systems covering the immediate area, and mobile and fixed guns from twenty-three all the way up to one hundred and thirty millimeters."

Ray could see a string of symbols laid out over a hilly landscape. A single two-lane highway crossed a trestle bridge at right angles. The bridge was down, but it looked like the Chinese were constructing a replacement pontoon bridge a short distance to the west. He wasn't familiar with the ground-unit symbology but could pick out vehicles filling the road north of the river and what were likely defenders arrayed on either side of the road. Biff pressed the "play" arrow, and new symbols appeared at the edge of the display. "Those are four F-22s, each loaded with eight Small-Diameter Bombs. Watch."

A few moments after the planes entered from the south, dozens of red circles appeared on the map. "Those are the targets for the F-22 weapons—the SAM batteries and gun radars," he explained.

The letters IP appeared and then, a few moments later, RELEASE. The aircraft symbols suddenly reversed course. "They've done a zoom climb and released their loads, then pulled out facing away from the target. Perfect delivery." Ray could hear the admiration in his voice. "While the Raptors are safe and heading away, the bombs are using their GPS guidance to correct their trajectory. Flight time with a nine-mile release was just under a minute." Ray noticed a timer in one corner, counting down the seconds.

"There." The circles flashed, then either turned bright red or black. There were more blacks than reds.

Barnes sighed heavily. "That strike should have taken out at least every radar and the short-range SAM vehicles. Instead, we got about half. We even doubled up on the HQ-9's radars, but they all missed!" He sounded disgusted. "Stealth got the planes in and out safely, but the only air-to-ground weapons the F-22 carries are GPS-guided. The Chinese have pulled their teeth. There was a squadron of Super Hornets thirty seconds behind the Raptors. The plan was to bomb the crap out of all that armor once the air defenses had been removed. The Hornet squadron commander had to abort, and the entire chain of command's saying he made the right decision." Barnes shrugged. "They had to try it, just to see how bad it would be."

Ray pointed to his watch. "Crew training in three minutes."

Biff stood up quickly, then paused for a moment and ran his hand over the stubble on his chin. "One second. I can't show up like this." He pulled open a drawer and took out an electric shaver.

As Barnes removed his overnight growth, Ray asked, "Would you have called for the abort?"

After a thoughtful moment, the captain answered. "Yeah, probably. It's too early in the fight to take that kind of risk. We could have lost four, maybe six, aircraft."

"And it could have been you in one of those Raptors—if I hadn't shanghaied you."

"I dunno," Barnes answered as he put the shaver away. "But, yeah. If I were in that squadron, I'd be out there, of course. And if the air force calls, I don't know what I'd say right now." He headed for the door and the stairs down, with Ray close behind.

Ray ventured, "You can do a lot more damage to the Chinese as *Defender*'s mission commander."

They clattered down the stairs. "I'll keep telling myself that. You just make sure that thing will actually fly."

U.S. Space Force Headquarters
Edwards Air Force Base
Battle Management Center
November 13, 2017

After the crew training was finished, Ray had decided to visit Jenny. Originally, she had been assigned to set up the command and control network that would support the mission. It was an immense job. She had to integrate links between the air force's Space Command, navy tracking stations, NASA, and even some civilian facilities. It had to be done quickly and with the real purpose secret.

All that data would be fed to a single point, the Battle Management Center, and her task had such an impact on the center that she ended up taking that over, too.

She'd done both jobs well, almost elegantly, but her progress reports had recently become pessimistic, and she'd missed her last milestone by two days. It was not a good trend.

They'd set up the Battle Management Center in a purpose-built prefab building. Located a short walk from the hangar, the BMC was separated from the rest of the facility by a double chain-link fence, reinforced by rows of concrete Jersey barriers that would stop a charge by anything but an armored fighting vehicle. The single gate was manned by armed Marines at all times, and there were spots on the roof for Stinger teams and heavy weapons.

Although work was well under way inside, more still needed to be done before the BMC was finished. Engineers were adding emergency diesel generators and a buried fuel tank, and technicians were doubling up the center's communications and data lines. Jenny was still debating the merits of a separate backup computer, at a different location, in case of a hardware problem with the system here.

The building itself already looked weathered and misused. The metal walls were primed pale gray but not painted, and modifications to the exterior were only roughly finished.

Jenny had met Ray at the door, standing proudly under a hand-painted sign that read BATTLE MANAGEMENT CENTER. He was glad to see her, of course. He'd smiled, and she smiled back, but it was a tired smile. He hadn't seen her in several days, and she seemed different. He realized she looked a little thinner, and wondered if the strain showed on him as well.

Ray tried to stay focused as Jenny Oh explained the BMC's status. He found her presence distracting and feared missing details as his mind wandered, but she was maintaining a professional attitude. He did his best to follow her example.

Jenny then led him down the main hallway, past security, past rooms crammed with electronic equipment or people hunched over workstations, into a large two-story open area surrounded by support spaces and offices. The central space held the main command displays. There was more security at the door to the operations center, and a vestibule that served as a security checkpoint.

An elevated scaffold had been erected that ran around three sides of the room. It was about fifteen feet wide, with a waist-high rail on the inside edge. The fourth wall was lined with gray equipment cabinets, and Ray could see more boxy shapes tucked under the scaffolding.

Jenny trotted up the steps to the scaffolding, putting them one story up, then led Ray along the walkway. Desks lined it, facing the center, with an aisle behind them. "This section's communications, that's electronic warfare, that's intelligence." They turned the corner. "This wall is spacecraft systems. We don't get a third of the telemetry that NASA gets, but we still monitor critical systems."

They turned the last corner, and she pointed to the final station, on the third side. "Admiral Schultz and his staff will sit here. I've got communications rigged to the White House, the NMCC, and to all the major commands."

He looked around the space. Everything was neatly arranged. The cabinets were fully installed. They'd even taken the time to paint safety warnings near the stairways. "It looks great, Jenny. You've done a wonderful job."

"Don't praise me yet," Jenny replied. "It's looked like this for almost a week. The real test is to see if the stuff inside works."

She walked over to one of the desks and picked up an augmented-reality headset. A headband held a clear lens in front of her right eye, and a small microphone came down the side. She slipped it on easily, and Ray heard her say softly, "Start test three bravo."

There was enough light in the center bay to see a smooth light-colored sphere, easily ten feet across. It hung in the air halfway between the floor and the ceiling, suspended on a monofilament line.

The projectors came on, and Ray barely had time to see it was white before it changed color, becoming a deep blue. Patches of blue lightened to a medium shade, then lightened more, shifting to brown and green. He realized he was watching the world being built, starting with the deepest part of the ocean. Then higher elevations were added, one level at a time.

Points of light appeared on the surface, and Ray recognized one as Edwards. Lines appeared circling the earth, and he knew they were satellite orbits.

Visually, it was stunning. The implications for command were even more impressive. It was the situational awareness a commander needed to fight a space battle.

"Here's the hard part," Jenny announced. A flashing symbol appeared in southern China, becoming a short red-line segment. A transparent red trumpet appeared around the symbol as it quickly climbed toward orbit. "This is a recording of their latest intercept," she told him. "Here's what we added."

A new point of light flashed, at Edwards. It started to rise, but then the display went dark.

The sudden blackness left Ray momentarily blind, and he heard a loud, "Damn it! I wanted that to work." He could hear the frustration and fatigue in her voice.

"The hardware was a piece of cake," she explained. "This display duplicates the one at Space Command, and I could get off-the-shelf components for nine-tenths of what we needed. Hooking it up was straightforward.

"But the software to support the new systems has been a pain in the ass. We have to be able to track *Defender* in real time. The display was originally designed to show a friendly unit's location based on GPS data. We can't depend only on that, so we're using radar and optical sensors all over the world to track her position. That information has to be collected, fused, and then sent to the display. That software is all brand-new." She smiled a lopsided smile. "I hear they're having a few problems at Space Command as well."

Ray waited for a moment, then asked quietly, "Is there anything we can get that will help you finish on time?"

She shook her head. "I wish I knew what to ask for."

Her tone shook Ray. He heard someone near the end of her rope. She'd accomplished miracles, but this gear had to be rock-solid. *Defender* needed guidance from the Battle Management Center. They didn't have the onboard sensors to see the entire engagement from the ship. Their upcoming fight would cover half the world. Information from the BMC would warn them of threats and tell them the results of their attacks.

He couldn't bring in more people. Not at this late date. They'd need time to get brought up to speed—time they didn't have. Jenny certainly didn't need any more gear. If she had the resources, then it was all about leadership.

"You can do this," Ray said carefully. "I can't give you a sunshine speech. Nobody's more committed to *Defender* than you, but I think you're afraid of failing. You care so much about the project that the fear of not making it is tying you up in knots."

She almost shook as she nodded. "I don't like to fail. I never have, more so than most. And this is important, really important. Peoples' lives will depend on it . . . including yours." Jenny's fatigue was more evident now as she leaned heavily on the rail.

Gently taking her arm, Ray led her over to a chair and sat her in it. He sat on the edge of the desk. He looked at her steadily.

"You've been a rock for me since the day this began. But also since that day, there hasn't been the time I'd like, for us. I've had to stay focused, and that's meant putting my feelings for you in deep freeze, until this is over. Your belief has kept me going. I hope my belief in you can do the same."

She smiled and looked up at him. "I want it to."

"Then it will." He stood. Ray tried to sound positive without being too enthusiastic. "We will make it, Jenny, and I'm glad you'll be here in the BMC when I'm up there."

U.S. Space Force Headquarters
Edwards Air Force Base
Battle Management Center
November 13, 2017

Glenn Chung's coworkers thought he was a good supervisor. Technically skilled but willing to delegate, he was interested in anyone he met. He loved camp gossip but was never mean or petty. He was a "people person" and would certainly be given more responsibility as the program developed.

He was obviously proud of his ethnic Chinese background. Chung often spoke of his extended family, spread throughout California and the western United States, as well as his grandmother and her immediate family, who now lived in Taiwan, after being forced to leave Vietnam. In fact, he'd heard there were still distant relatives living in northern Vietnam and spoke hopefully of getting them out, somehow. If they did exist, they would be way too close to the fighting.

It was not unusual for him to be seen all over the compound. His exercise of choice was power walking, and he'd often start his day crisscrossing the area several times. During the day, he could be found anywhere, expanding or fixing one of several networks that linked the Space Force with the outside world or that supported its internal workings.

Right now, Chung was toting his golf bag. After a ten-minute walk to the gate, he caught a shuttle to the Edwards main exchange, then a base shuttle bus to the golf course. He had time for practicing his swing.

One would think a golf course would provide thousands of possible spots for a dead drop—just pick a spot off one of the fairways. A couple of the earlier drops had done just that, but the grounds-keepers were everywhere, not to mention seekers of lost golf balls. Eventually, he'd chosen the driving range, which could be crowded to capacity on the weekends or nearly deserted during weekday working hours. And thanks to his flex-time work schedule, that suited him perfectly.

Another advantage to picking the driving range was that all types of golfers used it, both good and bad. This was ideal for Chung. He really wasn't very good, and he'd attract a lot less attention whiffing shots there than on the fairway.

There were two retirees practicing, and Chung greeted both before starting on his basket of balls. He had time, and, sure enough, both occasionally checked their watches. He practiced patience, as well as trying to get some consistent loft, and just before the half hour, they both picked up and headed for the first tee. He waited another five minutes, then took a break, drinking from a water bottle and stretching. Nobody was moving near the pro shop, much less coming in his direction.

The problem with choosing a dead drop was to make it easily accessible, but at the same time secluded. It should be possible to place or retrieve an item in seconds. The operative must be able to reach it quickly. Any special effort might draw attention. And while it must be easy to reach, it should be a place nobody would ever think to look.

The driving range was lit for nighttime practice. It looked perfectly natural to lean against one of the light poles, and, sure enough, the supports were hollow. A drain hole at the base provided a perfect-sized opening, and the rough edges discouraged casual exploration.

Going to one knee to retie his shoe, he'd already palmed the metal case containing the flash drive; he took one more scan of the area. All clear. In one careful motion, he fished inside the support and found an identical metal case. He drew it out carefully, being careful not to gouge himself on the unfinished edge. The new case was inserted in the next instant. Both were rough-surfaced and colored a dirty brown. Chung fought the urge to look around again and see if he'd been noticed.

Retying his shoe, he stood and pocketed the new case, then went back to hit a few more balls, both for appearance's sake and to work off the adrenaline.

By the time he was back at the Space Force complex, the case was tucked into a fold in the lining of his golf bag. When he entered the compound, his bag was checked, but the case wasn't found.

Chung had timed his trip so his roommate would still be working, and the trailer was empty. He still took the time to put the golf bag away and set up his tell-tales before opening the case and plugging the flash drive inside into his laptop. The flash drive he'd sent had been virtually full of information. Names, work, and even housing assignments were included, along with more technical data and software samples.

The new drive had only one file, and it decrypted normally, revealing a single short text file.

EXCELLENT WORK. YOUR INFORMATION HAS EARNED THE PRAISE OF OUR HIGHEST LEADERS.

1) HIGHEST COLLECTION PRIORITY IS PROGRESS TOWARD COMPLETION. A PLANNED LAUNCH DATE IS GREATLY DESIRED.

2) INVESTIGATE OPPORTUNITIES FOR SABOTAGE, EITHER BY CYBERNETIC ATTACK, USE OF LOCAL MATERIALS, OR EXPLOSIVES. TAKE NO

ACTION WITHOUT AUTHORIZATION UNLESS LAUNCH IS IMMINENT.
EXPLOSIVES ARE AVAILABLE WITH TWO WEEKS' NOTICE.
3) TAKE ALL MEASURES TO PREVENT DISCOVERY.

Chung automatically hid his surprise, even though he was alone in the trailer. First, he'd received rare praise. His last report must have made a real splash. Most communications from Beijing simply gave a list of desired information or collection targets.

The instructions were simple enough. He readily agreed with the last one, would do what he could about the first, and as for the second—he'd never used explosives in the field, although he'd had some training in their use. He was not a demolitions expert, though. He had other skills.

But their intent was clear. *Defender* must be stopped.

USS *Abraham Lincoln* (CVN-72)
VFA-137 "Kestrels" Ready Room
November 14, 2017

Commander Ian "Smurf" Murphy was trying to change the way his squadron did business and was learning more about orbital mechanics than he ever wanted to know.

The first question on everyone's mind was now, How many satellites will be in view during the strike? It dominated their tactics, even their navigation. Low-level approaches at night and bad weather were a lot harder now.

Everyone was frustrated and unhappy about having to abort their last attack. They'd tried a strike at night on a mechanized infantry division near Khon Pat, bunched up and waiting for a pontoon bridge to be finished.

A mobile armored formation was just about the hardest thing you could attack. Hundreds of individual armored vehicles, spread out across the countryside, many so tough that a bomb going off a few meters away might only scratch the paint. It had its own mobile AA guns and SAMs. Catching them at a river crossing was not a chance to be wasted.

The radar in Murphy's Super Hornet could see ground targets dozens of miles away. Because of GPS, the computer in his plane knew his exact position, and because of the radar, it knew the exact position of the targets. It would then tell the weapons where to fly. At least that was how it was supposed to work in theory.

In reality, it turned out to be a complete cluster. The Super Hornets couldn't launch their weapons if the GPS input sucked, and there were still a lot of operating SAMs in the area. The Raptor strike hadn't done the job, and with the air defenses still intact, he'd called his squadron's attack off. Murphy detested air defenses and did not consider them career enhancing, but aborting the strike was the hardest decision he'd ever made. The fact that he'd been correct was little consolation.

He was now planning for the next one. The Raptors would not be available for a restrike. The next attack would be in the daytime, but this time they would have full GPS 3D coverage. They would give up the concealment of night, but gain full accuracy for their weapons. They couldn't limit themselves to just one part of the day with adequate GPS coverage or the Chinese would be ready for them every time.

This time, a Tomahawk cruise missile strike would go in first, with his squadron following. The Chinese would either have to engage the cruise missiles, which would make them vulnerable to the antiradar missiles his planes would carry, or stay off-line and watch the Tomahawks carpet the area with antiarmor submunitions.

Almost a third of his planes would be tasked with destroying the Chinese SAMs and guns—not just "suppressing" them, but wiping them out. The PLA didn't have an infinite number of antiaircraft missiles, just a lot. And the Raptors had done some damage. His squadron would have to do the rest.

But since Smurf's squadron was flying in the daytime, he had to assign at least a flight of four planes as fighter escort. The Kestrels could take on any Chinese fighter that flew, but he wouldn't underestimate them, either. A fully loaded Super Hornet would be at a disadvantage against a Flanker.

So even with full GPS, planes that could have been destroying tanks or troop carriers would instead be hunting mobile guns and SAM launchers. Annoying, to be sure, but Murphy wouldn't send his strikers in on a target unless he was confident they had a reasonable chance of making it back safely.

It was a more complicated plan, and it reduced his squadron's striking power by at least a third, but if he did his job properly, his squadron would come safely back to the ship.

Murphy was also lowering his expectations. Survival in this type of environment was not a given. Mission accomplishment was worthless if he lost too many people, and in his mind one was too many. But with so many limitations, and Chinese air defenses operating at full effectiveness, one mistake or plain bad luck could cost him a lot of his guys.

Iowa Business Forum
Ames, Iowa
November 14, 2017

Rutledge's speech had been touted as discussing the common issues facing businesses in Nebraska, Iowa, and the other Midwestern states. He'd been spending a lot of time in Iowa. Not too much, though, because the elections were still a long way off. But he wanted Iowans to know who he was, and he wanted to have a well-established track record long before any of the other possible candidates showed up in the state.

The congressman gave them about three minutes on Midwest business issues before segueing smoothly into the potential economic effects of what was still being called the Vietnam War, in spite of historians' protests.

"Unfortunately, the biggest uncertainty facing the Midwest's economy, indeed the entire nation's, is the administration's reckless foreign policy. President Jackson has plunged us into a war with one of our largest trading partners and our biggest creditor. Is this supposed to be his answer to the Chinese attacks on our GPS satellites? That's like setting your neighbor's house on fire after his dog's peed in your yard.

"By the way, those satellites are still being shot down, one a week, with the cost of replacing them half a billion dollars each. Now, think about it, folks. The biggest problem with losing the GPS satellites is that our military can't fight as well. So what does the president do? Send our military into a fight with another superpower with one hand tied behind our back. And over a country that is not really a U.S. ally?"

Rutledge paused for a moment, taking a drink of water. "And while the president sends our brave men and women into combat, with the weakest of reasons and inadequate tools, his only answer to the original problem is a double boondoggle—a whole new air force command, and a secret 'space force' with some wonder weapon pulled out of thin air!"

Rutledge had worked on that line, polishing not only the wording but also the tone—mixing amusement with indignation.

"So as business leaders, while I would like to say we're in a great position for expansion and steady growth, thanks to the Jackson administration, you can expect your taxes to go up and the U.S. economy to become a target for Chinese cyberattacks and who knows what else. If you were selling U.S. products to China or selling to someone who does, well, that market went away with the first inaccurate bomb we dropped."

Gongga Shan
Sichuan Province, China
November 14, 2017

The visitors from the Ministry of State Security's Second Bureau
arrived precisely on time but were from a different branch than Shen
Xuesen had dealt with before. The general had worked closely with
MSS in the past. They had provided valuable technical information
vital to building the *Tien Lung,* but that had always come from the
Thirteenth, or Technical Investigation, Bureau. The individuals before him were from the Second Bureau's Operations Division, not
that they volunteered that information. A colleague in Beijing had
warned Shen of the impending visit. And while the men had not identified their organization, they did come bearing impressive gifts: a
complete detailed technical description of the American *Defender*
vehicle and its launch facilities.

General Shen's intelligence liaison protested that the information
should have come through them, but the ranking intelligence officer, Senior Agent Wen Jin, brushed his objections aside. "I'm sure it
will arrive in your office eventually, but we don't have time to wait
for you paper warriors to wake up from your naps. This is an operational matter."

Wen's response confirmed what Shen had already been told: These
men were responsible for directing the actions of agents in foreign
countries. Senior Agent Wen then turned to Dr. Dong. "We'd appreciate it if you would take a look at these plans. As an engineer, we
need you to identify places where a small explosive charge could be
placed to cause the most disruption."

"You mean, while it is on the ground?" Shen asked. "Wouldn't
that put your operative at risk?" He couldn't hide his curiosity.

"Do not speculate on that, sir," Wen replied sharply. Shen ignored
the disrespect. "Assume a small charge, a few kilograms at most, with
a timer that allows whoever placed the charge the opportunity to clear
the area. We need your recommendations as quickly as possible."

With that, they had the general sign for the documents and left. Shen's intelligence officer left as well, probably to complain to his superiors. Alone in his office, the general leafed through the pages, thinking about the agents' questions and what those questions meant.

Did the CMC now believe that *Defender* was a real threat? His own judgment, and that of Dr. Dong's, was that the vehicle would take at least a year to build, and that assumed everything went perfectly for the Americans.

After his confrontation with General Li, Shen definitely thought of the CMC as "them." Did they know something he didn't? He was not naïve enough to believe they'd tell him if there was a threat to the *Tien Lung*. There were still some in Beijing who'd love to see him fail, even now.

A chill ran down his back, and he tried to tell himself they were just covering all the possibilities. In any case, he'd give this new assignment his best effort.

17

Good News and Bad

Biff Barnes resisted the urge to shout or to give orders or any other kind of direction. These people were supposed to do their jobs on their own. He'd be too busy to give orders when the time came.

Jim Scarelli, the designated pilot, was off working on the real-flight control systems with the techs. Scarelli had been the Lockheed Martin test pilot for *VentureStar,* and there was no question of his ability to fly *Defender.* That part was easy.

The rest of them struggled to train on half-built systems in a jerry-rigged simulator. Six metal chairs mimicked the seats, and plywood and plastic boxes with laptops on them pretended to be control consoles. A plywood arch covered them, because many of the controls were positioned on the overhead. Network and power cables were tightly bundled but still required attention to avoid a misstep.

Steve Skeldon, the navigator and copilot, sat in the right front seat. A Marine captain, his time flying fighters was less useful than his master's degree in physics. This morning, he had taken over Scarelli's flight duties as well, which made him a very busy man.

Behind the pilot, Sue Tillman, the sensor officer, stared intently at the mock display screen, scanning the earth and space. The display was a montage of inputs from the impressive array of infrared, visible light, and radar equipment being installed in *Defender.* Hopefully the real systems would act as effectively as the simulated control panels. She also took care of the voice and data links that would tie *Defender* to the ground-based sensors she needed.

The weapons officer on the right was Andre Baker, a captain in the U.S. Air Force. Although he had no space-flight experience, he did know lasers, and he was a ballistics expert as well.

Biff sat in the rearmost row. As mission commander, he didn't need to look out a window. The displays on his console gave him the big picture. From the back, he could also watch his crew.

Ray McConnell's chair, for the flight engineer, was on Biff's right, also in the rear. It was empty as well. Ray was able to train only occasionally, but that was the least of Biff's worries.

Barnes worked the master console at his station. In addition to simulating his own controls, he could inject targets and create artificial casualties for the team to deal with. Right now, he was just trying to get the simulator's newest feature to behave.

"Sue, tell me what your board sees."

"Bingo! I've got an IR target below us bearing two seven zero elevation minus four five. Shifting radar to classification mode. I'll use the laser ranger to back up the radar data." She sounded triumphant, and somewhere behind Biff, a few technicians clapped.

"Velocity data is firming up. It should be showing up on the master contact display."

Biff checked his own console and said, "Yes, it is." He'd dialed in a *Tien Lung* target for Sue to find, and she had. Considering they'd just installed the software for the infrared detection feature at four in the morning, it was a significant achievement.

Despite the frustration and lost time, Biff smiled, pleased with the results. More than procedural skills, simulators taught the crew to work together through shared experience. These experiences weren't what he'd planned on, but the result was the same.

"It's good to see you smiling, Biff." Ray's voice would have startled him a few moments earlier, but Barnes felt himself relaxing a little.

Ray sat down in his designated chair, then clapped his hands. "Attention, please! We're short of time, so we can't arrange a ceremony, but I believe these are yours."

Everyone's eyes followed Ray as he handed a small box over to Barnes. As Biff's hand touched it, a photoflash went off, and he turned in his seat to see a photographer behind him, smiling, his camera at the ready.

He opened the small dark box to see a pair of golden oak leaves.

"We thought *Defender*'s mission commander should be at least a major." Admiral Schultz stepped into Barnes's view, reaching out to shake his hand.

Barnes, surprised and pleased, automatically tried to stand, but was blocked by the overhead console.

"At ease, Major." Schultz smiled. "I'm glad to be the first one to say that." As Biff took the admiral's hand, both automatically turned their faces to the cameraman, and the flash popped again.

"Thank you, sir."

"Don't thank me—thank Ray. He's the one who insisted you should wear oak leaves. I just had to twist some arms. A full year ahead of zone, isn't it? And by the way," Schultz said, raising his voice so the flight crew could all hear him clearly, "you're all going to get astronaut flight pay, backdated to the day you reported here for duty."

It was Ray's turn to look surprised. Schultz just smiled. "You had a good idea. I had a good idea."

CNN Report
November 21, 2017

"The newest Chinese tactic is called 'sidestepping.' Although both the U.S. and China have declared trade embargoes against each other,

Chinese goods are still arriving at U.S. ports, via shell corporations and merchant ships flying 'flags of convenience.'"

The image shifted from the newscaster to an anchored merchant ship. The camera was at water level, a short distance away, and as it passed down the length of the vessel, the gray hull towered over the observer. "This is the Chinese general cargo ship *Bao Jiang,* at least that was its name two weeks ago."

The camera, being carried in a small boat, reached the end of the hull and circled, showing the stern of the vessel. Freshly painted lettering read MARITIME VENTURE 3, SRI LANKA.

"Sometime after November first, *Bao Jiang* was purchased by the Maritime Venture Shipping Corporation, headquartered in Sri Lanka, and renamed. She is shown here unloading in Long Beach, California. Her manifest shows that her cargo originated in Myanmar, but all of the goods unloaded so far are of Chinese manufacture.

"Newly formed 'false front' shipping companies are appearing throughout Southwest Asia and Africa, with newly purchased, formerly Chinese merchant ships. The most likely source for the money to establish these firms is China herself.

"Cargoes from China are transshipped in neutral ports like Dawei onto a newly renamed ship, or sometimes the ship, with the cargo aboard, is simply purchased by the front company. Their manifests will either falsify the country of origin or claim the goods were purchased from China before the start of hostilities.

"The incentive is great. Because of the embargo, Chinese products are commanding three or more times their normal price in the USA, if they are available at all. A legitimate market in Chinese-made goods available outside China has helped mask and confuse the vastly larger shadow trade.

"We tried to find out whether any U.S. firms are employing similar techniques, but there have been no recent transfers of U.S. flagged or owned ships to other nations. Both the U.S. authorities and the American companies we contacted refused comment.

"U.S. companies are also complaining that foreign suppliers are stepping in to replace American firms shut out of China by the embargo. In addition to the lost business during the conflict, they are concerned that continuing political tensions afterwards will prevent them from ever reestablishing their business.

"Unemployment figures held steady for the month of October, but it is certain the news for all the economic indicators in November will be bad. Gold prices have risen sharply since the Chinese invasion began.

"President Jackson's job approval ratings, although low, have held steady, for the moment. Immediately after U.S. forces were committed to the defense of Vietnam, the country was almost evenly split, with forty-three percent approving of the president's decision and forty-five percent disapproving. Two weeks later, the numbers are forty percent and forty-six percent, almost unchanged. Some pundits believe that only a quick victory over its superpower rival in Asia will prevent them from dropping sharply."

U.S. Space Force Headquarters
Edwards Air Force Base
Security Office
0815 hours
November 22, 2017

"There." Colonel Evans froze the video. The color image showed someone half-kneeling near one of the light standards on the driving range. "That's Glenn Chung yesterday at seventeen forty hours. After we were sure he was back in his trailer and that no one visited the spot immediately after him, I went out with one of my people last evening, and we found this, right inside that light pole."

The colonel handed Ray McConnell a clear plastic bag. Inside was a small metal case, just a few inches long. It had a rough texture and was colored a dirty brown.

"My God," muttered Ray. He handed it to Geoffrey Lewes, who studied it silently.

The three of them were seated in Evans's office. The door was locked, with a guard posted outside.

"You get the credit for this one, Geoff," Evans remarked. "If you hadn't come to me with that one incident, I wouldn't have even known to start looking. Once we started watching him, it slowly became clear. It's all in knowing where to start." After a pause, Evans added, "I'm sure you felt bad reporting that incident at your desk with Chung."

"I did," Lewes admitted, "but his explanation just didn't quite ring true."

"Well, that was enough. Chung was very careful; it took us over a month before we had conclusive proof that he was passing messages. And while the guy has rarely left Edwards AFB, he's been all over the place. At the food court, dry cleaners, power walking past base housing. Being a support contractor, he has more time off than the engineers, and it's perfectly natural for someone to want to get away from this place for an hour or two after their shift. It wasn't until you showed us the recreation records that we realized the best place for his dead drop would be the golf course."

Lewes almost cringed. "Please, quit praising me! Chung always struck me as a great guy. Even knowing what he's doing, I'm finding it hard to dislike him. Is there any way we could be wrong?" Lewes's tone was earnest, almost pained.

Evans took the bag back and tapped the case inside. "We brought this back here at nineteen forty-five last night. My people have been working on it all night. As soon as we're done here, this goes back into the lamppost, just like we found it."

Lewes started to ask, "What if someone comes . . . oh, you're watching it. Of course."

Evans nodded. "Hidden cameras are watching the drop site, with people in striking distance, just in case. I'd rather keep these guys in the dark, though, and see who the contact is and where he takes it. But if someone shows up at the dead drop before this is back, we'll grab him and Chung as well and shut their operation down."

"You said you'd been working on it since last night, right? So what the hell is it?" Ray prompted.

Evans grinned. "Look at this." Handling it through the plastic of the bag, he pressed a seam that ran along the side of the case. It popped open easily. In one half, nestled in a foam cutout, was a flash drive. The number 3 was hand-painted on it in white.

"We had to do some serious tests before we could even put it into a computer, but turns out it wasn't booby-trapped. Once we could take a peek, we found numerous files, encrypted, of course. We sent them to the NSA late last night, and they sent us the decoded material about an hour ago. That's when I called you two."

Evans turned to his computer and pressed a key. "This is a list of the files we found on the flash drive."

- TENTATIVE KILL ASSESSMENT METHODS FOR ABL AGAINST NON-ATMOSPHERIC TARGETS
- NEW ORGANIZATION CHARTS FOR SOFTWARE DEPARTMENT
- INTEGRATION MILESTONES FOR CONFORMAL RADAR
- ESTIMATE OF CHINESE ASAT VEHICLE MANEUVERING CAPABILITY

In all, there were over twenty files. Ray recognized most of them. He'd even written a few. Almost all were classified, but the ones that weren't still worried him: a schedule of food service deliveries, a list of personnel who'd arrived at the base in the past week, along with their work assignments.

Ray fell back in his chair and exhaled heavily, as if he'd been struck. "They know everything."

Evans replied, "They know a lot. Chung goes to the golf course at least once, sometimes twice a week. That was our clue on how he signaled his partner that a drop had been made. During those weeks he goes twice, there is always a two-day gap between the two reservations; that's when the exchange of flash drives likely takes place.

Based on that theory, this is Chung's third drop since being assigned to Space Force.

"We already started poring through the golf-course reservation records to see if we can determine the name of his accomplice. I doubt they'd be that inept, but we still need to check. We've also been looking at Chung's work log to see if there is any obvious place for a network tap. The guy has been as busy as a beaver on speed; he's done an unbelievable number of install jobs all over Building 151. We haven't found anything so far, but we've only scratched the surface. You have no idea how many fiber-optic cables and server farms have been run throughout this building, and the layout map isn't exactly the greatest."

Ray nodded. "But, Jack, even with *just* three drops, the amount of data compromised could be huge. At a minimum, we have to assume the Chinese have a good idea of *Defender*'s characteristics, her weapons and sensors, and, most importantly, her status. I'll have to brief the admiral about this, right away—and Dawson. Chung came to us from Lock Mart. Who knows how much information he stole there before he came to us? They have a need to know."

"I agree," Evans replied, "but nobody else. Right now, the three of us are the only ones with the complete picture. Even the people I had working on this last night weren't told where it was found, or who it belonged to. In addition to the NSA, I've also notified the DCIS and FBI, as required."

The colonel then turned to Geoffrey. "And you're going to get some more bodies for your support staff, as well as in the IT department. They'll be security people, of course, but from outside the command. He may have taken the time to mark all of my people. I would."

"To keep him under surveillance," Lewes said. "Fine. I'll make sure they're placed in different sections: food service and recreation, primarily, but maybe a couple of others."

"Good. I'll make sure the new IT guys are assigned to work with Chung, on a rotating basis, of course. His company has been grooming him for additional leadership responsibilities, so this won't be unexpected. Hopefully, it'll cramp his style for the near term—reduce his ability to compromise more information. And there will be a few more security guys that nobody knows about, except me," Evans continued. "We're getting new people in here all the time, so a few additions won't attract any attention."

Evans leaned forward, speaking softly but earnestly. "I know you both will keep your mouths shut, but, believe me, don't spend too much time thinking about Chung. I'll do all the worrying. If you see him, or God forbid he speaks to you, don't try to 'act natural.' Just deal with whatever it is, then come see me as soon as you're clear. Remember that from now on, he'll be watched constantly. If Chung talks to you, one of my people will be nearby. Think of them as backup."

"Ray, you'll have to begin a formal investigation, as required," Evans reminded him.

"More paperwork!" Ray groaned. "I certainly don't need this right now."

"You'll survive," Evans told him. "Now if you'll excuse me, I have an errand at the golf course."

U.S. Space Force Headquarters
Edwards Air Force Base
Admiral Schultz's Office
1000 hours
November 22, 2017

Hugh Dawson watched the video, looked at the photographs, and read the list of decoded files. Then he asked to see the video again. He used the tablet's touch screen to expand Chung's image until it filled the screen. It was grainy, but definitely Chung.

He handed the tablet back to Ray, searching for words, trying to readjust what he knew. The implications were mind-bending.

Schultz was watching Dawson carefully, and he could see Ray

McConnell waiting for him to speak. Finally, the executive offered, "I'm sorry."

The admiral said, "I didn't think this was your fault, Hugh, even though he came from Palmdale."

Dawson, feeling a little lightheaded, answered, "But I feel responsible. Certainly our security people failed to catch a spy. We cleared him, and he's been working in one of our most highly classified facilities for over three years. Heaven knows what he's stolen and passed on." He shivered. "I'm having a little trouble absorbing this. The more I think about it, the worse it gets."

"Your security people will have to account for themselves, of course. We're assuming you'll brief your chief of security as soon as you get back, but only him. Have him coordinate with Colonel Evans, who is in charge of the investigation. Our main concern is finding out who Chung's contact is and tracking their network," said Schultz.

"Nobody's picked up the case yet?" Dawson asked.

Ray shook his head. "No. Evans said he'd text me the instant that happened."

"And then the hunt will be on," Schultz observed.

Dawson handed the admiral a stapled sheaf of paper. "Here's a hard copy of his Lockheed Martin personnel record. I was curious about why you asked for it, but I couldn't imagine it was for this. Chung's only worked for us. We got him fresh out of college."

Dawson paused, then continued. "Or, maybe he got us. He's had three years to send who knows how much back to China. Just thinking about it makes my head hurt."

"Well, he's stopped spying on you to spy on us, so count your blessings."

"What do we do? What can I do?"

Ray answered. "Evans says we watch and wait. From now on, we'll be able to read his mail. Once the contact picks up the case, we'll follow him back and see where he leads us, who else is involved."

"And please let them not work at Palmdale," Dawson added prayerfully.

"Which is why Colonel Evans doesn't want your security people to do anything, at least until we know one way or the other."

"I understand," Dawson assured him. "I don't want to tip these guys off, either."

The depressed executive left, and Ray and Schultz sat silently for a moment. Ray finally said, "A spy. It doesn't seem real."

"This from a guy who's building a spaceship?" Schultz smiled.

"I can't tell Biff, or Jenny."

"I agree. Biff will understand, and I'll vouch for you with Jenny. We'll keep any champagne bottles well out of her reach."

"You heard about that?"

CNN Report
November 22, 2017

The screen showed a map of northern Vietnam and its border with China. Pulsing red arrows moved south through mountainous terrain, converging on the city of Lang Son.

"The Chinese capture of Lang Son does more than just gain them a vital road junction south of the mountains. It means that the U.S. has missed its best chance to slow or stop the invading armies and is apparent proof of the effectiveness of the Chinese 'anti-GPS' strategy."

Arrows appeared, heading south and southeast. "From Lang Son, the Chinese columns can advance on Hanoi, the capital; Haiphong, a major port; or any number of other coastal cites. The country opens up considerably, and it will be difficult for the Vietnamese forces to establish a strong defensive line, especially if U.S. airpower has been weakened."

The scene shifted to fuzzy color video of jets diving and firing missiles at something off the bottom of the screen. "This is Chinese video of a U.S. attack during the daylight hours." The image was replaced by a pile of tangled metal. "The same video says this is the remains of a U.S. attack plane shot down during that raid. There was no mention of the pilot. U.S. losses in their air attacks have been light, so far. Observers believe that the American commanders have been cautious, feeling their way carefully as they find out what works and what doesn't. We asked our CNN consultant, retired air force general Blake 'Sandman' Sandus, for his assessment."

Sandus was standing in front of a wall-sized video screen. Photos of U.S. planes flashed across it, changing every few moments. He wore a conservative blue suit, and the camera zoomed in for a moment on his tie clasp, a miniature F-15.

"This is the first time in decades that the U.S. has not had complete air supremacy. In military terms, this is not a 'permissive air environment,' which in plain English means there is a real risk that our aircraft could get shot down."

The screen split, and the news anchor asked, "And this is because we've lost so many GPS satellites?"

Sandus nodded vigorously. "It's actually a double whammy. The precision of GPS weapons made it easier to neutralize any air defenses and then made sure a high percentage of the ordnance dropped actually hit what we wanted. My friends tell me that wing and squadron commanders are still looking for the right mix of weapons and tactics. Until then, they're playing it safe."

The anchor asked, "Isn't that just being wise?"

Sandus shrugged. "In one sense, yes, but playing it safe won't win a war. Air warfare used to be about attrition, with the losses we suffered justified by the damage we inflicted on the other side. Nowadays, we can't afford even moderate losses. We lose airplanes and pilots that are very difficult to replace, the other side may get a hostage, and the administration gets a black mark."

"Are you saying that there has been political pressure to keep casualties low?"

"All I'm saying is the higher the casualty count, the more heat the president's going to get about coming in on the side of the Vietnamese. It's a principled stand, but following one's principles gets harder and harder as the losses rise. That's why we haven't committed any ground forces to help the Vietnamese."

"General, since the air attacks aren't as effective as we hoped, should we commit ground troops? Certainly they won't be affected as badly by the lack of GPS."

Sandus smiled and shook his head. "Don't ask me. I was air force, and my opinion on that question isn't worth much. But you know what they say about ground wars in Asia."

U.S. Space Force Headquarters
Edwards Air Force Base
Hangar
November 23, 2017

Ray had resisted calling it "Laser Day," but the admiral had overruled him. "It's a milestone, Ray. Let everyone share the moment."

Geoffrey had laid it on as a minor celebration. The cafeteria, still called "The Hangar" despite operating from a newly erected prefabricated building, would offer a special menu, and he'd organized a laser light show on the side of the hangar, accompanied by the "appropriate music."

But it was an important step, a visible step. At thirteen-ten that afternoon, the actual hangar's overhead crane had lowered the airborne laser assembly into *Defender*'s cargo bay. He lost track of the number of steps that had led up to this point: structural modifications to the vehicle's spaceframe, laying power and fiber-optic cables in the bay—all the while refurbishing the laser's optics and its combustion chamber. That had been a technical challenge. It would now be exposed to vacuum, and the temperature extremes of space. It had never been designed for that, and in the end they'd had to reinforce the shell and add insulation.

It had taken only a few minutes to lower the laser into position, then mate it to the spaceframe with some very large, but very ordinary-looking, bolts.

Four days ago, he'd watched the one test the laser would get, hurriedly mounted on a steel framework and connected to a portable generator for power. Fuel tanks used for the original ground tests over thirty years ago had been located, tested, connected to the test rig, and filled. They held enough of the chemicals for two shots.

The earliest satellite window after they were ready had been at zero four-thirty. Ray had briefly considered skipping the test in favor of sleep, but it wasn't in his nature. He had to be there, and had watched as the last of the test instrumentation had been attached.

There was a hundred-yard safety zone in case of a breach in the combustion chamber, and they'd all watched from a slit trench as Amy Sloan, head of the laser section, held a silver box with two buttons. She pressed the first, and it lit, meaning laser fuel was free to move from the tanks to the chamber. She pressed the second, and the laser fired.

There was enough moisture and dust in the air that one could see the beam, a pale red spear that flashed and disappeared in a fraction of a second. It was aimed straight up, toward the zenith. Hoots and applause celebrated the sight, but Sloan concentrated on her watch, counting the seconds. The engineers had calculated the optimum interval to test the chamber, and just a few moments after the first shot, she fired it again. A second faint red flash came and went, and Ray found himself exhaling with relief.

The beam would be invisible in space, of course, and even if it were visible, they would all be in the cabin. A remote camera would be trained on the laser in the bay, but mainly to make sure the mechanism that moved and aimed the mirror was operating properly.

He'd listened for a noise, too, maybe a "pop" as air rushed into the space where the beam has passed, but the angry whine of the pumps had masked anything else, real or imagined. He was glad they wouldn't be able to hear that in the cabin.

At the "Laser Day" celebration, Ray mingled and watched every-one. Geoffrey's cooks had prepared a Cajun menu, with many "laser-blackened" items, as well as a very good bouillabaisse. He limited himself to small portions, since he still had a few more pounds to lose before he'd be at what Barnes called "flight weight."

People were definitely enjoying themselves. He heard laughter and animated conversation, although it often seemed to be technical. He knew many would go right back to work after the laser show, hope-fully refreshed.

He spotted Glenn Chung, sitting and chatting with several oth-ers, and did his best to look away. He'd seen Chung several other times during the past few days, bound on some task for the IT division. Ray had done his best to ignore Chung, but it was hard, knowing what he was. Was he gathering information right now, some frag-ment about someone's progress? It was a common topic, after all, and their common goal.

Ray's clenched jaw relaxed a bit when he realized that one of the people at the table with Chung was one of Evans's security team. The thought comforted him, but also made him doubly self-conscious. Then he spotted Geoffrey Lewes near the serving line. He seemed to be looking at the same table Ray had been. Ray tossed his plastic plate and utensils into a trash can and walked slowly over to the mo-rale officer.

"It's hard, isn't it?"

Lewes, startled and a little embarrassed, turned to Ray and said, "Tell me the food is good. I need to think about something else."

"The food really is good, Geoffrey. A party like this is almost as good as a day off."

"I like it when they're smiling, Ray. I can't help build *Defender*. I can barely check the oil in my car."

"But you know you're making a difference."

Out of the corner of his eye, he saw Chung get up from his table with several others and head for the exit. He saw Lewes tracking Chung's movement as well. Ray felt himself relax a little, since if Chung wasn't around . . .

"You know, he's going to notice if you're trying this hard to not look at him."

Coming from behind, Colonel Evans's voice startled Ray so much he would have jumped, except the colonel's hand was on his shoulder, steadying him. Evans's other hand was doing the same for Lewes, who was just as surprised.

Ray took a deep breath. Lewes said, "Sorry."

"No harm done this time," Evans said softly, "but next time, just leave. Don't wait for him to go."

"Has anyone picked up the item?" Ray asked quietly.

"Not yet," Evans replied. "It's all good right now. The longer we can leave him in place, the better for us."

Lewes nodded silently and headed for the back of the serving line. He had the right idea, Ray realized. Focus on what you could do.

He left the tent, headed for his office. Spy stuff was hard. He'd stick to building spaceships.

18

Break Point

CNN Report
November 23, 2017

"General Blake Sandus has been helping us understand the extraordinary events of this morning when we woke up to find we were in a full-fledged naval war with the People's Republic of China. Until yesterday, the U.S. had limited itself to air and Tomahawk strikes on Chinese units inside Vietnamese territory. General, is that correct?"

Sandus's thin frame barely filled a blue polo shirt embroidered with U.S. AIR FORCE and a set of pilot's wings. His mostly gray hair was still kept short in a pilot's crew cut. His voice was strong and clear, although he looked tired. The day had started very early.

"Jane, that's right. Attacking only Chinese troops that had crossed into Vietnam allowed the Jackson administration to correctly claim that they were only defending China's neighbor from aggression. It also gave the Chinese a way out, which they could have taken if they had suffered too many casualties."

"Do you think this new escalation is because American airpower wasn't enough to stop the Chinese? After all, the Chinese have taken Lang Son. Reports put them as much as thirty kilometers south of that city."

Sandus stepped over to a large flat-screen display of Vietnam. He tapped an icon, and the view zoomed in to show red arrows well south of the Vietnamese city, spreading south toward Hanoi, a hundred kilometers away, and southeast toward the coast. He tapped the latter arrow. "This is what may have given the Joint Chiefs the idea to take the war to sea. This column is driving on Haiphong, a major port. The road net across Vietnam's northern border is thin and is still vulnerable to interdiction, even if the Chinese spearhead is now in open country. If the Chinese capture a major port, it would let them supply their invasion by sea. It's the same as the D-day invasion in 1944, when the Allies' first goal was the French port of Cherbourg."

"Aren't naval forces affected by the loss of GPS?"

"Not to the same extent, Jane. Aviators need accurate three-dimensional location data—an aircraft's altitude demands it—while sailors who operate at sea level only need two. And they've had ways of navigating long before satellites appeared. Antiship weapons also have to hit moving targets, so they tend to use active radar homing rather than GPS guidance."

"And that puts us back on an equal footing with the Chinese?"

"Better than equal, I'd say. We still have an edge over the Chinese navy in several important warfare areas, although they have the advantage in numbers. We are operating in their own backyard, after all."

"So this new strategy is to block the invasion's supply lines?"

"Yes. For instance, a group of Chinese amphibious ships with their escorts were attacked off Cam Pha." He tapped a spot on the Vietnamese coast just south of the border with China. "They may have intended to land near Haiphong and catch the Vietnamese in a pincer, but a U.S. submarine wolf pack appears to have sunk both amphibious ships and some of the escorts.

"But this naval strategy is much more than that, Jane. If the navy had limited itself to just attacking Chinese warships in Vietnamese waters, that would have been the kind of small-step escalation that we tried in Vietnam." He grinned. "I know all about that. I was there."

Sandus zoomed the map back out to show the western Pacific and the South China Sea. He pointed to the south. "Instead, here at the exits of the Strait of Malacca, Lombok Strait, and Sunda Strait, U.S. warships are stopping every Chinese merchant ship they can find and sending them north to Vietnam. Other U.S. ships are doing the same in the South China Sea. Since the Vietnamese submarine fleet has already done some damage to China's shipping, America joining in will virtually shut down the shipping lanes in that area, at least for Chinese merchant ships."

He shifted the map to show the Chinese coast.

"American subs have taken positions outside several Chinese ports and naval bases and have already torn a patch out of the Chinese fleet and their merchant marine." He checked his watch. "As of ten hundred hours here on the East Coast, we know for certain of five merchants and two major warships that have been sunk, in addition to the ones lost off Cam Pha." He tapped the map in several places along the Chinese Pacific coast.

"What will the Chinese do to respond?" the news anchor asked.

"Well, they're screaming bloody murder, of course, and they'll try to find and sink our ships and subs where they can. But China's become a world power, which means their economy depends on importing materials from abroad and selling goods overseas. They've become vulnerable to a naval blockade, although the buzzword for it these days is 'containment.' The advantage of the naval strategy is that we can put pressure on the Chinese without attacking anything on Chinese soil. In fact, as far as I can tell, all the ships that were sunk were outside Chinese territorial waters."

"But isn't such a major escalation risky?"

"It's very risky," Sandus agreed. "But the president's committed the U.S. military to 'stopping Chinese aggression before it goes farther,' according to his press conference this morning. But aside from the risk to our military forces, other nations have axes to grind with China. It's a big country, and it has a lot of territorial disputes with its neighbors."

Sandus pointed to the Himalayas. "While China is busy, what if

India decides to score some points along their common border? The Vietnamese would love to take back the Paracel Islands they lost in 1974. It might seem strange for them to make an attack while Chinese troops are coming south en masse, but the Chinese garrison on the island is tiny, and taking them back would embarrass the Chinese and give the folks at home a boost in morale. Think of the Doolittle Raid over Tokyo at the beginning of World War Two in the Pacific."

"Is there a chance that Taiwan might use this opportunity to declare independence?"

"Well, that is the Big Question." Sandus scratched his jaw thoughtfully. "I'm just an old fighter jock, and the people who thought about that stuff were way above my pay grade."

The anchor smiled. "General, you commanded the U.S. Pacific Air Forces for two years before you became chief of staff of the Air Force."

"And one thing I learned was that predicting the behavior of a country's decision makers is fraught with peril. Right now, with Chinese ground forces involved in Vietnam and the U.S. Navy shooting at Chinese ships, it might seem to be the perfect time. But this war is really a test of strength between a rising China and what it believes is a weakened America. If Taiwan, or anybody else, decides to act, it won't be until China is clearly losing."

"Is that what you believe this is about? A test of strength?"

"Yes, Jane, at its most basic level it's about China feeling its oats and deciding to knock the U.S. out of the dominant position in the western Pacific. President Jackson has repeated over and over again that he's out to stop Chinese aggression. Do you have that clip from his speech this morning?"

The image shifted to show the president in the East Room of the White House. The sound cut in just as the president said, "Armed aggression against any country, whether it is a formal U.S. ally or not, is cause for deep concern. If we did nothing, and Vietnam fell to the invading armies, would China be weaker or stronger? Would they be satisfied with their single conquest, or would they look at other countries in the region? None can stand against the Chinese military by themselves. We cannot wait until they attack one of our allies at a time of their choosing. We must show China, prove to them, that aggression is not only futile but will cost them far more than they could ever hope to gain."

The picture shifted back to show the anchor and General Sandus watching the image. "Do you agree with his philosophy, General?"

"He's got a good speechwriter, and on one level, he's correct, but national leaders rarely tell you the real reasons for a war." Sandus paused for a moment, then carefully explained. "The Chinese began this confrontation by shooting down our satellites, which they are still doing, by the way. They believe that without GPS, our military is too weak to stop them from doing what they want. The invasion of Vietnam is a demonstration of Chinese power—a land grab. If we don't turn them back, then China becomes the big kid on the block. Every U.S. ally, not only in Asia but around the world, will have to rethink their relationship with us, and every U.S. adversary will see new opportunities to advance their cause at our expense."

"You make it sound like our survival is at stake."

"As a superpower, Jane, yes it is. The most dangerous time for a superpower is when they stop being one. If we lose this war, we'll find out what that's like."

U.S. Space Force Headquarters
Edwards Air Force Base
November 24, 2017

Ray McConnell was in the hangar when an engineer shouted to him from one of the side offices. "Mr. McConnell, the admiral wants to see you in his office ASAP." Schultz rarely summoned him like that, so Ray hurried to the admiral's office on the fourth floor.

The door was open, and Schultz waved him in. "You need to see this," he explained without prompting, and gestured toward and empty chair. As Ray sat down, the admiral pointed a controller at the flat screen mounted on his office wall.

The frozen image came to life, and Ray saw Congressman Thomas Rutledge at a podium. A brightly colored banner across the bottom said, "Breaking News," and the anchor's voice-over said, "Congressman Rutledge is speaking at a press conference in the U.S. Capitol. He's joined by Congressman Clayton Ashford, a Mississippi Republican, in demanding hearings by the House Armed Services Committee on the *Defender* program and the U.S. Space Force.

"The White House, the secretary of defense, and the Pentagon have all remained doggedly silent, refusing to acknowledge their existence even after their disclosure on the Internet some weeks ago. Let's listen to what Congressman Rutledge has to say." The sound cut in just as Rutledge leaned forward to speak into the microphone.

"These hearings need to explore the extent of the Jackson administration's misconduct, including his failure to effectively respond to the Chinese attacks on our navigational satellites, and instead apparently creating a whole new branch of the armed forces without formal congressional approval and spending unknown billions— that's billions with a *b*, folks, on a scheme of questionable merit. If that response wasn't inappropriate enough, the Jackson administration's also started a war with China, not only risking the lives of our brave men and women in uniform, but virtually guaranteeing a recession—and that's whether we win or lose."

The screen flashed back to the news anchor. "This is not the first time that Representative Rutledge has called for congressional hearings on *Defender* and the U.S. Space Force. Inquiries on the possibility of convening such a hearing have been sent to the House Minority Leader, Representative Thad Preston, and the ranking Republican on the House Armed Services Committee, Representative Rick Nussbaum. We've received a short joint statement this morning that acknowledged that 'Congressman Rutledge's concerns have merit, and consideration is being given to convene a hiring on the topic,' a rather lukewarm response, to be sure.

"Joining me in the studio are two widely recognized experts on congressional issues. The first is a political columnist with *The New York Times . . .*"

As the image shifted to a pair of analysts, Schultz hit the power switch. The admiral said in warning, "If a hearing is convened, it will be nothing but trouble."

"We'll have to testify, won't we?" Ray asked.

"I'm the head of the U.S. Space Force, so I'll be near the top of their list." Schultz grinned. "You're at the top, of course." He grinned. "It isn't like they haven't been looking for you."

Ray sighed. "Everyone with their name in the *Defender* document has been approached."

"And may be subpoenaed," Schultz concluded.

"My house is being watched. That's when they started following Jim Naguchi, when he went back to get some stuff for me. He's gotten the worst of it."

"Well, you certainly couldn't go."

"I haven't left the base in weeks—really, since we arrived here. I haven't wanted to leave, but this media hunt makes me feel like a fugitive." He shrugged. "Not that there's anywhere I need to go."

"Especially with Jenny here," teased Schultz.

"You don't seem to be very worried about these hearings," Ray observed.

"It's as great a danger as the Chinese," Schultz countered. "Just preparing for and attending the hearings would cost us time we can't afford. And even though it would be classified, there would be leaks. And with the legislative branch of the government fully engaged, Congress could pass legislation shutting us down or establishing a special prosecutor, or, God forbid, making us part of the air force."

"And there's nothing we can do," Ray complained.

"There's nothing *you* can do," Schultz corrected him. "One of my jobs, as head of this organization, is to keep stuff like this out of your face so you can focus on more important things. I'm working the system back in Washington, and we have other friends who are doing their own thing. Luckily, it doesn't take a lot to slow Congress down. Our one advantage is that they don't know our timeline. If we can stall them for just a little while, the whole thing will be moot."

Ray was about to ask how long it would take for Congress to issue subpoenas when Schultz's phone rang.

"Admiral Schultz," he said after picking up the handset. "Yes, Colonel, he's here." The admiral's head snapped toward Ray. "Thank you, I'll tell him."

Hanging up the phone, Schultz chuckled. "That was Colonel Evans. He asked me to tell you he's going golfing."

Colonel Evans said, "If I knew you were going to show up at my office this fast, I would have sent a text message from the golf course." He was smiling, though.

"Which I wouldn't get until after I left the SCIF!" growled Ray.

"Exactly!"

Ray shook his head wearily and asked, "You've still got the camera set up, right? You're going to watch him make the pickup?"

"Of course," Evans replied. "It will be evidence at his trial, as well as monitoring his actions."

"I wanted to see him make the pickup," Ray explained. "This still just doesn't seem real to me."

"And seeing another video on a computer screen will make it real?" Evans asked flatly. "Right. Anyway, Chung usually does his business after he hits a few balls. I'll let you stay that long, but I want you well away from here after that."

Ray almost laughed at Evans's parental tone but fought the urge and nodded solemnly.

Evans's flat screen had six windows set up, each showing the driving range from a different angle. Most were wide-angle views, but two were tightly zoomed in on the dead drop—the light pole and its support.

"There." Ray pointed to one of the windows. The camera was pointed across the width of the driving range, showing all the tees, which were empty. Chung walked into the frame, set up his clubs near the light post, grabbed a driver, and teed up a ball. Ray noticed how Chung kept his head up, using every motion to scan a different part of his surroundings. He hit a few balls, taking his time to verify he was all by himself. His attention drawn to the surroundings, he sometimes missed hitting the ball altogether. The other cameras confirmed he was alone. After a quick basket, Chung put the driver back in his golf bag. As he bent over to pick up his bag, his right hand lingered out of view for the briefest moment. "There." Evans tapped the screen. "He's opened the concealed pocket in his bag."

"If you say so," Ray answered. "It fooled me."

"It's supposed to," Evans replied, "but he made exactly the same motion last time he was there. Now he will go over and lean against the light standard while he ties his shoe."

Chung did exactly as Evans predicted. Ray watched as the traitor smoothly recovered a new flash drive with fresh instructions from his Chinese masters. Watching the act in real time had an unexpected effect on Ray. Suddenly, he grew ferociously angry, boiling mad. He wanted to charge out to Chung right now and grab him red-handed.

"It's real now, isn't it?" Ray noticed the colonel watching him, nodding slightly. "I've wanted to collar this sunuvabitch since we found him. But our patience has been rewarded. We've found out who his contact is, where his contact goes, and the FBI's now tracking that guy."

Ray's temper had cooled only slightly. Tersely, he asked, "When will you get the flash drive? I'm curious to see what the Chinese want now."

"About five minutes after he's back in his trailer. We know his pattern now. The accomplice isn't expecting to hear from Chung for another week or so, so we can move in at any time. The FBI will keep the other bastard under surveillance and hopefully track him to the next link in the chain. Now, don't you have something useful to do?"

The ringing woke him out of a dream. Confused, Ray fumbled to turn on the reading light, then grabbed the phone, unplugging it from the charger as he yanked it to his ear. Concentrating, he managed a passable "McConnell."

"It's Evans. Come to my office as soon as you can." He hung up before Ray could ask about what, and sudden anxiety propelled him out of bed. He focused his eyes on the phone in his hand. It was 2:10 A.M.

Ray's trailer was positioned close to the hangar and office annex, and he hurried through the early-morning desert chill toward the front gate and the security office. There were lights on in the hangar, but most of the complex was dark. He walked quickly, but halfway to the office, he heard a voice behind him. "Ray!"

It was Schultz, dressed in a gray sweat suit that read FLY NAVY across the front. Speaking softly, Ray asked, "Did Evans call you, too?"

"Yeah. Let's see what's worth waking us up for."

Evans was waiting and offered coffee to both without asking. Ray tried to wave it off, saying, "I'll never get back to sleep," but the colonel insisted.

"Too bad. I need you awake for this. We just got the decrypted contents of the flash drive back." He woke up his laptop and gestured to a list on the screen.

Ray started reading, and his heart sank. "It's a shopping list: current program status, communications frequencies and protocols, data-link vulnerabilities, the names and addresses of the families?"

"Oh, it gets even better," Evans remarked sternly.

Schultz and Ray watched as Evans brought up a separate file with detailed schematics of *Defender*. Ray gasped, "Look at this. 'Critical components in the hydrogen fueling system.' I recognize the diagrams, but someone's added these notations. Numbers and a Chinese character? Are these . . ."

"NSA says the character means 'kilograms.' Most likely, weights for explosive charges."

"Sabotage?" Even Schultz was stunned. "This is unbelievable!"

"This guy is being instructed to plant explosives on my baby!" Ray shouted.

"I know, incredible, isn't it?" Evans answered. "Well, now we know, categorically, the Chinese are worried about what we're doing here."

The colonel started pacing as the two senior officials looked on. "Chung has had way too much access for a civilian contractor. While I was waiting for you two to show up, I've been drawing up new security procedures. Except for a select few," he said, nodding to Ray and the admiral, "no one person should have access to everything. This is what happens when speed is the overriding priority. These new protocols will probably slow things down a bit. I'm sorry, but it can't be avoided. We've already paid too high a price for our mistake."

Schultz nodded his understanding; he was the one ultimately responsible. "The effectiveness of security is inversely proportional to its convenience," he quoted.

"Well put," Evans replied. "They can use this as a case study for future security-manager training." He shrugged. "Maybe they will, someday."

"Then that's it! We take Chung down now!" Ray demanded.

"The technical term is 'arrest,'" Evans observed. "We already have a plan to take him into custody, but I need to let my DCIS and FBI liaisons know first so they can put extra agents on the messenger. Even though Chung isn't expected to make contact for a little while, we still need to take precautions."

"Do we know who the runner is?" Ray asked.

"You don't have a need to know that, and frankly neither do I," answered Evans. "The FBI knows, and since they have jurisdiction off base, I won't stick my nose in their knickers."

"So sometime tomorrow they'll snag his contacts. What about Chung?"

"He's mine. Oh, there will be an FBI agent present, but I reserve the honor to put the cuffs on that asshole myself."

Looking at them both, Evans asked formally, "Do I have your permission to arrest him?"

The two looked at each other, and the admiral nodded to McConnell. "You say, it, Ray."

"Permission granted." Ray's expression held grim pleasure. "And I hope you use rusty handcuffs."

Evans nodded acknowledgment and said briskly, "Admiral, Ray, thank you for coming and making the decision so quickly. This simplifies my job immensely, but I've got some arrangements to make, so if you'll excuse me."

"One question, Colonel," injected Schultz. "How are you going to keep this quiet? You just can't nab Chung in front of everyone. How do you intend to keep his arrest a secret?"

Evans's face developed a wicked smile. "Oh, don't worry about that, sir. I have the perfect diversion." With that, Evans shooed them out of his office. Reluctantly, Ray and the admiral complied and began walking silently back to their trailers. Schultz was already yawning. He said, "I'll see you later in the morning, then," and turned to leave, but Ray had to ask, "How can you sleep after making a decision like that?"

The admiral smiled tiredly. "That was an easy one, Ray. And there's nothing else to do, so I'm going back to bed. I advise you to do the same. You were going to stay up, weren't you? Is something about this worrying you?"

"No. I agree it was the best thing to do, but there's just so much to think about."

"Ray, if you're going to be a leader, and not just an engineer, then learn to let go when you can, or you'll burn out. It will all be there in the morning. Good night."

Schultz headed for his trailer, and Ray did the same. He had been planning on staying up, tackling the mass of work that always waited, but really just marking the hours until Chung and his cohorts were arrested. But if he'd learned anything, it was that the admiral gave good advice.

Ray barely felt his head hit the pillow.

U.S. Space Force Headquarters
Office Annex
1100 hours
November 23, 2017

Glenn Chung had been fielding trouble calls all morning. Like most information techs, he regarded them as a pain, since most user problems were self-inflicted. On the other hand, it took him all over the *Defender* complex. Besides, this latest call might be an actual problem. Several people in the laser section had reported a 'sharp, acrid smell' near one of the servers. Sometimes, user descriptions of the problem could be a little vague, but this one sure sounded like a hardware failure.

The server for the laser section had one of his special "black boxes" on it. It was probably all right, but there was always the chance it was the source of the smell or that it had been damaged. He had a replacement ready, and a good story if the laser-lab supervisor was curious. Chung remembered his name: Al Sawyer. He was good with names. It was an asset in his profession.

Chung didn't bother knocking, but when he opened the door, he didn't recognize the man waiting next to the server bank. It certainly wasn't Sawyer, who was African American. This man was white, and taller—much taller. His name tag read RANDOLPH.

Mentally shrugging, Chung said, "Hi, I'm Glenn. Did you report the acrid odor?" As he offered his hand, he turned to look at the unit. Randolph took his right hand in an unexpectedly firm grip, almost painful. Reflexively, Chung started to pull away, but Randolph wouldn't let go. Before Chung could say something, another man came up from behind him and snapped a handcuff over his free wrist.

Confused, Chung felt a flash of panic. The hand with the cuff was still holding the toolbox, but he felt a sudden tug, and the box was sharply pulled from his grasp. Randolph then forcefully pushed the other wrist behind Chung's back to his unseen assailant. The man grabbed the wrist and pulled it into position. The feel of cold steel and the sound of sharp clicks sent Chung's heartbeat racing. Once his hands were secure, the other man quickly twisted him about. Still dazed, Chung soon found himself staring into Colonel Evans's fiery eyes.

"Gotcha, you traitorous scumbag," hissed Evans. He then shoved Chung toward Randolph and said, "He's all yours, Special Agent Randolph."

Spun around again, Chung found himself staring at the huge FBI agent. He had a large grin on his face. "Glenn Jing Chung, you are under arrest for violations of U.S. Code 2381, treason against the United States." Randolph's voice was flat, emotionless, but his expression clearly showed what he thought. "You have the right to remain silent. Anything you say . . ."

While Randolph gave Chung his *Miranda* warning, Evans and another agent searched him thoroughly. Randolph's steel grip effectively pinned Chung's arms behind him. His pockets were emptied and his belt removed.

It took a moment, but the word "treason" cleared away Chung's confusion. The panic remained, and he worked to calm himself. This was always a possibility, no matter how careful he was. He remained passive and did not struggle or speak. He had nothing he could say to them.

He realized now it had been an ambush, a setup. How much did they know? Had they arrested his contact as well? They would search his trailer. He could only hope that they made a mistake when they examined his laptop.

They finished their search, putting his belongings in a pouch that

Randolph sealed and tucked under his arm. Evans and the other FBI agent took firm hold of Chung's arms, while Randolph retrieved his toolbox. Their grip made it clear that any attempt to resist would be unwise. Their expressions matched Randolph's, and he realized he'd be seeing a lot of faces like that from now on.

Randolph pulled a radio from his belt and keyed the mike. "We're ready. Execute." He nodded to the other two, who silently nodded back.

A klaxon suddenly filled the building with harsh sound. It gave three short bursts, and then a recorded voice said, "THIS IS A DRILL. SECURITY ALERT, SECURITY ALERT. EXECUTE FACILITY-LOCKDOWN PROCEDURE. FOLLOW THE DIRECTIONS OF SECURITY TEAM MEMBERS. THIS IS A DRILL."

Chung knew the procedure. Colonel Evans insisted on holding emergency drills for fire, medical emergencies, or, in this case, terrorist attack. Everyone was supposed to stay in their offices or get into one, lock their doors, and not leave until the "all clear" was given.

A few moments after the alarm sounded, someone quietly rapped on the door, and Randolph opened it. Colonel Evans's deputy, in body armor and carrying an automatic weapon, gestured silently to Randolph, who stepped quickly through the door. Evans and the FBI agent hustled Chung out of the room, then down the hall at a fast walk, almost a trot. A heavily armed pair of Marines led the way.

Additional security personnel were waiting at the stairwell, reporting "Clear" as the group approached. Chung was virtually carried down the stairs, with Evans now in the lead, after being relieved by a third agent.

They reached the bottom level, and a black van, side door already open, was only feet away from the stairwell exit.

Chung was wordlessly muscled into the van, the three FBI agents climbing in with him. Their hostile silence amplified the slam as the doors closed, cutting off all light except what came from the windshield and forward windows.

The van started moving, and while he was curious where they were going, Chung didn't ask. They might not answer, and, besides, it didn't matter. His fate was set, and nothing he said would change it.

"That's it, then, he's gone," Evans reported with uncontained satisfaction. "I've briefed his supervisor. Josh will tell everyone that there was a sudden family emergency, and he's not sure when he will be back. As far as I can tell, the FBI took him into custody and got him into the van without anyone seeing him."

"Good," Schultz replied, sounding just as pleased, and very relieved. "With any luck, the Chinese won't know he's been arrested for a week, maybe two if we're lucky."

Ray added, "And we avoid the distraction of a Chinese spy being discovered in our midst."

"The distraction, and the publicity—the last thing we need is publicity," Schultz agreed.

"Where will they take him?" Ray asked.

Evans shrugged. "Probably the supermax prison in Colorado. He'll be held incommunicado there until after *Defender*'s launch." The colonel held out a hand, forestalling questions. "Don't worry, he'll be arraigned, and charged, and probably assigned a government lawyer, once we can get one read into the program."

"What if he wants his own lawyer?" Ray asked.

"That's for the Justice Department to sort out with the DoD Judge Advocate General," Evans answered. "It's unlikely Chung will even ask. He hasn't spoken a word since he was arrested."

"Treason," Ray said, testing the idea in his mind.

"I looked it up," Evans explained. "'Aid and comfort to the enemy,' and that definitely includes espionage. If he's convicted, he could get the needle."

"I'd gladly shoot him myself," Schultz added harshly. "He's put the lives of people under my command in jeopardy." He turned to face Evans. "I'm sure you're doing your best to help the FBI and make sure there are no mistakes, but your highest priority is finding out what he told the Chinese."

Evans straightened, almost coming to attention. "Yessir. I'll make sure FBI forensic guys understand what's at stake. Two of my people are with the FBI, searching his trailer right now, while his roommate's at work. By the time he's back, Chung's stuff will all be gone."

Ray said, "At some point, I'll have to tell Biff and the flight crew about this, and the department heads, in case he's done something that will affect the mission."

"Let's wait and see what the investigation finds out," Evans cautioned. "It won't take that long."

The wicked grin suddenly popped up again on Evans's face. "Don't worry, Ray. I'll make sure Jenny knows it wasn't your idea to keep her in the dark. No champagne."

"Does everybody know about that?"

19

Incidents

USS *Santa Fe* (SSN 763)
Yalong Bay
Hainan Island, China
November 30, 2017

"Ten seconds, Skipper." The XO's voice held a warning. Lieutenant Commander Jeff Kerry was the nervous type, but right now he felt it was an appropriate response.

"All right, down scope." Commander Leigh Taylor, captain of *Santa Fe,* shook his head. "The coast to the north is littered with lights. Picking out any navaids, even when you know where to look, is virtually impossible." He tapped the chart. "But I got a laser range and bearing to this pier on the eastern side of the harbor."

"It's good, Skipper," Lieutenant Mark Larson, the navigator, reported. "The bearing's consistent with our dead-reckoning position. We're steady on course zero two zero, depth under the keel is twenty feet. Yeshu Island is eleven hundred forty yards to the northwest, bearing two nine two. Set and drift unchanged, just over one knot east with the flood tide."

"Very well." Taylor acknowledged the report.

"The intercom buzzed. "Conn, Torpedo Room. Third salvo is ready."

Taylor nodded, and the XO pressed the "talk" switch. "Torpedo Room, Conn. Understood. Good work on the fast reload. Stand by."

The captain was already standing at the door to the sonar shack. "COB, what's the closest contact?"

Master Chief Sonarman Patrick McCarthy was not only the senior sonar technician, he was chief of the boat, the senior enlisted man aboard. Taylor was sure *Santa Fe* had been given this assignment because of McCarthy's skills. He was a small man, but his flaming red hair and Boston accent testified to his Southie upbringing.

"Sierra five two is now six hundred yards away, closing with a slight right bearing drift. She's likely outbound for the western gap in the breakwater. The next closest is Sierra five seven at eight hundred yards, but she's pointed south and away from us."

Taylor nodded and hit the intercom switch. "Torpedo Room, Conn. Launch Slims seven through nine." Raising his voice slightly, he announced, "As soon as they're away, I'm going to take her as close to the bottom as I can and increase speed. We'll get out from in front of Sierra five two."

The fire-control technician called out the tube as the Slim was launched. With the third one, Taylor issued a quick reminder. "Diving Officer, keep a steady watch on the trim forward."

"Aye, sir, watch the trim forward. I'm being very careful. I don't even like Chinese food." Chief Harris was using the weight of water in the sub's trim tanks to keep her on an even keel. The sub had just lost a little over two tons out the torpedo tubes, almost seven tons overall. If the chief didn't bring in the same weight in water, *Santa Fe* would be buoyant. This close to the surface, she might "broach," or accidentally surface. Doing this in the middle of a hostile naval base, in fact right in front of an approaching patrol boat, would be a Bad Thing.

Taylor laughed with the rest at the chief's quip. The navy called it a "Mark 67 Submarine Launched Mobile Mine." But "Slim" was a lot easier to say. *Santa Fe* had just sent three of them into the Chinese base in Yalong Bay. Actually, it was the third set of three. The

torpedo room was loading the last salvo now, making twelve altogether.

Based on the old Mark 37 torpedo, it would swim to a preset point,
shut off its motor, and wait on the bottom for the right combination
of pressure, sound, and magnetic field—for example, the kind made
by a large Chinese warship or submarine.

The little Haiqing-class subchaser coming toward them wouldn't
be enough to set one off. She only displaced four hundred tons. A
fifteen-hundred-ton frigate, or an even larger destroyer, though,
would trigger an explosive charge big enough to break her in two.

"Sierra five two is at four hundred yards, bears zero eight six, speed
six knots."

"Make your depth eight five feet, increase speed to six knots."

"Sir, the harbor shelves sharply ahead. We can hold this course
and speed for just over a minute."

"Understood, Mark."

Santa Fe had been at three knots, bare steerageway, while she
launched her mines. Doubling that speed was risky but would get
the sub to one side of the patroller's path.

"Sir, given the listed draft of a Haiqing-class, their keel should clear
our sail. Barely. Maybe five feet."

The navigator added, "That's about all we have under us." He
didn't sound happy.

Larson's report was immediately followed by a rhythmic *whoosh,
whoosh* that quickly grew in volume and then faded just as quickly.

"Make your depth seven zero feet, make turns for three knots."

The helmsman acknowledged the order. Larson didn't say anything but looked relieved. The acoustic intercept receiver chirped
madly in the background, diligently warning *Santa Fe*'s crew of all
the active sonars in the area.

Taylor asked, "Sonar, Conn, was Sierra five two still using a search
ping interval?"

McCarthy nodded emphatically. "Conn, Sonar. Yes, sir. No change
in the ping interval. She sailed on by and is continuing on course.

No indication they detected us, although we were in the main lobe for a few pings."

"With luck, our return blended in with the bottom," Taylor remarked.

"That or the sonar operator didn't know what he was looking at." Kerry grinned. "The return was probably pretty mushy. Our hull coating is particularly effective against those high-frequency sets."

"What's he doing now, XO?"

"He's in our baffles, Skipper." Kerry shrugged helplessly. The noise from a ship or sub's engines would blind a sonar if it tried to look aft. It was called "the baffles" because the builder actually installed a noise-absorbing baffle in the sonar dome to block any sound from that direction. Sonar would be of no help.

Nodding his understanding, Taylor stepped up to the number-two scope, raised it, and brought it around to face aft.

They all watched the television repeater that showed the periscope's view. Low waves lapped over the lens as it emerged, just inches above the water. The captain panned the scope to the left a short distance, then right. "There," he announced. The green-black low-light image showed the patrol craft's starboard quarter. "Still headed for the western exit," Taylor concluded.

Kerry said, "If he was curious, he'd have turned by now."

Taylor ordered, "Down scope," and pressed the intercom switch again. "Torpedo Room, Conn. How much longer on the fourth salvo?"

"Conn, Torpedo Room. Two down and one to go. The third Slim is going in now, sir. Another minute, tops."

"Understood."

"Captain, that increased speed for a moment moved us a little farther north than planned for the last salvo, but we're still within margins."

"Conn, Torpedo Room. Reloading complete. We're ready down here, sir."

Taylor looked over at Kerry, who nodded. "We're clear, sir."

"Then launch Slims ten through twelve," Taylor ordered. "And good riddance. When I shoot something, I like to hear a 'boom' right away."

Taylor waited for the report from the torpedo room before changing course. "Conn, Torpedo Room. Mines away, reloading with Mark 48 torpedoes."

"Torpedo Room, Conn. Understood. Stand by." Taylor glanced at the chart. Larson pointed at the sub's track. "Planned course of one six zero is still good, sir. It's fifteen hundred yards to the firing point. That's fifteen minutes at current speed. The tunnel entrance will bear zero five five at sixteen hundred yards."

"Very well. Helm: Right fifteen degrees rudder, steady on course one six zero." The new course would not only take them to their next waypoint inside the harbor but also closer to the southern exit, a three-hundred-yard opening in the breakwater on that side of the harbor.

"I think Mr. Larson and I will both feel better if I take a fix." Checking the chart, the captain said, "I'll take a range and bearing to the south corner of the main pier. After that, I'll increase speed to five knots. That will still give the torpedo room enough time to finish reloading."

"Bearing to the south corner of the main pier should be zero nine five, Skipper." Larson reported.

The XO took up position, watching the television monitor that would display the scope's image, and the clock, while Taylor turned the periscope, still down, to the eastern bearing. "Raising number-two scope."

On the television screen, the black-green image of the main pier was part of a confused muddle of lights; then Taylor upped the magnification, and the rectangular shape was clearly visible. He aligned the crosshairs squarely on the south corner and pressed the button under his thumb. "Bearing, mark. Range, mark."

"Bearing one five one, range two seven double-oh yards," Larson reported.

They waited for the captain to lower the scope. After a moment, the XO said, "Ten seconds, Skipper."

"Stand by," Taylor answered, and swung a little to the left. The image shifted on the screen and then flashed from green-black to natural light. Kerry tried to interpret the image, but the captain ordered "Down scope" sharply and snapped the hoist control ring to the down position.

The XO was already rewinding the video, then stepping through it in slow motion. The changing magnification made it more a succession of still images than a video, but after a few moments, he stopped the image on the main pier.

"Yes, that's when I saw it," Taylor commented. "What do you see moored at the pier?"

Kerry answered, "A sub, and a lot of activity on the pier." There were what looked like cranes, as well as lights that looked bright green in the false-color image.

Taylor ordered, "Step forward a beat."

Now the image was centered, and larger. "That's too long to be a diesel, or even a nuke attack boat," the XO commented.

"I concur. Step forward some more."

This was where the captain had shifted to natural light. Now the image was bathed in white light, and while the scene was darker, it was somehow easier for the eye to interpret. Bright lights bathed a long jet-black hull while cranes worked aft of the sail. "That is a Type 094 Jin-class ballistic missile submarine," Kerry said, almost reverently.

"At the main pier. In the open," Taylor added quietly. "And it looks like she's loading missiles." He paused only for a moment. "Helmsman, come left to one seven zero. Make turns for five knots. Observation, stationary target, main pier. Stand by for bearing and range."

Even while the scope was going up, the XO said, "Skipper, our orders are to torpedo the tunnel door, trapping the boomer inside."

Taylor steadied the scope and called out, "Bearing, mark! Range, mark! Down scope!" As the scope was sliding back down, the captain replied, "But remember our briefing? The intel weenies said they couldn't guarantee it would be inside. This removes any doubt. Where's Sierra five seven?"

"Still heading slowly south, probably for the same exit we are, range is twenty-one hundred yards." Sierra five seven was also an escort vessel, one of the new Type 056 corvettes, larger and with better weapons and sensors than the older Haiqing patrol craft.

Taylor stepped down from the periscope stand and looked at the paper plot, then the fire control display. "Hmmm, he's just in the right place to be a major pain in the butt. We'll have to plug him at the same time as the boomer."

"That's close to minimum enable run, Skipper," the XO warned.

"Then we'll shoot quickly. First we shoot tubes one and two at the Jin, cut the wires, then tubes three and four at Sierra five seven. Two weapons each. Set the acoustic seekers to 'off' for the first two weapons, high speed. The Jin is stationary, no Doppler, and the seekers would pick up too many echoes from the pier. The magnetic fuse will be good enough." Taylor was speaking quickly but carefully. "Send out the second pair at medium speed, forty knots, minimum enable run. By the time the weapons hit the Jin, the others will have acquired the 056 and will be homing."

The XO acknowledged the orders and relayed them to the fire-control technician.

Taylor then announced, "Firing point procedures. First the Type 094 SSBN, tubes one and two, then Sierra five seven, tubes three and four."

"Ship ready," called out the OOD.

"Solution ready," barked Kerry.

"Weapons ready," said the weapons officer.

"Stand by for final observation on the SSBN, up scope!" Taylor yanked on the hoist control and waited for the barrel to rise. Snapping out the handles, he quickly placed his forehead against the eyepiece. "Bearing, mark! Range, mark!"

"Bearing, one four five degrees. Range, two one double-oh yards."

"Solution matches!" Kerry exclaimed.

"Ready, shoot!"

As the scope was lowered, the hull shook twice as the two Mark 48 torpedoes were expelled from their tubes.

"Impulse return, normal launch. Torpedo course one four five, speed six five knots, acoustics off," reported the fire control technician.

"Conn, Sonar, own ship's weapons are running normally." McCarthy's voice was just as steady as it was during their last exercise.

Taylor barely acknowledged the report when they all heard a faint rumble.

"Shift targets. Shoot on generated bearings, Sierra five seven, tubes three and four," Taylor ordered.

Once again, *Santa Fe* shook as she launched more torpedoes.

"Conn, Sonar. Second set of weapons running normally. Also, the rumbling is off our starboard quarter, assessed as the reflection of an explosion aft, possibly one of our mines going off."

"Sonar, Conn. Aye. Report status on Sierra five seven."

"Conn, Sonar. The contact's blade rate is increasing, bearing rate is drifting to the left. Yep, Sierra five seven is zigging to port."

"Detect. Detect. Detect. Homing. Both weapons have acquired the target," the fire-control tech sang out.

"Then his turn won't matter." Taylor ordered, "Cut the wires on tubes three and four and close the outer doors."

Suddenly, two extremely loud and near simultaneous detonations rocked the boat. Everyone in the control room grabbed on to something to steady themselves.

"*That* was the boomer," Kerry observed looking at his stopwatch. Taylor only nodded. There still was the business with the escort to conclude.

"Conn, Sonar. Weapon number four has sped up and is closing on Sierra five seven," announced McCarthy. "Weapon number three has drifted away from the target and slowed down; it's executing a reattack search."

By the time Taylor acknowledged McCarthy's last report, another loud explosion shook *Santa Fe*. Only one torpedo had hit the corvette, but that would be more than enough.

"Observation. Up scope," Taylor ordered, and had the scope pointed straight at their second victim as the lens cleared the water. Low-level light and visible light images both showed the warship on its port side, its stern missing, covered in flames.

Once he was sure he'd gotten a good picture, Taylor panned the scope left. The Type 094 SSBN was gone, only debris and a large fire marked its last-known position. Facing south toward the open sea, the two lights that marked the opening in the breakwater were visible. Taylor took bearing and range to both, calling out "Mark" each time.

"Port light bears one six nine degrees, range seventeen hundred yards. Starboard light bears one seven eight degrees, range one six eight zero yards," Larson reported.

"Helm, come left to course one seven four. XO, how does that match the HF sonar?" All U.S. subs had a high-resolution mine-avoidance sonar fitted to look forward. It was designed to show underwater obstacles.

"I show the gap between one six eight and one seven eight degrees. The image is clear."

"Very well. Mark, what's the water depth?"

"One hundred feet here, sir, sloping down to one hundred and fifty at the breakwater entrance, and deeper once we're outside."

Taylor ordered, "Make your depth nine zero feet. Increase speed to twelve knots." He saw some concern on the XO's face and explained. "We were supposed to be a lot closer to that breakwater before we fired a torpedo."

"We're going to leave a wake on the surface, Skipper."

"It's night, and the wake's next to a sinking corvette." The captain glanced at his watch. "And we'll be outside the harbor in five minutes. Keep your eyes on the HF array, XO. I want to split the uprights."

"Keep my eyes on the display, yes, sir!" They were going too fast now to use the periscope. They would have to depend on the display to keep them from ramming the breakwater.

After a few minutes, the XO reported, "Slight left drift. The southern opening bears one six five to one nine seven, recommend coming right to course one seven nine."

"Helm, come right to course one seven nine."

"Conn, Sonar. Faint explosions to the south."

Taylor nodded while keying the mike. "Sonar, Conn. That should be Captain Walsh in *Columbia*. Are the explosions consistent with torpedo detonations?"

"Yes, sir!" shouted McCarthy from the sonar shack.

Taylor was ready to celebrate, but they weren't out of the woods just yet. One SSBN, one corvette, and possibly one something else sunk or damaged. *Not bad for a night's work*, he thought.

Santa Fe had snuck in, using stealth and darkness to hide her entry, but there was no time to be subtle. Her squadron mate USS *Columbia* was blowing a hole in the ring of escort vessels outside the harbor and, in general, creating a ruckus to draw Chinese attention away from *Santa Fe*. And if the air force was doing its part, U.S. fighters had entered Chinese airspace to shoot down any ASW aircraft that might be overhead.

The opening in the breakwater swelled on the mine-hunting display until there was nothing but open water on the screen ahead of them.

And they were out.

Oval Office
The White House
December 1, 2017

"It was Vietnam's taking the Paracels back that started this." Hugh
Cambridge was President Jackson's secretary of state. He sounded
exasperated more than unhappy. Defense Secretary Peck and General Kastner, Chairman of the Joint Chiefs, nodded agreement, but
Kastner added, "Don't forget the Spratlys."

Cambridge waved the general's words aside. "The Philippines already had troops on Thitu Island when the shooting started. They
just reinforced the garrison."

Peck backed up the general. "I disagree, Hugh. A few months ago,
the Chinese would have raised a major stink about a military buildup
on a contested island."

"Both those situations are different than the issue before us," President Jackson declared. "Vietnam recaptured territory from a hostile state. Our only role was making it too dangerous for the Chinese
to intercept the landing force."

General Kastner added sarcastically, "We didn't even find out
about it until our patrol planes spotted the ships coming out of Da
Nang. There was no notice, and absolutely no cooperation between
us and Vietnam."

"In the second case," Jackson argued, "the Philippines, a U.S.
ally, reinforced the troops on an island they already possessed.
The Chinese may claim it, but they can't bully the Filipinos right
now."

"The critical words are 'right now,'" Secretary Cambridge argued.
"Once this conflict ends, what's to prevent the Chinese from revert-
ing to their old ways? They fought a battle in 1974 to take the Paracel Islands away from Vietnam. Will they try it again? And this latest
move is just going to make it worse."

"So your recommendation is that I tell the Japanese no," Jackson
stated.

"I didn't say that, sir," Cambridge protested. "There are consequences with either answer. If we say we're against it and they occupy the islands anyway, that only reinforces the notion that we have no influence in the region."

"At least they told us what they're doing, before they do it," Peck observed.

"When they're two days away from sailing," Cambridge countered acidly. "And it wasn't so much asking for permission, as it was, 'By the way, we plan on placing military forces on Uotsuri Island. We'd like to coordinate with any operations you have planned in the area.' They don't really need our help. The Japanese task force includes two of their Aegis destroyers."

Peck nodded. "They can take care of themselves, as long as the Chinese don't concentrate too many assets against them."

"Will the Chinese do anything at all?" Jackson asked. "Firing on a U.S. ally that currently isn't involved in the war? China has enough problems without adding the Japanese to the list of combatants."

"They're already mad about our ships and planes operating from Japanese bases," Cambridge pointed out.

"And have done nothing," Jackson responded. "We haven't attacked targets within China. If they strike Japan, all bets are off. General, are there any military implications of the Japanese operation that we should be aware of?"

Kastner grinned. "If the Japanese are going anyway, I'll make sure PACCOM has good comms with their people. It's part of the Chinese coast I won't have to worry about."

"Look at it from China's point of view," Cambridge protested unhappily. "After all, that's what you pay me for. First, we start shooting up their navy, which they were going to use to exert control over the South China Sea. Now, while we're keeping their fleet busy, all the smaller nations are using the opportunity to grab disputed territories. It's all about the fishing rights and the oil and mineral deposits," the secretary observed. "Did you know there are three oil-exploration ships getting ready to sail from Japanese ports? Each from a different company?"

"Mr. President, as far as I can see," Peck argued, "this is all part of that 'cost of aggression' you included in your speech. It's certainly more than they bargained for when they started shooting down our GPS satellites."

"Which they are still doing. We lost the fifteenth satellite today," Jackson observed. "And they show no intention of stopping. All right. Whether or not we say yes, the Japanese will seize the Senkaku Islands and formally make them their own. Their nationalist prime minister chalks up a win, along with their economy. It will be another loss of face for China and another crimp in their future plans for economic expansion." He paused. "I'm not unhappy with that. Hugh?"

"I can make it work, Mr. President." The secretary of state sounded resigned.

Secretary Peck was more positive. "I'm in favor of anything that gives the Chinese heartburn."

"I'll take that as a yes," Jackson replied.

U.S. Space Force Headquarters
Edwards Air Force Base
Office Annex
December 2, 2017

They'd all heard the news of the incident before being summoned to the fourth-floor conference room. Every video screen on the base that was tuned to the news showed the same thing: rolling explosions and waves of orange flame billowing out of a chemical plant in Indiana. It was a bad one.

Ray waited, along with Schultz, Colonel Evans, and Josh Blake, the head of the IT section, for the *Defender* department heads to arrive. Biff Barnes, as the mission commander, was also present.

Given the urgency of the summons, most of the senior people had shown up within minutes, but Ray insisted on waiting until every department was represented. It was a very full room, with eight of nine department heads and the others at the front. Ray tried to not look too much at Jenny, representing her C3 section, but they did exchange smiles.

A large flat-screen display at the front of the room showed the Indiana chemical fire, less than an hour old. The sound was muted, but a banner across the bottom read, "At least fifteen dead, dozens wounded."

The last to arrive, breathless, was Gail Summers, deputy head of propulsion. "Sorry, Aaron can't stop what he's doing."

"Then you'll have to brief him," Admiral Schultz replied. "Go ahead and take a seat."

Ray didn't even wait for her to sit down. "The chemical plant explosion in Indiana was not an accident. The Chinese defense ministry has taken responsibility for the explosion, calling it 'a strategic attack on the U.S. war machine.' It says more will follow."

Ray saw the reaction on many of their faces, but they were quiet, waiting. He only paused for just a moment, then explained, "That's bad news, of course, but we didn't call you here because of just that." He nodded toward Admiral Schultz. "But because it's a cyberattack, the admiral and I have decided you all need to know that eight days ago we arrested a Chinese spy, here at the project."

They'd remained silent at the news of a Chinese cyberattack, but now almost everybody expressed surprise. A few started to ask questions, but Ray, raising his voice slightly, said, "We've kept it quiet this long because, as far as we know, the Chinese don't know he's been arrested. Colonel Evans will explain what happened."

There was immediate silence as Evans spoke first about the suspicions of a spy, without mentioning Lewe's role, then about the dead drop and the use of video surveillance to get confirmation. Evans kept it short and left the spy's identity for the end.

"It was Glenn Chung, in the IT section." That provoked another verbal reaction from the group, but Evans kept talking, and they quickly fell silent. "We briefed Josh immediately after the arrest, of course." He motioned to the IT section head.

Josh Blake was in his late thirties and a little overweight. Glasses and premature baldness only emphasized his round face. He held up a plastic envelope with a small black plastic box inside. "We found six of these attached to hubs on different secure servers. They capture and record anything that passes by. The FBI has the other five. I'll pass this one around. Do not break the evidence seal. If you do, Colonel Evans will make whoever does fill out the paperwork."

He handed the device to Ethan Kirsch, head of the power section, who examined it and passed it on. Blake said, "My people, assisted by others from the FBI and other three-letter federal agencies, have checked every network and transmission line, and we appear clean. But after this latest incident, we're checking everything again."

Evans added, "Note that it looks handmade. We don't know if Chung built these himself, but virtually all our IT gear is off the shelf. If you see anything else that looks homemade, of any size, contact me immediately, and I mean it. If you see any strange behavior from your IT systems, or from anyone working on your IT systems, call me first, then call Josh for tech support. Put me on your speed dial, if I'm not there already."

The colonel paused for a moment and looked to Schultz. The admiral stood and said, "Some of the material Chung sent could be used to facilitate sabotage"—he held out his hand to forestall the immediate questions—"which is why there were bomb dogs all over the complex last week."

Schultz added firmly, "I believe that if the Chinese were able to sabotage *Defender* or make some sort of cyberattack on us, they would have already done so. There's no indication that Chung placed any other devices, electronic or explosive, outside of the computer networks, and we didn't find anything after a most thorough search. But we can never be one hundred percent certain. Which is why we're telling you now."

Ray said, "For the moment, this stays at the department head level, although you can brief your deputies," he said, nodding toward Gail. "But nobody else, and don't even discuss this with each other. If you see anything that seems off, contact Colonel Evans immediately and let him make the call about whether it was your imagination or not."

U.S. Space Force Headquarters
Edwards Air Force Base
Office Annex
December 3, 2017

Ray heard the klaxon in his office. It was a security alert, but this time, there was no announcement over the loudspeaker. He ran to the window but couldn't see anything. Then the three short bursts sounded again, followed by the PA announcement of an unidentified approaching aircraft.

His first thought, of the hydrogen and oxygen tanks at the pad, was so frightening that his mind raced. Then he heard machine gun fire, close by. Desperate to know what was happening, he dashed down the stairwell next to his office and ran outside.

Others were standing outside the annex, tasks forgotten as they pointed to the west. He didn't see where the firing had come from. The hangar doors, normally open, were closing.

An open-topped Humvee loaded with armed Marines roared up. An officer waved frantically and yelled, "Everyone get inside. Take cover!"

A pair of Marines jumped out and started herding them back toward the annex, but one of them recognized Ray. "It's Mr. McConnell, hold up," and pointed toward the officer.

Ray nodded his thanks and headed for the vehicle at a trot, but as he approached, a Marine began firing a heavy machine gun mounted on the roof. The sudden noise almost knocked Ray off his feet. The officer, a lieutenant directing the fire, spotted Ray and pulled him off to one side.

"It's a full alert. Radar's detected a slow-moving aircraft headed for the complex. It's already inside the prohibited zone, and the pilot won't answer on the radio."

McConnell heard machine-gun fire again and realized there must be several guns. The one nearest him fired again, and the gunner was pointing his weapon up. Ray followed the line of tracers, and saw a small speck. It looked like a light plane still a few miles away.

"He can't hit anything at that range," Ray shouted.

"He's trying to warn him off," the officer shouted back. The lieutenant picked up the vehicle's radio microphone. "This is Hall. I can see him. It's a light plane, a Cessna or something like it. It's at low altitude, and it's headed straight for the hangar."

"What's that fool doing?" asked Ray.

Hall shrugged. "You tell me. It could be a suicide attack or loaded with commandos. Or he could just drop leaflets that say, 'Save the Whales.'"

The radio squawked, and Ray couldn't hear what was said over the firing, but the lieutenant had a headset. He said, "Understood," then reached in to tap the gunner on the leg. When he stopped firing the lieutenant told him, "They're not taking the hint. The major says, 'Bring him down.'" The gunner nodded and began firing again.

Ray could see other squads racing into position, and more weapons opened up on the approaching plane. It was closer now, and he could hear the plane's small engine snarl as the pilot opened up the throttle. Its speed increased slightly, and he lowered the nose. Was he going to crash into the hangar?

Tracers surrounded the plane. Ray knew intellectually how hard it was to hit even a slow aircraft with a machine gun, but right now he was infuriated with the gunners who couldn't hit something that large, that slow, flying in a straight line.

It was closer now, and he could see it was a high-winged civilian plane, a four-seater. He'd flown them himself. It was nose-on, headed straight for him. The drone of the engine increased quickly, both in pitch and volume.

Although he couldn't see any weapons, he suddenly felt the urge to run for cover. They hadn't planned on an air raid. And the hangar would provide poor protection; it wasn't designed to withstand a direct attack.

Something fluttered out from the side of the aircraft, and for a moment Ray thought the machine gunners had actually hit. Then he recognized the shape as one of the side doors. A parachute jump? But they were too low, no more than a few hundred feet.

They were almost over the hangar, and Hall shouted, "Hold fire!" then repeated the order into the radio. He explained to Ray. "If we hit it now, it could crash into the hangar."

Assuming that isn't their plan, Ray thought.

McConnell watched the aircraft's path, wishing it would vanish. It didn't, but at the last moment it did veer a little to the left. He saw a man-sized object leave the plane and drop toward the ground. It had fins on one end and a point on the other. It looked like nothing so much as a giant dart.

Ray stood and watched the object fall, looking even more dartlike as it fell nose-first. Out of the corner of his eye, he saw that the Marines, with better reflexes, were all hugging the ground.

It struck almost exactly in front of the hangar, exploding with a roar. The concussion was enough to stagger him a hundred yards away, and misshapen fragments cartwheeled out from the ugly brown smoke cloud.

Ray was still standing, dazed and unsure of what to do next when a pair of Marine Super Hornets zoomed overhead in pursuit of the intruder. His eye followed the jets as they quickly caught up with the Cessna, still in sight, but now headed away at low altitude.

One of the Hornets broke off to the right, then cut left across the prop plane's path. McConnell heard a sound like an angry chainsaw, and a stream of tracers leapt from its nose in front of the trespasser.

The other jet was circling left, and had lowered its flaps and landing gear in an attempt to stay behind the Cessna.

Lieutenant Hall's radio beeped, and he listened for a minute before turning to Ray. "They've ordered the pilot to land, and he's cooperating." Glancing at the lethal Hornets circling the "slow mover," Hall said, "I sure would."

Remembering the bomb, Ray ran toward the hangar. Acrid fumes choked and blinded him, but he ignored them, then almost stumbled on the debris littering the once-smooth surface. Slowing down, he picked his way over metal fragments and chunks of concrete. His heart sank when he saw the hangar door through the clearing smoke. Buckled and peppered with jagged holes, half of it had been torn from its tracks.

Admiral Schultz appeared out of the clearing smoke and stood beside Ray. He saw Schultz look him up and down, then ask, "You look fine. Is everyone okay?"

Ray stared at him for a moment, then replied, "I don't know."

"What about *Defender*?"

"I haven't checked yet."

Schultz shook him by the shoulder, not roughly, but as if to wake him. "Ray, snap out of it. We've got to check for casualties and see about the ship. Stop gawking and get moving!"

Ray nodded and started to check the area. He spotted people he knew and set them to work. He saw Marines working as well, moving from person to person, making sure everyone was all right, helping some who were hurt.

A few minutes later, Lieutenant Hall trotted up to Schultz and saluted. "Sir, they've got the intruder lined up for landing."

"Right, let's go, then." He called over to McConnell. "Ray! Get over here!" Ray had overheard the lieutenant and was already heading for the Humvee.

The lieutenant drove almost as fast to the runway as he had to the hangar. A sentry at the end of the airfield spotted the Humvee's flashing light and waved them onto a taxiway, pointing to the far end. A cluster of vehicles surrounded the Cessna, and the two Hornets whooshed overhead, as if they were daring it to take off.

Ray spotted Colonel Evans, standing to one side as armed Marines secured the plane. Its two occupants were being half-dragged out of the plane and efficiently searched. A man and a woman, both were in their early twenties, dressed in fashionably ragged jeans and T-shirts. To Ray's eyes, they looked like a couple of college students, straight off the campus.

"Don't put weapons in space!" yelled the man as he was searched.

"Down with *Defender*!" the girl shouted. "We won't let you turn space into a battlefield."

Ray was in shock. He wanted to grab both of them, show them the damaged hangar, the injured being taken to the hospital.

Evans's face was made of hard stone, and Schultz looked ready to order two executions on the spot. But neither man moved or said a word. Maybe they couldn't for fear of losing their cool. Ray didn't, either. He watched the Marines cuff the two individuals and lead them away.

Later that day, Ray reported to the admiral. Schultz's office was filled with people. General Norman, down from Camp Pendleton, occupied the only other chair, and an air force JAG officer, the public affairs officer, and *Defender*'s security officer took up most of the remaining floor space. They'd all been waiting for Ray.

Ray didn't bother with introductory remarks. "The engineers say they can fix the apron where the bomb struck by tomorrow evening. They'll use the same material designed to repair bombed-out runways. It won't last, but it will be fine for the moment.

"The hangar door took the brunt of the blast and stopped most of the larger fragments. They've found twelve pieces of shrapnel that penetrated the door and bounced around inside the hangar. Two fragments hit *Defender*. One hit the floor and ricocheted into the belly,

and the other struck the leading edge of the port wing. The prelimi-
nary reports indicate no internal damage, and they're already prepping for repairs. Both will take a little time to fix, but shouldn't delay
the launch. Other fragments wrecked some test equipment, and there
are a few dents in the far wall."

"Thanks, Ray," said Schultz flatly, holding in his rage. He turned
toward Evans.

The colonel began his report. "They're not Chinese agents—or,
if they are, the Chinese are making some bad personnel choices. Their
names are Frank and Wendy Beaumont, and they're siblings, students at Berkeley. They're well-known peace activists at the school
and belong to several political organizations. The plane is their father's, and both have been taking flying lessons."

"We think they had help with the bomb, probably from an engineering student. It was an improvised shaped charge. The boy, who's
a sophomore and a political science major, described it in detail and
claims he did it all himself, but I doubt it."

Schultz nodded, then looked at his public relations officer, an air
force captain borrowed from Edwards's staff. They'd added the new
billet after *Defender*'s disclosure on the Internet. His job was more
accurately described as "public opinion officer," since, officially, *Defender* still didn't exist.

The captain said, "The press is having a field day with this incident. Half the headlines read, MARINES FIRE ON COLLEGE STUDENTS,
and the other half say, MARINES FAIL TO PROTECT SECRET SPACE-
CRAFT. Either way, we can't win. Some Web sites are speculating that
Defender was badly damaged, and of course we can't show them that
it isn't."

Schultz replied quickly. "Let them say it. If the Chinese think we're
hurt, that's fine. But make sure you show them the people who were
hurt in the blast." The admiral continued, "I just got off the phone
with the hospital. We had five personnel hurt, one seriously enough
to need surgery to remove a bomb fragment. All of them are expected
to recover fully."

"I'm grateful nobody was killed," General Norman rumbled. "But we can't assume that there won't be another attack. I want to personally apologize for letting that plane get through. It won't happen again. The commandant has told me I can have anything I need to protect you and this base. I'm bringing more people down from Pendleton. For as long as you need it, we will stay at full alert. We're keeping fighter patrols and helicopter gunships overhead twenty-four/seven. There will be no further interruptions."

20

Final Push

Rayburn House Office Building
Washington, D.C.
December 5, 2017

Congressman Tom Rutledge left the chambers of the House Armed Services Committee disappointed and angry. It had been over a week since he had publicly demanded a hearing on President Jackson's rogue actions, and the chairman of his committee had yet to put one on the docket. When Rutledge protested, Chairman Nussbaum merely advised patience, as there were many high-priority issues the committee had to deal with. He did pledge that Rutledge would get his hearing as soon as it was practical. The Nebraska representative recognized stalling when he saw it, and he resented being pushed aside so casually. He had legitimate concerns on the constitutionality of the president's orders, and, despite his consistently strong public statements, only a few of his colleagues seemed to take him seriously.

Rutledge had welcomed the opportunity to be out front on the whole China-GPS crisis. He relished being the "lone voice in the wilderness," boldly taking on the administration and its misguided response. The fact that he and the president were from the same party would only enhance Rutledge's image that he wasn't just playing partisan politics. But thus far, no one had seriously responded to his numerous warnings of the executive branch's overstepping its constitutional boundaries.

The Republicans seemed quietly amused—that was to be expected—but even his party's senior leadership had downplayed the whole issue, paying only lip service to his calls for a congressional investigation. Were they so blinded by party loyalty that they couldn't see Jackson's empire-building agenda? Rutledge had been fully prepared for a fight, and he expected one after he'd thrown down the gauntlet. But what he hadn't anticipated was that no one would say anything in return; it was as if he was being intentionally ignored. And the one thing Representative Thomas Rutledge wouldn't stand for was being ignored.

Fuming, Rutledge walked briskly, trying to purge himself of some of his pent-up frustration when his cell phone buzzed. It was a text message from Ben Davis, his chief of staff: "PLEASE RETURN TO YOUR OFFICE. URGENT MATTER WAITING." Strange. Davis never sent anything to his boss that could be perceived as a directive. Even his strongest recommendations were couched as polite suggestions. *Something big must be going on*, Rutledge thought. Pocketing his cell phone, the congressman picked up his pace.

"All right, Ben, what the devil is going on?" barked Rutledge as he burst through the office-foyer door.

Davis's face was stern and worried at the same time; his expression encouraged the representative to quiet down. "You have visitors," he said quietly.

"Who?" Rutledge asked impatiently. He was in no mood for games.

"Ah, Tom! Good to see you're back. We'd like to have a word with you in your office, if you please."

Rutledge looked up to see Thad Preston in the doorway to his office. Standing next to the Democratic minority leader was the Speaker of the House, Bernard Terpak. As surprised as he was,

Rutledge managed to maintain a neutral poker face. Having *both* senior house leaders waiting in your office was usually a bad sign.

"Certainly," he said nonchalantly. As he approached the door, Rutledge called out to his chief of staff, "Ben, please see to it we're not disturbed."

Once inside, Terpak closed the door behind them. Turning to face his visitors, Rutledge asked lightly, "To what do I owe the honor of this visit?"

"Surely that is not a point of debate, Congressman Rutledge," replied Terpak tersely. The speaker's formal tone confirmed Rutledge's suspicion that he was about to get his ass chewed. Preston raised his hand, quickly intervening.

"Tom," began the minority leader, "for the last two months, a number of us have quietly counseled you to give the president a chance to deal with the China crisis. Russ Urick has spoken to you, Rick Nussbaum has spoken to you, as have I, on numerous occasions. And yet you seem hell-bent on raising the issue with ever-increasing volume. Your public statements have become more and more shrill, and quite frankly many of your colleagues are losing patience with your grandstanding."

Rutledge's nostrils flared with indignation. *It's my duty to speak out! What the president is doing is illegal,* he said to himself. Struggling to keep a level tone, Rutledge fired back, "Nobody else has had the courage to demand that the president be held accountable. He has bypassed the House and Senate with the formation of the U.S. Space Force . . ."

"Are you sure of that, Congressman Rutledge?" Terpak injected. "Do you seriously believe that the silence concerning the Space Force meant that none of us had a clue as to what was going on?"

A sharp chill suddenly went down Rutledge's spine. The speaker's stern tone told Rutledge that his questions were rhetorical, but when did the president consult with Congress? For the first time, doubt crept into Rutledge's mind.

Preston saw Rutledge's confused expression and explained. "Tom, before the president gave the order to form the U.S. Space Force, he called the top senior congressional leadership to the White House, briefed us on his plans, and asked for our approval. There was a lot of debate, but the gist of the agreement is that the president was given the go-ahead, but, once this crisis is over, formal congressional hearings will be held and the issue put to a vote on both floors. President Jackson also agreed to a condition required by the Senate majority leader that if Congress didn't approve, the Space Force would be rolled back into air force. So your claims are not correct. The president did consult *members* of Congress, and he was given tacit approval to proceed with his plans, provided that the more formal process is followed later."

Rutledge was stunned. Why hadn't he been consulted? As a member of the House Armed Services Committee, he should have had a role in that discussion. The wanton disregard for traditional protocol astounded him. "What basis did he have for circumventing Congress's proper role in this decision? How can we spend several billion dollars on this harebrained scheme without formal congressional approval?"

Preston rubbed his forehead and sighed. Terpak, being an old crusty navy vet, would have none of it. "If you'd paid any attention to the intelligence briefs given to your committee, you'd realize there is a war on, Mister. If we follow the normal bureaucratic protocol, it would be at least a year before any real action could be taken. By then, China would have a lock on East Asia, and our ability to defend our interests in that region would be severely compromised. This is an information-age war, Congressman Rutledge; we don't have the luxury of time."

"But the polls show . . ."

"The opinion polls are damn-near split fifty-fifty, Tom," argued Preston, his voice harder. "That means it's a nonissue. Regardless of what the president does, half the citizenry of this country will not be thrilled. President Jackson made a strong argument that we needed to act while we still could, and while we had the best chance to win.

The vast majority of the members of Congress present during that meeting agreed with him, myself and the speaker included."

That last sentence told Rutledge he would have no top cover if he continued speaking out. He would be on his own. For once in his political life, Rutledge found himself without words.

"And as a side note," Preston continued, "the Space Force hasn't been anywhere near as expensive as you've implied—less than two billion so far. Sure, the president basically gave Admiral Schultz a blank check, but the admiral has been diligent in trying to keep costs down where he could. For a major DoD acquisition program, it's one of the better ones I've seen, despite its hurried nature."

"It's also damn far cheaper than losing several B-2s in a questionable attack on that mountain complex," Terpak noted sharply. "And that's in terms of both money and lives."

Preston continued, "The bottom line, Tom, is that *Defender* is our best option, as crazy as it sounds. If it fails, we lose our access to space. Not just the GPS constellation, but our intelligence collection, communications, and weather satellites as well. If this 'harebrained scheme' doesn't work, we're totally screwed."

Sea Hawk Flight
Paracel Islands
South China Sea
December 6, 2017

Commander Wang Gao's eyes shifted focus according to a well-practiced drill. Check altitude, heading, and speed. Conduct a quick visual search ahead and above, just in case any enemy aircraft were in the area. Then glance left and right to check on the rest of the formation. Repeat. Lieutenant Kuan Yu in the backseat alternated between his own visual searching and looking at the radar-warning receiver. With their aircraft's radar in standby, there was nothing else for him to watch.

Wang's squadron of JH-7A fighter-bombers had taken off from the Sanya air base on Hainan Island, dove down to the deck, and proceeded under strict electronic silence toward their target. Somewhere near Yongxing Dao, or Woody Island as it was known to most of the world, was a Vietnamese convoy bringing supplies and air defense batteries to reinforce the island—an island that was, until a week ago, Chinese territory.

The squadron leader frowned under his mask. He needed to pay attention to what he was doing and not let his nationalistic pride get all wound up. Traveling at just under the speed of sound a mere twenty-five meters above the ocean demanded his complete attention. If he made a mistake, he wouldn't even have time to blink before his aircraft plowed into the water.

Fortunately, it was a very short flight. Their air base was less than two hundred nautical miles from Yongxing Dao. It was the main reason why the South Sea Fleet commander had chosen Wang's squadron for the attack. That, and the fact that American submarines were running rampant throughout the South China Sea, sinking everything they ran across. The daring attack at Yalong Bay had been a very rude awakening.

"IP in two five miles, sir," announced Kuan.

"Understood." In three minutes they would come up to their search altitude and see what the Vietnamese had brought to the party. The prestrike intelligence report estimated between eight and twelve ships, including escorts. The type and number of ships determined how many YJ-83K missiles they'd need to launch to achieve the desired degree of damage, and this in turn determined how many aircraft would be required to carry out the attack.

Wang had his men work through the antiship strike-planning software, and they came up with eight aircraft carrying four missiles each. He added two additional strikers just to make sure there were enough missiles to give them a good chance of sinking everything that floats near the island—especially if there were more ships present than they thought. The other two aircraft in the squadron would carry electronic countermeasure pods, just in case the Vietnamese had some SAMs already in place, or should there be any American ships in the convoy.

"Mark IP," said Kuan.

Wang toggled his mike, "Sea Hawk Leader to Sea Hawk Flight, climb to designated altitude and energize radars. Eagles One and Two, take point and report all electronic contacts." As his pilots acknowledged their orders, the two ECM aircraft accelerated and began climbing rapidly. As soon as they had cleared the rest of the formation, Wang pulled back on his stick and started his ascent. He felt himself begin to relax a little as he watched the altimeter spiral upward, away from the cruel and unforgiving sea.

As the squadron passed two thousand meters, the lead ECM aircraft reported in. "Eagle One to Sea Hawk Leader, hold three air search radars in the direction of Yongxing Dao; two Positiv-M and one P-15M. The signal strength on the P-15M is strong. It's very likely it's detected us."

Wang nodded approvingly. The intelligence estimate had been spot-on. Two Vietnamese Gepard frigates were part of the escort screen, and there was at least one Pechora-2M surface-to-air missile battery on the island. But there was no mention of any Americans in the formation. "Sea Hawk Leader to Eagle One, understood. Are any Americans nearby?"

"Eagle One to Sea Hawk Leader, I hold one SPS-49 and one SPY-1, radar bearing two two eight. Range approximately one five zero nautical miles."

Wang smiled. A U.S. Aegis cruiser was to the south-southwest but too far away to respond to his squadron's sudden appearance; the Vietnamese were on their own. Still, the Pechora-2M would be a problem. The SAM was a heavily modified SA-3 and had the ability to intercept cruise missiles. It would have to be suppressed.

"Sea Hawk Leader to Eagles One and Two, begin jamming the Vietnamese air-search radars. Sea Hawk Flight, scan for targets; prepare to launch missiles."

USS *O'Kane* (DDG 77)

Captain Bradley Alberts slid down the ladder, hit the deck, and started running toward the combat information center. "Gangway! Make a hole!" he yelled, forcing sailors to plaster their bodies against the bulkhead so he could pass unhampered. The general alarm was still reverberating throughout the ship, and sailors were scurrying to their battle stations. Lunging through the door into CIC, Alberts took his seat in front of the two main flat-screen displays next to the tactical action officer. The picture showed twelve new air contacts.

"TAO report," he ordered.

"Captain, EW has multiple JL-10A radars in surface-search mode. The bogies are concentrating their search on the ships around Woody Island, but there have been a few scans in our direction. There's a low probability they picked us up at this range. The contact data on the main display is from *Cowpens* to our southwest via the CEC data link. SPY-1 and all weapons are in standby."

"Very well, TAO." Alberts studied the evolving tactical picture on the two large Aegis displays; his ship was sixty miles off the Chinese aircrafts' track. Given *O'Kane*'s reduced radar cross-section, he agreed with his TAO's call that they probably hadn't been detected. The cooperative engagement capability, or CEC, data from *Cowpens* was very good: Both her SPS-49 and the SPY-1 were tracking the incoming flight. Alberts's ship had an excellent fire-control solution and could shoot on remote data alone.

"CIC, Bridge. Battle stations manned. Material condition Zebra is set throughout the ship," squawked the intercom.

Alberts nodded to his TAO, who acknowledged the report. His ship was ready to fight. "TAO, engage tracks eight five zero one through eight five one two with SM6 missiles, single shots." Seconds later, the ship rumbled under the vibration of twelve missiles being launched from both the fore and aft vertical launchers.

Sea Hawk Flight

"Radar contact, eleven medium and large ships, bearing one one seven, range six eight miles," reported Lieutenant Kuan.

"Understood," replied Wang. Everything was going according to plan. Each of the strikers had selected their targets, and with the Vietnamese air-search radars jammed, they wouldn't know what hit them—now to evict those intruders. "Sea Hawk Flight, launch missiles."

Kuan hit the launch button, and the first YJ-83K dropped from its pylon; seconds later, its turbojet engine kicked in and it streaked away from the aircraft. Wang looked around at the formation and saw that the first wave of missiles was well on its way toward their targets.

USS *O'Kane* (DDG 77)

"All stations, TAO. Bogies have launched vipers! Repeat, missiles are heading toward the Vietnamese formation."

Alberts's blood started flowing a bit faster. There could be as many as forty antiship cruise missiles on those aircraft. And since they weren't heading toward *O'Kane,* he'd have precious little time to engage them.

"TAO, time to enable?" he asked.

"Sir, our birds will go active in ten seconds."

"Very well. Light 'em up, TAO. Engage inbound vipers; fire at will."

"Aye, aye, sir! Air, TAO. Illuminate with the SPY-1; track bogies and vipers. Break. Weapons Control. Shift Aegis to automatic and engage vipers!"

Sea Hawk Flight

"Sea Hawk Leader, Eagle One. SPY-1 emissions, bearing due south! Very strong signal strength! An Aegis ship is very close!"

Wang heard the fear in the man's voice. The tone annoyed the squadron leader, but the warning couldn't be ignored. An American air defense ship had been laying in wait for them; his squadron was in great danger. But before he could key his mike, the radar warning receiver began chirping madly. "Missile alert!" shouted Kuan.

Two bright flashes suddenly blossomed in front of him, grabbing Wang's attention. Both ECM aircraft had exploded, flaming debris spinning wildly downward.

"Break formation! Evade!" Wang radioed to his comrades, and then pushed the yoke down sharply. "Lieutenant! Launch countermeasures!"

The tight formation immediately began to scatter, but not before three more of the fighter-bombers were hit. In less than ten seconds, Wang had lost nearly half his squadron. With his aircraft in a steep dive, he yanked hard left; the loud pops and shudders told him Kuan was ejecting chaff at a rapid rate. His efforts were wasted.

A loud explosion, followed immediately by a body-wrenching jerk, caused Wang's helmet to slam into the canopy. Dazed by the sudden impact, he tried to focus his eyes. The controls were sluggish, and there were a host of warning lights and alarms. Both engines were gone, and the hydraulic system was failing; his plane was bleeding to death.

As he struggled to keep the aircraft steady, he shouted at Kuan over the intercom. "We're hit! I'm losing control. Eject! Eject!"

There was no response. "Kuan! I said eject!" Again, he heard nothing. Wang had to look over both shoulders before he could see Kuan's helmet; the visor was covered with blood. His backseater was either unconscious or dead.

Wrestling with the yoke, Wang groped for the ejection system handle with one hand. Once he found it, he released the yoke, grabbed the handle with both hands, and pulled upward. A fraction of a second later, the canopy was blown off, and Wang was brutally flung into the air. The jerk from the deploying parachute sent a stabbing jolt of pain down his left arm; his head thumped mercilessly.

As Wang drifted slowly toward the sea, he tried to look around and see how many planes had been hit. Spinning about on his chute, he thought he counted seven smoke trails. Including his own aircraft, that meant that two-thirds of his squadron was gone, destroyed by those American bastards. Distress welled over him, as he could see only a few parachutes—were all the others dead? Wang shook his head, the pain rousing him from his anguish. He had to stay focused. The sea was getting bigger and bigger. He had to keep his wits about him and prepare for when he hit the water. Then there was the long swim home.

U.S. Space Force Headquarters
Edwards Air Force Base
Office Annex
December 7, 2017

Ray stumbled into his office and headed straight for the minirefrigerator in the back corner. Grabbing a cold bottle of water, he plopped himself into his chair and guzzled the contents. Half-sitting, half-lounging, Ray looked at his in-box and felt like crying. It had grown by several inches while he had been at training. Training? A better description would be torture.

Immediately after their casualty-drill session in the recently upgraded simulator, Barnes announced a surprise PT test and proceeded to run the whole crew longer and harder than ever before. Only Skeldon truly seemed to enjoy the arduous PT workout, "Oorahing" his way to the finish line. *Marines*, thought Ray, *they're all raving lunatics!* That was the only logical explanation he could come up with.

While they'd all passed the surprise test, some of them had just barely made it, including Ray. Of course, Biff wasn't satisfied and warned them they'd do it all over again in a couple of days. *He's trying to kill me,* Ray said to himself, wincing as he sat up straight. *It's his revenge for all those black programs I made him wade through.*

Ray reached for the first report on the top of the stack and opened the folder. He felt disgusting, with a fine layer of encrusted sweat and dust on his skin and clothes. A shower sounded really good right now, but he had to review some of these final subsystem-test reports and get them out of the way before the next batch arrived.

In fact, he had to review and approve all of them before *Defender* could be rolled out to the launchpad and prepped for launch—and that was to happen within the next couple of days! The thought came as a shock; *Defender* would start her journey out to Area 1-54 tomorrow. By Saturday, she'd be erected and hooked up to her gantry. The scheduled launch date was just over a week away.

Ray stopped and shook his head in disbelief. The whole idea seemed so surreal to him. His people had been busting their asses, working long shifts to make that demanding date a reality. They'd made a lot of progress, solving one technical problem after another, and in record time, but there had been frustrating setbacks as well.

The navigation system report Ray had in front of him was one of the pieces of good news. The system had been fully checked out and deemed flight ready. The nav team had come up with a way to integrate all four satellite-navigation systems so that *Defender* would not have to rely on GPS fixes alone. And just in case everything went to hell in a handbasket, two stellar sextants had been installed. Come what may, *Defender* would know where she was at all times. Then there was the bad news.

Both the sensor fusion and data link teams were struggling with software glitches that were proving to be annoyingly difficult to isolate and correct. The last series of tests of the command-data link between *Defender* and the BMC had gone badly, with poor connectivity and data-transfer rates. Jenny had been visibly disappointed and frustrated at the results. Ray heard she had even hurled her clipboard across the room when the test was shut down. After the outbrief, she'd left the briefing room silent and angry, descending back into the command bunker. Ray hadn't seen or heard from her for the last two days.

Ray was signing off on the maneuvering thruster report when a series of sharp raps broke the silence. "Morning, Ray, I'd like to . . ." The admiral came to a complete stop as soon as he got a good look. "My God, man! You look like shit!"

Ray immediately regretted the rapid head motion as he looked up. He waited while the pain passed, then said, "Thank you, sir. I didn't think you'd notice." A slight smile popped on his face.

Schultz placed the stack of papers in his hand on the desk and pulled up a chair. "Looks like Biff is running a tight ship," he remarked.

"Yes, sir. We've nearly tripled the training schedule. Biff still has us reviewing basic procedures, but he's got us working casualty drills at least twice a day now. He's trying to cover every possible contingency."

"As he should." Schultz smiled. "He's doing exactly what he's supposed to be doing. As unpleasant as that may be."

"We've talked off-line, away from the other crew members. He's worried, Admiral."

"About anything in particular?"

"No, just everything," Ray replied while slowly sitting back. "*Defender* is unproven, the weapons are unproven, the command and control is unproven, and the crew is unproven. We've tested each individual subsystem to death, but the integrated whole gets its first real test when we take her up in a little over a week."

"You getting cold feet, Ray?" asked Schultz. There was a serious tone to his voice.

"No, sir. I'm just trying to be realistic. In theory, this should work. But we both know the path from theory to practice can be a bit bumpy at times. Under normal circumstances, I'd be ecstatic with how far we've come. But things aren't normal, are they? And there's an awful lot riding on this mission."

Schultz nodded. He knew where his technical director was coming from. "Ray, there is a risk of failure in every human endeavor. But in war that risk is considerably higher because you aren't in control of a big chunk of what's going on. You can plan all you want, strive to minimize the possibility of failure, but in the end you can't guarantee success. That's why it's called a calculated risk." The admiral rose and started pacing.

"Both you and Biff realize the risks associated with this mission are higher than we'd like, and you're both doing your damnedest to knock that risk down, but we're running out of time, and we'll have to take our chances. If it's any consolation, I don't believe in kamikaze missions. I wouldn't condone a fight with a high chance of failure and crew loss. But, even with the risks, we are still the best bet in town. Our mission has the highest probability of success and the lowest for casualties of all the other options, save giving up."

"Tell that to Jenny," responded Ray quietly.

"She's not happy, I take it."

"We've talked several times—or, rather, she's talked and I've listened. As much as she supports the mission, and as proud as she is that I'm flying, she's still scared to death, and she's told me so. She knows she can't have it both ways, but that's just how she feels."

The admiral sighed and shook his head; this was a major disadvantage of having a loved one cleared to know what was going on—they knew the reality behind their fears. "Jenny's a big girl," Schultz finally replied. "She'll find a way to deal with it."

Ray nodded silently.

"Now you go hit the shower. We'll talk about the command datalink problem after you've washed up," ordered Schultz.

"Yes, sir. I shall cleanse myself and cease to be an affront to thine eyes," Ray teased.

"My eyes!?" countered Schultz. "It's my nose I'm worried about!"

Gongga Shan
Sichuan Province, China
December 8, 2017

Shen grumbled as he read the latest progress reports, a typical mixture of good and bad news. The army had done reasonably well, having reached the outskirts of Hanoi slightly ahead of schedule. But recent messages reported PLA units had started running into stiffer resistance as the terrain became more urban. Intelligence reports also indicated that the Vietnamese were establishing strong lines of defense south of Hanoi near the cities of Vinh and Dong Ha. The first was not as well fortified or manned as the second, indicating it was more of a delaying tactic—a speed bump to slow the advancing Chinese columns. Estimates put the defenses at Dong Ha as being far stronger—and, further, it was being fed daily by fresh shipments of arms and supplies through the port of Da Nang, a port kept open and active courtesy of the American navy.

The Americans had turned the South China Sea into a meat grinder, with the Chinese navy and air force taking significant casualties fighting for control of that strategic body of water. Despite the best efforts of the People's Liberation Army Navy, the seas along the front remained contested. U.S. submarines seemed able to strike at will up and down the Chinese coastline. And under the coordinated cover of an American-carrier strike group, the Vietnamese navy boldly seized Yongxing Dao—a tremendous embarrassment to the PLAN and China.

A hastily thrown together air strike was sent out to stop the Vietnamese from consolidating their position, only to be butchered by an Aegis ship that lay silently nearby. And while the navy pilots courageously pressed their attack, they only succeeded in causing moderate damage to the ships in the convoy, at a cost of nine fighter-bombers shot down and another two damaged beyond repair. Virtually an entire squadron sacrificed for *nothing*! Shen crumbled the report into a ball and threw it at the wall in frustration. The war was turning into a conflict of pure attrition, something he had carefully sought to avoid.

"If only those fools would have listened to me!" he shouted to himself. Shen jumped out of his chair and began pacing frantically, trying to read between the lines of the sterile daily reports. The personnel losses were worse than he had imagined, and even if the Vietnam campaign continued on its favorable course, the navy and air force would emerge from the war in a weakened state. The longer the war went on, the weaker they would be.

Still, his anti-GPS campaign was proceeding perfectly. The Dragon's Mother had only moments ago claimed her sixteenth victim. In less than a month, the U.S. would have only a few hours of 3D coverage left, and none during the night. With their long-range precision-strike capability neutralized, the Americans would have to rely on other methods to execute their attacks—methods that would increase their casualties. Shen was convinced that as soon as the body count started climbing, the Americans would sue for peace.

A sharp knock at the door disturbed the general's train of thought. "Enter," he snapped.

Colonel Hsu, Shen's intelligence officer, opened the door and walked into the office. "Excuse me, General, but I have a report that the Americans have launched another GPS satellite from Vandenberg."

Shen sighed deeply; the news was annoying, but not unexpected. "You've confirmed this?"

"Yes, sir. We have U.S. news coverage of the launch, as well as space-radar data. The satellite was placed into a standard GPS orbit."

"Very nice of them to tell us what they're doing," remarked Shen cynically. "Well, that should be their last one. They shouldn't get another one for many months now. Anything else?"

"No, sir. Is there something the General wants?" Hsu asked.

Shen frowned. He hadn't seen a new intelligence report on the *Defender* vehicle in over a week. There could, of course, be fresh reports still making their way through official channels, but the general had specifically asked that anything new be delivered expeditiously. It wouldn't hurt to ping the system. If new reports were coming, he'd at least be informed of that.

"Yes, Colonel, check with your colleagues to see if any new intelligence reports on *Defender* have been received. It's been a while, and I wish to be kept up to date with any developments."

"Certainly, sir. But I thought you believed *Defender* would take far more time before it can be launched?"

Frustrated and tired, Shen thundered impatiently. "Yes, Colonel, I still believe that, but that doesn't mean I wish to remain uninformed! Wisdom demands that we must consider the alternative, even if it's impossible!"

"Yes, sir! At once, sir!" replied Hsu as he rushed from the office.

Stewing, Shen found himself considering dark thoughts. If *Defender* were real, if it could interfere with his GPS campaign, then the war would likely go on longer than his current estimated timeline. Such an outcome would not bode well for China.

The Reveal

www.Defenderwatch.com
Posted December 8, 2017

Apologies to all for the site being down yesterday. It was another cyberattack, but we've gotten a lot of practice recently at protecting our files and recovering from misguided hackers. At least it wasn't the Chinese. Nothing blew up.

For the people who haven't bothered to read the FAQ, let me say it here:

THIS SITE DOES NOT TAKE SIDES ON
- The ongoing war with China
- The issue of government secrecy/transparency
- The *Defender* program as a response to the GPS satellite attacks
- The weaponization of space

We really don't care.

So leave us alone and go shout at someone who gives a frack.

People interested in discussing these extremely controversial topics can click <u>here</u> for a list of appropriate forums.

The only position this site does take is that *Defender* exists and is being built in California at Edwards Air Force Base.

Thanks to the leaked *Defender* design document, we have a fair idea of the spacecraft's characteristics, although those of us with experience in the aerospace community know that there can be, and usually are, many changes between the drawing board and the runway (or in this case, launchpad).

Many of the postings lately have been about when big "D" will fly. Estimates range from weeks (the Krazy Glue and duct-tape crowd) to months to never. Instead of trying to guess when, let me ask a better question: How will we know when they're getting ready to launch? Personally, I'd like to be as close to Edwards as they'll let me if and when she flies.

Since the Beaumont incident, the impressive security at Edwards AFB has been tightened still further, and getting into the not-supposed-to-exist "U.S. Space Force" base inside Edwards is virtually impossible. My friends in the industry with access to Edwards say the area around the old Airborne Laser Program facility looks like a Marine firebase. There are no signs saying USSF, by the way.

An aside to potential "truck watchers:" Since the appearance of the *Defender* document online, people with more spare time than sense have attempted to get clues about the activity at the USSF base by monitoring truck traffic in and out of Edwards, recording license plates and company logos, as if they'd spot a rocket engine hanging out the back. I've had posts from four individuals saying they'd done this, and all four have been questioned—and three briefly taken into custody—by federal agents who have absolutely no sense of humor.

Let me explain this to you all. Remember that Edwards is an air base. They have runways, lots of *long* runways. Anything big or important will be flown in. At night.

The launch, especially at night, should be visible from as much as one hundred nautical miles away, so that includes Bakersfield to the northwest, Riverside to the west, and possibly Los Angeles and Long

Beach to the south, depending on the pollution and sky glow. Barstow is fifty miles to the east, and should provide an excellent viewing spot, given that the vehicle will arc eastward as it climbs. One California poster is already looking for good spots along Highway 58.

But he needs a little warning time to get in position. So I've created a new thread in the forum: How will we know when they're close? Contributions from Chinese sources are welcome.

U.S. Space Force Headquarters
Edwards Air Force Base
0315 hours
December 9, 2017

"You know, moving her at night isn't going to make any difference. As soon as she's on the pad, she'll be seen," Barnes observed critically.

"It gives us a few more hours," Ray answered. "We kept her in the hangar for as long as possible, but she has to go to the pad now."

They watched as *Defender* was slowly towed from her hangar down Taxiway A toward the launch complex in Area 1-54 some twenty miles away. Everything was going smoothly. The recently repaired concrete apron in front of the hangar had held, and Jerry Peters's crew had marked the turn points along the route in paint. Security was tight, with armed fighters patrolling overhead and Avenger air defense vehicles in front of and behind the procession. They were camouflaged, of course. And in the darkness, they looked like utility trucks, until you spotted the box missile launchers pointed skyward.

"I don't like what it's doing to the training schedule," Barnes complained. "I agree that the flight crew needs to be involved in bringing her to the pad, but they're losing a lot of sleep. It'll be well past dawn by the time she's in position, so they won't be able to get any sleep."

"What is this 'sleep' you speak of?"

"Ray, don't joke. I don't often agree with the flight surgeon, but stuff like this can mess up your circadian rhythm, and the effects last. You're dragging for the next few days, no matter how much sleep you get the next night. You haven't been in the astronaut program for very long. We make an effort to keep ourselves as close to perfect health as possible. You can't ignore the physical demands . . ."

"Biff, I understand, really. Was there a better way to do this? You didn't suggest one when we planned this out."

"No," Barnes admitted.

"Then why are you complaining?"

"Because I have to complain to someone, and complaining might make them not like me. You already don't like me, so there's no harm done. Besides, you're handy."

The two were following the convoy and *Defender* as it moved at a brisk walking pace. They'd become separated from the rest of the group, mostly department heads, who were either walking or riding farther back. Jenny was in the BMC, using this opportunity to test communications.

Barnes seemed glad for the late-night exercise. Not content to simply follow the convoy, he would go to one side of the road and then the other, looking from different angles, all the while monitoring Peters's radio communications. It kept him at a half jog.

"Would you like to take over for one of the tractors?" Ray asked. "Or would you just like to push from back here?"

The pilot laughed and nodded. "I normally don't feel like this until just before a flight—I mean, in a fighter. It's when I'm prepping, when I'm going through my preflight routine. I get pumped, and I expect it. I want it. I can use the adrenaline."

"At least you've been in space before."

"Not on a combat mission. Not with so many unknowns, and not with so much at stake."

"I think my nervousness is more about how I will react to space flight. I've read enough about it, heaven knows. Some can't handle it."

Barnes nodded. "It happens, rarely. But since we're likely to be shot at as soon as we're in orbit, you'll be too busy to throw up." He grinned. "Or down. In space the direction's irrelevant. But aren't you worried about *Defender*?" Barnes asked.

"Not really," Ray stated firmly. "I'm confident she'll fly and do well; the other stuff, not so much. But what about the rest of the crew? You've spent more time with them than I have. Are they as wound up as we are?"

"As you are," Barnes corrected him. "Scarelli's a test pilot. He's coping by memorizing every fact about *Defender* he can lay his hands on. Steve Skeldon's got one combat tour in Super Hornets. He's like a kid waiting for Christmas. I had to chase him out of the simulator last night. And Andre and Sue won't stop asking me questions about my own experiences in space."

Ray didn't say anything for a minute, silently following *Defender,* then declared firmly, "Biff, we need to change the training schedule. Let's add some group games: basketball, soccer, stuff like that."

"The six of us? And I suck at soccer."

"Then baseball," Ray suggested.

"Seriously? Three on three? You're just trying to get out of weight training."

"I am not," Ray insisted indignantly. "We need to get rid of these nerves, or we won't have an edge at all. Physical activity as a group is a great stress reliever. Just consider it."

Barnes was silent for a dozen steps. He said, "We don't have the time," but he said it softly, as if debating with himself. Then, "What if someone gets hurt?" And again, "There's no time!"

Finally, Barnes announced, "Volleyball. Twenty minutes right before lunch. We'll play a couple of fast nine-point games. It's a big, relatively soft ball, and the risk of injury is low. And Sue can play with the five men on equal terms. She's taller than everyone except Jim."

"Okay, but I haven't played since grade school," Ray admitted.

"Then you'll probably lose a lot, but that's not really the point, is it?"

Gongga Shan
Sichuan Province, China
December 9, 2017

Senior Agent Wen seemed almost breathless when he appeared at the door to General Shen's office. It was a long flight from Beijing, even in a high-performance jet.

Shen didn't wait for him to speak. "I know. The Americans have moved the *Defender* vehicle into launch position."

Wen nodded. "Yes, General. My superiors are asking for your opinion on when she will be ready to launch."

"*My* opinion?" Shen asked sarcastically. "I didn't think anybody in Beijing cared what I thought."

"General, with respect, the Ministry of State Security did not take sides in your 'discussion' with the Central Military Commission. Our task is to gather, analyze, and share information."

Shen sighed. "Can you tell me anything new about the vehicle's status? Systems that aren't operating properly, or equipment that hasn't been installed yet?"

"No, General, there's been no new information for some time now."

"Your source has been arrested then," stated Shen.

Wen nodded sadly. "It's likely he is lost to us. We haven't been able to reach his handler for over a week. In such cases, standard procedure is to send a message directly to the agent, through a safe channel, of course. The agent is supposed to respond within twenty-four hours." After a small pause, Wen reported, "He has not responded."

"So we can expect nothing more from that source," Shen concluded.

"And our technical means are extremely limited," Wen added. "Is there any chance that this is a deception plan, a bluff of some sort?"

Shen almost laughed out loud. "What? To what end? I thought that issue was settled earlier."

"Please excuse the question. My superiors were instructed to explore every possibility. The entire politburo is now convinced that the American vehicle is a credible threat."

"And faced with the reality, they're scared. They're still looking for some way to make it disappear."

"But we come back to the basic question. When can the Americans launch?"

The general scowled. "Considering I didn't think they'd be ready for nearly a year, I may not be the best man to ask. But, practically speaking, the original *VentureStar* vehicle was designed to simplify launch preparations and reduce turnaround to a minimum. There's no booster or strap-on fuel tank. If the modifications the Americans intended to make are complete, then all they have to do is fill its fuel tanks, and they're ready to go."

Wen observed, "Normally, a country making a space launch is required to publish a Notice to Airmen and Mariners in advance, but there has been a standing notice of 'tests' over Edwards for some time now."

Shen smiled and shook his head. "The Americans wouldn't make it that easy."

The security agent added, "We have increased our monitoring of cell phone traffic in the region, but so far it has not provided any useful information. We may get lucky, but we can't depend on it."

"The only thing we can depend on," Shen replied, "is that we will know when it is launched. They can't hide that. With the media hovering like they are, it will be broadcast over the news channels in moments. I've already instructed Dr. Dong to expedite the preparations at Xichang, and, of course, we're also getting another *Tien Lung* ready for launch. I do have one thought, however."

Shen gestured to a timer on the wall of his office. It read "134.28.12." The numbers were counting down. "The Americans know as well as we do when we will launch the next *Tien Lung*. If they want to stop us, they'll have to launch by that time, or wait another week for the next cycle. And I'd wait until right before we launch, so we won't have time to react."

Wen nodded his understanding. "If they don't launch by the time we do, we kill another American satellite, and there's no reason to launch for another week. But if they launch too early, before the *Tien Lung,* it gives us time to react to their presence."

"Precisely," the general replied. "If they wait until we launch and commit to a target, and then take off themselves, it gives them the best chance of intercepting and destroying the *Tien Lung* vehicle."

Wen stood and bowed. "Thank you, General. I will report your conclusions to my superiors. I'm sure the politburo will find them very helpful."

After the agent left, Shen grumbled, "Now they listen."

U.S. Air Force Chief of Staff's Office
The Pentagon
December 9, 2017

"You know they've moved her to the pad."

"Yes, sir." General Maureen Ryan couldn't tell whether her boss was pleased at their progress or disappointed. Everyone knew that General Warner would never wish the *Defender* team to fail. Not only were they working to defeat the Chinese, they'd also acquired a large following who admired their daring. For a generation that had been raised on NASA's methodical, almost exhaustive thoroughness, the Space Force's speed and innovation were breathtaking. But it was clear that General Warner wished they were part of his air force.

General Ryan was Warner's deputy chief of staff for logistics, installations, and support. Although this meeting was supposed to be about supporting the air force wings involved in the Chinese war, Warner had already asked twice about resources that could be devoted to the new Aerospace Defense Organization.

There were a lot of cynics and "experts" on Capitol Hill who called the new organization a bluff or a sham, political cover for the president's failure to stop the GPS shoot-downs. They should sit in her chair and listen to the chief of staff, try to answer his questions, assist him in his search for talented people, and scrape together money for those people to work with.

Money was always scarce, and it was no different when the ADO was created. Warner had to "reprioritize"—Pentagon-speak for taking money away from someone to whom it had already been promised. There was some possibility of additional funding from Congress, which was angry over the Chinese attacks, but funding the ADO couldn't wait for Congress to act. There wasn't time.

But when the shooting started in Vietnam and then spread, the only thing that mattered was supporting the troops in the theater. Still, Ryan managed to find a few people who were smart enough but couldn't join the fight. And they'd just have to get by with almost no money at all.

"And they christened her, just like a ship. It had to be the navy." Warner sighed. "Well, we gave the B-2s names," he said philosophically.

"What will we do if *Defender* is successful?" Ryan asked carefully.

"I'll cheer along with the rest and give Barnes the medal he will certainly deserve." Warner grinned. "Then try to lure him back to the fold. And if *Defender* fails," the general added, "heaven help us all."

U.S. Space Force Headquarters
Area 1-54 Launchpad Complex
December 10, 2017

They trained aboard *Defender* now, testing the hardware and software at the same time as they drilled on the equipment they would actually use. From the point of view of the crew's control panels, they were in space.

Defender's control system was actually a large group of computers networked together. Systems or specific functions could be assigned to one machine or shared by several depending on the workload.

And if one computer failed, another would automatically pick up the slack. While the crew trained, those computers were disengaged from the ship's hardware and instead plugged into laptops that responded to the crew's orders in the same way that the ship's equipment did.

When Jim Scarelli, the senior pilot, fired the engines or reaction thrusters, the commands went from the propulsion computer to a laptop instead of the engines' pumps and valves. The laptop reported that the engines were firing, and the propulsion-control system was none the wiser.

Although the laptops were not as powerful or sophisticated as a purpose-built simulator, they still allowed Biff to create equipment failures and insert artificial targets into the weapons control system.

Sometimes the crew decided ahead of time what the failure would be, and they'd discuss and practice until they figured out the best way to respond. At other times, Biff would just throw something unexpected at them and watch the fun.

Jim Scarelli sat in the traditional left-hand seat in front, with copilot Steve Skeldon on the right. This was purely tradition, since *Defender* did not have a window forward. This was part of the original *VentureStar* design and solved a lot of technical problems with the heat shield. Instead, the front end of the crew compartment mounted a large flat-screen display, which showed the view from several cameras, as well as the vehicle's navigation system and flight instruments. Scarelli could view the information in separate subwindows or fuse it into one combined image. Ray wondered if it was the same brand as the one in his house.

Sue Tillman and Andre Baker, the sensor and weapons operators, sat in the second row, while Biff and Ray were in back. Having the mission commander in the rear let him watch the crew as well as his own displays. Ray had been designated second in command, over his protests that it should be Scarelli. But Ray had a better overall knowledge of *Defender*'s systems.

The six sat in padded chairs, not ejection seats. Not only was ejection and return from orbit impossible, but so, too, was a safe exit even when *Defender* was in the atmosphere, since it would usually be flying at many times the speed of sound.

The only door from the crew compartment lay behind and between Biff and Ray. It led to a passageway heading aft, past a microscopic bathroom on one side and an area for food storage and preparation on the other. The passageway had two exits: A pressure hatch led straight aft into an airlock and then into the cargo bay, and the other exit elbowed left to the hatch for external crew access. Although pressure-tight, it was not an airlock.

A locker with survival gear was located next to the hatch in the unlikely but hopeful event that the craft crash-landed in a remote location and the crew survived. In the equally unlikely event that they had time and were able to bail out from a damaged craft, another locker held six parachutes. An escape rail, similar to the one on the shuttle, would get them away from the vehicle. It was a nice thought, and Ray was glad it was there, but things happened pretty quickly aboard a spacecraft.

Ray glanced to his left at Biff, who was smiling, just a little. With Biff, smiling wasn't always a good thing. It was time to check the systems again, anyway. With more time, more of the fault detection would have been handled by computers, but on this flight, the flight engineer would have to manually search for anything but the most obvious errors. And Ray wanted to catch any problem before it became obvious.

Ray checked his displays in what was becoming a well-practiced routine, systematically stepping down several levels in detail in each subsystem. Nothing was immediately apparent, but Ray saw Andre, working with the laser, and watched those subsystems in detail, then the attitude control system as Scarelli simulated using the reaction thrusters. There. Just after the thrusters fired, there was an overpressure. He announced, "There may be a problem with RCS number seven, starboard aft. Pressure is above norms."

In the headset, he heard Scarelli's voice. "I didn't see any problems during the burn."

"Which is good, but overpressure is not," Ray answered. "Adjusting starboard RCS pump speed. Pressure will be lower, but still sufficient for a burn."

Biff nodded, and his smile widened. "Twenty-three seconds to spot it, Ray. Nicely done."

The simulated flight continued, their fifth of the afternoon. It felt good to be in the real spacecraft, practicing for what would soon be the very real thing, but it also gave Ray a surreal feeling. He tried not to think too much about his role in *Defender*'s creation, but it could surface in the strangest ways—for instance, at the christening ceremony, which had been held the night before she'd been towed to the pad.

While some work continued, there was a brief pause for many of the engineers and technicians, and they'd gathered near the nose. Secretary of Defense Peck and General Kramer had both flown in to actually see the vehicle and add their presence to the occasion. There'd been one very short speech by the secretary, who spoke on behalf of the president. Most of the off-shift workers had gathered in the hangar as well to watch the ceremony, and Peck told them that, although they were secret, they were not forgotten. Everyone in the government who knew about *Defender* was watching them, and in the not-too-distant future, the entire world would see what they'd accomplished.

Then he started singling people out. Biff Barnes was congratulated for his leadership, Geoffrey Lewes for making everyone's life smoother, Colonel Evans for his "fierce protection of *Defender*," and then finally Ray McConnell, "not only *Defender*'s inspiration and lead builder but now part of her crew."

Peck clapped, and everyone there joined in the applause. Ray felt his face flush and knew he must be bright red. He was embarrassed because the praise was early, since they hadn't flown the mission yet, and because everyone had been involved. Yes, it had been his idea, but Jenny was right. Nobody owned it. Or maybe they all did now.

A maintenance platform had been placed next to the starboard-side nose, and Admiral Schultz and his youngest daughter, Genevieve, who had been briefed into the program for this special purpose, climbed the steps that took them just over two stories above the hangar floor.

Near the platform, the white-painted hull of *Defender* was covered by a form-fitting panel, also painted white. White cloth also obscured the side of the ship almost back to the tail. An aide handed Schultz's daughter a magnum of California sparkling wine, and, with a nod from her father, she gripped it with both hands and lined up on the panel. Her voice echoed in the hangar, but it was clear enough to hear her almost shout, "I christen thee *Defender*. May you fly high and far."

The bottle shattered, and the panel dropped away, pulling the white covers off the side of the ship. Her name was painted on the front in glossy black letters, as close to the nose as the heat shield would allow. Farther back, the LOCKHEED MARTIN and NASA emblems had been replaced with UNITED STATES SPACE FORCE and an American flag. The hull next to the crew-access hatch listed the names of the six crew members.

Schultz gave the official photographer ten minutes before ordering work to resume, but he insisted Ray be in many of the photos. Jenny, smiling brightly, reminded him, "Once *Defender* goes public, these will be all over the Web."

Ray tried to push it all to one side and focus on the engineering display. He didn't want fame. Right now, all he wanted was to learn everything he could before launch time. He had a hunch things would be a whole lot more complicated after they launched. *Please, Lord, don't let me screw up.*

www.Defenderwatch.com
Posted December 10, 2017

This will be my last post for the day and part of tomorrow. Don't expect anything new until midafternoon Pacific Standard Time. Here's the best picture I could find of *Defender,* now on her launch-pad at Edwards Air Force Base. It's from a series of twelve shots taken by a CNN photographer.

The FAA and military are still arguing about whether or not the plane violated the exclusion zone around Edwards, but it's no accident that the plane CNN hired for the run was a surplus F-100F—a two-seater, owned and flown by a retired FedEx pilot who wanted to fly something more exciting than an Airbus. He gets gas money by doing movie work, so the rear seat was already fitted with a serious long-range camera.

Photos of the pilot, plane, and backseat rig are available here, and they have a coolness quotient just slightly less than the shots of *Defender* herself.

Luckily, the hardware surrounding the spacecraft is much reduced from the NASA/Saturn days. Instead of a huge gantry, there's a simple erector. *VentureStar* was designed as a second- or even third-generation spacecraft, completely reusable and with a fast turnaround. It's still a complex vehicle, but automation, improved design, and better materials have turned a one-shot rocket into what you and I would call an honest-to-God spaceship.

They make almost all the prelaunch preparations while the ship is horizontal and sitting on her landing gear. Once they're ready, they'll push her onto the erector and bring her to the vertical. Then they'll fill her tanks with liquid hydrogen and oxygen, and she's ready to fly. They'll fill the tanks for the chemical laser with hydrogen peroxide and potassium hydroxide (her "ammunition") after she's upright, as well.

The CNN pilot must have planned his run like a recce mission in hostile territory. He had not only clear weather (not too hard in

Southern California) but also the sun in the right position to light the ship well, so we got a good shadow.

Not that we can tell all that much. There are no obvious changes to the external configuration. Didn't really expect anything there. All the good stuff is tucked inside the cargo bay. She's surrounded by gear, but it's all small stuff, the kind of thing you'd expect to see near a high-performance aircraft getting ready for a flight.

And note her position, members. She's on the erector but still horizontal.

According to the accumulated wisdom of our posters (I love crowd-sourcing), it only takes minutes to bring the vehicle upright, and only a few hours to fill her tanks.

So she could fly in as little as six hours from the time this photo was taken, which was yesterday afternoon. The Chinese have been regular as clockwork, sending up one *Tien Lung* a week, and it's five days until the next one flies.

I believe *Defender* is ready, loaded for bear (or dragon, in this case), and will launch about the same time as the Chinese vehicle. And if that's the case, then I'm outta here. I've got my camping gear, and I even bought a solar charger for my laptop and phone. I'll be posting updates as events and power allow.

There are already a fair number of space-launch junkies parked along the highway. I'm meeting several posters along Highway 58, and we'll take turns keeping watch. I don't think we'll have to wait long. BTW, is there such a thing as tarantula repellent?

Why am I going? Because it's the first launch of a new space vehicle, or course, but more importantly because it's the first U.S. move in a battle with the Chinese that will take place somewhere way over our heads. *Defender*'s crew won't see or hear us when they launch, but we'll be there, cheering our guys.

22

Anticipation

Biff Barnes knocked twice on Ray McConnell's trailer door. The fighter pilot wasn't happy. The trailer lights were on. When Barnes didn't get a response, he tried the knob. The door was unlocked, and, as he opened it, he heard the sound of someone typing. Ray sat hunched over his laptop keyboard, pounding away in his pajamas.

"Ray, this is supposed to be a wake-up call. Remember?" admonished Barnes. "We had this discussion earlier, didn't we? Something called 'crew rest'?"

"I remembered something early this morning that I had to deal with," Ray answered, his attention still focused on the screen.

"After working last night until one o'clock." Barnes dropped onto the edge of the bed. "I need you alert and at peak for tomorrow, Ray. When did you wake up this morning?" His question had an edge to it.

"Four."

"So you think three hours of sleep is enough?"

"Okay, I'll take a nap after lunch."

"That's when we're supposed to review the new sensor-handoff procedures."

"Oh, yeah, sorry." Ray stopped typing, a grimace popping up on his face. He'd forgotten all about the procedure review.

"Join us halfway through," Biff told him, shaking his head in frustration. "Now, get moving. I'll see you at crew breakfast in fifteen minutes."

Barnes left, and Ray quickly showered and got dressed. In spite of his fatigue, it didn't take any effort to hurry, and Ray wondered what percentage of his blood was composed of adrenaline. He'd been running on nerves for way too long.

Feeling like an impostor, he put on the blue flight suit Barnes had given him. The left shoulder had a patch of the Stars and Stripes, while the left breast had a leather name tag with MCCONNELL, FLIGHT ENGINEER and U.S. SPACE FORCE on it in silver lettering. The right breast had a colorful patch of the spacecraft with a laser shooting out of the cargo bay, the name *Defender* embroidered underneath. Although the patch was attractive, if flashy, Ray didn't remember approving the design. When asked, Barnes had told him that some things were better left in the hands of fighter pilots.

Barnes had insisted that Ray wear the flight suit at all times during the last week before the launch. "Of course it makes you stand out. You're flight crew, and that makes you different. Let everyone see it. You not only supervised the design and building of *Defender,* you've got the balls to fly in her as well. That's the ultimate vote of confidence, and your people will appreciate it."

The Hangar restaurant looked better and better. Geoffrey had changed the décor again, this time from Southwestern to a space theme. Posters of star fields and spaceships filled the walls, and the classical music was appropriately grand.

Ray hurried over to the crew table and was gratified to see he was not late. Steve Skeldon and Sue Tillman were also just sitting down. Both of them wore military rank insignia on their flight suits that made them look natural. Ray thought he probably looked all right, as long as he stood close to one of them. Inside, he still felt like a pretender.

Instead of going through the cafeteria line, Ray checked off what he wanted on an order form, and they brought his food to the table. The theory was that the crew should be doing useful work instead of standing in line, but Ray felt it was just another perk, a way of making them feel special. Biff had argued the minor distinction was good for everyone's morale, not just the crew's. Ray had agreed reluctantly.

They did do work while they ate, with Barnes drilling them relentlessly on safety procedures, equipment locations, technical characteristics, and each other's duties. His favorite trick was to ask one question, then quickly ask another in the middle of the answer. The victim had to answer both correctly, and in order, within seconds.

At first Ray thought Biff was deliberately picking on him, grilling him repeatedly on engine-out procedures. Then after watching him work over the others, Ray thought Barnes might have been cutting him some slack.

The recital continued throughout breakfast, and Barnes prepared to take the crew to the simulator. Ray really wanted to go with them but knew there were many last-minute issues that still needed fixing.

Part of him couldn't wait for tomorrow morning. The rest of him wanted the day to go on forever. He needed the time.

CNN Report
1000 hours
December 14, 2017

Mark Markin was as close to the Area 1-54 launch site as he could get, which meant standing just outside the far eastern end of Edwards AFB, fifty yards off U.S. Route 395. But the launchpad with the mysterious space vehicle still lay six miles to the west, just over the horizon. Farther to the west, far out of sight, lay Edwards Air Force Base proper, with the mythical USSF complex nestled safely within.

Markin desperately wanted to set up his gear on the small rise to the south; from that vantage point, he'd have a clear line of sight to Area 1-54. Unfortunately, the hill was within the base's fence line, and the Marines already had an observation post on that coveted piece of real estate.

The nearly empty landscape along the fence line was dotted with clusters of TV trucks and other vehicles. Markin had positioned his cameraman so that the sandbagged guard post, manned by heavily armed Marines, was visible in the background.

As Markin began his report, the camera shifted from the guard post to an approaching Humvee, then centered on the sentries as they approached the vehicle. It continued on its patrol route after the driver talked briefly to one of the guards.

"Following the attack ten days ago, the U.S. Army and Marine Corps detachments here have increased security to extraordinary heights. Civilian traffic on and off the base has been severely restricted, and most of the traffic into the base has been for official government business.

"All our attempts to contact senior Department of Defense officials regarding the damage inflicted by the Beaumonts have been fruitless. The Coalition Against Military Space, which claims responsibility for the action, says that the launchpad was destroyed and a nearby hangar damaged. Major Dolan, the Edwards Air Force Base public relations officer, still denies the existence of *Defender* and is therefore 'unable to discuss damage to something that doesn't exist.'"

A fuzzy, pixelated color image replaced Markin and the sentries. It showed a square building with rails leaving one side. They led to a flat rectangular area with the white triangular shape of *Defender* in the center. The image was skewed, as if the camera had been tilted well off the vertical.

"This photo was taken from a CNN plane flying just beyond the prohibited area near the base and has been viewed by millions on the Internet. Using computer enhancement, we were able to expand this image of the "nonexistent" hangar and launchpad. While there is little that can be seen at this distance, the hangar and pad appear intact. Presumably, *Defender* is also undamaged, since she has been moved into launch position. CNN news will monitor developments at the base closely and let you know the instant that there are any new developments."

U.S. Space Force Headquarters
Edwards Air Force Base
Admiral Schultz's Office
1010 hours
December 14, 2017

Admiral Schultz angrily turned off the flat-screen TV. There was little pleasure in pushing a button. What he wanted to do was push in Markin's face. "War in a fishbowl," he grumbled.

Colonel Evans, *Defender*'s security officer, heartily agreed. "Radar's tracked several civilian planes flying just outside the prohibited area. There's a good chance at least one of them is a CNN plane with a long-range TV camera aboard, waiting for us to launch."

"Which is no surprise," Schultz muttered. "But when *Defender* takes off, all they'll really need is a pair of eyeballs and a cell phone."

"But it's the cameras that concern me, sir. CNN's broadcast will be seen all over the world. The Chinese will have a front-row seat without having to risk another operative." Evans seethed. "Allowing someone to tell the enemy what we're doing flies in the face of every OPSEC technique I've ever been taught! I just can't see the Chinese letting us put *Defender* in orbit and doing nothing about it!"

The admiral heard the frustration in Evans's voice and was entirely sympathetic, but there was precious little they could do. It was completely impractical to cordon off an area that extended for over one hundred miles in every direction. Stewing, the two men sat in silence. But after a short pause, Schultz suddenly began smiling. "Then let's give them something to look at."

As Schultz explained his idea, Evans's face began to light up.

"I'll need to talk to the base commander, General Norman, and Commander Oh," stated Schultz as he leapt from his chair.

Evans asked, "How about McConnell?"

Schultz shook his head. "No, he can't help with this, and he's got a busy day coming." He stifled a yawn. "And once *Defender* is safely back home, I'm taking a long nap."

U.S. Space Force Headquarters
Edwards Air Force Base
Battle Management Center
1030 hours
December 14, 2017

Schultz found Jenny Oh hard at work, testing and refining the tracking software so critical to the upcoming mission.

Now she sat at the chief controller's desk, considering Schultz's idea. She was tired and worried, but it was an intriguing plan, even if it complicated the last few precious hours.

"We've run similar drills, sir," she replied carefully. She couldn't give Schultz a resounding yes, much as she wanted to. She needed to think it through herself. "And my programmers could continue running their tests separately."

"I don't want to do anything that interferes with readiness for the launch tomorrow," the admiral reassured her.

"It would mean transmitting on the launch frequencies," warned Jenny.

"We have more than one set, don't we?" he asked.

"Yes, sir, but only a limited number. Once they've been used, we have to assume the Chinese, or anyone else for that matter, will be able to monitor them."

"But they're encrypted," Schultz replied.

"I don't assume anything, sir," Jenny answered firmly.

"You're right, of course, but I believe this will be worth it." He looked at his watch. "I want it nice and dark, so you'll need to be ready by zero five-hundred hours."

"Not a problem, Admiral. We'll be ready."

Gongga Shan
Sichuan Province, China
December 14, 2017

General Shen paced a racetrack in the launch center. The staff, familiar with the general's moods, gave him a wide berth and paid attention to the preparations for the upcoming launch. Wisely, he left them to their work. Events were taking their own course. He was no longer in complete control of the situation, and he hated it.

The launch base, always on alert for attack, was now on a full war footing. Every man of the garrison had been turned out, and patrols went out twice as far as usual. Flanker fighters ran racetrack patterns overhead.

They had cause to be concerned. American strikes up and down the coast had hurt the People's Liberation Army badly. Vital bases were damaged, ships had been sunk, and dozens of aircraft destroyed. The politburo had forbidden the services to discuss casualty figures, even among themselves.

The general was still trying to accept the fact that the *Defender* vehicle was actually going to fly, and, by every indication, probably very soon. Having his initial judgment proved wrong did not worry him so much, but wondering what else he may have been wrong about did.

He was an engineer. Building a gun that would shoot down satellites was easy compared to predicting your opponent's behavior. He hadn't been able to comprehend why the Americans were launching replacement GPS satellites, until he'd received the news about the American spaceship being sighted on the launchpad. They were not beaten, and they did not believe they were helpless. The Americans were waging a subtle delaying action—buying time to finish *Defender*.

There would be a fight in space; he was certain of that, but he and Dong had taken steps that should destroy *Defender* soon after her launch. But nothing in a battle was certain. Would the *Defender* vehicle attack them here? Shen knew they would if they could, especially since this was where the real battle lay. But he and Dong were not going to let the American crew live.

Shen was almost eager for the Americans to launch. Its appearance would resolve so much of the uncertainty he had lived with. Its failure would break their will.

U.S. Space Force Headquarters
Edwards Air Force Base
Defender Simulator
1700 hours
December 14, 2017

Barnes had driven them hard, training until an hour before dinner. He'd just finished his last critique when he suddenly declared, "That's it. You're ready." Skeldon and Ray had both protested, suggesting, almost demanding, additional drills, but Biff had flatly refused. "You're just as well trained as when I went up. Unless you can tell me exactly what the Chinese are going to do or what part of the ship will definitely break, there's nothing more we can do to get ready."

Ray had bristled a little at the suggestion that something on *Defender* might break, but he yielded to Biff's experience. Barnes's pilot wings had an astronaut badge in the center. That carried a lot of weight with Ray and the others. The other five would receive their astronaut insignia when they came back.

Biff gave them ten minutes to change and then ran them over to the volleyball court. They ran in the same arrangement they sat in *Defender*: Scarelli and Skeldon in the lead, then Tillman and Baker, with Ray and Biff in the rear. "We'll play six-on-six today," Biff shouted as they jogged. As they neared the court, Ray and the others could see a group waiting for them next to the net. It was more than six people, a lot more, although some of them were in athletic gear. Ray didn't recognize them, but Scarelli, then Sue Tillman, suddenly called out and sped ahead of the group. A moment later, Andre Baker called out, "Helen!" and took off at a full run.

The two groups merged in a chaos of hugs and introductions. Ray was quickly introduced to a husband and grandfather, two wives, an uncle, and two sets of parents. Five of them had suited up in borrowed USAF sweat suits for volleyball, while one wore navy PT gear. "The major said you guys were soft and needed a good workout," Sue Tillman's husband explained, grinning. Lieutenant Brad Tillman was also in the navy—a SEAL. He was the crew's most dangerous opponent, although the sheer distraction of the crew seeing their family members gave the newcomers' team an edge.

In between sets, Biff pulled Ray aside and explained. "I invited Jenny, but she said she couldn't break away and that you would understand."

Ray nodded. "I do—and besides, let's be fair. I've seen Jenny often during our time here. The rest of the crew's been separated from their people for months."

"She also said she didn't want to crush your delicate male ego."

"Too late," Ray answered. "But wait a minute. Jenny has a clearance. These folks do not. Or were they all read into the program for this volleyball game?"

"Admiral Schultz said that as of your flight tomorrow, the wraps are off. He was the one who signed off on them coming here. They'll stay on base until after we return," Barnes reassured him. "As long as we don't talk shop over dinner, it will be fine. Even if we did, Colonel Evans took all their cell phones and such, so they're off the grid. Now that's enough of a break. They're waiting for us."

In the end, they only had time for two sets before dinner. While the families rode in blue air force vehicles back to their quarters to change, Biff, this time in the lead, ran the others back, almost sprinting and daring them to match his pace. Ray and the others took the challenge, with Andre Baker coming in second. Ray was fourth, but he was not disappointed. A couple of months ago, a run like that would have killed him.

"The Hangar" staff had expanded the area for the mission crew to accommodate their families. After hearing stories about The Hangar's food, they'd all decided to have a regular dinner from the cafeteria line, but Lewes and his staff had added some special touches: name cards, wine, and a fancy salad waiting on each plate.

Ray saw a card and a place for Jenny set next to his, but it was empty. He was beginning to feel a little alone, surrounded by so much family togetherness, but Jenny arrived while they were still working on their salads. Her "sorry, I'm late" was followed by a round of introductions and some slightly embarrassing questions, but Ray endured the interrogation quietly. He was just happy she could be there.

She seemed irritated at his relief. "A girl's got to eat, doesn't she?" she demanded, but Ray knew it had taken a huge mental effort to step away from the BMC. On the other hand, he was glad that she would also get a chance to clear her head, even if only for a short time.

Several family members started to ask questions about details of the mission, but by unspoken agreement, the crew steered them away from specifics. Biff shared many of his experiences on his single space flight, and between family news, base gossip, and stories about the coverage of *Defender* "outside the wire," the meal rushed by, until the chef brought over a freshly baked apple cobbler for dessert.

Jenny, in an act of self-discipline on several levels, excused herself and returned to work. With her gone, Ray ate his dessert and listened to the conversation, but his mind was filled with tomorrow. One part of him wondered if the families' presence might not be a distraction. He thought of the bomber crews in England in World War II, in the pub one day and over Germany fighting for their lives the next.

Ray firmly believed the risk of his screwing up was far greater than of his dying, either through Chinese actions or some system failure, but this was still a combat mission. Nothing was certain. But what was the risk of some spouse or relative saying the wrong thing or breaking down in tears compared to a chance for the crew to spend time before their mission with the ones they loved? And if, heaven forbid, it literally was their last night on earth, these memories would be all the more precious.

After the meal, the crew loaded their family members back into the cars and waved good-bye. As they walked back to their trailers, Ray wasn't the only one yawning. "I see my diabolical plan is working perfectly," Biff observed.

"Diabolical but obvious," Ray responded. "And necessary. I'm trying hard not to think too deeply about tomorrow."

"What's to think about?" Biff shrugged, smiling. "We wake up; we go." After a short pause, he added, in a more serious tone, "Events are in motion. Give yourself over to them. Accept them, focus on your part, and you'll do well."

"Is that what you did on your first space flight?"

"No, that's what I wish I'd done. I was so worried about screwing up, I hardly got any sleep at all."

Ray laughed softly and offered his hand. "I won't let you down, boss."

"That's not going to happen," Barnes said, shaking Ray's hand. "Now go get some sleep, and no working tonight, mister. Clear?"

Georgetown
Washington, D.C.
December 14, 2017

Tom Rutledge sat in his study, flipping randomly from channel to channel. Coverage of *Defender* was ubiquitous and uniformly irritating. The media drumbeat reminded him of his defeat—no, his humiliation—by his own party.

He'd told his staff he'd be out of touch while he "considered his next move." He might actually do that, eventually, but first he intended to get drunk. He wasn't wasting honest whiskey on it, either. Vodka, with lemon and sugar. It went down easy, and he'd have less of a hangover in the morning.

Not that he had anything planned for the morning. Ben Davis and the others were under orders to respond "no comment" to any questions about GPS satellites, the Space Force, the air force's program, and especially the upcoming *Defender* launch. If pressed, they could add, "We fervently hope that the GPS satellite shoot-downs can be stopped somehow."

It just hadn't worked. Usually there was enough political space for a "maverick" to carve out an issue and make it his. The whole Space Force–*Defender* thing had looked like a perfect ticket to the national stage. If you stay on message and sound authoritative, people start listening. Your influence grows. Pretty soon, they start asking you about other issues, and your power grows some more. Then someone with an issue to sell comes to you, asking for your support. And Mrs. Rutledge's son never did anything for free.

Rutledge took another pull on his drink and flipped the channel again. Another cable news channel, another set of talking heads filling dead air, speculating, predicting, while the networks waited for the "money shot": *Defender* blasting off. Then they could start with a whole new question: What was actually happening up there, in orbit? It would be a new kind of war, horrible and fascinating, but sure to raise ratings.

He flipped again. Nope, they weren't waiting for the launch. Somebody had a computer-animated *Defender* firing a laser from its nose at an animated *Tien Lung* projectile. Nobody knew exactly what the Chinese weapon looked like, so they'd used something that looked like the shell from a gun, painted red, of course. The Chinese animation fired back at the American vehicle, and the show's host was asking a question about damage to *Defender*'s heat shield from this hypothetical weapon.

If and when this thing actually flew, somebody would be sure to run a video of it blasting off, followed immediately by one of him blasting the administration. He was on the record calling the program "an idea bound to fail," and a "deliberate waste of the taxpayer's money." More than on the record: He'd made it his signature issue.

And if he hadn't been told to shut up and sit down, he might have been on that TV set, ambushed by the video, then trying to answer embarrassing questions like, "What do you think now, Congressman?" Those were a reporter's favorite. Nothing helped ratings more than catching a politician with his position exposed.

Maybe the House leaders had done him a favor. He'd called *Defender* a boondoggle, the Space Force a money trap, and the air force's new organization political cover for the Jackson administration. Normally, he didn't regard being wrong as a great handicap, but being so completely and publicly wrong could condemn him to judging hog contests for the rest of his political life.

But, dammit, the whole space issue was perfect for him! It had no effect on his local base, and national-level interest a mile wide. Bottom line, he just hated seeing all that TV coverage wasted. He could have been in front of those cameras, except he'd picked the wrong message.

They were running the animation again, this time asking questions about how the two opponents would have to maneuver. Like anyone knew. And if a battle actually was fought, would anyone remember this crap? Little stuff like this wasn't worth remembering, but they'd remember "Rutledge and *Defender*."

Reporters were still calling his office, as late as it was, asking for a statement or reaction to the latest factoid, but word was spreading about his meeting with the speaker and minority leader. Nothing stayed secret in Washington forever. If he didn't find some way to spin that, if it became common knowledge . . .

Wait. Not if, but when. Getting "taken to the woodshed" was a popular spectator sport in Washington. What everybody watched for was the subject's reaction afterward. Denial was common, if futile. Defiance was another choice, but was usually taken as a sign of weakness. The winning play was humility and a display of party loyalty, followed by laying low and waiting for a fresh opportunity.

But the opportunity was now! He'd tried the "voice in the wilderness," gambit but hadn't gotten any traction. Where could he go after being so publicly wrong?

Rutledge took another drink. Okay, so if he couldn't change the situation, maybe he should run with it instead. Not just admit he'd been wrong but embrace it. A politician who'd changed his mind and was willing to talk about it was worth a round of interviews right there. And then become *Defender*'s biggest supporter. Instead of "the maverick," play "the convert."

Whether or not *Defender* beat the Chinese, the U.S. Space Force would need friends in Congress in the days ahead. He could become their best friend, someone they needed. And Mrs. Rutledge's boy never did anything for free.

U.S. Space Force Headquarters
Edwards Air Force Base
Battle Management Center
2130 hours
December 14, 2017

Ray waited for a minute or two after Biff left, and he didn't grab his doorknob until he heard the door of Biff's trailer open and close.

Peeking out a side window, he saw the lights in Barnes's trailer come on and then realized he was being foolish. He felt like a kid sneaking out the night before exams. Biff might be mad that Ray didn't immediately go to bed, but Ray didn't care.

It was a ten-minute walk to the BMC, during which time Ray had to show his ID four times: first to a roving patrol, then at the BMC's perimeter fence, and again at the entrance to the building. The last time was at the entrance to the actual command center, after he found out Jenny wasn't in her first-floor office.

Ray was in his flight suit, of course, and everyone he passed, including the security guards, wished him "good luck" or "safe return" or "give 'em hell." It felt good.

The Battle Management Center was partially manned, and the projectors had turned the blank white globe in the center into a real-time replica of Earth, including weather, displaying the tracks of the remaining GPS satellites. It was a far cry from his earlier visit. Ray just stood and admired it for a moment. If you looked carefully, you could see the day-night terminator moving across the surface.

He spotted Jenny sitting at her second-level command desk. She was smiling and waved down to him. He waved back and then trotted up the stairs to the catwalk.

He sat down in the second chair at the command desk. "Maybe instead of a spacecraft, I should have just designed a really cool RV."

She laughed and waved an arm toward the globe. "Then what would we do with this? Although, I have to admit, the RV sounds nice." She smiled warmly.

"Well, this is pretty cool, too," Ray conceded. "I didn't get much of a chance to talk to you at dinner. I wanted to wish you luck tomorrow and tell you how much all your work has meant to me."

"Well, thank you, Mr. McConnell. Is that all you have to say?" She was smiling, but Ray realized there were rapids ahead.

"I should also mention that you are beautiful and intelligent, and I will be thinking of you every moment that I'm in orbit."

She laughed brightly. "Don't you dare! Focus on your job, or you'll end up as a big greasy smear somewhere, and I would really hate that."

"Then I will think of you as I fall asleep tonight. Which will be very soon."

"Good," she said approvingly.

"And why are you still here?" he asked.

"Just some last-minute tests," she replied, but she wouldn't meet his eyes.

"Is there a problem? Has something cropped up? The admiral and I both saw the last test verification report, and the BMC was certified as 'mission-ready.'" There was concern in Ray's voice.

Jenny shook her head sharply. "No, nothing is wrong, but I almost wish there was. Nothing this complicated is ever completely bug-free, and I have this recurring nightmare about the whole system crashing with you up there."

"Jenny, I have faith in your ability not only to build this thing but also to test it within an inch of its electronic life. Let me walk you to your quarters. You need sleep as much as I do."

Sighing and nodding, she shut down her console and followed him down the steps and out of the BMC. They both collected more good wishes from the staff, which they answered with, "good luck to us all."

Outside the perimeter fence, he took her hand and turned toward her quarters, but she stopped and said, "Your trailer is that way." She let go of his hand to point and then pushed gently on his chest. "Go."

Jenny turned and started walking, but Ray protested. "I said I'd walk you to your quarters first."

"Uh-uh. It's a ten-minute walk each way, and that's twenty minutes less sleep."

"But ten minutes less with you," he countered.

"Let's squeeze it into a minute, then," and she stepped closer and kissed him.

They didn't move for what seemed like both forever and just a few seconds, and then she said, "Now go. And remember: You said you'd think of me."

Ray kept his promise.

23

Bait and Switch

Edwards Air Force Base
Hangar 1600
0330 hour
December 15, 2017

Admiral Schultz watched the Marine pilot go through the preflight of his F/A-18E Super Hornet. It was dark on the flight line, but the illumination from the open hangar doors and the rigged spotlights was adequate for him to conduct his inspection. The drab gray camouflage scheme reflected the light poorly and made the aircraft look like it was made from alternating light and dark, angled shadows.

The fighter was unarmed but carried three of the big 480-gallon drop tanks. The pilot and several NASA technicians were paying a lot of attention to them, particularly the centerline tank that was a little larger than the other two. Oddly, there was a thick coating of frost on it.

General Norman had also joined Schultz on the flight line. "It seems so simple," the general said, looking at the plane's payload. But his face betrayed his skepticism.

"It'll work just fine," Schultz reassured him. "This idea is based on a problem we used to have with the old A-6s and F-14s back in the day. In fact, once the pilots found out how to do it intentionally, we had to explicitly forbid the practice. This setup is basically the same thing, only on steroids."

"Okay, but what I don't understand is why you need to have liquid oxygen in the centerline tank?"

Schultz's face broke out in a wicked smile. "Your basic reporter won't realize there's a different color in the flame shooting out of a rocket engine, although a retired engineer or shuttle astronaut might say something during an interview. But our opponents manning the Dragon Gun aren't stupid. They would spot it immediately.

"We need to have a blue flame coming out the back end if we're to fool them, and any fuel will burn blue as long as there is enough oxygen. So by carrying liquid oxygen and spraying it out behind the bird, we can ensure an oxygen-rich atmosphere when Major O'Hara dumps the fuel. It'll look very impressive and make a hell of a lot of noise—just like a rocket being launched."

The smile waned, and the tone of the admiral's voice hardened. "But we are talking about dumping several tons of JP-8 along with lots of oxygen directly behind his aircraft. This will be one hairy ride. And there are risks with this stunt."

"Which Major O'Hara tells me he understands," Norman remarked. "But I'm taking all this on faith. I'm just a dumb grunt."

"And I'm just an old pilot." Schultz grinned at him. The admiral looked down at his watch and noted the time. "I'm needed elsewhere. Would you care to join me, Carl?"

"I'd love to, Bill," replied the general.

U.S. Space Force Headquarters
Edwards Air Force Base
0330 hours
December 15, 2017

Suiting up for the flight was still a novelty for Ray. He'd practiced donning his ACES suit twice before, as well as learning how to use it during a high-altitude bailout in case something went wrong during launch or reentry. Like the shuttle crew, they could work in a shirtsleeve environment once in orbit, but for this mission they'd wear the full rig the whole time. This wasn't a supply run to the international space station or a scientific expedition. It was a combat mission.

The advanced crew escape suit was the standard attire for most space shuttle flights, and even though it wasn't rated for extravehicular activity, it was a full-pressure suit with thermal insulation and liquid cooling layers. Under normal conditions, the ship supplied the oxygen for the crew to breathe, but the ACES suit also had two emergency oxygen bottles fitted in the same harness with the parachute and life raft. Colored a very bright orange, the international color for distress, the ACES suit was affectionately known as the "pumpkin suit."

Ray moved through the morning's activities in a total haze. He felt detached from what he was doing, just an observer, guided from one station to another by a helpful technician. Everything had happened so fast. His role in building *Defender* and preparing her for flight was over, and now he had to switch to his new role as astronaut. But Ray was so used to the immense pressure of the deadline that he still felt it weighing on him. Like taking final exams, it took a while to accept that they were over.

Added to that delayed realization was the fulfillment of a lifelong dream: He would fly in space. He'd flown before, of course, in light planes that he piloted and had taken joyrides in high-performance jets. This would be much different. He'd see and feel things he'd never seen or felt before.

Ray knew he was afraid. There were risks, of course. Mechanical failure or human error could bring them all to grief, but it was the importance of the mission that really frightened him. Did they have the right tools to do the job? Ray had become so closely tied with *Defender,* he felt as if he were part of her, and the thought of her failing almost paralyzed him. He then remembered his talk with Jenny and tried to say to himself the words he'd said to her.

U.S. Space Force Headquarters
Edwards Air Force Base
Battle Management Center
0345 hours
December 15, 2017

The visit was just as important as fueling *Defender* or loading her software. Led by Major "Biff" Barnes, *Defender*'s crew filed up onto the scaffolding surrounding the slowly rotating globe of the earth. They were all dressed for the mission, wearing their orange ACES suits and, purely for photo purposes, carrying their helmets.

Although no one announced their arrival, someone, then several people, and finally the entire center began clapping and cheering as they made their way to Admiral Schultz's position.

Ray felt embarrassed and proud at the same time. The BMC staff was applauding the crew, their faces beaming with pride, but Ray knew the crew would depend on these people while they were up. In fact, without them, he and the rest of the crew wouldn't be able to accomplish their mission. They were a closely linked team, but Ray also understood that he and the others were the ones taking the risks.

Biff Barnes understood it better. There'd always been a special bond between the people who maintained the planes and those who flew them. *Defender*'s crew was here to acknowledge that bond and to let the ground-support staff have one more look at the crew before launch. They were the stars of the show, and stars need to let themselves be seen. It was good for morale.

Admiral Schultz also wanted to say his good-byes and wish them luck as well. After this, the crew would be bused out to the launchpad and would then strap themselves into *Defender*. With the crew in place, the final launch preparations would begin; there'd be no time for ceremony then.

Schultz shook everyone's hand and had a few words for each member of the crew. When Ray took his hand, the normally outgoing admiral was silent for a moment, and he finally just said, "Good luck."

Behind Schultz, Ray saw Jenny. She was smiling, but swallowing hard at the same time. Her eyes were alight with pride, but Ray also saw the tears welling up. She was struggling to keep her composure, and Ray suddenly wanted to go over and hug her. But that was the last thing she wanted him to do, and she had made that desire clear in no uncertain terms. They'd had their good-bye the night before. On the BMC watch floor, she was just another member of the staff, and even though everyone knew of their relationship, any "public displays of affection" would be inappropriate.

She nodded her approval as Ray held himself in check. Then, silently, she mouthed the words "I love you." Ray echoed his feelings to her.

Suddenly, a hand grasped Ray's left shoulder and gently started tugging on him. "Time to go, Ray," whispered Barnes.

Edwards Air Force Base
Area 1-54, Launchpad Complex
0415 hours
December 15, 2017

The crew left the ready room together and walked outside. Only a few people saw them, but they clapped and waved at the six as the crew approached *Defender*.

Ray had visited the Kennedy Space Center several times and loved the huge vertical assembly building and the massive tracked transporter that carried the assembled shuttle on its six-mile-per-hour crawl to the launchpad. They were tremendous technical achievements, needed because of the shuttle's boosters and fuel tanks. They were also tremendously expensive. *Defender* required neither.

Late last night, they'd rolled the supporting shelter away from *Defender* and positioned her at the launchpad. Two rails helped them guide her onto the pad, where she was elevated to the vertical for launching. Fueling began as soon as she was locked in place. With a midnight rollout, she'd be ready for launch at zero six hundred. The sheer simplicity of the launch preparations still amazed him.

The spacecraft was still an overall white, a broad snowy wedge that reflected the work lights. The swept-back wings at the rear made her look wider and taller. The ship sat on a short framework over a large pit to deflect the exhaust gases; the beam used to elevate her was once again lowered.

The crew-access elevator took them two-thirds of the way up fuselage, where the square black of the open-access hatch led them inside. The technicians helped the crew into their seats and ensured their five-point harnesses were securely fastened. After a pressurization test of the ACES suits and a communications check, the technicians began filing out. The senior engineer gave Biff a thumbs-up and closed the hatch. A few minutes later, a slight bump told the crew the elevator had been disconnected. *Defender* was ready to roll.

"All right, people, let's start going through the final prelaunch checklist," ordered Barnes.

Ray grabbed his operating-procedures manual from its storage rack, opened it up, and started running down his checklist.

Edwards Air Force Base
Main Runway, 04R/22L
0445 hours
December 15, 2017

Major Tim O'Hara lined his Super Hornet up on the centerline of the main Edwards runway. Nighttime takeoffs always required extra caution, and this one would be a little trickier than most. He was following directly behind a pair of F-16s taking off to relieve the standing combat air patrol. The Marine kept his eyes glued to the two fighters in front of him. They'd led him down the taxiway and were now positioned some eighty feet in front of him. He set his brakes and listened for the air-traffic controller to clear the Falcons to take off. As he waited, he checked his radio, again. The transmit switch was off and would stay off until he was ready to land.

The runway was dry and clear, and the weather was perfect. The skies were absolutely clear, no clouds at all, with a thin waning crescent moon providing little light. The upcoming show would be visible for dozens of miles. O'Hara fought the urge to double-check his armament display. He did double-check that his navigation lights were off. He wasn't supposed to attract any attention, which is why he would be following close behind the air force jets. The tower would keep all other traffic clear as the new CAP section took off. O'Hara heard the controller vector the standing fighter patrol to the other end of the base.

"Acme Six, you are cleared for takeoff, runway Two Two Lima," squawked the radio.

"Roger, Tower." O'Hara recognized the voice of the lead F-16 pilot, and as soon as he saw the aircraft's navigation lights flash twice, he released the brake and moved the throttle forward. The F-16s were already moving quickly down the runway when their afterburners kicked in. The racket from the air force fighters would mask his Super Hornet's departure. The runway lights slid past him on either side, quickly becoming streaks. With long practice, he pulled back on the stick, feeling the ship almost leap off the runway. He cleaned her up, bringing up the flaps and gear.

Throttling back, he stayed low and started his first turn to the right, away from the rest of the base and open territory. After passing NASA's Dryden Flight Research Center, O'Hara turned sharply to the right and reduced his altitude to only one hundred feet. Once over Rogers Dry Lake, he spotted the brightly lit launchpad some sixteen miles to the southeast. He lined up his ship and slowed down to two hundred knots.

Even at this relatively slow speed, he crossed the parched lake bed in just under two minutes and spotted the IP ahead. They'd decided to use one of the rocket-engine test stands just three quarters of a mile to the northwest of Area 1-54. The test stands were almost on the exact same bearing as the launchpad from the news cameras' perspective; the difference in distance would be imperceptible in the darkness. Turning to the east, he lined up for a straight shot to the orange blinker lights. O'Hara then heard the tower vector the F-16 CAP to the west to "investigate" an unidentified contact. That was the code phrase for the fighter pilots to make a nuisance of themselves with the CNN aircraft loitering just on the other side of the closure-area perimeter.

As he passed Area 1-42 to his left, O'Hara pushed the throttle to full military power. The jet built up speed and quickly passed over a small service building he'd noted on the map. It marked the spot where he had to begin his climb.

O'Hara pulled the nose up sharply, the g-forces pushing him down into his seat. By the time he'd reached the vertical, he was directly over the engine test stand. He hit the afterburner and, an instant later, the "dump" switch on his drop tanks. Fuel and compressed oxygen sprayed out of the extended nozzles on the back of the tanks and was immediately ignited by the jet's exhaust. The view from the cockpit went from total darkness to a vibrant blue glow. The noise was beyond description.

Accelerating, O'Hara wrestled with the controls, concentrating on keeping the nose straight up, and watched as the altimeter spun wildly upward. Even from his limited viewpoint, he knew he was putting on a damned impressive airshow. Bouncing about in his harness, the Marine knew he'd be sore for the next few days. He could only hope that someone was getting a really decent video.

CNN Urgent Report
0502 hours
December 15, 2017

"FLASH. This is Mark Markin, CNN News, outside Edwards Air Force Base. We've just seen a huge flame rising to the west." Turning to someone off-camera, he shouted, "Is it still there? Get the camera on it!"

Markin's face was replaced by an intense blue-and-yellowish streak moving against a black background. Jerky camera motion gave the impression of an object at a great distance. The end of the streak flickered and wavered as the "vehicle" climbed skyward. It seemed to be going very fast.

"Less than a minute ago, a bright blue flash appeared in the direction of Area 1-54, the launchpad used by the *Defender* program. The flash shot up into the sky at terrific speed and is now fading at high altitude.

"Without any official announcement, and presumably to protect the American GPS constellation, *Defender* has launched.

"I repeat . . ."

U.S. Space Force Headquarters
Edwards Air Force Base
Battle Management Center
0505 hours
December 15, 2017

General Norman watched CNN's transmission, grinning. "That's what you get for peeking over fences," he joked at Markin's image. The CNN reporter was rehashing the recent event yet again.

Schultz was listening on his headset and watching Jenny move among the launch controllers. Instead of paying attention to their screens, they read from a paper script. Normally used for training, it drilled the controllers in what they were supposed to say at each point as they guided *Defender* during its launch. They'd practiced the procedure dozens of times, but this time their transmissions were being broadcast. Because the transmissions were encrypted, it was extraordinarily unlikely anyone would have a clue as to what the launch controllers were saying. But if someone were listening in, they'd pick up the sudden jump in radio traffic, which is exactly what they would be expecting to hear if a spacecraft had indeed been launched.

Gongga Shan
Sichuan Province, China
1710 hours
December 15, 2017

From the look on the controller's face, Shen knew it was an urgent call. He took the headset and heard Dong Zhi's voice. "The Americans have launched. It's all over CNN."

"What did they show?" Shen asked impatiently, motioning to one of the technicians to bring up the news feed. Along with the rest of the Dragon Mother's staff, Shen watched the launch and heard Markin's commentary. The video coverage was impressive, but the flame looked like it had too much yellow in it.

"Time of launch was two minutes after five local, about ten minutes ago," reported Dong. "We've also received word from the Second Bureau of the General Staff of a significant increase in radio traffic from Edwards. It would appear the Americans have launched *Defender*. We're calculating the intercept position now."

"Are you sure, Doctor? Didn't the flame look a little odd to you? Do we have a good idea of what the exhaust from this new Aerospike engine should look like?"

"General, I appreciate your diligence, but the video from multiple networks showed a deep blue flame indicative of a high-oxygen-combustion process. A number of the videos did show some yellow, but others did not. Combined with radio traffic analysis from our intelligence arm, it argues strongly that the launch has taken place."

"Very well, Doctor. We're still seventeen minutes from launch here," said Shen, checking the time. He could feel a prebattle excitement building inside him. The Americans had moved. Despite all his reservations, the Americans had somehow managed to launch *Defender* within the timeframe they had set—a most impressive feat.

"I recommend holding your launch until we finish the intercept," the scientist replied. "I don't want the staff having to deal with two vehicles attacking two distinct targets at once. Without worldwide tracking, we'll have to move fast once the American appears."

"All right." Shen was reluctant to hold the launch but agreed with Dong. He knew the staff's capabilities. "I'll wait for your word."

Dong reassured him. "Preparations for the booster have started and are on schedule. It should launch in ten minutes."

Shen broke the connection and turned to find his launch crew suddenly busy at their posts. He should be worried about the American spacecraft, but he felt relief instead. The uncertainty that had plagued him was now gone. He really hadn't expected the Americans to launch their vehicle so soon. It would have a short life.

U.S. Space Force Headquarters
Edwards Air Force Base
Battle Management Center
0530 hours
December 15, 2017

Wrapped up in the launch sequence, Ray was almost irritated when Schultz's voice came over the communications circuit. "BMC to all stations, SITREP, people," Schultz announced. Conversation stopped immediately, and the admiral continued, speaking quickly. "We've got a launch from mainland China."

Ray cursed their bad luck. Was their timing off? Intel had firmly assured him that they would be able to launch before the Chinese sent up another ASAT vehicle—maybe by less than an hour, but they needed that time to get into position for an intercept.

Then Ray saw it was from Xichang, south of the Dragon Gun's location. The thin red line grew slowly, angling east and steadily climbing in a graceful curve. He heard a controller announce, "It's faster than a *Tien Lung*."

"A bigger gun?" wondered Ray amazedly.

"No, that's one of their space centers," replied Barnes. "The one that's been associated with ASAT ops. It has to be a standard booster. But what's on top?"

While the crew all studied their displays, Schultz explained about the decoy launch and the massive coverage on CNN. "It must have fooled the Chinese as well, and they've tipped their hand early.

"We'll continue with launch preparations while intelligence tries to sort it out. Continue the countdown, T minus fifteen minutes and counting."

It was less than five minutes later when Schultz interrupted their preparations again. With only a few minutes until ignition, Ray knew it would be important news. "The launch was from their Xichang space complex, and the telemetry is consistent with a Long March 2F space launch vehicle. That's one of the rockets they use for manned launches, but it's moving too fast for a manned spacecraft. We think it has a much smaller payload."

"Aimed at us, no doubt," Barnes remarked. "An orbital SAM."

"Aimed at what they thought was us," Schultz corrected him. "That fireworks display was more useful than we thought."

"With that much energy, they may still be able to engage us," Ray countered.

"And with what?" asked Barnes.

"Probably another *Tien Lung*," guessed Ray. "But it could be mod-ified."

"Nukes?" Barnes didn't look worried, but some of the other crew did.

"Anything's possible. We're at war, remember?"

Schultz asked tersely, "Are we go or no-go? We can hold on the pad."

"With that thing waiting in orbit for us? No way," Ray responded. Suddenly he remembered he was on a live mike. Barnes should be the one to answer for the crew. Ray looked at the major and said, "I recommend we go, sir."

Biff nodded, then looked at the rest of the crew. All were silent, but they all nodded yes.

"They're still aiming at something that isn't there. Let's go now, before they get a chance to regroup. We're go," Biff answered firmly.

"Very well, we are go for launch. T minus ten minutes and count-ing," commanded Schultz.

Ray tried to keep himself busy as those last minutes ticked away, but he had a hard time keeping his mind on his display screen. All the checklists had been completed. All systems were operating normally. Everything was proceeding according to plan. There was really noth-ing to do but sit back and wait. When the count reached T minus 60 seconds, Ray felt his mouth become dry. He was breathing faster, and his heart rate could give a lab rat a run for its money. A bead of sweat ran down his cheek.

He was briefly thinking of opening his visor to wipe the sweat off when the launch controller announced, "Ten, nine, eight, seven . . ."

Ray saw the indicator light on his panel flash on; the main engines had just lit off. "Main engines start!" he yelled over the sound of the engines.

"Understood," acknowledged Barnes. Then the whole vehicle began to shake, a little at first, but then growing to a bone-jarring rattle. *Defender* was taking flight.

Ray barely heard the launch controller say, "Lift off," and he grasped the arms on his chair tightly. Vibrating in his harness he thought, *OH . . . MY . . . GOD!*

Gongga Shan
Sichuan Province, China
1750 hours
December 15, 2017

General Shen had left the CNN newscast on in the hopes that some additional information on the launch might be added, but after running out of ways to repeat themselves, they'd just started speculating. And while amusing, it wasn't very useful.

He was in an unusual—in fact, unique—situation. The Dragon's Egg projectile was ready; it had been for almost ten minutes, but they had not fired. Technicians sat idle, the gun crews crouched in their launch bunkers, and they waited. Xichang was still waiting for *Defender* to appear on their tracking radars, while the Long March interceptor raced to the best guess of *Defender*'s future position.

Shen found himself drawn to the CNN channel out of impatience. He needed something for his mind to work on. Much of the material shown was coverage of the war. Most was propaganda, but the coverage was extensive. He'd learned a few things that Beijing would certainly forbid them to discuss . . .

"FLASH. This is Mark Markin, at Edwards Air Force Base in Southern California." Markin's familiar image replaced the physics professor who had been explaining *Defender*'s engines.

"We have just witnessed another launch from the direction of Area 1-54, the launchpad associated with the *Defender* spacecraft." Markin looked and acted rattled and confused.

"The launch that took place just a few minutes ago was louder—indeed, the noise was 'shattering'—much, much louder than the event earlier this morning. What?"

Markin looked off to the side, then answered, "Good, put it up."

"Here is an image of the launch taken by a local resident who grabbed his camera when he heard the noise." The picture showed a dark sky with an angled pure-blue pillar, almost a cone, across two-thirds of the frame. A small arrowhead sat on top of the pillar.

Markin's voice said, "We're going to enhance the picture." A box appeared around the arrowhead, and Shen watched as it expanded, then rippled, and finally sharpened. Individual pixels gave it a jagged look, but he could see swept-back wings and make out clusters of flame at the base.

"Get me Dong!" he shouted to the communications chief, then stared at the image on the screen. "Somebody print that picture out, NOW!" he ordered as the chief handed him a headset.

"Dong! Are you watching it, too? I don't know what we saw earlier, but this one looks real enough. Yes, yes, we'll begin final launch preparations immediately." Shen signed off and blasted out orders to the launch staff to begin the final countdown. As they scurried about, a tight knot formed in the general's stomach.

24

High Ground, Part I

Defender
0550 hours

The experience of the launch filled Ray's senses. Every part of him, inside and out, was affected by the unbelievable sound, the intense vibration, and the acceleration that continued seemingly forever.

Early in their training, there had been time for each of the flight crew, except Steve Skeldon, who was already a pilot, to have one flight in a high-performance jet, with Biff in the front seat, coaching and explaining. He put each of them through a series of high-g turns, both so they could experience the sensation and so the flight surgeon could make sure the crew could tolerate the acceleration of a space launch. "You'll be lying in your chair, not sitting up, for the launch," Biff had explained to Ray as he pushed the fighter through another six-g arc. To Ray, the world seemed to be taking on a red tinge, and his vision was blurred.

"Lying down is the best way to handle acceleration, so we won't have to worry about red-out," Biff explained. "It will feel like there's a giant on your chest, but your body will do what's needed. Just take shallow breaths."

After they landed, Ray was almost too tired to climb out of the cockpit. "Maybe now you won't whine about the weight training," Barnes teased as he helped Ray down the ladder. "Your body is going to be pummeled in ways it has never experienced before and was never designed to handle. The best way to cope is to be in top physical condition, like me," he said, smiling broadly and striking a bodybuilder pose.

That had been right after Ray had been picked to be part of the crew, and the experience had stuck with him, not only as a motivator for the physical training but also as a question in the corner of his mind: *What will it be like?*

Ray watched the timer slowly tick off the launch burn, one slow second at a time. To throw the Chinese off, and make it as difficult as possible for them to do anything during their ascent, Barnes opted for the equivalent of a "combat takeoff," which meant a four-g burn for seven minutes. They could have gone up even more quickly; *Defender*'s two Aerospike engines had the smash for four and a half g's, but they'd have less fuel when they reached orbit, and they would need that fuel to maneuver.

Four g's felt like plenty, especially when it lasted not just for a short turn in an aircraft but for four hundred and twenty continuous seconds. One corner of Ray's mind said something about "time dilation," but the acceleration pushing him down was much more immediate. He found himself wanting to take a deep breath, in spite of Biff's advice, and fought the urge. The suit provided all the oxygen he needed. He forced himself to relax, to accept the increased sensation of weight.

A controller built into the chair's armrest let him scroll through the displays and operate the controls, but just moving a finger on top of the selector button required a deliberate effort. Still, he was the flight engineer, and he methodically stepped though the screens, watching for trouble. It helped pass the time.

Biff watched the crew, checking each member for signs of g-loc: gravity-induced loss of consciousness. He didn't expect anyone would have *that* much trouble during the ascent, but it wasn't wise to make such an assumption—the majority of the crew hadn't gone through the full-up astronaut training, and their acceleration was faster than a traditional shuttle launch. Turning his head to look over his shoulder to check on Ray was more than a little unpleasant. Barnes had forgotten just how much he hated the continuous acceleration. The physical sensation was not new to him, of course, but his mind was also filled with the responsibility he held—mission commander. He tried to take comfort in his training as an astronaut and combat pilot, but the rules were different. All the rules. Not just the acceleration, but sensors and weapons as well. He'd drilled himself mercilessly in the simulators, never sure if it was enough. Now he'd find out. At least he didn't have to pull lead.

Ray focused on the board, letting his body do unconsciously what he couldn't tell it to. All the systems were working well, although they'd have to deploy the sensors to really check them out. They'd traded payload for time and overengineered the shock mountings. He had a feeling that would pay off.

Engine cutoff was a bigger surprise than the acceleration. The sudden absence of weight wasn't obvious from inside the cockpit. There was no loose gear to float in midair, and of course they were firmly strapped in, so nobody rose out of their chair. But it still was easy to tell. Ray's inner ear told him, in a high, panicky voice, that they were falling, that it was a long fall, that the sudden stop would be painful . . .

Biff's only advice on avoiding space sickness had been to avoid sudden head movements. Moving disturbed the fluid in the inner ear, so Ray held his head as still as possible. But the sensation just went on and on, and Ray's brain engaged in a spirited argument with his inner ear. Strangely enough, his stomach did not join the discussion, which might have tipped the balance. Ray focused his thoughts on the chair he sat in, the displays, the straps that held him in place, and it seemed to work.

Similar discussions were being held elsewhere in the cabin. Andre Baker was in charge of opening the bay doors and extending the laser turret. He was doing it one-handed, though. He'd opened his helmet and was holding an airsick bag over his mouth. Ray couldn't tell if Andre had actually used it, and didn't want to know.

But the doors were opening. Both his displays and the sensations transmitted through the deck and the chair told him so. The laser turret also extended properly, thank goodness. It was a simple arrangement—just electric motors lifting the turret assembly clear of the cargo bay—but with no chance for a "shakedown cruise," every successful function, no matter how small, was a victory for Ray and all the people who had worked so hard on building *Defender*. He tried to remember how it felt, so he could tell his people, and Dawson's as well.

He touched a switch on his hand controller and shifted from the systems to the tactical display. Two screens simultaneously displayed a side and overhead view of the situation. The Chinese intercept vehicle, marked TL1 on the display, was above them, but eastbound. They had launched *Defender* to the east in a following orbit, but it was already lower and thus slower than the Chinese vehicle. It was still accelerating, ascending into a higher orbit. The *Tien Lung*'s high velocity would make it difficult to attack *Defender*. Of course, the same applied to *Defender*'s intercepting TL1.

Gongga Shan
0600 hours

General Shen had studied the intercept math as well. There were choices to be made. He pressed his point over the link to Xichang. "If we try to intercept *Defender* on the next orbit, the Long March *Tien Lung* will be out of our view for over an hour. We can't tell what the Americans will do to it during that time. Their ascent was faster than a traditional space shuttle launch; the engines on *Defender* are quite powerful. We clearly underestimated the vehicle's abilities. Instead, we should use the Long March weapon to kill another GPS satellite. Their orbits are fixed, and the weapon has sufficient energy for the intercept. I'll attack *Defender* with the Dragon's Mother instead."

"But General, that's our last shot for a week," Dong countered. "Shouldn't we use it to kill a GPS satellite? Two kills in one day, both while *Defender* is supposed to be protecting them, will embarrass the Americans."

Shen disagreed. "It's far better to destroy *Defender*, Doctor. We may have missed with the Long March, but that doesn't change the value of the target. If they lose the spacecraft, that's all they have. There's nothing else that can stop us."

It was Shen's decision to make, but the general wanted Dong to agree. Dong's people would have to handle the two intercepts simultaneously, but for only a short time. Although Shen knew they were capable, the general asked, "Can you do it?"

"Yes," Dong admitted.

"Then tell them to prepare. We'll be firing in less than five minutes." He raised his voice for the last sentence, and the staff in the center hurried to obey.

"We'll be ready for the complex maneuver, General. I won't let you down again," replied Dong. Then, with a contrite voice, he added, "I must apologize for my failure, General. I was wrong about the first launch, and my poor judgment has placed us in this awkward position."

Shen wasn't surprised by Dong's admission; the senior engineer had an impeccable reputation for honesty. But it still wasn't easy for a man of his stature to say it. "Don't concern yourself with that any longer, Zhi, the Americans fooled us all. One more thing," General Shen added quickly. "Tell Beijing we need to initiate the special attack." Shen lowered his voice without trying to sound conspiratorial. Security concerning the "special attack" was so tight that even his launch staff didn't know about it.

"Good," Dong answered, sounding relieved. "Liang has been af-ter me to use it since this morning, when we were fooled by that false launch."

Battle Management Center
0615 hours

Jenny noticed it first. She ran the whole BMC, but she always kept one eye on the communications display that monitored the data links. Without the crucial information those links passed, there was no way to manage the battle. They'd be blind. Consequently, she dedi-cated one of her displays to keep track of the data links from dozens of sites worldwide. These included command centers like NORAD and the NMCC, radar-tracking stations, and intelligence aircraft orbiting off the China coast. The BMC had no sensors of its own but took the data from all these sources and created the global situ-ation display.

The audio beep and the flashing red icon grabbed her immediate attention. She called one of the controllers on her headset. "Carol, check on the link to Kwajalein. We've lost the signal."

No sooner had the controller acknowledged her order than another link went red, this time the one to Pearl Harbor. Used to looking for patterns, she instantly compared the two but could see no similar-ity. Pearl Harbor was a command site; Kwajalein a radar station.

She started to detail another of her small staff to check out the link to Hawaii when a third one went red, this time in Ascension Is-land, and then others, coming so rapidly it was hard to count.

"Admiral, we're losing all our sensor data links!" Jenny tried to control the panic in her voice. She started to listen to Schultz's reply when Carol cut in with a report on the Kwajalein tracking station.

"I'm in voice comms, Commander. They say the gear's fine, but they're under electronic attack. Someone's hacking their network con-troller."

"That's impossible," Jenny exclaimed before realizing how silly that sounded. She paused, examining the situation, then suggested, "Their firewall must be down. They're supposed to reject anything that's not properly encrypted."

"They say this stuff is encrypted," Carol explained, "at least well enough to get through the firewall."

"We've got another launch," a different controller reported. "This time from the Gongga Shan complex."

Jenny saw the track appear on the globe and checked the sensor log. An air force surveillance aircraft, one of several off the Chinese coast, had made the detection. So far they hadn't been . . .

The globe, smoothly rotating in the center of the room, suddenly stopped, then moved jerkily before freezing again. What now?

Even as she switched her headset to the computer staff's channel, Chris Brown, the head of the computer section, reported, "We're being flooded. Someone's sending us tons of bogus tracking data over the links."

"Our firewall isn't stopping it?" Jenny asked.

"Not all of it."

Jenny walked over to Brown's console and watched him analyze the false information being sent from supposedly secure sites. "Here's the header data on one that got through. It's good."

"But they're not all getting through the firewall?"

"No, about one in ten makes it." He tapped his console, bringing up another stream of data. "This one has a similar header, but the encryption isn't quite right, and it was rejected."

"But the ones that do get through are enough," he continued. "They force our system to chew on each for a while before rejecting it, and for every real packet, we're getting hundreds of these fakes."

"Jenny, I need to know what's happening." Admiral Schultz's voice in her headset was soft, but insistent. She looked across the open space at the admiral, who met her gaze expectantly.

She answered over the headset. "We're under electronic attack, sir, through our tracking stations. It's sophisticated. They not only deny us sensor information, but they're piggybacking bad data on the links to bog us down."

Schultz's face had a hard frown on it; they hadn't anticipated that the firewall security would be compromised. "A parting gift from Mr. Chung, no doubt. How do we block it?"

Jenny sighed. "I'll have to get back to you, sir."

Chris Brown had been listening to her conversation with the admiral and spoke as soon as she signed off. "It's completely down now. We just lost sensor processing."

Defender
0620 hours

They were still setting up when Jenny called. The pilots, Scarelli and Skeldon, had opened the bay doors. Then Andre Baker, the weapons officer, extended the laser turret above the bay. Sue Tillman was running a systems check on her sensors. While the specialists readied their gear, Ray watched power levels and the health of the data link.

Ray had noticed the problem a few moments ago but had concentrated on checking the systems at his end. The thought of the BMC going down left Ray feeling very alone.

Jenny's message clarified the situation but didn't help solve it. "Ray, we've lost sensors. We're under electronic attack down here." Her words chilled him, but he forced himself to be silent, to listen. She explained the problem, but its effects were obvious. They were on their own. She could not say when they'd be back online.

Suddenly Ray felt vulnerable. Somewhere below, another *Tien Lung* was climbing toward them.

Biff Barnes looked at the display screens. They were flat and two-dimensional, nothing like the command center's fancy displays. He selected different modes, looking at projected paths and engagement envelopes.

While their link to the BMC still worked, the information was becoming stale, based on the contact's past movements, not its current position. If the new vehicle maneuvered, they'd get no warning.

Without the BMC's information, they were nearly blind, but only nearly. *Defender* had its own sensor systems, radar, EO, and IR, but their range was limited to line of sight. The *Tien Lung* that had just been launched from Gongga Shan was below their horizon, on the other side of the world. They'd have to depend on voice reports from the ground while Jenny and her team sorted out the data link problem.

Barnes ignored the new threat. They could do nothing about it, so he'd decided to work on the one target they did have.

Ray looked over at Barnes studying the display. "They've missed their chance at us. They'll have to go for a satellite."

"I agree," Biff responded. "Look at this." He sent the plot to Ray's console. It showed the remaining GPS satellite tracks and the area covered by the Chinese tracking radars.

"The easiest one to reach is SVN seventy-five, here." Biff highlighted one of the satellites. "If they make a course change anytime in the next half hour, they can nail it. The Chinese will be able to watch the intercept, as well."

Barnes waited half a moment while Ray studied the screen. He nodded slowly. "Concur," the engineer replied. It was Biff's call, but it never hurt to have someone check the math.

"We're taking it out," Biff stated. "Right now. Before it gets any farther away. Before TL2 shows up to ruin our morning. Pilot, align us on TL1. Crew, stand by to engage TL1 with the laser."

Ray watched the stars and Earth spin slowly as Scarelli oriented the open bay so it faced toward the Chinese spacecraft. The distance was a problem, but at least they didn't have to maneuver to keep the target in *Defender*'s limited weapons arc.

Sue Tillman, the sensor officer, went from busy to extremely busy. She fiddled with the radar settings, then chose one of a number of search patterns for the radar to follow. Everything had to be done manually, and that took time.

The lieutenant finally reported, "I've got a hit with the radar, one five one miles, bearing three three zero degrees relative by eight zero degrees elevation. Changing to track mode." A few moments later, she said, "Track established."

Checking another display, she reported, "IR confirms target is being tracked."

Ray suppressed the urge to express his satisfaction at the gear actually working.

By rights, the detection should have been automatically tracked and evaluated. But systems integration takes valuable design time. Instead, it was all done semiautomatically with a lot of help from a trained operator, and with each second the target moved farther away.

Captain Baker, the weapons officer, didn't miss a beat. He'd slaved the laser to the data sent by Tillman's radar. "Ready," he reported, as calmly as if he was reporting the weather.

Ray had seen the seven-ton laser turret tested on the ground. The motors made an unholy whine. Now, there was no sound, just a slight vibration felt through the ship's structure, as it tracked the target.

"It's at the edge of our envelope," Ray reminded Barnes.

"And I figured out what that envelope was," Baker responded. "We're good."

Biff ordered, "Shoot. Five shots."

Ray felt more thuds and vibrations as pumps pushed chemicals into a combustion chamber. The intense flash of their ignition "pumped" the chemical laser, and a two-megawatt beam angled out and away.

Inside *Defender,* Ray watched five seconds come and go. Sue Tillman, looking disappointed, turned to look over at Captain Baker.

The weapons officer watched a spectrograph slaved to the laser mirror. "Nothing," he reported.

Set for five shots, the laser automatically fired again. Ray watched a TV camera set to cover the bay. Puffs of vapor left the combustion chamber, and he could see the turret slowly moving, but it was a silent combat.

Both Baker and Tillman spoke this time. The army officer announced triumphantly, "I've got an aluminum line." The laser had caused part of the target to glow. Baker's spectrograph had seen that light, and told him what elements that part was made of.

Tillman confirmed, "IR's up now. It's a lot hotter than before."

But it's still there on radar?" Barnes asked.

She nodded. "Affirmative. Trajectory's unchanged."

"Continue firing."

The third and fourth shots, five seconds of intense energy, also struck the Chinese vehicle, but with no better results than before. Ray fought the urge to fiddle with the systems display or remind Barnes that the target was growing more distant with every shot.

They'd spent a lot of time trying to decide how they would know when they'd actually "killed" a target. You couldn't shoot down something in space, and at these distances, they couldn't see the effects of their attacks.

During the fourth shot, Biff asked, "Sue, can you measure how fast the temperature is rising?"

"No, sir. The equipment's resolution isn't that fine, and the target is pretty far away. Physics says it can't radiate heat away as fast as we're adding it, but we're also adding less heat with each shot, because of the increasing distance."

By the time she answered Barnes's question, the fifth shot of the salvo had been fired as well. They'd used up almost half the magazine, but the mission commander didn't wait a moment. "Keep firing. Another five."

Well, they were here to shoot down Chinese ASAT vehicles, Ray thought. He tried to stay focused on his monitors, watching for signs of trouble. It would be hell if a mechanical failure interfered at this point.

Tillman saw it first, on the second shot of the new salvo. "IR's showing a big heat increase!"

"Spectrograph's full of lines!" Baker reported triumphantly. "I've got silicon, nitrogen . . ."

"Secure the laser!" Biff ordered. "Silicon means the electronics, and nitrogen's either solid propellant or the explosive warhead."

"There's also hydrogen and plutonium," she added, her voice a little unsteady.

Barnes nodded as if he'd expected it. "After all, they planned to use that vehicle against us. The GPS satellite was a fallback option."

Ray shuddered at the thought of a nuke aimed at him.

"Multiple contacts. Radar shows debris as well," Tillman confirmed. *Defender*'s radar would have no trouble distinguishing individual pieces of wreckage.

"It's a kill," she announced formally, with satisfaction. Sue Tillman also handled voice communications with Edwards, and she said, "They're cheering in the BMC!"

Ray noted the time. They'd been up half an hour.

Gongga Shan
0625 hours

"It's gone, General!" The communications tech handed him the headset. Shen listened to Dong's report quietly. The Americans had destroyed the special *Tien Lung*. They'd made the kill at long range, on an opening target. Apparently, the cyberattack on their communications system had not affected them enough.

Shen worked to control his surprise and disappointment, making his face a mask. *Defender* had proved itself. Now more than before, it was vital that the second vehicle destroy the American spacecraft. Unfortunately, there was nothing more he could do to ensure its success. Like countless commanders before him, Shen could only wait for the dice to stop rolling.

25

High Ground, Part II

"It's a brute force denial-of-service attack, Commander." Chris Brown sat surrounded by display screens. Some showed packets of invading data. Others listed tables of statistical data—numbers of packets sent from each site, numbers rejected by the filter, amount of processor time lost, and many other values.

"They don't have our encryption completely broken, but they've learned enough to get through occasionally. See," he said, pointing to two invading data packets. "The body of the message is the same. And most of the header data is valid. All they have to do is vary the part they don't know. And they're getting better at it. Look at this curve." It showed the percentage of successful penetrations since the attack began, and the number steadily increased.

Jenny forced herself to think clearly, to ignore the rest of the center and the craft in space above her. This was a battle of minds.

"The encryption key is time-based," Jenny said. "To mimic it at all, they'd have to be monitoring our communications in real time."

"Then that's what they're doing," replied the computer analyst.

"But all of the communications from the ground stations are line-of-sight to the Tracking and Data-Relay Satellites. You can't receive the signals being sent to them from Earth." Jenny had insisted on that, for obvious reasons.

"They must have satellites within the field of view to monitor the comms stream. They can then upload spurious data directly into the TDRS system from ground stations in China," concluded Brown.

"And we can't shut the system down without losing contact to the ground stations and *Defender*," finished Jenny. The access to the worldwide data links and the ability to feed processed information to *Defender* were the reasons for the Battle Management Center's existence. She visualized the data flow: It went out from the ground station, intended for the BMC, but it was also picked up by an intercept antenna somewhere in space; the Chinese then fed back bogus information directly to one of the TDRS birds from SATCOM transmitters deep in China. The Chinese were using America's own relay satellites and codes against them.

"Chris, we have to change the encryption key."

"That won't help, ma'am. It would take too long to get all the stations switched to the new encryption key and the data links resynched. By the time we were done, the *Tien Lung* attack would be long over."

Jenny slammed the console with her fist. A Chinese ASAT weapon was hurtling toward *Defender*, toward Ray and the others, and she seemed powerless to do anything about it. Her thoughts raced as she tried to think of a way to reset the encryption in time. Then it struck her: *Screw the encryption.*

"Then I have an idea. Go ahead and start changing the encryption keys, but also instruct the ground stations to parallel their transmissions in the clear."

"In the clear, ma'am? They'd be completely vulnerable. The Chinese would see that . . ."

"Yes, I know. But it will take them a little time to realize it and react. In the meantime, we use the clean data to update *Defender*'s computers."

Brown's face lit up. "I get it! I reset the firewalls to reject *all encrypted data*; that'll cut off all the Chinese bullshit flooding our system. But that may work for only five, maybe ten, minutes."

"That's all we'll need, Chris. Use the secure voice channel and get the word out to all the tracking stations."

"Yes, ma'am. I'm on it," the analyst sang out.

Jenny hurried back to her own console, keying her handset as she went. "Good news, Admiral. I believe we have a temporary solution to our problem."

"How temporary, Commander?" Schultz's voice sounded stern and hopeful at the same time.

"Long enough to get us through this engagement."

"That's good enough, Jenny."

Defender
0645 hours

Jenny's unorthodox tactic had an immediate effect. Cut off from the BMC, *Defender*'s computers had been displaying the estimated position of the second *Tien Lung*. It had been close, but the uncertainty of the estimate had prevented them from taking any action.

Now the display flashed with the real position of TL2. A red arc showed its track history, a red dot its present location, and a red cone its possible future position. *Defender*'s orbit lay square in the center of that cone, and another flashing symbol showed the intercept point.

Intercept was only five minutes away. They couldn't hope to set up and kill it with the laser before it reached them. Barnes ordered, "Andre, countermeasures!" and then told the pilots, "Retract the turret and close the bay doors. Execute orbit-plane-change maneuver; assume this vector, full thrust, fifteen-second burn."

Scarelli's nav display showed the track that Barnes wanted him to fly. Ray watched as the radar decoys left the ship, a cluster of simple radar-reflecting corners, based on the intelligence community's best estimate of the design of the kill vehicle's sensors. Then the bay doors began closing.

They weren't armored, but the doors might protect the turret and other equipment in the bay against small fragments from the *Tien Lung* if it did detonate.

Big fragments were another issue. More than ever, Ray felt grateful for the data link. Without its warning, the Chinese vehicle would likely have killed them all. They weren't out of danger, but at least they could try and evade.

Scarelli had oriented the spacecraft so that its upper side faced the *Tien Lung*. They'd argued about it during one of the many strategy sessions and decided they'd rather have fragments in the doors and upper fuselage than in the heat shield. They could live without weapons and sensors, but they couldn't reenter without the heat shield.

Ray watched the indicators for the turret and the doors. The instant the turret locks showed green, Scarelli fired the main engines.

Ray saw the stars swing again, then felt pressure against his back as *Defender*'s engines came to life. They quickly increased to full power. The acceleration, a full-thrust maneuver, was stronger than takeoff, and this time mixed with uncertainty.

He watched as the line of *Defender*'s projected course slowly slid away from the Chinese track. The engines stopped, and Ray saw that they were just outside the Chinese intercept cone.

The arc carrying the *Tien Lung* did not change for two long minutes. It finally started to shift back toward an intercept on their new course. "Look at that," Barnes said, pointing to the display. "Their reaction times are very slow."

He waited for a moment longer, then announced, "They're not buying the decoys. All right, pilot, execute another orbit-plane-change maneuver; assume this vector, full thrust, thirty-second burn. Stand by for a long burn, people."

This time Ray was ready for the acceleration—and, better still, welcomed it. The Chinese lag in controlling the *Tien Lung* would be their undoing.

Barnes's new course zigged *Defender* away from the *Tien Lung,* exactly opposite to the course correction the Chinese vehicle was making. *Defender*'s engines were far more powerful than the *Tien Lung*'s thrusters. The Chinese vehicle had been designed to engage satellites, not maneuverable spacecraft.

"Past closest point of approach!" the copilot reported. Skeldon didn't sound relieved. The Chinese could always command-detonate the warhead if they felt there was a chance of damaging them.

They did, after another twenty extra seconds of distance. There was no sound of an explosion, but two sharp bangs, like rifle shots, sounded over their heads, and part of Ray's board went from green to red and yellow. One corner of his eye noted that the symbol for the second *Tien Lung* was now gone from the screen.

Ray reported, "We're losing pressure in hydrogen tank two."

"Continue the burn," Barnes ordered. "Move as much hydrogen out of tank two as you can before it escapes."

"Doing it," Ray responded. "It'll screw up our center of gravity," he warned.

"Compensating," responded Scarelli. "What about that other hit?" the pilot asked. "I'm losing thrust in engine number two."

"I'm trying to sort it out. Give me a minute," Ray replied.

Part of the electrical system flashed red, but what was the problem? Was it a component, or the wiring? They'd installed redundant lines on all critical systems. It was time to see if it was working. He started isolating components one at a time. His mind focused on the technical problem; he hardly noticed the acceleration.

There it was. "We've lost the number-two hydrogen pump," reported Ray.

But something else aft still had a red alarm indicator.

"That figures. Explains why we lost the number-two main engine," Scarelli continued.

"We can cope," Barnes reassured him. "We don't have another burn until we reenter. We can get by on one engine."

Ray continued tracing down the aerodynamic control system and found the last piece of damage. "Primary actuators for the starboard ailerons are also off-line. Backup system appears to be functioning nominally."

"You'll need to keep a close eye on that during reentry, Ray," Barnes commanded. "Joe, be on the watch for any sluggishness once we hit the atmosphere."

The remaining engine was cut off. Ray hadn't even noticed the sudden weightlessness. His stomach complained a little, but he mastered it.

Barnes asked, "Joe, how long until we're over Xichang?"

Scarelli checked his plot, then answered, "Twenty-three minutes. That last burn brought our orbit right over them!" He looked at Barnes with a "How'd you do that?" expression.

The major grinned. "I picked the first burn vector directly away from where I wanted us to end up. That way I could make the long burn in the right direction. Crew, set up for surface attack. Here are the targets."

Ray watched as he designated two points on the map display. Scarelli had to make one small burn to refine the course. Then he and Skeldon spun *Defender* so her cargo bay faced the globe of Earth below.

After that, they waited. Baker and Tillman checked out their equipment, and the pilots monitored their course. For the first time since they had taken off, Ray had a moment to realize he was in space.

His inner ear was still under control, and they were all strapped in anyway. No floating during General Quarters, he mused. He looked at the monitors, one of which showed the earth "above" them. They were over the Pacific, and he could see the weather patterns, with landmasses half-hidden by clouds. He'd seen enough pictures taken in orbit to know what it would look like, but he hadn't expected it to look so beautiful. The photos missed too much.

"Five minutes," Scarelli warned, and Baker and Tillman both acknowledged. Ray and Barnes both watched silently as the specialists worked.

Tillman reported, "Imaging first target," and changed radar modes. The signal easily found the Xichang space center, a cluster of large buildings. Ray selected the radar display and studied the buildings. They'd seen it all before in satellite photographs, and Tillman quickly picked out the administration buildings, the control center, the powerhouse, and the other structures. The synthetic aperture image was clear enough to show the chain-link fence that surrounded the compound.

Baker designated his targets, and Ray saw three small symbols appear over the control center, and two more on the antennas. The weapons officer reported, "Ready for Spike drop."

"Drop on the mark," Barnes ordered calmly.

"Roger, in ten," the weapons officer replied, and then counted the seconds down. "Stand by! Mark! Dropping now, Spikes away!"

Ray saw his board change but felt nothing.

The Spikes were not as noisy or complex as the laser. Each consisted of a standard two-thousand-pound penetrator bomb and guidance kit in the tail. The only special additions were a small retro rocket mounted on an ablative heat shield that fitted tightly over the nose of the bomb.

Springs ejected five of the projectiles in quick sequence from their rack in *Defender*'s bay, and Ray watched the stream drift clear of the ship.

As fast as they'd been ejected, their individual motors fired, slowing them and driving them down toward Earth's atmosphere and reentry. The motor and ablative shield would absorb the heat, while the guidance kit in the tail would receive navigation updates from *Defender,* keeping the bombs aligned on their targets. Eventually, the fins would also burn up, but by then the bombs would be on a steady course, with so much speed that nothing would deflect them.

The standard BLU-116 penetrator munition, the core of each Spike, could penetrate eleven feet of reinforced concrete when dropped by an aircraft. From space, the bomb reached terminal velocity and would strike with even greater force.

Xichang was still several hundred miles ahead of them, but of course the Spikes needed that time to cover the distance to the ground. That also made it difficult for the Chinese to predict the target.

"Two minutes to next target," Baker announced.

Gongga Shan
0715 hours

The call came over a standard phone line, not the command net. General Shen Xuesen took the receiver from the communications chief.

"General, this is Wu Lixin." Shen knew the man. He was one of Dong's assistants at the Xichang control center. He sounded absolutely shattered.

"Wu, what's happened?"

"They bombed us, sir. Dr. Dong is dead, and so is most of the staff. The center's gone, ripped apart."

"Bombs?" Shen repeated with disbelief. "Was it an air attack?"

"No, no airplane—nothing was seen. No planes, no missiles."

The general felt his heart turn to ice. It had to be *Defender.* So the detonation hadn't hurt them at all. They were still capable, still a threat.

Shen looked at their predicted orbit. She was moving from east to west, and . . .

"Out! Everybody outside right now! Head for the shelters!" he bellowed. Turning to the comms chief, he said, "Get the gun crew out as well." Theoretically, the gun and the control bunkers were hardened, but Xichang's control center had been hardened as well.

There was no way to tell when, or even if, an attack would happen, but Shen wasn't risking his people's lives. The instant he saw everyone in the center moving, he headed for the door himself.

He sprinted outside, heading for one of the slit trenches that had been dug nearby, but he made it no more than a dozen steps before the explosions began.

It wasn't from behind him but from the mountain, to his right. He turned just a little and saw a series of bright yellow fireballs ripple over the gun's location. Rocks and debris spouted into the air hundreds of meters high, and he could feel the concussions from over a kilometer away.

At least three deadly flowers blossomed at the base of the gun, right over the breech. Another four or five landed in a neat line on top of the barrel, and another three clustered closely around the muzzle. In the early-morning light, the mountain was outlined for several seconds by the flash from the explosions.

One of the first bombs must have found the liquid-propellant piping, because the entire building suddenly disintegrated in a huge ball of orange flame. Pieces of debris arced high into the air, and Shen suddenly found himself running again, diving headfirst into a trench as pieces of cement, steel, and rock began raining down on him and others nearby.

The deadly rain stopped, and Shen untangled himself from the people who had sought shelter with him in the trench. Reluctantly, he knelt, and then stood, a little unsteadily at first. Knowing and hating what he would see, he nonetheless had to find out what they'd done to his gun.

The breech building was gone, replaced by a hole filled with flaming debris. Most of the installation had been belowground, and the crater had carved a massive gouge out of the mountain's roots.

The slope of the mountain looked almost untouched, but a line of craters neatly followed the path of the gun barrel, and the mouth was hidden in a mound of loose rock.

Five years of backbreaking work. Ten years of convincing before that, after twenty years of dreaming—all lost. His friend Dong Zhi was dead, and many of China's brightest were dead with him. How many bodies would they find in the ruins?

Shen realized others were trying to help him out of the trench. Passively, he let them lift him out and steady him on the rough terrain. He turned automatically to head for the center and saw it was in ruins, flames outlining the ruined walls. He hadn't even heard the explosions.

It was finished. Shen was suddenly very sorry he'd lived.

Defender
1000 hours

With most of their fuel used up, they'd made one small burn to line up for reentry after two orbits. Now, with nothing to do but wait, Ray felt his sensation of unreality return. His mind and emotions sought to understand this new experience.

They'd fought and won a battle in space—the first one in the history of mankind. He'd played a role, a major one, in making it happen, but he knew he wasn't the only one. More important, others would now follow after him. Not all of them would be Americans, maybe not all of them would be friends, but warfare had changed, as it always does.

Along with Ray, Biff Barnes checked the systems displays over and over again, looking for the smallest fault, but the ship was performing well. Reentry was now only half an hour away. Scarelli and Skeldon were handling the preparations perfectly.

For some reason Barnes was having problems trying to determine how he would fill out his personal flight log. Would the *Tien Lung* count as a kill? Four more to become an "orbital ace"? He suspected there would be more missions after this one.

That one thought led to another, and then another. Barnes started to make a mental list of improvements *Defender* would need before she flew again.

Battle Management Center
1030 hours

Jenny Oh fought hard to keep her emotions under control. Her first cheer had been when *Defender* had destroyed the first *Tien Lung*. Her heart had leaped to her throat when she saw the symbols for *Defender* and the kill vehicle merge, and then it soared when Barnes reported they were all safe.

And that had been followed by the destruction of the Dragon Gun at Gongga Shan. They'd watched it all on *Defender*'s imaging radar, data-linked down to the BMC. The sudden transformation of the neat structural shapes to rubble had been clearly visible, and she'd yelled as loud as any of them. It was the success of everything they'd worked so hard for. *Defender* had proved herself.

Jenny had looked over at Admiral Schultz, who sat quietly, his head in his hands. He stayed that way, aware but silent, for some time. After the celebration had died down, he left the command center without saying a word, only to return in time to watch the reentry. He slowly walked over to Jenny's station, checking his watch as he approached.

"Check CNN," the admiral suggested, smiling. It was just 1030.

Jenny selected the broadcast and saw Markin's now-familiar face. Behind him was a commercial-satellite image of the destroyed gun. Markin was excited, almost frantic.

"This is CNN reporter Mark Markin with breaking news! Only a short time ago, a confidential source revealed the destruction of the Gongga Shan Dragon Gun by the United States Spaceship *Defender*. Also destroyed was another *Tien Lung* orbital-kill vehicle aimed at a GPS satellite. The Chinese attempted to shoot down the American spacecraft, using a second *Tien Lung* ASAT vehicle, but, according to my source, were unsuccessful after an extended battle."

"Extended battle?" Jenny wondered aloud.

"Well, it was extended, in orbital terms." The admiral's smile widened.

"*You're* his 'confidential source'?" Jenny asked, almost shouting, and then controlling her voice.

"This time, yes. I felt bad about bamboozling him earlier this morning. There's no more need for secrecy, and I figured the best way for the media to get it straight was to get it straight from me."

They watched Markin's piece together for a few more minutes, as he detailed the engagements in space and the damage to the Chinese installations. Finally, he started to repeat himself, and Jenny checked the status board. *Defender* was now in blackout, and would be until she finished reentry.

The admiral watched her for a moment, then said, "Congratulations, Jenny. You made it happen."

"Congratulations to all of us, Admiral. We all did it."

"We all believed we could make it work, Jenny, and busted our butts to prove it to the rest of the world. But you and Chris Brown saved the mission. Chris is a civilian, and he'll get a commendation for his civil service file. I'm recommending you for a Silver Star. Nobody fired a shot in your direction, but you were in the fight as much as anyone. Your quick thinking saved *Defender* and won the battle."

Jenny felt herself flush, and she automatically came to attention. "Thank you, sir!" Then she wavered. "But what about *Defender*'s crew . . ."

Schultz waved a hand, cutting off her protests. "Oh, yes, there'll be medals and parades and all the glory a grateful nation can provide. They've earned all of it."

"Do you think Ray will be able to get a little free time, sir?" she asked quietly.

Epilogue

Lancaster, CA
March 15, 2018

Ray was organizing electrical cords in the second bedroom when Jim
Naguchi called out from the living room, "It's all connected." Ray
arrived in time to see his giant flat-screen display, eight by sixteen
feet and covering one whole wall, come to life. The new "McConnell Digital Wall" was up and running.

At first, it showed a desert scene, magnified fourfold and almost
dizzyingly large, then four identical scenes, then a nighttime star field
so vivid and crisp Ray had to look outside to remind himself that it
was still morning. "Nicely done, Jim!"

"I just followed your directions, Ray." Naguchi waved a sheet of
paper over his head. Jim had been in charge of transporting Ray's
extensive electronics from San Diego to Lancaster and had then
managed the setup.

Jenny came down the hall. "Everything is up in the master bedroom," she announced triumphantly. "And guess what they're showing on channel ninety-three?"

"Ooh, wait! Wait!" Naguchi said as he typed quickly on a tablet
PC. A window appeared on the video wall, as large as a conventional

flat-screen television, with an image of officials gathered around a podium.

The banner scrolling across the bottom read, "U.S. Space Force Base Dedication—Edwards Home to Newest Armed Service."

"Gah! Not again!" Ray moaned. Still, he didn't ask Jim to turn it off. The news cameras had a much better view of it than he'd had as a participant.

Admiral Schultz was at the microphone, and as Naguchi increased the volume, they heard the admiral say, ". . . best to add to the illustrious history of what is now Edwards Space Force Base. Glen Edwards, combat and test pilot, represents exactly the type of individual we will need to face the dual challenges of technology and human conflict . . ."

Others heard the sound and came into the living room, standing where they could in the clutter of boxes and packing material. Ray negotiated his way to where Jenny was standing and slipped an arm around her waist. She leaned against him, just a little, as they watched the ceremony.

Secretary Peck and Hugh Dawson from Lockheed Martin stood next to Admiral Schultz on either side of the podium. Ray and Biff were both visible in the second row, if you knew where to look.

Jack Garber, from the San Diego contingent, asked, "They're still running that? That was two days ago!" Sue Tillman argued, "You should have been in front, Ray!"

"I thought it was nice of General Warner to come out for the dedication," Jenny remarked.

"Yeah," Ray answered, laughing. "He had the same smile on his face all morning. Maybe it was glued on."

"He was trying to be civilized about it," she insisted. "He didn't have to be there. He could have left the transfer to the base commander."

"You're right, of course," Ray conceded.

Biff Barnes said brightly, "Look, it's almost time for Rutledge's speech."

"Mute it! Quick!" Shouts from across the room were accompanied by pieces of cardboard thrown in Naguchi's direction. Luckily, cardboard exhibits poor aerodynamic properties. The impromptu assembly broke up and resumed their earlier tasks.

"I liked it better when he was trying to shut us down," Barnes said. "We didn't have to listen to him as much."

Jenny answered, "We would have had a lot harder time in the hearings without his support. Before we launched, he was leading the opposition, and when he suddenly reversed course, they didn't know what to do and just imploded."

Biff nodded. "You're right, but having to listen to him again may be too high a price . . ."

Ray cut in. "As far as I know, the last of the electronics is hooked up. With the important stuff out of the way, now we can bring in the rest of the boxes and the furniture."

"Don't worry," Jenny said, squeezing his arm. "With so many helpers, it will all be in by lunchtime."

"And I'd better get going. I have to organize a meal . . ."

Jenny held up a hand to stop him. "Geoff Lewes already offered to set up a buffet in the front yard. He left with a few others an hour ago to prepare."

"And how much will that cost?" Ray asked, but she waved the question away.

"With luck, maybe we'll get to meet some of the neighbors," she answered.

Brad Tillman came in the front door with a large box. "This one's just labeled WEDDING GIFTS. Where should I put it?"

Ray tried to remember the box's contents but drew a blank and just stared at it; Jenny looked over and spoke up. "I packed that one. It has the kitchen gifts we got." She pointed toward the appropriate door, then smiled. "We're lucky we got that stuff," she told Ray. "How could you not have a toaster?"

He shrugged. "I never needed one."

Shaking her head, she followed Brad Tillman into the kitchen to begin unpacking. Helen Baker said, "Let me help," and joined her.

Jim Naguchi was still fiddling with the display. There were almost a dozen subwindows covering the wall now, including three or four news channels, the basketball-tournament rankings, and a local map centered on their new house.

Two of the news channels were showing pictures of *Defender* and the dedication ceremony. The other two were covering the ongoing Chinese withdrawal from Vietnam. With the Dragon Gun destroyed, and the U.S. blockade cutting off virtually all sea trade, Beijing had seen no profit and great loss from her military campaign.

Pundits were coining terms like "the GPS gambit" for China's failed strategy. On one cable show, two experts were trying to guess how badly the Chinese economy would suffer in the next year. Their only disagreement was what percentage reduction best described "really bad."

And the media had been covering a lot of changes in the Chinese leadership, with many senior officials suddenly leaving, all at the same time, "for health reasons."

"Ray, don't get sucked in!" Jenny called from the kitchen.

"Right," he answered, tearing himself from the screen. He had to move, anyway. They were bringing in the couch.

In the end, they finished bringing everything in by lunchtime. Aside from the electronics, Ray's possessions had fit in a medium-sized trailer. Jenny didn't have much more, and with friends from both San Diego and Edwards helping out, it only took a few hours after lunch to put most of it away and clear out the trash.

Finally, the San Diego SPAWAR contingent had to leave for the long drive back, and the move party began to break up. Jim Naguchi and the others from SPAWAR were careful to get photos with Ray, Biff, and the other *Defender* crew members before they left, and most asked for autographs. Ray laughed inside at his new celebrity. If that was the price for so many helpers on moving day, he was more than happy to pay it.

The people from Edwards didn't have far to go at all, but they left, too, with calls of, "See you at *our* base tomorrow!"

Ray and Jenny strolled through their new home, suddenly empty of all the bustle and laughter. It was just a ranch house, with the obligatory red tile roof. One wall of the living room was glass, and sliding doors led out to the patio and the also-obligatory pool. Jenny had insisted on the pool. "It's good exercise, and now that you're in shape, I want you to stay that way," she said, poking him in the side.

"I'm sorry it was such a short honeymoon," Ray said, a note of disappointment in his voice. "A weekend in Sequoia National Park wasn't remotely long enough."

"Don't think that!" she argued. "The timing on the house was too good to ignore, and you've got that meeting with Hugh on the new *Defender* follow-on in two days . . ."

"But it's our honeymoon, Jenny!"

She smiled. "Who said the honeymoon's ended?"

Kelly Johnson's Rules and Practices

1. The Skunk Works manager must be delegated practically complete control of his program in all aspects. He should report to a division president or higher.
2. Strong but small project offices must be provided both by the military and industry.
3. The number of people having any connection with the project must be restricted in an almost vicious manner. Use a small number of good people (10% to 25% compared to the so-called normal systems).
4. A very simple drawing and drawing-release system with great flexibility for making changes must be provided.
5. There must be a minimum number of reports required, but important work must be recorded thoroughly.
6. There must be a monthly cost review covering not only what has been spent and committed but also projected costs to the conclusion of the program.
7. The contractor must be delegated and must assume more than normal responsibility to get good vendor bids for subcontracts on the project. Commercial bid procedures are very often better than military ones.
8. The inspection system as currently used by the Skunk Works, which has been approved by both the Air Force and Navy, meets

the intent of existing military requirements and should be used on new projects. Push more basic inspection responsibility back to subcontractors and vendors. Don't duplicate so much inspection.

9. The contractor must be delegated the authority to test his final product in flight. He can and must test it in the initial stages. If he doesn't, he rapidly loses his competency to design other vehicles.

10. The specifications applying to the hardware must be agreed to well in advance of contracting. The Skunk Works practice of having a specification section stating clearly which important military specification items will not knowingly be complied with and reasons therefore is highly recommended.

11. Funding a program must be timely so that the contractor doesn't have to keep running to the bank to support government projects.

12. There must be mutual trust between the military project organization and the contractor; very close cooperation and liaison on a day-to-day basis. This cuts down misunderstanding and correspondence to an absolute minimum.

13. Access by outsiders to the project and its personnel must be strictly controlled by appropriate security measures.

14. Because only a few people will be used in engineering and most other areas, ways must be provided to reward good performance by pay, not based on the number of personnel supervised.

Afterword

This story first appeared as a novella in the anthology *Combat* edited by Stephen Coonts and published in hardback in 2001. I enjoyed writing the story, but there were entire plotlines that had to be ignored given the limitations of a forty-thousand-word format.

This novel has been updated and fills out those missing plotlines. The story was originally set in 2010—i.e., then ten years in the future. As we write this (in 2013), we do have tablet PCs, but they're still working on the Silver line to Dulles.

Chris and I hope you enjoy it.

Glossary

AA: Anti-aircraft

ABL: Airborne laser

ACES: Advanced crew escape suit

ADO: Aerospace Defense Organization

ADP: Advanced Development Programs

AESA: Active Electronically Scanned Aray

Aerospike: An advanced-design rocket engine that can compensate for altitude, making it burn fuel more efficiently as the air gets thinner.

ASAP: As soon as possible

ASAT: Anti-satellite

AWOL: Absent without leave

Beidou: A Chinese satellite navigation system similar to GPS but limited in coverage to Aisa and the Western Pacific. A system with global coverage, called COMPASS, is planned to be operational in 2020.

BMC: Battle management center

BOQ: Bachelor officer quarters

C3: Command, control, communications

CAD: Computer-aided design

CEC: Cooperative engagement capability

CIC: Combat information center

CJCS: Chairman of the Joint Chiefs of Staff

CMC: Central Military Commission

CNO: Chief of Naval Operations

DCIS: Defense Criminal Investigative Service

DoD; Department of Defense

DSP: Defense Support Program. A reconnaissance satellite system designed to provide early warning of intercontinental ballistic missile launches.

EVA: Extra-vehicular activity

ECM: Electronic countermeasures

EO: Electro-optical

EW: Electronic warfare

FAA: Federal Aviation Administration

FBI: Federal Bureau of Investigation

FEMA: Federal Emergency Management Agency

HMMWV: High Mobility Multipurpose Wheeled Vehicle, acronym pronounced as "Humvee"

Galileo: A European satellite navigation system similar to GPS, funded by the European Union.

GLONASS: Global Navigation Satellite System. Russia's equivalent to the U.S. Navstar GPS.

GPS: Global Positioning System. A navigation system that uses a constellation of 24 satellites that sends precise timing signals to receivers on Earth. By comparing the time differences, the receiver can find its location. The constellation's orbits a arranged so that several are above the horizon at any given time. The more satellites that are visible to the receiver, the more precise the navigation fix. GPS is funded and run by the U.S. Government.

IP: Initial point

IR: Infrared

IT: Information Technology

JCS: Joint Chiefs of Staff

LED: Light-Emitting Diode

MoD: Ministry of Defence

MP: Military police

MSS: Ministry of State Security

NSA: National Security Agency

NASA: National Aeronautics and Space Administration

NAVAIR: Naval Air [Systems Command]

NIOC: Navy Information Operations Command

NMCC: National Military Command Center

NNSOC: Naval Network and Space Operations Command

NORAD: North American Aerospace Defense [Command]

PLA: People's Liberation Army

PT: Physical training

R&D: Research and development

SAM: Surface to air missile

SATCOM: Satellite communications

SCIF: Sensitive Compartmented Information Facility

SECDEF: Secretary of Defense

SIPRNET: Secret Internet Protocol Router Network

SPAWAR: Space and Naval Warfare [Systems Command]

SRB: Solid-rocket booster

STRATCOM: Strategic Command

Supergun: An extremely large-bore artillery piece. The technology for superguns was a specialty of Dr. Gerald Bull, a Canadian-born engineer who advocated their use for space launches, as well as military applications.

SVN: Space Vehicle Number

TAO: Tactical action officer

TDRS: Tracking and Data Relay Satellite

TEL: Transporter-erector-launcher

UON: Urgent operational need